THE
WEDDING
HITCH

A laugh-out-loud enemies to lovers rom-com

CLAIRE McCAULEY

Joffe Books, London
www.joffebooks.com

First published in Great Britain in 2024

Cover art by Becky Glibbery

ISBN: 978-1-83526-489-8

For Stephen.
Meeting and marrying you in under a year
was the best thing I ever did.

MAY

CHAPTER 1: AT FIRST SIGHT

'Sylverley is on the right, immediately after this bend.' Nate didn't react, so I added, fighting to keep my voice patient, 'Slow down, or we'll miss it, and there's nowhere to turn for ages.'

'Keep your hair on,' Nate said, decelerating the van from forty to thirty: still way too fast to slow in time. I caught a glimpse of the long driveway, winding up through parkland to the house, high on the horizon, as we sailed past the tall iron gates.

'Shit,' Nate muttered, his eyes shifting to mine, then back to the road we now crawled along. 'There's somewhere we can turn, you reckoned?'

'In about a mile,' I ground out. The fingers of my right hand moved to my left, and I twirled my engagement ring round and round. I'd borrowed the van to scout the route out the day before precisely to avoid problems finding the place.

We reached the lay-by and Nate circled the bulky van back onto the main road, facing the way we'd come.

'You all right?' he asked. We re-approached the gates a little more cautiously this time.

You all right was Nate's version of *sorry*. A wary acknowledgment that something could have occurred, that he might have had something to do with, that perhaps caused me to not be all right.

'I'm absolutely fine,' I said emphatically, because I wanted to be, and a moment later, as he swung into the opening and gave the whistle of appreciation I was hoping for, I was.

Honey-coloured Bath stone always looks its best in the summer, of course, and with the removal of several centuries of soot during the recent restoration, Sylverley glowed like old gold against the cloudless blue sky. Even the slate roof shone in the sunlight. Beneath it, the warm colours softened the stark Georgian grandeur of the house with its columned central elevation, flanked by symmetrical wings fanning out at each side. It was far from the largest, finest or most historically important stately home in Somerset, but it was certainly one of the prettiest and, if I executed my plan perfectly, would acquire the most personal significance to us as a couple.

Darting a look at Nate, I gauged whether to utter my burning suggestion in these initial, awestruck seconds. Then the front wheels reached a speed bump, jerking us. Not while we were in motion then, and anyway, it would be best to have his full attention.

Ahead there was a queue of vehicles, and Nate braked to a smooth halt, still staring up at Sylverley, sat perfectly atop the highest point within its grounds. Deciding to go for it, my heart rate reached a dizzying speed. I sucked in a steadying breath and placed my hand on his, resting loosely on the gearstick.

'Are you thinking what I'm thinking?'

His liquid brown eyes met mine enquiringly.

'This place is so beautiful, and barely anyone knows it's reopening. We should book our wedding here.' I paused, readying myself to deliver the next part of my prepared speech, that dealt in one fell swoop with the practicalities. My lips parted again—

There was a tap on my window. As Nate pressed the button to lower the glass, I scowled at the man now bent into view, noting the grey suit and teal tie — brand Sylverley.

3

'The trade entrance is back down the drive and round to the west,' the man said.

'Actually we're here to look around, not make a delivery,' I said, unsmiling. It was an error more suited to a stammering teenage part-timer than this man in his early thirties, like Nate and I. He was well-presented and eye-catchingly good-looking — which gave him no right at all to interrupt my speech to Nate.

'I'm very sorry for that misjudgement, madam,' he said, his eyes sweeping down to my pale tea dress, then up to my red hair, into which I'd woven a white silk rose, to give off subtle bridal vibes. It was impossible not to notice his expression adjusting in response. I tore my gaze away, berating myself for observing that the softening lines of his face made him even more attractive. 'Truly, I'm sorry. But unfortunately we're only open today to give invited guests a little sneak peek. If you hop onto our website, you'll be able to book to visit next weekend. Here — please accept a discount code.'

I ignored the flyer he held out, instead grabbing the thick, white envelope from where I'd tucked it for safe keeping on the dashboard. As I tipped out the contents, Nate leaned across me, his shoulder-length dark curls brushing my face as he accepted the flyer.

'That's decent of you, mate. We'll look forward to coming back.'

'No need for that.' I brandished the evidence from the envelope. Two tickets, printed with almost exactly the same words spoken by the accosting Sylverley employee: *Sneak Peek Entrance for VIPs*. Our names were handwritten beneath: *Róisín O'Reilly, Nathan Slater*. 'I know you're only doing your job,' I said through the window. 'But as you see, we're two of Sylverley's invited guests, so could you please direct us to where we should park without further delay?'

* * *

Only doing your job, I thought, as we continued up the drive. Only distracting me from what could have been the most important moment of my life so far with his annoyingly handsome face, more like. And now I was musing over another man rather than refocussing on my fiancé. I shook my head to clear it, and the rose in my hair dislodged. I flipped down the sun visor and peered into the mirror to pin it again. 'Nate? That idea of mine . . .'

He didn't bite, his mind still occupied with the interruption. 'How did you get hold of the tickets?' He grimaced. 'And I'm guessing I'm not meant to ask how much they cost?'

'Best not,' I said lightly, as we reached the fork in the driveway, and he steered right, as directed, his grimace deepening. 'That's a *joke*, Nate — they were a complete bargain.'

As expected, he immediately brightened. Nate's enjoyment of anything and everything had always increased in direct proportion to the percentage discount he'd secured. 'How much of a bargain are we talking?'

'The ultimate kind — freebies. Sylverley's marketing team offered them to hoteliers and tourism industry professionals, so Abi got a pair. But she's so tired at the moment so requested they be reissued to us as her representatives.'

Nate grunted at that. He wasn't keen on Abi's recently acquired husband, but since their sudden but very sweet wedding, and delighted pregnancy announcement he'd promised to stop moaning about him. And he very much approved of Abi, my friend and former employer, passing regular freebies onto us via *Historic Bath and Beyond*, her rather exclusive tour company, where I occasionally helped out during quieter periods in my historical fashion business.

'Anyway,' I said, trying again to get the conversation back on track. 'My idea, before we were interrupted . . .'

Nate pulled into the car park. 'Idea?'

I waited until he had manoeuvred the van into a space and turned the engine off, then pinned his eyes with my own, as I pictured the digital mood boards I'd been working on all week, entitled *Sylverley wedding ideas 1-5*. I smiled. 'Getting married here.'

He smiled back at me, and my heart leaped. 'Gorgeous place for a wedding, yeah.' He added, casually, 'Maybe in five years, if we save hard.'

'Five years,' I said flatly. 'You want to wait another *five years* to get married?'

'We've only been engaged since Christmas — and yes I know, *of course I know*, that we've been together for ten years, but if we want a big swanky wedding someplace like this, we've got to save.'

'When you proposed,' I began, and a look crossed his face that I couldn't interpret. 'What?'

'Nothing.' He raked both his hands through his dark curls leaving them as artfully dishevelled as ever. 'Listen Rosh, this idea of yours is great, but it would cost a small fortune.'

I launched into the part of my prepared speech that addressed the practicalities, wishing fervently that I'd not been diverted. 'A wedding at Sylverley wouldn't be as expensive as you think, not if we act quickly. Opening up in May like this, they've completely missed this summer's wedding season, and if they're not careful they'll miss next summer's too. So if we approach the events team here, requesting a really speedy date, and offer to write excellent testimonials, I reckon there's a good chance they'd cut us an excellent deal.' I paused deliberately on *deal*.

'Even if you're right,' he said slowly, 'They'd at least want a chunky deposit, and we don't have much in savings.'

'I've got that money my dad left me, to be used for my future wedding, remember?'

'Didn't your mother spend that on extending her house?'

'Mam *borrowed* it for her extension.' I kept my tone even, controlling the triumph surging through me. 'She said last week that she's saved it all up now, and I can have it whenever I want.'

Nate's hands raked his hair again, which was far from the response I was expecting.

'The thing is, Rosh,' he said eventually, looking over at the team of efficient-looking young women in grey pencil skirts and teal blouses, greeting guests as they left the car park. 'The thing is, that the kind of place where we get sent to the trade entrance because we've arrived in a van aren't going to consider us deserving of a wedding here.' He got more convinced by his own argument as he spoke, releasing his hair and sitting straighter. 'So I don't think they'd cut us any sort of deal, and that means there's no point even dreaming about it.'

* * *

I stayed back as Nate approached one of the staff at the front of the house. At any other time I'd have been entranced by the closer perspective of the elegant portico porch and the pair of stone staircases, one at either side, sweeping up to the huge front door at first floor level. But I was too wrung out from the tearful end to the conversation and our uneasy truce; Nate would reconsider my idea after I'd done more research — if I agreed to drop it for the rest of the day.

'Hear that, Rosh?' Nate hollered over his shoulder.

I dragged my eyes from the house and strode over. The woman holding our tickets parroted, for probably the fiftieth time that day, 'You've got the choice between two different sneak peeks — the rose garden and orangery, or inside the house.'

'The garden and orangery, I thought?' Nate said, as at the exact same time I said, 'I'd prefer to see inside, I guess.'

We exchanged a glance, cautious of further dissent.

'Apparently they've opened up the orangery for cream teas,' Nate said in an undertone. 'We could scope out the competition.'

'Your café's in Bath, six miles away — hardly competition,' I said mildly, wondering if I should suggest returning home immediately. Now that Nate had heard about the orangery, he'd focus on nothing but the quality of their scones and which jam supplier they'd chosen, and the last thing I felt like was eating.

Nate shrugged. 'We could split up for the tours, and meet to exchange notes once we've tasted — I mean *seen* — everything?'

Maybe that was best, I mused. The charms of Sylverley's gardens might succeed where I'd failed, and ignite Nate's excitement for a wedding here. So I mirrored his shrug. 'See you back here in an hour?'

The young woman directed me to the mass of people climbing the steps of the portico. My phone rang from deep within my cross-body bag. Digging in to silence it, I encountered the discount flyer we'd been given. It cheered me slightly that Nate would be keen to return, since we could do so cheaply. Reaching the top of the steps, I took in the elevated view. Verdant lawn surrounded the house, with the car park situated behind the cover of trees. There was a thicker spread of trees over to the west, and an array of historic outbuildings. Around it parkland stretched from horizon to horizon, bisected by the gentle curves of the driveway.

A tour guide piped up from within the entrance foyer: 'Sylverley is a Palladian house, built in the 1750s on the site of a smaller property.'

I stepped through the vast oak doors onto a floor of white marble. Aside from a modern reception desk, the space had no furniture. Light flooded in through the tall sash windows behind me, opposite which were three sets of double doors.

'But Sylverley is also much more than just a house. It's a small estate, a slice of living history and, for over two hundred years, the country home of the late Edward Sylvers and his ancestors.'

Blocking out the rehearsed tour patter, I strolled to the far end of the foyer, which was dominated by a fireplace so huge I'd only need to dip my head slightly to stand within it. The carving on its mantel comprised a heraldic salamander within a flame — part of the Sylvers' family crest, according to the research I'd done since getting the tickets. Though since the reclusive old Edward Sylvers had died eighteen months ago, a trust had been managing the place, and over-seen the restoration.

The guide opened the most significant pair of double doors and I moved to re-join the group. They were set within such deep walls that there was a panelled embrasure beyond, enclosed by curtains on the far side. They sprung apart, reveal-ing the magnificence of the domed ballroom, and the sight ren-dered its audience instantly silent. I understood why; the excess of gilt and frescoes caused my breath to catch in my throat.

Unfortunately, at that moment my phone rang again, and the guide glared at me, as if the spirits of the deceased Sylvers line could be raised with a ringtone.

'Sorry,' I muttered. Freeing my handset from my bag, I checked who was trying to get hold of me so persistently. Not Nate, as I'd half expected, but my mother. Rolling my eyes, I clicked to accept the call, retreating further back into the empty foyer as everyone else pressed into the ballroom. 'Mam, I don't have long.'

'Aoife's engaged!'

I infused my voice with an air of infinite patience, in an attempt to indicate quite the opposite. 'How *lovely* of you to ring me, Mammy. *I'm* very well *thank you*, how are you doing?'

'Are you deaf or something? *Aoife's engaged* — and she's getting married next year, in August! You'll need to do an extra wee trip over next summer.'

I visited Northern Ireland each March, for my birthday, but Mam was forever coming up with spurious reasons for me to fly back for extra visits. Her random work colleague's wedding was particularly extreme though. 'I don't think I'll manage that.'

'You can't *manage* it?' Mam spluttered. 'Can't even man-age coming home to see Aoife wed?'

I smothered the retort that Derry wasn't my home. She refused to understand that by moving the family away from London, back to her hometown, while I was at university, she'd left me without a home. Until I created one later, with Nate.

9

'Hang on a second, Mam . . .'

I'd discovered the side of the long reception desk was stuffed with brochures for other local attractions, and I'd come prepared for such an opportunity. I checked the coast was clear then pulled two sheaves of promotional postcards from my bag. One pile advertised Nate's café, and the other my own specialist services, designing and making authentic historical costumes. I removed two sets of Roman Baths leaflets to create space for them.

'Listen Mam, I've really got to run. I'm out, and you told me about Aoife getting engaged to that fellow from the fish counter ages ago. I don't think I've ever met her, so I really can't go to the expense of flying over just—'

'Jesus, give me strength. Not Aoife from work. *Our* Aoife — your wee sister! Young Connor took a notion, and proposed. They booked their ceremony in at St Columba's before they even told us, they were that excited, and I've just arranged the Foyle Hotel for the reception. It's a bit dear, and they don't have a penny, but since you haven't set a date yet, I thought the money I'd saved can go for their wedding, and I'll start saving again for you after, and sure that's much of a muchness.'

My phone slipped from my grasp.

A split-second later it concluded its plummet with an almighty crack against the marble.

The glass screen fractured into so many pieces it resembled crazy paving, but it took more than that to silence an Irish mother, and her voice still emanated from the handset. *She wants her sister and sisters-in-law as bridesmaids of course . . . I still can't get my head around her getting gone out of my back bedroom, but he's a nice wee lad . . . They're thinking that band that your brothers both had for their dancing; you know, them'muns with the fiddles from Donegal way . . .*

Suddenly I couldn't take any more. I crouched, shakily seized my handset, and bashed it against the marble, and again, harder, until Mam's voice cut off.

I'd moved so abruptly and thudded my phone down with such force that my open bag spilled over in the process.

10

I scrabbled to retrieve a tampon, lip-gloss, my purse, then reached for the discount flyer, which had drifted the furthest. I glanced at it, mechanically noting the fifty percent discount. Definitely enough to tempt Nate to return, but what was the point, without cash for a deposit? Negotiating a deep discount felt doable, but negotiating an entirely free wedding certainly did not.

I refolded it, my fingers still trembling. The other side of the glossy paper was revealed, a picture of the house, and a different offering: *Win your dream . . .*

I flattened it to reveal the whole thing.

Win your dream all-expenses-paid wedding at Sylverley House and Estate. Free entry. Fill out the form below and pass it to any member of staff by May 31st.

JUNE

CHAPTER 2: BREATHTAKING

'Something's definitely off with you,' Gemma said, dunking one of the biscuits I'd brought over from the café into her mug of black coffee. 'Are you going to spill about what's wrong?'

'No.' I sipped my tea, which was too weak. 'Not now at least. Maybe later.'

Her eyes shot to mine. 'Oh, I get it . . . you'd rather tell Joe.'

'No,' I said again, quicker this time. It wasn't that I didn't want to confide in Gemma, but that I'd rather her husband were here too. I'd discovered back in our university years, when the three of us shared a flat, that Joe's optimism and Gemma's caustic bluntness balanced out into oftentimes perfect advice. Especially when it came to Nate, who Joe had known since school, and I'd met at their wedding. 'But when will he and Esme be home?'

'Ha! I knew it,' Gemma said, dunking the second half of the biscuit. 'Her physio appointments aren't long. They'll be here soon.' She swallowed it and took another from the box. 'Open the window, would you, this humidity's a nightmare. And then tell me what's wrong. I promise to stifle my gobby instincts and channel Joe's sympathy.'

I'd risen to help myself to a better cup of tea, and pushed the window open. The air remained still and heavy, so I opened the back door for good measure. Returning to the table, I decided to open up while I could; it would be impossible in front of Esme, their inquisitive six-year-old — and my goddaughter.

'Remember a few weeks ago, when Nate texted to say my phone was off being repaired?'

'Yep. Mishap at a museum, or something? It sounded like such peak-Róisín that it really made me laugh.'

'Thanks,' I said dryly. 'And we weren't at a museum but Sylverley — that Georgian estate, just south of here? A huge restoration project is finishing up, and it's breathtaking. And, it's opening for all the usual money-making activities. Cream teas and tours . . . *and weddings*.'

'Weddings, as *in* . . .'

'As in, Sylverley is the perfect location for the Regency-themed wedding that I've always imagined,' I explained, trying to keep my voice light, to conceal my misery. 'An idea which, shortly before I broke my phone, Nate shot down in flames.'

'Remind me on *Regency*. You know I forget which era is which.'

'Oh *come on*, Gem. The end of the Georgians.' At her blank look, I added, 'All the best historical romances we've binge-watched have been set in Regency times. It's the pinnacle of romance.'

'So, like, Pride and Prejudice, or Bridgerton?'

'Both!'

'Sylverley resembles the big houses in those?' She finally looked impressed. 'That would be amazing for a wedding. You'd need flowers absolutely everywhere for the ceremony, then a reception styled like one of those balls, with all the formal but flirtatious dancing. And an empire waist wedding dress would really suit you.'

'It's almost like all of that would be so perfect that I spent years dreaming of it.'

She ignored my rolled eyes, and the jibe. 'But Nate won't go for it, you say? So it's a non-starter.'

I stared at her for a moment. Despite not a scrap of make-up, and drowning in one of Joe's old shirts, she looked as beautiful as ever. I'd been there the night, in fresher's week, that she and Joe had met. He'd dazedly announced, 'Face of an angel, mind of a barracuda, and one day I'm marrying her,' when she went to the loo, and four years later they were indeed married. All of which meant she had no experience of how Nate's ambivalence towards committing to me, throughout our relationship, had left me feeling. It took months for him to call me his girlfriend, four years for us to move in together, and another five after that before he proposed. And now the cycle seemed to be continuing with actually getting married.

'Something else happened, that same day.' I moved my gaze to the dregs of tea in the depths of my mug. 'Mam told me she no longer has the money to repay the wedding fund I inherited when Dad died.'

Gemma put her mug down so firmly that the table rocked slightly. 'That's not on. You need to put your foot down on the conservatory, or whatever it is this time.'

'It's not something I can say no to. In fifteen months, Aoife's getting married, and Mam's already putting down deposits.'

'*Noooo* — Aoife's just a baby!'

'Twenty-two, like you were when you married?'

'That was different. I was wise beyond my years, and Joe was just about smart enough to know his own mind. Whereas Aoife . . .'

'Only learned to tie her own shoelaces about five minutes ago, has Mam do all her laundry, and got fired from at least six jobs in as many months. Exactly!' I folded my arms on the table and let my head flop forward to rest on them. 'I hope she and Connor have a lovely wedding, and are really happy together, I honestly do. And I'm proud of Nate and me, celebrating a decade together, getting engaged, and running two just-about-profitable businesses between us. But I

feel like such a pitiful failure that all my younger siblings —
even bloody Aoife — will be hitched and settled before me.'

Gemma contemplated another biscuit, before returning
it to the box. 'Yeah, you're right, you really needed Joe for
this.' Her hand landed on my shoulder, digging in rather
painfully. 'The only reassurance I've got, is that as the married sister, what I feel about my single sister is very much
closer to envy than pity.'

'Hello, darling,' Joe said mildly, appearing at the back
door. 'I heard that.'

I sat up, bracing myself just in time, as Esme appeared
behind her father.

'Fairy Godmother!' she shrieked, whizzing down the
home-made ramp and across the kitchen. Her wheelchair thudded into my legs, and then she was bending forward to clasp me
round my neck. 'I haven't seen you for months and months.'

'Less than one month,' I corrected, hugging her.

'It felt like months and months,' Esme said, releasing
me. She had her mother's fine blonde hair and heart-shaped
face, and her father's slightly protuberant pale blue eyes.

'You two had a nice catch-up?' Joe asked. 'What led to
the marriage-bashing?'

'Nothing,' I said quickly.

'Well, that's not true,' Joe said, looking at Gemma.

'Honestly, Róisín, your face is too honest for lying to
people who know you.' Glancing back at her husband, she
continued briskly, 'Marriage came up because Aoife wants
Róisín to be her bridesmaid.'

'Lucky me,' I said stonily, before recalling that Esme was
listening, and pasting a smile on my face. 'I'll probably get to
make her dress and all the bridesmaid dresses too.'

'Is Aoife another future sister-in-law?'

'Both her brothers already got married,' Gemma said
impatiently. 'Aoife's the ditsy little sister.'

'Well, then a bit of independence will probably be the
making of her, assuming her fiancé's a bit more . . . switched
on.'

17

'Let's just say,' Gemma said, sniggering, 'that their first holiday together was to Costa Rica, which they only realised isn't in Spain as the plane took off.'

'They'd have still had a lovely holiday,' Joe said. 'Costa Rica's meant to be beautiful.'

'Not for a long weekend,' I said with a pained sigh. 'They spent all but nine hours travelling one way or the other.'

Joe cringed at that, as Gemma cackled, and Esme, stoutly ignoring them, met my eye. 'Daddy took me to the phys-ee-oh,' she sounded out carefully. 'It was boring. I don't want to have silly muscles anymore.'

I flicked my eyes to her parents, who had gone quiet. Gemma darted a look at Joe, who gestured for me to keep the conversation going. I swallowed, then spoke softly. 'Thanks for telling me that. We don't get to choose lots of things about what our bodies are like, but you doing all those physio exercises makes your muscles . . .' I bit back *better*. With cerebral palsy, she would always have some degree of motor problems. 'Helps your brain and muscles work together better.'

Esme's face contorted in indignation. 'But I keep doing them and now I need the wheelchair nearly all the time. Before I keeped doing them I didn't need one at all.'

Gemma choked and buried her face in her hands, her shoulders shaking. It was so long since I'd seen her overcome with emotion, that I froze.

Esme looked aghast. 'Mummy! Mummy, what's wrong?'

'She's sneezing,' Joe said heartily. 'Get her the box of tissues from the lounge, would you, pumpkin?'

Esme examined her mother doubtfully, then nodded. Dropping her hands to grip the wheels flanking her legs, she manoeuvred her wheelchair out of the room. The seconds before she returned gave Gemma the opportunity to splash water on her face, and as Esme swivelled back over the threshold she gave her daughter a watery smile.

'Sorry about that. I guess I'm coming down with a cold.'

'Is that what made you go all leaky like that? Are you all right now? Do you want more tissues, look I gotted the whole box—'

'Esme,' I said. 'I've just had a brilliant idea. How about we send Mummy and Daddy off for a walk in the sunshine, so we can play on our own?'

Esme cheered and Joe mouthed '*thanks*', but Gemma looked between the clock, high on one wall, and the whiteboard, on the other, displaying a colour-coordinated schedule. 'It's standing time, and it's vital she keeps to the programme.'

'Perfect,' I said. 'We wanted to play with the dollhouse anyway, right, Esme?'

'Right,' she said emphatically.

* * *

Esme's doll's house was mounted on a console table in the corner of the lounge, at the perfect height to play with while leaning on her frame. It was painted white, with black stripes like embedded beams, and tiny roses around the doors and windows. She was compliant while Gemma strapped her in to spend her mandatory time on her feet, distracted by telling me the latest adventures of the dolls inside.

'I've got someone who wants to meet them properly,' I said, waving her parents off. 'Can you get them lined up in a row, to shake the hands of a beautiful lady who's moving in?'

As she rearranged the figures, I got out the latest little doll I'd sewn for her. She crooned over it, debated names, then christened her Lady Rhubarbia Custardy, but once she'd introduced her to the other occupants her usual barrage of questions started up.

'Where's Nate, and why was Mummy so sneezy and who is Eva marrying and why did you look like that about being a bridesmaid and who is Eva anyway and—'

'Whoa — remember the rule I taught you last time?'

Esme sucked in her cheeks, considering that. 'The one about only three questions at a time? No, I don't remember that even one little bit. It won't stay in my brain. We prob'ly should choose a better rule, like always asking as many questions as we can think of. Don't worry, not just me — you can ask them too.'

'Why thank you, but I prefer my rule,' I said firmly. 'Only three questions on any one subject at any one time. So have a long think before you decide what to ask about.' I was pretty certain that she wouldn't waste them on her mother's *sneezes*, but I could bombard her with hay-fever facts if I had to.

As she opened her mouth, my phone rang. I checked the screen, in case it was her parents, and seeing it was a local landline, declined the call. After pocketing it, I glanced back at Esme, who ran her tongue over her small white teeth, which shone like a string of pearls.

'Question one, please will you tell me everything about the wedding you told Mummy about.'

I snorted. 'You're a tricksy one. Okay — fine. My sister, *Aoife* — with a fff sound, not a vvv sound — has got engaged to her boyfriend. That means she's promised to marry him, you know? They plan to get married in a year and two months. And she wants me to be her bridesmaid. And that's all I told Mummy about her wedding, because so far it's all I know.'

Esme took in a determined breath. 'Question two, why did you look kind of saddycross about being a bridesmaid?'

I smiled at the compound word she'd created. 'I'm neither sad nor cross, exactly. It's more . . . more that I'm a bit bored of the bridesmaid thing. I've been one twice before, at my brother's weddings, and it's like . . . like watching someone else have a go on a game on the iPad. It's only fun for a short while, you know?'

'And then you want your own turn,' Esme said knowingly.

I bit my tongue, hard, between my teeth, emitting a small, non-committal squeak.

'Oh, Fairy Godmother,' she said suddenly. 'The wedding is the game and you need a turn. We have to find someone for you to marry!'

I turned my choke into a cough. 'I have someone to marry, Esme,' I managed eventually. 'Nate proposed to me at

Christmas — remember this emerald ring he gave me, that used to belong to his grandma?' When I'd announced our engagement with startled happiness as her family arrived for Boxing Day lunch, she'd objected to Nate giving me an old ring rather than buying one, so I rushed on. 'I love history, so an antique ring is perfect for me. And getting an heirloom like this is really special.'

She examined it, then her relentless gaze returned to my face. 'Question two—'

'Nice try, but we both know you're on your third and final question.'

She giggled. 'Question three, then. Can I be Aoife's bridesmaid instead of you?'

I opened my mouth, then snapped it shut against the hasty promise that she would be my bridesmaid once we'd saved enough money for Nate to agree to a date. It wouldn't be fair to dangle that with no firm plans. Instead I detailed the impracticality of her plan based on the wedding taking place over the sea in Northern Ireland, then managed to get her reabsorbed with the new doll, so I could check my phone.

There was no voicemail so, mentally running through my sales pitch, since a local landline almost always meant a costume enquiry, I put my finger to my lips. Once Esme had acknowledged that I needed silence by mirroring the gesture, I pressed to return the call.

'Yes?' It was a male voice, but I could tell no more from the single word.

'I had a missed call from this number — I'm Róisín, the fashion historian?'

'Sorry?' It was the passive-aggressive type of sorry, that actually meant get off the line, you cold-calling idiot. 'Hold and I'll connect you to reception.'

It was a struggle to keep my voice polite. 'I don't know who I should ask for at reception, since it was this number that called my phone.'

'Sorry?' This sorry was one of confusion. 'I don't recall—'

'In the past ten minutes.' There was no hiding my impatience anymore. 'I presume you're after my historical costume-making service?'

'The only call I made was to . . .' There was the sound of papers rustling. 'Ms O'Reilly?'

'That's me. Róisín O'Reilly.'

There were a few beats of silence, then he swept on. 'What an awkward mix up. I'm sorry about that.'

Noting that he sounded sincere, and that he'd finally used sorry for its rightful meaning, I relented a little too. 'No problem, but . . . I actually still don't know who you are.'

'Tristan Nash, the general manager at Sylverley. As it happens I have some rather good news for you, Róisín. You've won a competition we were running. For your dream wedding, all expenses paid, here at Sylverley House and Estate.'

'What?' His words were so extraordinary that I couldn't capture them for long enough to understand what he was going on about. 'Hang on, would you . . . could you please repeat that?'

'You entered the dream wedding competition we held here at Sylverley.' His voice was steady and patient. 'And this morning we randomly drew a winner. That winner is you. Uh . . . Ms O'Reilly, are you still there? I know it's a lot to take in.'

'Fairy Godmother?' Esme said uncertainly. 'What's happening?'

I came to my senses suddenly, and smiled at her, breathing deep and slow in a vain attempt to slow my racing heart. 'I'm here . . . sorry . . .' An idea struck me so hard it made me flinch. 'This isn't some kind of prank, is it?'

'Not at all. This is absolutely genuine.'

It was finally sinking into my consciousness. Marrying Nate in the beautiful surroundings of Sylverley, just as I'd pictured — and with every expense paid. 'This is amazing — I can't thank you enough!'

'No need to thank us, but we would appreciate getting you and your fiancé over here without delay, so we can present you with the prize formally.'

'That's fine,' I said, and then, 'Oh my God — my fiancé! I've got to tell Nate!' My fingers twitched, but I resisted the urge to end the call so I could phone him. Instead I pulled my phone from my ear and typed a text as rapidly as my quivering thumbs would move: *WE'VE WON A WEDDING!!!!* In one swift motion I sent it and returned the phone to my ear.

'. . . is that all right?' he was asking.

'Umm . . . I should think so?'

'Good, good. As for the practicalities, I've got your email address, from your entry, and we'll send through the prize details. You have a full calendar year during which your wedding can take place, but we don't want to risk a double booking, so the sooner you let us know your preference, the better. Not necessarily when we see you later, of course, but as soon as you decide.'

'Right,' I said. And then, 'What was that about seeing us later?'

'You said you thought you and your fiancé could attend this evening to formally accept the prize?'

'I did indeed,' I said, cursing myself for missing something vital in my haste to message Nate. 'Remind me what time you suggested; I forgot to note it down.'

'Seven p.m. Miranda Pangbourne-Perkinson, our head of events, will meet you beside the portico.'

'Meet Miranda Pangbourne-Perkinson at Sylverley's portico at seven,' I chanted, as if I was laboriously writing it out. 'Got it — thank you for that — and for the prize!'

'You're very welcome, Róisín. And please let me take this opportunity to congratulate you and your husband-to-be on your upcoming nuptials at Sylverley.'

The line went dead. My phone was still pressed to my ear. I couldn't breathe. And I was standing in the middle of Gemma's lounge, with Esme in my sole charge.

I had to sit down before I fainted . . .

'Why are you praying, Fairy Godmother?'

'This isn't praying. I've got my head between my knees because I thought I might pass out from the shock.' I raised my neck slowly, to check on her. 'I'm okay though. It's good news — the best news!'

'You won something,' she said. 'I listened. Was it from the rumbola, like Mummy?'

'Wha— oh no, not a tombola. It was a competition, which I'd pretty much forgotten entering because . . . well because I never even dreamed of winning, I suppose. But I did, I won!'

'Was it a pink candle, like Mummy got?' she asked politely. 'It was the first prize, and she asked the lady to swap it for the second prize because wine's better than candles, but the lady said no.'

'It's even better than wine. I won a wedding!'

Her face lit up. 'Can I come? Will it be tomorrow? Will there be balloons and a carousel and face-painting? What can—'

'You're confusing weddings with a carnival, I think. Weddings have dancing and cake and pretty dresses. And they take a while to plan, so first Nate and I will choose a date and then we'll send you an invitation, but you'll definitely get to come.'

'Do I get a pretty dress?'

While there were many details I couldn't confirm alone, there were a few matters that were solely the bride's prerogative. So I reflected her expectant grin back at her. 'You'll definitely be getting a pretty new dress, Fairy Goddaughter. Because I would absolutely love it if you'll be my bridesmaid?'

CHAPTER 3: THE ONE

Our maisonette covered the upper floors of a Georgian townhouse, within a parade on the periphery of Bath city centre. We could only afford it because of what was beneath us on the ground floor: the bakery that Nate's mother had founded. When his parents retired to the coast he'd taken over the lease on the whole building, and we'd moved in upstairs. Nate capitalised on the gentrification of the street by adding café seating, while I'd turned my twin obsessions of history and sewing into a business from the room above. The entrance was squashed between the glass frontages of the café and our boutique charity shop neighbours, and I'd screwed a brass plate beneath the letter box: *Róisín O'Reilly, Fashion Historian — Costume Designer — Seamstress*. I rarely passed it without giving the brass a quick buff, but I didn't even spare it a glance as I peered through the door of the café.

'Nate around?'

The lad behind the counter shook his head. 'Left a while ago.'

Nate had got my text, then, despite not replying, and was awaiting me upstairs. I unlocked our front door and listened intently as I discarded my sandals. Nate was rarely quiet, yet the place was silent.

I checked the large room leading off from the landing on the first floor. Nate's parents referred to it as the drawing room, as though the place was still one grand house, rather than long since carved up into bakery and maisonette, but we called it our office and used it for various aspects of our work, from my sewing and client meetings, to Nate's admin and staff interviews.

The period features were impressive, but more importantly gave me plenty of light to work in, thanks to the south-facing sash windows and high ceilings. We'd kept the furnishings simple, with an oak table for my sewing machines under the window, huge sideboard for storage, and a three seat velvet sofa, which flipped out into a double bed for our occasional guests. Usually Nate spent any work hours when he wasn't serving or baking downstairs on the sofa, his head on one armrest and his ankles hooked over the other, his laptop precariously perched on his chest as he typed menus or ordered supplies. But the sofa was unoccupied.

'Nate,' I yelled, nipping back to the staircase and bounding up to the next storey, which encompassed our bathroom and bedroom; both doors were open and both rooms empty. The final flight of stairs was steeper than those below, indicating that it led to the original servants' quarters. It opened straight into our living area, which had been knocked through at some time in its past. A galley kitchen was crammed into one end, bookcases and armchairs at the other, and a small dining table in between. I could see instantly that Nate wasn't at home.

I returned to the office and sat at the table, drumming my fingers as though short of ideas of what to do next. It was a performance only for myself, because there was really only one way to distract myself until Nate turned up. I flipped open my laptop and read the email from Sylverley, my eyes skipping over the details in my excitement, so I had to re-read it several more times before I absorbed everything. *Any Sylverley wedding package . . . full choice of premium extra services.* I typed *Sylverley weddings* into the web browser. Their website displayed more of the teal and silver-grey branding, and had a silhouette of the house on each page I clicked through. Civil ceremonies could take place in the rose garden or library and seated receptions in the orangery or ballroom, with a maximum seating capacity of four hundred and fifty guests. I was dubious whether Nate and I were acquainted with that many people, even between us. But knowing him, he'd get excited about maximising on freebies and insist on inviting the largest possible numbers. We'd probably end up with my dozens of aunts, uncles and cousins there, I thought, smiling, even though I'd never met most of them, and all Nate's regulars from the café.

An alert popped onto the screen: *Incoming video call from Aoife O'Reilly.*

I clicked to accept, and my youngest sister came into focus, sitting on her single bed and flicking her hair, which had once been the same shade of red as mine, but was currently bleached to the shade of straw.

'Congratulations, sis!'

Her thick eyebrows lowered, then rose again. 'Aye thanks, it's wile good to make it through training. Mo — the boss, who owns the place, says my only problem is mixing up them there wee buttons on the tills but there's loads of them and—'

I intervened quickly. 'I wasn't congratulating you on work, Aoife, though it's great you made it through a probationary period.'

'What, then?'

I pushed my hair behind my ears, wondering if Mam had been pranking me, then discarded the thought. Mam developing a sense of humour was a lot less likely than Aoife having missed the point. 'I heard that your relationship with Connor took a major step forward?'

She squealed. 'It's mad, isn't it, I know! I can't wait to get married!' The whole screen was taken over by pink flesh. 'Isn't it *gorgeous*? He chose it himself and got down on one knee and everything.'

Squinting, I made out that she was showing me her index finger. 'I can't see your ring at all, you need to angle your hand to the left a bit more . . . No, that's your thumb — try the other left. Perfect, hover it there.' The band was white-gold, with a tiny solitaire diamond set within a claw, but even a small solitary diamond had a sparkle, so I was able to tell her entirely honestly how pretty it was. 'Though it will look even lovelier on your hand when you're not sunburned.'

She retracted her hand. 'It's the start of a tan, so I won't look like death warmed up in white. And I'm on a diet, too.'

'You don't need to lose weight, Aoife, and you know redheads burn instead of tanning.'

Her mouth pursed with indignation. 'Jesus wept, Róisín. You know full well I haven't been ginger since I was sixteen.'

'Dying your hair doesn't stop—' I halted myself as we'd had that discussion before, and I glanced out the window for a change of subject. Wisps of grey clouds were thickening in the sky. 'It looks like the forecast is right for once, and it's going to rain here at last.'

She turned her head sharply, so I saw her profile. 'It's already raining, you eejit,' she said with scorn.

'I live three hundred miles south-east of you. The weather's different.'

'Seriously?'

I gave up entirely. 'Is Mam there?'

'Still at work. Why?'

I sucked my teeth. I really, really wanted to talk to someone about my own wedding. Ideally Nate, but anyone was better than no one. But Mam would murder me if I told my sister before her. 'I've got some news, too. Tell you what, I won't tell you, but let's see if you can guess.'

Aoife nodded with enthusiasm, then said, 'What is it?'

'That's what you've got to guess.'

'But I don't even know what it's to do with.'

'It's to do with the subject I congratulated you about.'

'I don't remember what . . . oh aye, my job. No, my wedding. So, umm . . .'

Beep, beep-beep. The horn blared from the back of the house, where we had a parking space. It was Nate's habitual announcement that he'd arrived home, and the most irritating manifestation of him generally being heard before he was seen.

'I've got to run, Aoife.' My heart leaping in my chest, I slammed down the laptop then turned in the swivel chair, listening hard.

There was a bang as Nate closed the front door behind him, and thuds as he dropped his messenger bag and kicked off his Chelsea boots. This was often followed by whistling or sighing or some other indication of his mood as he climbed the stairs. On this occasion it was the metallic chime of his keys clinking against the loose change in his pocket.

'You back yet?' he bellowed.

'In the office!' I called, rising from the desk chair. Reaching the top of the stairs, he grinned at me, and leaned against the door frame in his loose-limbed way. I drank in my first look of him as the man who wasn't just my fiancé, but was finally, *imminently,* going to be my husband. The strength of my emotion suddenly overwhelmed me, and tears filled my eyes.

He stepped into the room. 'Hey, don't cry.'

'Just happy tears.' I scrubbed my eyes with the heels of my hands. Every time I cried it triggered hiccups, and I really didn't want to hiccup my way through the delights of our first wedding planning discussion. 'Beyond happy, really. Amazed. Overjoyed. *Bursting* with happiness.'

Meeting his eyes, I discovered not elation, but puzzlement, and I groaned. 'You didn't see my text.'

'My phone's out of juice.'

It was more romantic this way anyway, I thought, rising to plant a kiss on his lips. 'Did I remember to mention filling out a flyer, a few weeks back, to enter a competition?' I asked against his neck, his curls tickling me as his arms encircled my waist.

'Mmmph? Don't think so.'

'Okay. So to cut a long story short, it happened that day at Sylverley, when it looked so beautiful for a wedding.' I gathered myself, then drew back slightly, smiling so wide at him that my cheeks ached. 'The competition was to win our dream wedding. An hour ago I got the call informing me that I won; *we* won. Within one year from today, on a date of our choosing, we'll become husband and wife at Sylverley, with all our expenses paid.' I felt more than saw the breath leave his body in a shocked exhalation of air, and laughed. 'I was surprised too. I'd dismissed any thought of winning, so it wasn't like I had a proper heads up.'

Nate held me tighter, keeping me steady as he took a few steps backwards then collapsed us onto the sofa. I rested my head against his chest, tucking my legs up under me.

'Say it again . . .' he said shakily. 'You entered a competition to win yourself a wedding?'

'To win *us* a wedding.'

'And you . . . *we* won.'

'Exactly!' I snuggled in closer. 'We've got a whole year before it expires, but I don't see any reason to wait long. With no need to save up we could even go for later this summer. It wouldn't leave me long to make all the clothing for the bridal party, but aside from a gown for me and a suit for you, I'd be happy to cut some corners. To be honest, I'd even cut corners on our garments — I'd marry you in a bin bag.'

'I wouldn't.'

I laughed again. 'Just as well neither of us will need to wear a bin bag, then. You know — we could make it a Christmas wedding, if we want the planning to be a bit less manic . . .'

He unfurled his arm from around my shoulder. 'Even December is very soon. I don't want to compromise our arrangements for the sake of an arbitrary time scale.'

'Arbitrary time scale,' I spluttered, sitting up. 'Has this not sunk in for you yet? It's a whole, *free* wedding. Look on the laptop — their basic package starts at twelve grand — and we're not limited to the basic options. Food, booze and flowers are all included, as well as exclusive use of the whole house and gardens. We even get a healthy budget to hire in musicians — or a band or DJ, but classical musicians would better suit the location.'

He raked his hands through his hair, sweeping the curls back into a short ponytail, which he held for a few seconds before releasing it and drawing his hands round to his forehead to begin the motion again. It was a nervous gesture I recognised from awkward conversations of the past, and it caused me to draw back uneasily.

I settled myself against the arm at the opposite end of the sofa, and twisted my engagement ring round and round, reassuring myself with its solidity and warmth and lustre that it was real. And since it was real, the fear that was creeping up on me was ludicrous.

'Nate, I'm imagining . . . ridiculous things. Please, reassure me that underneath the surprise, you're happy about this?'

He swivelled until he was leaning back too, his legs bent on the cushion between us as he mirrored my position. He didn't speak, just stared up at the ceiling, his face miserable. 'What is it that you're imagining?'

'That when . . . when you said you don't want to marry me wearing a bin bag, or plan our wedding to an arbitrary time scale, you actually meant . . .' I paused. Once completed, the idea would be out there, non-returnable. And worst of all, I'd get an answer. I raised my knees and wrapped my arms around my legs, then swallowed back the burning in my gullet. 'Did you actually mean that you don't want to marry me at all?'

His eyes shot to meet mine, but a verbal response was slow. 'I don't know,' he said eventually.

'Yes you do.' I forced the words out against the sensation of needing very badly to vomit. 'You do know. And you need to tell me.'

'I love you, Rosh. I really love you.' Something about the bleakness of his tone, like he was announcing a death, warned me what his fatal next word would be. '*But*—'

I flinched, and he bit into his lower lip, so hard that when he released it there were indentations from the bottom edge of his incisors, and a bead of blood.

'But what,' I said shakily. 'Fucking but *what*?'

'But I don't want to get married.'

* * *

I had once slipped on the icy street outside the café and hit my head so hard that I gave myself concussion. Nate's admission triggered the same roaring in my inner ear, and a rush of even worse disorientation. And all of a sudden I couldn't bear to be so close to him, and sprung up from the sofa.

I tore out of the office, slamming the door shut so hard that it reverberated in its hinges as I took the stairs three at a time, hiccupping painfully.

I'd have run outside immediately if my feet weren't bare. As it was, I ignored the gladiator sandals I'd worn earlier, with complicated laces, and shoved my right foot into one of my running shoes. Unfortunately, it was the left shoe and with my sight blurred by tears, by the time I'd released it and rammed in my left foot, I heard Nate's quick, heavy tread on the stairs.

'We have to talk about this. Rosh — you can't just storm out.'

The tongue of my trainer scrunched up, and I tugged it free, then wrenched the suede up over my heel. 'Watch me.'

'The last thing I've ever wanted is to hurt you,' he said, as I reached for the other trainer. 'I'm just . . . I like our lives as they are right now. All the conventional bullshit won't make us any happier.'

I stared up at him. 'Conventional bullshit?' The shoe was in my hand, and his head was in view. I hiccupped, then threw it at him, as hard as I could.

He caught it in one hand, and raised an eyebrow. 'Seriously?'

'Chuck that back to me — I'm leaving.'

'No.' He sunk onto one of the bottom steps, my trainer captive on his lap. 'Not until you let me explain properly.'

'There's no explanation,' I choked, 'that will make sense of *marriage is conventional bullshit* in light of you proposing to me at Christmas.'

32

'I didn't mean to propose,' he said, so quietly that I wasn't sure he intended me to hear.

'What the hell?' My breathing was ragged. 'I was there too, funnily enough, so you can't wriggle out of it like that. You gave a long spiel about your grandma, how back in your teens she told you to keep this ring to give to *the one*, when you found her. You thought that was ridiculous, and nearly sold it for beer money, but your mother realised in time and put it in her safe. And after ten years together you asked her for it back, wrapped it and put it under our Christmas tree, with my name on it.'

'And you opened it and said, *oh my God, you're proposing at last, YES!* and put it on like an engagement ring. Apparently without noticing that you were answering a question I hadn't asked.'

'But you told me . . . you said I'm the one.'

'You are the one, Rosh,' he said, his eyes intent on me. 'I know that, I *feel* that, with every fibre of my being. I was trying to do the right thing by telling you that, as I gave you the ring. I planned to go on to say that I didn't want . . .' His jaw snapped shut.

'The conventional stuff?' I breathed.

He gave a curt nod. 'Joe kept telling me I should bite the bullet and propose, or else make it clear that I never would. I was trying to do that gently — to explain that marriage wasn't on the cards, but that I love you, and always will.'

I stared at the ring. An imposter on the fourth finger of my left hand. A lie.

'You didn't correct me,' I said, in a voice that didn't sound like mine. 'If I was really wrong about it being a proposal, you'd have corrected me.'

His gaze had dropped to my shoe, and I held my hand out for it. He stood and passed it over, then returned to the same step. 'I didn't . . . I didn't want to upset you like that. Not on Christmas Day. But then you'd announced our engagement to absolutely everyone, and I thought . . . well I thought that maybe nothing really needed to be said. We could have a long engagement, and by then . . .' His elbows were on his knees, his head in his hands. 'Maybe I'd have stopped hating the idea of marriage and babies. Or even better, you'd have gone off it.'

Marriage *and babies*. It had been going to be my next question; whether this unspoken antipathy was solely to marriage, or if it also applied to my other dream, for far into our future. And he'd confirmed it. He loved me, *but* . . . no marriage, and no babies.

My ring had always been slightly loose, so removing it was the work of only a moment. 'Here,' I said, taking one long stride and dropping it into his palm.

'It's yours — keep it. Whatever happens between us—'

I was already shaking my head. 'You say I'm the one. But you're wrong. Because if I'm your one then you're mine.' A sob hitched in my chest. 'And that's impossible, because the one for me wouldn't keep me hanging, knowing that he doesn't share my dreams, but never admitting it. The one for me wouldn't let me think he was proposing, nor let me tell everyone how happy I was to be marrying him. And the one for me wants what I want . . . to build an authentic life together, with all the *conventional bullshit* that entails.'

In one swift moment I turned and opened the door. Without glancing back, I hiccupped and limped into the street, with one shoe on my foot and the other in my hand.

CHAPTER 4: I DO

My throat was tight as I finished my stammering explanation of everything that had happened.

'What's the chance . . . ?' Abi began.

At the same moment Herbie, her husband, said from where he was stirring gloopy green soup at the hob, 'It feels like . . .'

Abi and Herbie stared at each other, engaging in one of the wordless conversations they'd developed during the short span of their time together. It hit me suddenly that their relationship had been nine years shorter than mine, yet Nate and I had never managed this sort of intense, silent communication. Whenever I locked eyes meaningfully with him, he'd ask what I was pissed off about rather than attempting to interpret what I meant. It was a small sign of the bigger problem with communication that had ended so ignominiously in an accidental proposal.

Both pairs of eyes returned to my face as Abi spoke. 'Do you think there's any chance he'll change his mind?'

There was a lot I didn't know, like where I was going to live and work, having lost my fiancé, home and workspace in one go, but I was certain of the answer to that voiced question. 'None at all. He was clearer than . . . well, than he's ever been before about anything.' I'd thought I'd cried every tear my body could produce on my march through the rain to their house, but as I spoke, hot tears spilled from my eyes again. Abi, empathetic at the best of times, and now with all the emotions of early pregnancy, cried too as she hugged me.

Herbie pointed the wooden spoon at me. 'I was wondering something . . .'

'Shoot,' I croaked.

Horror crossed his face, and he dropped the spoon into the saucepan, where it sank into the bubbling gloop. 'Oh, I wouldn't do that. I promise, that was a spoon — not a weapon.'

'You're freezing,' Abi murmured. 'Let's find you some dry clothes.'

* * *

I'd peeled off my sodden dress and was scrubbing myself dry with a towel as Abi tapped on her bathroom door and passed garments through.

'Here's a selection of my tops, but my trousers will be too short for you, so try this skirt, or otherwise I think these trousers of Herbie's will do.'

She was little over five feet, so her denim skirt barely covered my underwear. It would have to be the harem pants, probably tie-dyed by Herbie himself. I pulled them on, doubling the waistband over and rolling up the leg hems. I had no choice but to put my wet bra back on, and over it I wore the largest of Abi's tops, oversized on her tiny frame, so only slightly tight on mine. It was black cotton with long sleeves, and emblazoned with *I look this good because I'm vegan*. I scraped my wet hair into a topknot then approached the kitchen, where Abi and Herbie were engaged in a low-voiced discussion.

I glanced between them, sensing strain. 'I'm so sorry about landing on your doorstep like this.'

They both blinked. 'Well, you don't need to be,' Abi said. 'I feel bad that you walked all that way, but of course you weren't thinking straight enough to stop and phone us.'

'I wasn't even thinking straight enough to remember my phone.'

'I'll pop round tomorrow to collect everything you need urgently,' Abi said, as Herbie nodded.

'And then you must stay here for as long as you want,' Herbie said.

'I appreciate that, but I don't want to impose.' Even as I turned them down, I screamed at myself inside. Where the hell was I going to stay if not with Abi and Herbie? They, at least, had a spare bedroom, unlike Gemma and Joe and most of my other friends, as well as being unencumbered by a separate friendship with Nate.

'Herbie's right, you're staying here until you get fed up with us,' Abi said, not meeting my gaze.

'You don't look convinced . . .' I queried softly, and her eyes sprang to mine.

'I am about that. Don't freak out, but Nate just rang.' I stiffened from head to toe. 'I didn't tell him you're here. I think he's calling round everyone you know, in a panic. He said to say, if you turned up, that he's sorry for hurting you. But just . . . but just that.'

I dropped into a dining chair. 'I don't want him to know where I am.'

'I know.' Abi covered my hand with her own. 'That's what I was telling Herbie.'

'Well, I think we should tell him something,' Herbie said, paying great attention to not spilling the steaming soup as he inched over to the table, though he didn't seem to notice that the end of his long ponytail had dipped into it at some point, and was now dripping green sludge onto the floor. 'If we say we heard from you and you're safe, he won't worry all night.'

Nate really didn't deserve his sympathy; he referred to Herbie as a pound shop Jared Leto, taking the piss out of everything from his waist-length hair to his business, knitting and selling shapeless hemp jumpers. 'I had another idea too,' Herbie said, before closing his eyes and inhaling the fetid smell of the soup with evident pleasure. I'd thought it impossible to get a vegan recipe emitting a strong stench of eggs until I'd encountered Herbie's cooking.

'What's that, hun?'

He opened his eyes. 'Spinach and fennel soup.'

'I meant your idea,' Abi said, with no hint of either impatience nor repulsion.

'Right. Well, I thought, Róisín might need to borrow one of the minibuses, to get there in time.'

'Sorry — to get where in time?' I asked.

'To the appointment to accept the prize.'

'Herbie,' Abi said, noticing that his hair was covered in soup. She wiped it off with the sleeves of the hideous green and yellow striped cardigan she was wearing, which was doubtless one of Herbie's hemp creations. 'Why on Mother Earth would Róisín go all the way to Sylverley to discuss marrying a man she just broke up with?'

He frowned as he ladled the gloop into three bowls. 'I didn't realise the prize was to get married to Nate at Sylverley. I thought it would be a wedding, to anyone she fancied marrying. So it seemed like she should go and explain, to see if they'll still let her have the prize, ready for when she meets the perfect person.'

'I imagine it's the latter,' Abi said slowly. 'But she said it had to be taken within a year.'

'Exactly! A *whole* year. Which is loads of time, since when you know, you know.' He gave her the sweetest of smiles. 'Like I did.'

'You're right,' Abi said, her eyes widening under her heavy fringe. 'We met eleven months ago, and look at us now! Róisín, what time's this appointment?'

'Seven,' I said. Their heads swivelled in unison to glance at the digital clock on their oven: 6:25. 'And I'm not going anywhere. The last thing I want to think about is a wedding.'

'Bu—'

'*I'm not discussing it.*'

They murmured apologies and busied themselves with the final preparations for the meal; Abi rooting in the sink of dirty dishes for spoons, then wafting them under the cold tap, Herbie hacking at a loaf of seeded bread with a blunt knife.

'Getting carried away like that was insensitive,' Abi said, returning with the spoons. 'It's just that Sylverley's so pretty, and a wedding there would be so perfect for you — I can so easily see you getting married there.'

I knew what she meant, because I'd spent so long imagining it myself. I'd daydreamed about a wedding somewhere along the lines of Sylverley for years and years, and then spent all those hours on five different digital mood boards of Sylverley wedding schemes in the week prior to my disastrous visit with Nate. I could even close my eyes and picture the wedding photo that would adorn the front of my album. Me, silhouetted in front of the perfectly proportioned house, in a beautiful Regency dress, looking at my groom with the unashamedly loving expression that Herbie and Abi gave each other. My groom's face was in shadow, so I couldn't identify much about him, except that, for the first time in the image in my mind's eye, he was certainly not Nate.

Opening my eyes, I curled my hands into fists. 'I hate Nate for destroying my opportunity to get married there.'

'Only actually to marry *him* there,' Abi put in mildly. 'He hasn't — *he can't* — stop you getting married there altogether.'

'If I meet someone else,' I said bleakly.

'If you meet someone else,' she agreed. 'And you've actually accepted the prize.'

I knew she was right when nerves kicked in, but then I recalled what I was wearing. 'I can't go anywhere,' I said, accepting a spoon. 'I look a complete state.'

'So?' Herbie said, tucking into his soup. 'You'll be chatting with a couple of people about the prize. It won't matter that your hair looks like a nest or that your eyes are all red like that or—'

I intervened before he talked me out of it entirely. 'Does it matter how I look, Abi?'

She squinted, scanning from my damp, messy bun down to her husband's harem pants, hanging off my hips like clown clothing, then back up again. 'Honestly? I can't see why. And if you're going to make it anything like on time, you've got to go now.' She trotted over and lifted a key ring from a hook by the back door. 'Come on — we'll take the red minibus.'

* * *

If I was driving, I'd have turned back as soon as I realised that Bath was snarled with more traffic than was usual for a Saturday evening. Partly because it was making me late, and I had more than enough to apologise for without that too. But even more because it gave me more time to absorb the insanity of what I was doing; informing Sylverley's head of events that I would like to accept the generous prize of a wedding . . . despite becoming suddenly single.

I stared out of the side window, swallowing hard. *Single.*

'We need to go back,' I blurted.

'No, we don't,' Abi said blithely.

After one attempt at wimping out, it became easier. 'I'll be half an hour late at this rate, so the woman I'm meeting will have given up on waiting for me — please, just move into the other lane, so we can turn back.'

'You won't be anything like as late as that — we'll be through this junction any second, and the roads should be clear the rest of the way.' The lights switched to amber, and she grinned at me, shifted into first gear and put her foot down.

She was right, and we made up some time, even in the lumbering minibus, but my dread increased with the speed.

'I honestly don't think I can go through with this. Not tonight.'

She circuited a mini roundabout, turning onto the B-road that wound down through a village, skirting first Sylverley's eastern wall, then part of the southern boundary, before passing the main entrance. 'You have to. I know what you're like — if you put it off once, you'll keep putting it off forever.'

'Then let me use your phone? I'll call them and apologise, explain what's happened and ask—'

'Alerting them on the phone makes it too easy for them to make up some bullshit terms and conditions to deny you the prize. Honestly, the way to get away with this is to ask in person.'

'You're not listening to me.' The words tore from my chest in a whimper. 'I *can't do it*. Even thinking about it is making me . . .' I raised my trembling hands.

She glanced at them, then shifted her gaze back to the road, her voice softening. 'The shakes are a bit of shock. Only to be expected, after the day you've had. But we're really close now, and I'll stick by your side while you inform these people what's happened. Keep it short and sweet, and with any luck we'll be zooming home shortly after, safe in the knowledge that you've secured your prize. And yes, I know the last thing you feel like is finding someone else — someone *better* — to marry, but the point is that you'll have the option open, as and when you meet someone.' Abi's hands were so tight around the steering wheel that her knuckles were white. 'You got angry about Nate destroying this opportunity for you, and I'll be angry if you destroy it for yourself.'

I plaited my fingers together. 'You'll really stay with me the whole time?'

'*Absolutely.*'

Her strength quelled the writhing in my guts, though I couldn't speak much more than to warn her that the entrance came up fast.

She slowed enough not to overshoot the wrought-iron gates, and turned into the driveway, gasping at Sylverley on the horizon, this time with the sun low in the sky beside it. In the mild summer evening, now the rainstorm had passed, it looked even more magnificent than I'd remembered.

Ahead, a barrier had been erected across the drive, with a wooden hut immediately to its left. A stout man in his fifties, with a face like a weather-beaten shovel, lumbered out.

I groaned. 'If we're redirected to the trade entrance, we really are leaving.'

Abi shushed me, lowering her window. 'Good evening! We're here to discuss the prize my friend has won.'

'You're the girl who won the wedding?' the man asked, his voice warm with West Country burr.

'My friend is,' Abi said, louder.

He half-turned, spoke into a walkie-talkie, then stooped down to the window, this time speaking across Abi.

'Róisín O'Reilly? They're waiting for you urgently.' He returned his attention to Abi. 'You've special permission to drop her at the front of the house. Then circle back to park in the upper field.' He pointed towards Sylverley as he retreated, as though otherwise we might miss it.

'We'll park first — I'm staying with my friend,' Abi hollered after him, but I shook my head.

'Just drop me,' I said through clenched teeth. 'Then walk up to the house. It's not far, and I can manage alone for the first ten minutes.'

'You sure?'

'I don't want to keep them waiting even longer.'

She was tapping her nails against the steering wheel as we neared the house, and the tyres crunched over gravel. 'You're still shivering. Take my cardigan — I mean it, put it on.' She'd discarded her ugly cardigan before starting the engine, and the time in my footwell hadn't improved either its looks or its odour. But I didn't want her to worry about me, so I draped it around my shoulders, avoiding the sleeve with which she'd mopped up spinach soup from Herbie's hair.

'Don't rush back and trip over,' I called, as I opened the door and leaped down. 'If I'm not still beside this portico—'

'I'll ask a staff member to help me find you,' she said. 'I'll see you shortly.'

I spared one forlorn glance after the departing minibus, then breathed in, long and slow. Unfortunately I caught a whiff of the soup and almost gagged. There was nothing I could do but hitch my overlarge trousers up and speed march toward the steps of the portico, hoping the breeze would eliminate the worst of my odour.

'Arriving looking like you've been dressed from a lost property box is bad enough,' I hissed at myself, as I started up the steps, my eyes scrunched against the sun, 'without stinking like you're doused in Eau de Eggy Spinach.'

I crashed into someone. A woman about my own age, in the grey skirt suit and teal blouse of Sylverley's uniform, whose large-toothed smile dropped off her face when she clocked the mess of my clothing — or maybe my smell.

'Enjoy your visit to Sylverley,' she said, stepping lower and calling to a smartly-dressed young couple who were strolling, hand in hand, past the portico: 'Are you Róisín and her fiancé?'

As the couple responded blankly, and she began to scan around again, I saw the polished bronze oval pinned to her lapel; *Miranda Pangbourne-Perkinson, Head of Events.*

I slithered the cardigan from my shoulders, folding it over my arm, and moved up a step, so I was downwind of her. 'Excuse me? I'm . . . uh . . . I'm who you're looking for. I'm really sorry I'm late.'

Her eyes stretched wide. 'You're Ms O'Reilly?'

'Yes. Do call me Róisín.'

'In that case, you must call me Perky,' she said briskly. 'Everyone always does.'

'Sorry, *Perky?*' I couldn't quite believe my ears, and thought her accent was perhaps to blame. She spoke with one of those upper-class drawls that distorted vowel sounds, so *always* sounded like awl-whizz.

'Oh, you heard right,' she said, already heading up the steps, and beckoning for me to follow. 'My full name's such a mouthful that at boarding school I became Perky Perkinson, and I've never thrown it off since. Róisín, excuse the impertinence, but where is your fiancé?'

'He couldn't make it after all. Because of . . . the short notice.' I didn't know where the words came from, beyond a sudden certainty that I wouldn't . . . *couldn't* utter the real

43

explanation until Abi was back at my side. 'But my friend accompanied me. She's just parking and then—'

The walkie-talkie at Perky's waist crackled. She unclipped it and moved it swiftly to her mouth. 'She's here, and alone. Mr Holt was correct . . . Yes, bringing her straight in.'

She marched me to the top of the steps and into the foyer. It was deserted, except for a cluster of Sylverley staff beside the largest double doors, leading to the ballroom, which were open a crack.

'Uh . . . Perky? Could someone please direct my friend to wherever we'll be?'

She side-eyed me as she clicked in her high heels across the polished marble. 'Probably best for her to meet you afterwards.'

Before I could object, the group of staff surged towards us, each individual reacting with a split-second of amusement or horror at my clothing before controlling their faces and introducing themselves by their job titles, things like head of PR or vice-head of visitor experience. They were mostly young women, and despite their array of shapes and sizes, all very much alike, sharing chic Sylverley uniforms and an abundance of self-confidence.

'Which just leaves the boss — Tristan Nash, general manager of Sylverley,' Perky said briskly. 'Tristan, come and meet our prize winner,' she called to a tall man who had lingered by the double door, his back to us as he engaged in a conversation through the crack.

He pivoted and took a few steps, and instantly the writhing in my stomach returned.

It was the eye-catchingly attractive man who'd tried to send Nate and me to the delivery entrance. The man I'd been so incensed at for interrupting my speech about getting married at Sylverley. The man, now immaculately dressed and outstretching his hand, whose face betrayed nothing of what he thought of my outfit, until he focussed on my features and could no longer control his surprise.

'We've already . . . met.' I didn't know if his words were for me, Perky or himself, as I gave his hand one brief shake.

His palm was rougher than I expected for a man in such a well-cut suit. It was made of the same grey fabric as the rest of the Sylverley staff, but I'd tailored enough men's clothing to recognise that the three pieces had been custom-made for the perfect fit. His teal silk tie was knotted into a half-Windsor, his blond hair had been recently trimmed, and his firm jaw was double shaved.

I willed myself not to flush, as I became even more acutely aware of what I must look like. Damp hair, scraped up messily, my eyes rimmed with red, and horrendous tie-dye trousers paired with white trainers and topped by a T-shirt with an obnoxious slogan.

His eyes met mine. They were an ambivalent hue, set between straight eyebrows and high ridged cheek bones. 'I understood on the phone that your fiancé would also be joining us this evening . . .' He paused and cleared his throat.

I filled my lungs, steeling myself to answer honestly. *I have no fiancé anymore.* But it was like my tongue was numb; I couldn't form the words.

'Unfortunately he couldn't make it at such short notice,' Perky said. I was half grateful for the rescue, and half annoyed that she'd perpetuated my lie. Admitting the real situation would be even harder now.

Say it, say it, I urged myself.

I parted my lips just as someone opened the double doors fully. 'It's time!'

'Righty-oh,' Perky said, with a clap. 'Róisín, let me take your . . . err . . . coat.'

I clutched the stinky cardigan tighter. 'I'm fine.'

'Really, I insist,' she said, whipping it from me then urging me close to the wide doorway, which was nearly a metre deep, the sides inlaid with wood panels. Heavy curtains in red brocade were now the only barrier between us and the ballroom beyond. 'Tristan, you'll have to escort her in.'

'What? Why—' I began, but several staff members hushed me, and someone gave me a push, right between my shoulder blades, so I had to step forward into the panelled door embasure. Tristan paced so close to my side that I could smell his oaky aftershave. He straightened the cuffs of his jacket then crooked his elbow.

'Shall we, Róisín?'

The curtains sprang open. For an instant my eyes swam, and all I could take in was lilting harp music, and the low, steady hum of multiple conversations.

Then my vision cleared, and I saw that the ballroom was crammed with people, splendidly dressed in evening wear, interspersed with Sylverley staff holding trays of champagne flutes and canapés.

And at that moment, the music stopped, and every head swivelled towards us, like we'd been picked out by a spotlight.

A young man dressed like a footman piped up into a microphone. 'Please welcome our honoured guest — Sylverley's prize winner, Ms Róisín O'Reilly, together with her fiancé—' Tristan shot him a look of appalled disbelief and he coughed. '*Sorry*, together with the general manager of Sylverley, *Mr Tristan Nash*.'

The sea of people broke into applause. The noise startled me into an attempt to whirl around and flee, but Perky and the other young women were pressed too closely behind me. Numbly, I slipped my arm through Tristan's, and let myself be swept into the room and through the clusters of people.

'Stage fright?' Tristan murmured out of the side of his mouth, and I knew my shivers had started up again. 'Don't worry, we'll only be on the dais briefly. You just need to sign that you formally accept the prize and then we'll get you some champagne.'

'I can't stay,' I hissed back at him, suddenly frantic. 'My friend's outside, I have to go to find her.'

'We'll help you do that in just a few moments.'

He inclined his head at women dressed in Chanel and Dior gowns, and I cringed.

'I'm really sorry, Tristan. I missed a bit of what you said on the phone — I had no idea this would be so public. And then I got caught out in the rain and had to borrow clothes.'

'It really doesn't matter,' he said, though I thought I heard a little relief at my explanation, and then we were taking a high step onto a platform, and spinning back, facing the crowd from behind a lectern, on which was laid a sheet of paper and a fountain pen.

The footman with the microphone announced more details . . . *Róisín won our wedding day of your dreams competition . . . formally accepting the prize now* . . . To avoid the scrutiny I was getting, I pinned my eyes to the visual focus of the vast space — the domed glass lantern that took up most of the ceiling. Dusky light cascaded through it, causing the gilded frieze surrounding it to glitter.

'I don't recall your fiancé's name,' Tristan whispered.

My eyes shot to the paper. It was a simple contract, stating the prize of a wedding, all expenses paid, to take place at Sylverley House and Estate within the next calendar year. Beneath it was *Bride: Róisín O'Reilly*, with even the fadas in the correct places. His pen was poised beside the word *Groom*.

My head span. 'I can't sign something on his behalf . . .'

'Good point.' He considered, then left a gap where a groom's name should have been.

'Sign at the bottom,' he said, passing me the pen. 'And then the wedding's yours.'

'There's a . . . complicating factor I need to check with you first,' I breathed, swaying slightly.

'Whoops,' he said, laying a gentle hand on my shoulder. Once I was firm on my feet again he released his hold on me. 'Sign it quickly, and I'll have you whisked out of here with a glass of water, to find your friend.'

I stared at the paper that committed me to accepting a wedding.

'Is there a problem, Róisín?' Tristan asked in my ear. 'You do actually want this prize?'

It committed me to accepting a wedding, I thought, *but not to marrying Nate.*

I set my jaw. 'I do,' I said, and scrawled my name.

CHAPTER 5: HIS MISSUS

I'd started over twice before in my life. The first time was solely down to my parents, since I was three years old when my father got an engineering job in London, and they moved from their house in west Derry to a flat midway up a high-rise. I hated that Mam cried a lot, not having a garden, and the lift, which smelled of what I later identified as piss and meth. But I loved the views out over the city and I came to love growing up in London, so that first fresh start was something I'd always viewed positively.

The second time came as my history degree ended. I'd studied in London automatically, because a degree was what came next on the educational treadmill, and staying near home was essential with my father gravely ill. Dad died in my second year, and within weeks my mother had sold up and taken my siblings back to Derry. But I was busy with my course and cleaning job, and settled in a flat share with Gemma, Joe and a rolling succession of other students, so the losses didn't fully hit me until graduation approached. Joe had accepted a teaching job and Gemma a traineeship at a solicitor's firm, both in Bath, where they could live with his parents, and other friends would live at home to study for a masters. When I was rejected for every role which could have earned me enough to stay in London, sharing bunk beds with Aoife while working in a supermarket in Derry felt unavoidable. Until I went to Bath for the weekend for Gemma and Joe's wedding, met Nate, and decided on my second fresh start. Within a month I'd met Abi, in her messy little house, where we came to a quick arrangement — I'd conduct as many tours as she could book, at a low hourly rate, in exchange for staying in her spare bedroom.

And here I was, holed up in Abi's spare bedroom again, cowering from the smoking ruins of my life with Nate. But this time I couldn't stay for four years — even if I could cope with the chaos of her and Herbie's well-meaning hospitality, they'd need their spare room for their baby. And anyway, returning here felt like a step backward, when what I needed was a third completely fresh start. But even planning that was difficult, when as much as I didn't want to, I was missing Nate so badly. After so long together it felt like I'd lost an organ — probably one of the ones involved in oxygen circulation, as sudden waves of agonising breathlessness kept crashing over me.

It was in the middle of a bout of painful gasps of grief that I decided to open up a conversation about the lingering practicalities by texting *hi* to Nate, on the basis that I couldn't feel any worse anyway. His reply blinked back almost instantly.

—*I'm worried about you, Rosh. Are you ready to talk?*

I instantly knew I'd been wrong; it had been possible to feel worse.

It was a few days later before I managed to reply.

—*No interest in talking. We need to organise splitting the joint savings account.*

His response was neither angry nor cajoled me to return, instead insisting that I took over our small deposit of savings, and assuring me that there was no rush for me to move the rest of my belongings out. It was just as well, as the spare room was too small for much more than the suitcase of essentials Abi had done a mercy mission to collect for me. But I couldn't earn until I had space to sew, and that meant renting a place big enough to live and work, so even as I replied with a brief *thank you*, I knew I had to push aside my grief for long enough to sort my life out. Somehow.

In the middle of one sleepless night I put pen to paper and scrawled a list: *find a cheap spacious place to rent, get in touch with Gemma and Joe, tell Mam about the break-up, solve Sylverley problem.*

In the morning I ripped off the bottom item. Even in the warm light of a summer's day it was too intimidating to face the fact that I was single and contracted to get married. Plus, Abi might read my list, and when I'd hustled her out of Sylverley's foyer she'd assumed I'd explained my single status and that they'd graciously assented to giving me the prize anyway. I still hadn't put her right.

I began with the easiest item, and checked online adverts, ascertaining that no miraculously cheap flats had become available for rental. The second easiest was loading the family chat group. I ignored the recent messages, which were all about Aoife's wedding, and ignored my stinging eyes as I typed that I'd broken up with Nate, moved back in with Abi, was doing fine.

Which left Gemma and Joe to deal with. Nate had alluded to telling them about his reluctance to marry me, but in all the hours I'd spent in angsty discussion about how long he was taking to propose, they'd never given me any hint of that, and the betrayal smarted. But Esme was my goddaughter, so I had to sort it out with them at some point.

'Just not today,' I muttered, truculently.

The next day Abi and Herbie returned, rather shell-shocked, from her twelve-week scan, clasping a grainy image of twins. I knew I needed to give them some space and wandered around Bath's fashion museum for a while, before calling Gemma.

'You're meeting me at a wine bar,' she snapped. 'Tonight.'

I assented, but vowed to myself that if I caught even a whiff of an attempt to take Nate's side, I'd walk out.

* * *

Perched on a barstool, I watched warily as Gemma entered.

'At least you threw something at the prick,' she said in place of a greeting. 'I just wish it was something harder than a trainer — and that you hadn't missed.' Almost unwillingly, I started to laugh. 'What?'

'That was pretty much the opposite of what I was worried about you saying.'

'You thought I'd take Nate's side?' She draped her jacket on the stool next to mine. 'Fuck that. I'm furious with him.'

I ran my finger around the rim of my glass. 'Does that mean he had or hadn't told you that he never planned to marry me?'

She glanced up from the drinks menu, casually enough that I was sure she was innocent. 'I swear he never told me. And Joe only confessed that he knew it after we heard what happened last week. What's that you're drinking?'

'Dunno what it's called.' I lowered my voice. 'The bar manager brought it over, on the house — don't go staring at him like that! He's a semi-regular at the café, so either he thinks I still live there with Nate and it's one of the freebies that food service people give each other, or he's heard we broke up and it's a pity cocktail.'

'Or he heard you're single and wants you to notice him.' Gemma's voice had a speculative edge that made me scowl. 'Fine, fine.' She waved for his attention, enquired about my drink and established that it was a rhubarb daiquiri, declared it too sweet and ordered a vodka soda. 'Light on the soda,' she called after him.

I stirred my drink with a straw, wondering precisely what Joe knew, and when. It hurt, but in that weirdly satisfying way, like obsessively pressing on a bruise.

'Gemma? How did Joe justify reassuring me all those times that Nate would man up and ask me to marry him, knowing he didn't want to?'

'Because he didn't *know it* know it. Apparently it only ever came up when they were drinking, so he assumed Nate was overstating the strength of his feeling about marriage and would work through it, given enough time.'

'Given enough of my time,' I muttered, as she accepted her glass from the barman, with a wink.

'How much is that, or do I get a freebie too?'

'Of course, it's on the house,' he said, glancing at me. 'Róisín, you—'

'I'm still going with this one, uh . . .' I couldn't remember his name. 'Thanks.'

'Thing is,' she said after a sip. 'Joe's such an optimist that he's shocked the two of you are over. Whereas I only knew half of what he knew, and am barely surprised.'

I pushed my drink a little up the bar, to remind myself not to finish it for a while. Whatever the barman's motivation, I didn't want to accept another freebie. 'Really?'

'I thought the writing might be on the wall about a year before the engagement, with what he gave you for Christmas.'

'The make your own soy sauce kit,' I said, wrinkling my nose. 'When I hate cooking. And I've never told you the worst thing.'

'What, he made it himself and served it downstairs in the café? He got it free in a Japanese restaurant?'

'Maybe all that too, but worst of all was the wrapping.' I had to pull the drink back and take a glug of the rhubarb-infused rum. 'We had some wrapping paper left over from his birthday. So to save him buying a Christmassy gift bag he wrapped it in that. It had *Happy Birthday* printed all over it. Realising I might object, he added *Jesus* in a matching colour at the end of every *Happy Birthday*.'

Her jaw dropped open. 'He could have got a gift bag for what, a quid?'

'I guess it adds insult to injury,' I said into my cocktail. 'Him hating the idea of marrying me, even with a totally free wedding.'

'Don't talk to me about that flipping wedding. Esme's broken-hearted about not being a bridesmaid after — shit, Róisín, I was exaggerating. Seriously, don't cry — or between the tears and the hiccups the cutie behind the bar will think you're hammered, and stop serving us. Honestly, Esme's *fine* now. I explained that her fairy godmother will undoubtedly be swept off her feet by someone perfect within a few years, and be in dire need of her bridesmaid services again.'

'Absolutely, I will. In fact, if I meet anyone even halfway perfect, I'll snap him up just to follow through on my promise to her.' I pressed under my eyes with the napkin she'd thrust at me. 'It could even end up being at Sylverley, within eleven and a half months.'

'Pardon?'

I shook my head. 'Ignore me.'

'There's literally no way you get out of explaining.'

I groaned. If there was any sure-fire way to divert her, I'd have done it — even if it meant propositioning the barman — but she'd have only returned to the topic afterwards, like a dog with a buried bone. 'Ugh, *fine*. So when Nate and I ended, the wedding at Sylverley seemed like a non-starter, obviously. But then . . . well, then I got angry about Nate ruining my chance at the only prize I'd ever won, and let myself be persuaded to go along and request to keep it, in case . . . well in case I meet someone between now and then.'

'Persuaded by . . . oh, Abi and her eco-warrior, who saves the planet one hemp sweater at a time?'

'Don't. I've come to really like Herbie — despite him trying to poison me several times a day.' At her astonished glance, I added, 'He stirs vegetables into combinations that make them taste like rancid eggs.'

'Must be bad, for you to notice,' she muttered. 'Oh, come on. At uni, whenever it was your night to cook we got those crappy sausages that come in a tin with baked beans.'

Now she'd reminded me, I quite fancied a tin of them. 'If you'd rather discuss my lack of culinary skill . . .'

'No, carry on. The herbivorous lovebirds had a crazy idea, and what, accompanied you to ensure you enacted it? Abi's got the gift of the gab, but a nice sincerity with it. I bet she told the sob story on your behalf, and no one there liked to say no to her?'

I downed the rest of my cocktail. 'Not quite. She did come with me, but there was a hideous mix up . . . actually that part's all incidental.' Explaining what had happened wasn't as excruciating as experiencing it, but it wasn't far off. I finished on one breath, to get it over with. 'Basically, I got split up from Abi, wimped out and signed a contract to accept the wedding without telling anyone at Sylverley that I'd just become single.'

Gemma choked explosively, nearly dropping her glass in the process. Then she stared at me, motionless.

I stiffened, steeling myself for her response, but she shook her head mutely, then finished her drink in several swallows, and held it up, high, in the direction of the barman. 'I have to cross-examine this defendant. We need more booze.'

* * *

We were on our third round before the inquisition was over. While Gemma was unsure whether I'd signed a contract or something purely ceremonial, she'd established that there was no way it could be legally binding. She hadn't worked as a solicitor for three years, giving up soon after Esme's diagnosis, but her previous experience, and quick call to a former colleague, put my mind at rest.

'In essence you've ended up with an option; the right, but not the obligation, to a free wedding at Sylverley. Goodness knows how their management will react, but you do need to apologise, and inform them as soon as possible.'

'Fury. Ire. Burning coals and pitchforks,' I said morosely.

'Not necessarily. If you don't go through with the wedding, they don't have to supply one — it saves them money. On the other hand, presumably there's a reason they ran the competition in the first place, and they'll lose out on whatever that perceived upside was.' She broke off to purse her lips around the paper straw she'd stuck in her vodka soda, her cheeks hollowing as she sucked. 'And of course, it's not impossible that you meet someone, and the wedding goes ahead?'

'For a stupid moment,' I admitted quietly, 'when Abi and Herbie were all loved up, and I was half in shock from the break-up, I imagined bumping into a man in a library and locking eyes as he tells me he's a historian—'

Gemma snorted. 'Serendipity isn't what'll get you a husband. If you really wanted this prize, you'd have to go for it properly.'

'What d'you mean *if* I really wanted this prize? Of course I want it, Gem.' The alcohol was getting to me, making it easier to expose myself. 'I want a beautiful wedding day, in the dream location, to the love of my life. But Nate doesn't want any of that with me.' As I spoke, I made a wish that one day I'd become accustomed enough to that thought that it wouldn't cause the painful constriction in my stomach.

'So you need to find the one who does.' Her eyes wide and intense, never had the resemblance to her daughter been stronger. 'Not by relying on the historian in a library bullshit, but by putting yourself out there until you find him.'

I stared at her. 'Did you start on the vodka at home or something?'

'This isn't inebriated frontal cortex impairment, if that's what you're implying. Listen, there's no reason you can't have this wedding — dating is just a numbers game, and if you meet enough eligible men, you'll find him. The one. And I'll help you!'

'You really are serious.'

'You always look amazing, and you're kind and bright,' Gemma said in a burst of feeling which she immediately balanced by adding, 'Lots of men will dig the history-nerd stuff, and you can keep quiet about your shit cooking until you've suckered them in.'

'I don't need lots of men. I just need one.'

'Exactly! Meet loads, to end up with one — easy-peasy.' She narrowed her eyes as she considered. 'Online dating's the easiest way to line up a load of dates, but that's how my sister got that stalker, so then . . .' She narrowed her eyes at me. '*My Single Pal*.'

'That's me.'

'No, that's the name of the matchmaking app where friends or family set someone up on blind dates. My sister got nervous after the stalking, so I downloaded it and wrote her a profile. It was so easy to read the profiles of single men written by their loved ones, choose potential matches and then send her off on dates with them. And—' she stretched her lips over her teeth in a menacing smile — 'if a bloke steps out of line, I was in contact with his relatives. So I'll do a profile for you, and start booking in dates — simple.'

I stared at her. Flinty eyes shining with certainty beneath her blonde curls. 'Maybe you're right . . . maybe I should think about that . . . Once I'm over Nate.'

She did such a long, loud groan that the barman glanced over with evident alarm. 'I take all the compliments back. You're not bright at all Róisín — in fact you're completely dim.'

'That's not nice!'

'If you valued *nice* you wouldn't have made friends with me in the first place.'

'True enough.' I sucked up some more of my drink, thinking hard. 'Gemma? Do you . . . do you really think this is doable?'

Her eyes bored into mine. 'Hell yes. As long as you get on with it, and don't sit around licking the wounds Nate inflicted. Time's already short, and I know what you're like for putting things off. And anyway, you'll get over Nate faster by getting yourself out there, don't you reckon?'

'Maybe,' I said, slightly to my own surprise, though Gemma just nodded, satisfied with her own powers of persuasion. 'So . . . I guess, if you can find anyone decent for me, that would be okay.'

'Of course I can,' she said, waving a hand dismissively. 'Literally all you're meant to give me is your consent, and what kind of man you want blah blah blah, but I know all that.'

Blah blah blah. A qualm hit me. 'Maybe I should tell you anyway, just in case? I want someone local, and who likes history—' I anticipated her objection and sped on. 'Or if that's hard to find, then someone who can at least appreciate old buildings and things like that. I want him to . . .' It had been on my lips to say *be the opposite of Nate*, but that wasn't right. Nate and I had worked for as long as we did because some of our traits matched. What I needed to swerve was where we didn't match. 'I want him to actively want to settle down, and not be scared of marriage.'

She waved at the barman. 'Can we look at the drinks menu? I need something stronger — I don't feel in the slightest bit tipsy.' Gemma had always been good at holding her drink. Whereas I was feeling the effects of three to the extent of thinking my bodily functions were interesting, and loudly announced that I needed a wee.

'Good for you. Here — leave me your phone, so I can sync us with this app.' Gemma took it then flipped it and held it out, expectantly. I pressed my finger to unlock it before wandering off to the ladies'.

When I returned, Gemma thrust my phone under the bar, but I was closer to sobriety, from holding my wrists under the cold tap, and I'd already seen that her thumbs were rapidly pressing across my screen.

'Surely you can write my profile from your own phone?' Gemma glanced up at me. 'So suspicious.'

'With good reason — what did you do?' I'd only asked again to provide a distraction as I pounced to snatch it.

'Hey — I'm not finished!'

I stared at the screen. She'd not only loaded up the email I'd been ignoring, entitled *Afternoon Tea with your fiancé*, but she'd had the gall to write a reply.

Hi Miranda, thank you for this invitation. I'd love to come to Sylverley for afternoon tea and to discuss potential wedding dates. Unfortunately I'll have to come alone, due to an additional matter I need to discuss with you, so the sooner the better from my perspective.

Tally ho! Róisín

'What the fuck,' I spluttered. 'Tally ho?'

'I repeated the same sign off as Miranda Hyphenated-Mouthful, or whatever her name is. You can change that, but then you have to send it.'

'No one calls her Miranda, either. But I'm not—'

'Yes, you are. As the closest thing you've got to a legal representative, I assure you it's in your best interest to 'fess up as soon as possible. I could come with you and—'

'No need,' I said, shuddering. 'Okay, fine, look, I've edited and I'm pressing send. We'll fix a date between us and I'll go along and tell the Sylverley people I'm single.'

'Single but actively searching, remember.'

'Single but actively searching,' I echoed, as she ordered two espresso martinis.

'Coffee's too bitter—' I began.

'Don't care. You need waking up. It was a rookie error to leave me with access to your phone like that. Seriously, what were you thinking?'

The barman's eyes boinged between us as we continued squabbling while he made the martinis, then approached and slid them across the bar. 'I added plenty of sugar to yours, Róisín.'

'Oh. Thanks.'

Gemma grasped the one he'd set nearer her, and sipped cautiously. Her pale eyebrows shot up. 'But an extra shot of coffee in mine. You're good at telling what people are into.' The speculative glint in her eyes concerned me, and I nudged her knee.

He raised his shoulders. 'Lots of experience with hearing people's problems, I guess. It helps me to recommend a drink based on their personality. Or, when they know exactly what they want, to amuse myself working out why.'

'So what do you conclude about someone who orders vodka sodas?'

He leaned forward on the bar. 'You're in it for the booze. Without the calories. Or the taste. Drinking as a means to an end.'

She considered that. 'Maybe we don't even need the app,' she mused. I bashed her knee with my own again, harder, but she ignored me. 'Want to take Róisín out for dinner?'

'Gemma!' I cringed so hard that I felt, for a moment, like I'd turned myself inside out. And the aghast expression on the barman's face didn't dispel the idea that I might just have exposed all my internal organs.

'I'm . . .' he stammered. 'Is this . . . ? I'm not saying that she's not pretty and all. But Nate would kill me if I took out his missus.'

CHAPTER 6: SAVE THE DATE

I stepped out into the scorching sunshine, from the minibus I'd borrowed from Abi with a vague murmur about a trip to Sylverley. She hadn't asked questions, distracted by the imminent arrival of her in-laws. My suggestion of ordering lunch in from a deli was soundly ignored, but I'd at least been able to tidy up while Herbie fussed over the lentil-stuffed marrow.

'Róisín — hullo.'

I looked for Perky, and discovered instead a woman who was a bit younger and much taller, but with an almost identical drawl. She could have been one of those I was introduced to outside the ballroom, but their names and faces had blurred into one, so I just waved in reply.

'Amelia Legg, head of marketing,' she said promptly. 'We met when you were here a fortnight ago. And may I say, you look lovely today.' The *today* made me wince slightly, and her brow furrowed. 'I rather put my foot in it there. I heard we inadvertently ambushed you with that ball — and anyway, you really do look lovely — where's your dress from?'

'I made it,' I said, smoothing the skirt of my floral halter-neck. I'd spent the day prior trying on every outfit in the limited wardrobe I had available, searching out something that gave an apologetic impression. But the linen shift dress I'd had in mind was still at Nate's place, and not wanting to arrive under-dressed again, I'd gone for the nicest dress Abi had packed for me, which had a tiny daffodil print.

Amelia continued chatting as she led the way along a path snaking round the east of Sylverley house, pausing every now and then only to fan herself with a sheaf of paperwork. The uniforms, usually so elegant, were far from ideal for the heatwave. I learned that her line manager was Perky, who had a few other hats, on top of heading up events. Perky, in turn, reported into Tristan, who was ultimately in charge of every aspect of the estate, having been appointed by Ashgrove, the trust that ran it. I intervened when she seemed on the verge of listing the names, roles and responsibilities of everyone at her level of management.

'Have you had many wedding bookings yet?'

Her answer was cut off by a large tour group approaching from the other direction. We pressed into a bush to give them space. Once they'd passed, Amelia flicked a leaf from my skirt, then rotated slowly, so I could check her.

'Thanks,' she said, as I pulled a bit of twig from her hair. 'And what was that — oh, weddings. Unfortunately, none yet. It's early days of course, and we knew it would take a while — that's what gave us the idea for the competition. To spread the word that we're doing weddings now, and—' I caught her considering, sidelong glance.

'And?'

Her smile was cautious. 'If it's okay with you and your fiancé, we're very much hoping you'll give us permission to use photographs of your special day in our marketing campaigns.'

I swallowed. 'Ah,' I croaked. 'Right.' My confession had become instantly more awkward, I thought rather desperately: *Yes, you can photograph my perfect Sylverley wedding for marketing purposes . . . but there is a significant risk of no groom.*

My lack of reply hadn't gone unnoticed. 'I'm so sorry if that's overstepping,' she said quickly. 'Oh dear, I should have waited for Perky to ask you.'

'That's not the issue at all,' I said, as we approached a fork in the footpath. At the end of one of the branches, I could see the glass of the orangery glinting in the sunlight. 'I'd be happy to allow photos to be used however you need, except that—'

'Perfect timing,' Perky said, approaching from another branch of the path, just ahead of Tristan Nash, who stretched his hand out. His fair hair shone in the sunlight.

'Róisín, nice to meet you again,' he said. 'Amelia — Mrs Holt tells me that you've reserved the best table and ordered a special menu — I can't wait.'

During a few minutes of fast but unfrazzled efficiency, I was ushered up to the large orangery, whisked inside and introduced to a beaming, rotund woman. Mrs Holt, whose polished brass badge declared her Sylverley's head of catering, didn't stop talking as we filtered past tables filled with guests enjoying afternoon tea. She seated the four of us in upholstered chairs at what seemed indeed to be the nicest table. It was at the rear of the orangery, set squarely between floor-to-ceiling windows, with an unimpaired view of the rose garden that stretched toward the house, and the panorama of criss-crossing hills in the distance.

Tristan drew my attention from the view by clearing his throat, as Mrs Holt trundled off. 'Róisín — thank you, we're grateful.'

My bemusement must have been clear on my face, as Perky prompted, with her large-toothed smile: 'Amelia was just saying you kindly granted permission for use of your photos.'

Tristan nodded. 'It should help immensely with our efforts to take more wedding and event bookings.' In such bright, clear light, the colour of his eyes wasn't as ambivalent as I'd previously thought. They appeared light grey, like the trunks of the trees spaced along Sylverley's driveway. And although the set of his mouth and the straight line of his brows were controlled, they already seemed less severe than during our previous encounters.

Suddenly aware that his eyes had alighted on mine, I flicked mine away. The orangery was walled on the north side, which when this place was built, predominately for growing warm-climate plants, would have protected them from winter weather. Long, large windows lined the southern and westward sides. Air entered through the entrance at the east side, and with the help of overhead ceiling fans there was a slight but welcome breeze.

'This place is stunning,' I said.

'Glad you think so, given it's one of your options for a sit-down reception.' Perky nodded for Amelia to pass me the paperwork. 'One of the brochures shows all available options dressed as if for a wedding breakfast. After you've plumped for a date, which of those best suits you will be the next choice.'

'About the date,' I said. I exhaled some fear and sucked in a new breath, keeping my eyes on Amelia, who was by far the least intimidating person at the table. 'I need to pencil in as late as is possible — a full year from now. Because—'

'A full year from when you were awarded the prize is the latest allowable date,' Perky corrected, leafing through a large leather diary. 'That was on the thirteenth of June. Next year, the thirteenth is . . . a Friday.'

A wedding on Friday the thirteenth would pretty much sum up this whole debacle. 'I'd prefer a Saturday — the seventh, would that be? But as I said in my email, I need to explain why I'm alone for—'

'Pardon me, Tristan,' Mrs Holt interjected, bustling over. 'Mrs Sylvers is upset about a painting she wants to hang.'

A micro-expression of some strong emotion flitted across his face. It was gone again before I identified it, replaced by a veneer of politeness. 'I'm so sorry, but you'll have to excuse me,' he said, rising. 'Duty calls.'

He strode away, straight backed, making much faster progress towards the exit than Mrs Holt, without appearing to be in any rush as he wove between tables and planters containing small citrus trees. An older man stopped him, and, presumably looking no further than his suit in Sylverley colours, asked for a menu.

'My pleasure, sir.' Tristan said, collecting one from another table and handing it to him. 'My colleague will be over to take your order in just a moment.' Before exiting, he mentioned something in an undertone to a young waiter.

I glanced between Perky and Amelia. 'Mrs Sylvers? I hadn't realised any of the family were still . . .' I bit back the word *alive*. 'Still . . . in residence at Sylverley.'

'Suzanne Sylvers is the last of them,' Perky said briefly. 'She was married to Mr Edward Sylvers, who died last year.'

I frowned, attempting to fit this with the family history I'd read during my initial research. I was sure there had been something about Edward Sylvers' wife dying suddenly, and speculation that it had caused the tragedy in the next generation. I'd had to dig deeper to find the details online — their only child, Edward Sylvers junior, had left home after his mother's death, spiralled into drug addiction, and died before his thirtieth birthday. 'I thought Mrs Sylvers passed away several decades ago.'

'That was Edward's first wife,' Amelia explained. 'He married Suzanne in his sixties.'

'Is that why he didn't leave Sylverley for her to manage — she's very elderly?'

'Not exactly — she was some years younger than him.' The way Amelia's mouth twisted revealed more than her light words. It wasn't difficult to conclude that Mrs Suzanne Sylvers was generally hard work for the staff. 'Though not young enough for them to have a child, so with no heirs, leaving the estate in the hands of a trust was the only long-term option, if it was going to survive in any form.'

The young waiter stepped up to Perky. 'You ready to be served, or you'll wait for Tristan?'

'Goodness knows how long he'll be,' Perky said crisply. 'Whenever Mrs Holt's ready is fine. Right, what's next?' She consulted a piece of paper beside her. 'Ah, yes — Róisín, you wanted to explain why your fiancé couldn't attend today . . .'

Playing for time, I reached for the water jug and filled all our glasses. The only thing worse than explaining my single status once was having to say it twice. 'Shall we wait for Tristan, so I don't need to repeat myself?' I realised the error of framing that as a question, as Perky's mouth opened before I'd even finished, so I rushed on. 'I'd love to look at these brochures, to get a proper feel for the options for locations. Which are your recommendations for a strong Regency feel?'

Deferring to Perky had been the correct diversion, and she started on the relative merits of the orangery versus the domed ballroom for a ceremony, before concluding that ultimately it came down to numbers. A small crowd might feel overwhelmed in the ballroom, but a large one would certainly feel too crammed here in the orangery. 'How many guests are you and your fiancé planning to invite?'

I sipped my water rather desperately. *Actually, I've no idea how many friends and family the groom has . . . because I haven't met him yet.* 'To be honest, I'm more elastic on numbers than on the aesthetics. I'm a professional seamstress and tailor, you see, specialising in historical fashion, and I studied—'

Amelia's eyes bulged. 'I *thought* I recognised your name! Perky, remember that postcard I've got pinned to my notice-board? It's advertising Róisín's business — she makes historical garments, which we thought would be so amazing for us, for future swanky events.' Returning her gaze to me, she rattled on. 'We feel rather out of place in our uniforms, with guests dressed up and looking amazing — or almost all guests . . . oh, I'm sorry, but you know what I mean.'

I inclined my head, amused rather than offended. 'I do. It's fine. So . . . you thought historical costumes? It's an expensive way to solve the problem — much cheaper to wear dresses you already own, or even buying some teal ones off the peg, if you should all match.'

'But guests would love us all dressed up. We did that at Drumlanrig Castle — where I used to work, and it always became a real talking point. In fact, we got asked who made

65

them all the time — I believe the seamstress got a lot of work off the back of it.'

I could well believe that, having secured new clients in the past through word-of-mouth referrals. And a lot of people would be coming through Sylverley . . . I sat up straighter. 'Is this something there's serious interest in, Amelia?' Although my words were directed to the younger woman, my eyes were on Perky, who spoke next.

'It would be jolly nice. But we're only in the market for costumes that are properly authentic — we have too many history buffs through our doors to get away with anything else.' I smiled at her — *properly authentic* were my watchwords. 'And we don't have a large budget.'

It was an effort not to let my smile instantly drop. Authenticity and low budgets didn't go together, and I had long experience of the deterioration in people's enthusiasm for my work when they learned my prices. It wasn't obvious up-front how much time it took to meticulously research and design each garment, even before I got going making the pattern and then onto the laborious sewing.

'I tell you what,' I said evenly. 'I've got testimonials, photos and approximate costings here on my phone. I'll email them to you both in case it seems the right kind of thing for your needs at any stage.' I fished for my phone in my pocket then forwarded them my carefully prepared potential-commission package, with zero expectation. Nineteen out of twenty prospective clients who warned of budget constraints never even got back to me. And that was without the added complication of the confession they'd soon hear.

The waiter returned with a tray of bone china and silverware, and laid four place settings on our table. As Amelia flipped her tablet open I let my attention wander to the view. There was an ornate fountain in the centre of the rose garden, and I thought it was Tristan beside it, his arms moving fluidly as he interacted with a smaller figure: a raven-haired woman dressed from neck to toe in black. I stood and wandered closer to the window, but the distance remained too far for me to identify anything more about Suzanne Sylvers.

'These costumes are truly amazing,' Amelia was saying, her head bent beside Perky's as they scrolled through my document.

Perky's assent sounded grudging rather than enthused, and her head jerked up sharply when they reached the price list. 'These prices are way beyond us, unfortunately, Róisín.'

I smothered an unsurprised sigh as I returned to my place. 'No problem at all. As I'm sure you saw, all my pieces are made to measure and historically accurate. It's an expensive process.'

'If it was a smidge beyond what I could afford, I'd talk to Tristan, see if he'd sign off on a slight uplift on the budget,' she said slowly, her lips pursed. 'I really haven't seen anything else half as good. I wonder . . .'

The one commission in twenty from someone without money to burn came like this, where the distance of my price point seemed to encourage the exclusivity and therefore desirability of my services. With what was looming, I knew it unlikely to pay off, but I grasped the opportunity to at least show some willing, in hope of buttering her up ready for my confession. 'Given the circumstances, I could offer a ten per cent discount if you were to commission five or more costumes.'

'That sounds really—'

Perky spoke over Amelia. 'Could you stretch to twenty per cent off the total?'

'I wish I could. But honestly, I can't afford it right now. I'm . . .' *Stay honest*, I ordered myself internally. 'I lost my workspace recently, and committing to a new one's expensive.'

Her high forehead creased, but Amelia grew in excitement, until she was virtually bouncing up and down on her chair.

'I've had the *most* inspired idea. You have the skills we need and we have plenty of the space you need. So why don't you give us a large discount in exchange for us giving you workspace?'

Before Perky or I could respond, the waiter arrived with two three-tier cake stands, covered with linen napkins. I'd seen them on other tables, laden with the scones that had met even Nate's exacting standards, alongside little pots of clotted cream and butter, pastries, cakes and chocolate fondants. My stomach rumbled in anticipation as I calculated the depth of discount I could offer in the slim likelihood that Amelia's idea was a goer.

'Oh good, perfect timing,' Perky called, and I followed her gaze; Tristan was making his way back towards us.

'Apologies,' he murmured, taking his place as the cake stands were installed in the centre of the table.

'You placated her?' Perky muttered back. At his nod, she returned to normal volume. 'Róisín, we've got a little surprise for you.' She indicated the covered tiered stand nearer me, as Mrs Holt bustled over to stand behind her chair, grinning broadly. 'There isn't much to suit you on the afternoon tea menu, and Mrs Holt thought that would never do.'

'Sorry?'

'We all noted what your clothes said,' Amelia pronounced with pride.

Puzzled, I glanced down at my dress.

'The last time you were here,' Perky clarified, and with a sinking feeling, I recalled the top I'd worn to the grand reopening party, borrowed from Abi and declaring *I look this good because I'm vegan*.

'Here at Sylverley we don't miss anything,' Amelia burbled on. 'And the stupendous Mrs Holt devised a special plant-based afternoon tea especially in your honour — ta-dah!' She whipped the napkin away, revealing tiers filled predominately with green.

Mrs Holt leaned in. 'Spinach scones with nut butter, courgette and lemon loaf cake and avocado chocolate mousse pops.'

My lips parted to explain . . .

'Best of all,' Perky added briskly, 'new menus have been printed, with the vegan option named after our prize winner. She flipped open the large menu; half of the far page was headed *Róisín's Romantic Afternoon Tea — PB*.

'Actually I . . .' Glancing from face to face, I realised there was no way of letting them down gently. I'd make them feel ridiculous for going to all the effort, and they'd remember what had happened every time they glanced at a menu. It didn't matter, anyway; not compared to the important confession. 'I can't believe how . . . healthy this all looks. And seriously,' I added, hoping I'd misheard. 'There's avocado in the chocolates?'

'Yup — try one!' Amelia urged, biting into one herself.

I accepted one of everything, then cut it all up small on my plate, as Mrs Holt wandered off looking pleased, and Perky caught Tristan up on our discussion. 'We didn't get much wedding planning done,' she said. 'We were diverted by the realisation that Róisín is the fashion historian I'd been hoping to commission.'

Amelia passed him her tablet. 'Look at her work, Tristan — by far the best we've seen.'

I balanced a crumb of spinach scone on my fork, eyeing it sourly before popping it in my mouth and swallowing without chewing. There was no eggy aftertaste, so I slowed down enough to taste the next piece. It wasn't Herbie-level unpleasant. But it was nowhere near a buttery scone topped with clotted cream and strawberry jam.

Tristan had reached my prices. 'Maybe next year,' he said, shutting the iPad off rapidly. Perky and Amelia both started speaking and he raised his hands. 'What am I missing?'

'Róisín's prepared to give us a discount, but she can't go deeper than ten per cent, because she needs a new workspace. And we have plenty of space . . .'

Perky intervened. 'We have a whole suite of empty rooms on the ground floor of the east wing.'

'We do indeed. And they're as yet un-renovated, with woodworm multiplying so fast that my foot went through a floorboard yesterday,' he said dryly. 'Oh — thank you.' The waiter was back with a bottle of champagne in a silver ice bucket.

'Fine. What about one of the cottages? They're a decent size, and half-renovated at least.'

'*Half*-renovated,' Tristan repeated. 'Maybe we should ask Róisín how interested she'd be to live in a *half-renovated* old cottage?'

'*Work* there — she wouldn't have to live there,' Perky corrected.

At the exact same moment I said, 'I could *live* there as well?'

There was a loaded pause around the table. All I could think, against the background sounds of clinking cutlery and low conversation from distant diners, was free workspace *and* free rent. *Free workspace and free rent.*

Then Tristan smiled, and popped the cork on the champagne. 'Looks like we might be able to drink to more than just a wedding, here.'

As he filled the flutes, and Amelia whooped, Perky began to haggle over the discount for my services.

'If it worked out, I could cut at least forty percent from the invoice,' I assured her. 'Maybe a bit more.'

'You wouldn't have any utilities to pay . . . and your fiancé can stay there with you, if you want.'

I grimaced at the reminder of what I still needed to get over with, as Tristan passed me a champagne flute. 'Is the reality of a half-unrenovated cottage kicking in, Róisín? Please take some time to think about it—'

'It's not that,' I said. 'To be honest, if there's a small amount of space for me to live in, and at least one large room for me to work in, I'd accept willingly, whatever state it's in. But there are complicating factors, and once I've explained, I don't . . . well, I don't think this is something that'll work for all of you.'

'Oh, complicating factors,' Perky said dismissively. 'In my experience, things are only as complicated as we insist on making them.'

My throat was dry, and in desperation I took a gulp of champagne rather than a sip. The bubbles burned their way down my gullet. 'I can't do this anymore.'

'Can't do what anymore?' Perky asked, her eyes boring into me, as Amelia gaped at me and Tristan pinched his lips together, so they narrowed almost to invisibility.

I wondered if I could spring up and make it out of the orangery fast enough for none of them to catch up with me.

But Mrs Holt was over at the door. And the young waiter midway across the room. I'd never make it out without challenge.

So I heaved in a deep breath and laid my hands flat on the tablecloth. 'You might . . . you might have noticed that I'm not wearing an engagement ring. I had one when I entered the competition. Nate — that's my . . . well, the man I thought I was going to marry. He gave it to me last Christmas. But when I won the prize — that afternoon, just before I came here and accepted it . . .' I could only finish in a whisper. 'Nate said he didn't want to marry me. So . . . I'm single.'

Perky made a sound that I could only describe as a whimper.

'But I need you to save the date for me anyway. The date for my wedding. Because I'm going to find him . . . going to find *the one*, and marry him here. I promise.'

JULY: ELEVEN MONTHS TO GO

CHAPTER 7: GHOSTED

'I just don't get why you assume they've ghosted you, after they took your confession so well?' Abi was sprawled back on her sofa, dunking a cucumber stick into a jar of peanut butter.

'Because Perky said she'd be in touch in a day or two, and it's been three weeks. Anyway, *so well* is a bit of an exaggeration,' I said.

Amelia's open-mouthed shock had been the strongest reaction, but once she recovered, she'd blamed Nate rather than me. 'The cad. The swine. The unreliable scoundrel.'

Perky was astonished, but after one deep breath she switched to making the best of it. 'If you find the one in time to marry him here, the PR opportunities are boundless. I've got a contact at *The Telegraph's* weekend supplement—'

Tristan, who had betrayed no surprise at all, had intervened to suggest Perky not get carried away, then turned to me with a close-lipped smile. 'Of course we'll save you that date, and best of luck with your quest.'

Abi herself had been more cross with me, when I arrived at the flat and finally confessed it all to her, while scrubbing the marrow-encrusted baking dish that she'd slung back in the oven. But she'd mellowed quickly, whereas I hadn't heard a word from anyone at Sylverley ever since.

'Maybe Mam's right, and I should get away from it all for a while, and fly over for a visit.'

'That would be running away from your problems,' Abi snapped. 'Anyway, Sylverley really can't pretend you never existed, barely a month after introducing you to hundreds of people as their prize winner. And stop pacing — it's really getting on my wick.'

The other end of the sofa was within splat range of her peanut butter. And she'd sat in the armchair for her last snack, of very crumbly seeded bread, so it more resembled a bird table than a seat. But I'd recently vacuumed the hemp rug, so I settled down on it, and checked my phone. No new emails, and the only unread text was from Nate. It wasn't new; despite our careful avoidance of anything emotional, every contact with him enflamed my misery at our break-up, so I hadn't opened this one from earlier in the day.

I dropped my handset and thumped my forehead onto the rug. 'None of them reacted like it was impossible for me to meet *the one* in time for the wedding, but maybe after I left they laughed themselves silly about it.'

Abi licked the last of the peanut butter from the cucumber, discarded it and dipped a spoon into the jar. 'That's what I was cross about, y'know. Not what you'd let them believe initially, but that you promised them you'd work hard to find *the one*, to the extent of setting Gemma onto finding you dates. Romance doesn't happen like that.'

I fingered the tassels edging the rug. 'Maybe not. She was insistent that dating's a numbers game, but she hasn't come up with a single date yet.'

Abi squinted from beneath her heavy fringe. 'Gemma knows nothing about dating — she's been with Joe since her teens. Whereas I was actively dating until I was thirty-four.'

I wasn't convinced that made her more qualified. Abi had much more dating experience, but if the purpose of dating was finding and securing the one, surely it was Gemma with a track record of speedy success? Instead of voicing that, I changed the subject. 'How are the twins?'

'We're not calling them that anymore. Herbie's reading this book on free-range parenting, and reckons child psychologists say tw— uh, multiple-birth babies need their own identities.'

'That doesn't sound *not* right.' That was as strongly as I was prepared to endorse one of Herbie's suggestions. 'But surely that's tricky while they're scrunched up side-by-side inside you?'

'Which is why we're using their names.'

I glanced at her doubtfully. 'You've chosen them names before they even have faces?'

Abi struggled to sit up. 'Of course they have faces! Have you missed how adorable they look in the ultrasound pictures on the fridge?'

Adorable . . . if blobs of undercooked meringue were adorable. 'I forgot, sorry. But you're seriously choosing their names more than five months before they're born?'

'Not their ultimate names. But now we know they're one boy, one girl, we can start trying out potential names and see which ones seem to suit. Today they're Cassiopeia and Cedar.'

'Oh.' I added, with caution, 'Will it be c-names every day?'

'We're making our way through the alphabet. Tomorrow they'll be—' she wrapped her arms around her stomach, like she was covering their ears, and lowered her voice — 'Dharma and Dune. The day after is trickier.'

'Emma and Edward?'

She wrinkled her nose. 'Boring.'

'Fine then. You two like vegetables, so . . . Edamame and Endive.'

'Interesting. Keep going.'

'Uh . . . can't think of any more names for veglings. But there's plenty more that are food inspired. Enchilada and Empanada . . . Eclair and Espresso . . . or to keep it short and sweet, Egg and Eel.'

'Egg and Eel, in a vegan family?' she spluttered. 'Really Róisín, be serious — and while I remember, please don't ask

76

Herbie again how he knows that almonds don't have just as many feelings as cows. I hate seeing him cry over breakfast.'

'Sorry,' I said. 'Tea with almond milk just isn't the same. It makes me grouchy.' I glanced at my phone; no emails, no texts, no missed calls in the ten minutes since I last checked. 'Argh, at this stage I'd rather hear a flat no about the commission and cottage, rather than this waiting.'

Abi dropped her spoon, tried to catch it, and missed. It clattered onto the floor. Before I got there to pass it back, she shrugged and stuck a finger directly into the jar, scooping peanut butter up then sucking it off. I repressed my flinch; if there was anything that a month of living with a pregnant woman had taught me, it was to never, ever get between Abi and whatever foodstuff she was obsessed with. Also that my showers couldn't last more than ten minutes, because she was desperate for a wee at least that often.

As if she'd read my mind, she groaned and asked for a hand up. 'Cedar's bouncing on my bladder. Fine, son, you're not a Cedar, I've got the message. But your sister seems to be responding well to Cassiopeia, so maybe it should go on the shortlist.'

I clasped her wrists and heaved. 'How about Cassie instead? Cassiopeia would have been shortened to Pee-er at my school.'

'Like mother, like daughter,' she said, sniggering as she headed for the bathroom.

My phone, beside me on the rug, began to buzz.

And the call had a Somerset dialling code.

My stomach flipped. 'Róisín speaking.'

'Hullo! Perky here.'

'Hi. Uh . . . this is a bit of a surprise.'

'Is it? I promised I'd be in touch. Now, can you make six historical outfits by early December? We'd want forty-five per cent off the final invoice, less costs for materials, paid half up-front and half on completion. In return for which you can have a Sylverley cottage rent-free until the renovation resumes next summer.'

My breath had caught in my throat, and I had to cough before I could reply. 'You're serious?'

'Entirely. I'll email my ideas for the garments through in a moment, and we'd appreciate a decision immediately after you've viewed the cottage.' Relief burned through me. Work was the distraction I needed from the Nate-sized gap in my life, and with the bonus of a cottage in the grounds of gorgeous Sylverley, there was no way I'd turn her offer down, whatever the cottage was like. 'When can you come to look around? I'll warn you, there are minimal mod cons, but it's fully furnished and . . . Róisín, are you still there?'

'Still here. But not for much longer. I don't need to view the cottage to agree to the deal. When can I move in?'

* * *

There was a funereal silence in the maisonette. I supposed it was apt, since Nate and I were gathered together for a death ritual. That time honoured ritual marking the death of a relationship by separating belongings.

I'd arrived early, my arms full of flat boxes, and packed up the obvious things while Nate was busy with breakfast service down in the café. My books, then sewing machines, overlocker, mannequins, and box after box of fabrics, buttons, ribbons and all manner of haberdashery ephemera. I purged the bathroom cabinet of my half-finished toiletries and wiped it clean behind me, before starting on my wardrobes in the bedroom. I owned a lot of clothing, almost all of which was vintage or I'd made myself. I zipped my historical gowns into garment bags and folded clothing into suitcases, dragging each of them out to the narrow landing when I could squeeze no more inside.

Nate came upstairs at ten, and hovered in the doorway as I emptied my belongings from the top half of our chest of drawers.

'You all right?' he asked.

'Fine,' I said.

A few minutes later I asked how the café was doing.

'Also fine,' Nate said.

It went on like that for a while. Me packing, him watching, and occasionally each of us thinking of a way to break the silence. Only, when we did, rather than igniting a conversation it had a deadening effect, so that afterwards the silence seemed deeper.

'Cuppa?' he tried eventually.

I shook my head as I tucked my umbrella and rain mac into the gaps in the case I'd filled with winter coats and boots. 'No thanks.'

He considered me for a few moments. 'I think that's the first time you've ever turned down a cup of tea.'

I smiled, like he'd cracked a joke. The truth was that my stomach was tight and painful. If I tried to swallow I might vomit up my entrails.

He clocked my cardboard boxes and began assembling them. Thunking each out into a square, unreeling parcel tape and snapping it off the roll, then spreading it along the crack on the underside and crunching it down.

Maybe he thought that the noise would be a distraction, but instead it somehow highlighted the silence between us, until our wordlessness stretched so thin that I could almost sense a faint reverberation.

When the boxes were all built, he jerked his chin toward the landing. 'I could start taking the suitcases down for you.'

'If you wouldn't mind,' I said, already knowing that he wouldn't. Nate had never objected to hard work. And anyway, it was his escape from this atmosphere.

He shrugged, and I tossed him the key to the minibus. *My* minibus, for the next year, thanks to Abi. It was the only help I'd accepted, going forward, from my friends. Herbie and Joe had each offered assistance to move, but I'd turned them down. Partly because it was time to stand on my own two feet, and partly because of Nate — it would be painful, in different ways, to witness him sniping about Herbie every time he turned his back, or exhibiting how pally he was with Joe.

Completing the chest of drawers, I recalled buying the early Victorian bedside tables with my birthday money from Mam one year — but I was moving somewhere furnished. I contemplated for a moment, then decided I'd collect them at a later point if I needed them. The patchwork throw I'd made to shroud the garishly upholstered armchair filled the rest of the box, and then the bedroom I'd shared for more than five years was shorn of anything made by me.

Nate had emptied the landing by the time I moved on to the open plan living area, in a rare occurrence of our sense of timing being in sync. It was just as well, as this was where negotiation would be necessary, since most of the items had been acquired together. Pushing the barren bedroom from my mind, I dumped a few of the empty boxes on the small dining table, planted my hands on my hips and stared around. The drawers and cupboards beneath the wooden work tops were full, as were the shelves on the built-in dresser spanning the wall behind the table, which displayed mismatched but complimentary china that I'd chosen from charity shops and an occasional auction.

'I'll start on the bits and pieces I brought when I moved in. If you move things that you had before I came to the far end of the worktop — no, by the oven — then we can work out how to split up the rest.'

Nate started moving items in line with my suggestions, as I sought the things that I remembered Mam passing onto me, when I left the old flat for my uni house share, or that I'd bought while living with Abi. Most of the Ikea utensils had expired, aside from cutlery and a battered saucepan, its non-stick coating long ago worn off. Shifting over to the dresser, I reached up for the blue teapot.

Nate glanced up, then did a double take. 'That one's mine.'

'No, it's not.' I pulled a sheet of the *Guardian* free, and wrapped the teapot's lid. 'I brought it with me.'

'It's Denby. My parents left it when they moved out.'

'They left you three blue Denby mugs,' I said coolly. 'I happened to own the matching teapot.' There was no sign of recognition on his face. 'You laughed when I unpacked it, and showed me the matching mugs.'

He screwed his face up. 'Maybe that rings a vague bell . . .'

I added the wrapped lid to the box, and folded paper around the teapot itself, not saying that he hadn't just laughed. He'd said, pulling out the evidence of our matching set: *It's a sign! We match each other perfectly!*

And it was far from the only item that had sentimental memories attached. There was the bottle opener I bought him on the fifth anniversary of our first date. The crystal wine glasses someone sent us as an engagement gift, and the plastic tray that must have been one of the other things his parents left here, as the cutesy picture of hens in a farmyard was in no way Nate's style. He'd carried it through to me in bed, a cup of tea perched on it, pretty much every morning.

I turned my back on him, blinking away the sudden pricking in my eyes. Then I raked through ideas for how to get this over with without triggering any more nostalgia. Maybe I could walk away from the rest of the contents of the kitchen cupboards altogether. Even when I'd purchased them, with Nate doing all the cooking they'd become his over time. My self-appointed role had been turning this place from a rather tatty maisonette into a nicely decorated and clean home and workspace, but I couldn't suck the paint off the walls, nor prise away the tiles I'd set around the sink.

Decisively, I swung back to Nate, who was rooting in a drawer for the set of silver teaspoons he'd owned since his christening. 'Splitting all this could take forever. So how about, I'll take everything else on the dresser, and you keep everything in the kitchen cupboards.'

He sucked in his cheeks. 'But that would mean I had all the stuff for cooking and you had all the nice dishes for serving food on.'

I gritted my teeth. 'We can debate the provenance of each item instead if you want.'

His phone pinged an alert, and he turned aside to glance at it. Taking that as assent, I lifted a Fortnum's teacup down from the dresser and cocooned it in newspaper.

As I finished the highest shelf, Nate was still absorbed with his phone. Leaning forward onto the worktop, his hair had dropped over his face, so I couldn't see his expression as he typed rapidly with his thumbs, waited for a response, and typed again.

'Who's that?' Before my lips had even relaxed from shaping the words, I regretted blurting the question. It could be anyone, about anything. He might even be seeing someone else, and with Gemma intent on setting me up through *My Single Pal*, I had no right to the stabbing sensation the thought had caused me. 'None of my business — sorry,' I added quickly.

'It's Joe,' he said, shooting a puzzled glance at me.

'Oh.' I wondered whether Joe knew that Gemma was searching for the one for me, and if he'd tell Nate, but before I could subtly probe, he put his phone down and strolled over to join me at the dresser. We didn't talk, but the silence was more contemplative than the awkward atmosphere between us earlier.

I stowed the final item. 'That's it now, I think.'

'In the whole flat?'

'I meant in here, but it's not far off everything. Just the big linen cupboard to go. Any ideas on splitting up the bed linen and towels?'

He heaved one of the boxes up. 'Literally all I bought were my gym towels. You were the one invested in waffle versus towelling, and how high a thread count. Take all of it if you want.'

'And leave you without any sheets?' I said, following him onto the landing.

'Not unless you take the one currently on the mattress.'

'I wouldn't do that.'

He paused at the top of the stairs and smiled at me for the first time all day. 'I know.'

I opened the armoire, so the door shielded me from his smile and a few seconds later he thudded away. I grabbed everything I wanted to keep, doubling each sheet, towel or duvet over and over, until it was a neat square.

When he returned, he said my name hesitantly.

'Yes?'

'You know, before . . .' he began. 'Actually, don't worry — it doesn't matter.'

Then he sighed.

I sucked a breath in, between my teeth. 'It sounds like it matters?'

'It doesn't,' he said. 'Don't worry about it.' He raked his hands through his curls, the whole way over his head, and then grasped the back of his neck. Then he dropped his arms back to his sides. 'Actually . . . I think you're right. I think I need to ask something.'

'Yes?' I said again, fighting to keep all emotion from my voice.

'When you asked who was on the phone, and then said it was none of your business . . . it sounded like you . . . You didn't assume I was already seeing someone else, did you?'

I tried not to squirm. 'I didn't assume anything.'

It was only when he raised his chin and met my gaze full on, that I realised he'd been avoiding locking eyes with me like this all day. 'Good.' His throat bobbed as he swallowed heavily. 'You know I wouldn't do that, right?'

'Do what?'

'See someone else.'

His large brown eyes had always been my favourite of his features, but now it was like they were devouring my own.

I wrenched my gaze away. 'Why not? Nate, you're free to see whoever you want. We ended weeks ago.'

He sank, looking defeated, to sit on the stairs.

'It wouldn't be fair, though,' he said, his voice hoarse. 'Not when I'm still in love with you.'

I froze. But it wasn't the words he'd just spoken that had shocked me into immobility. It was a flashback to the similar phrase he'd used last time I was in the building. The phrase that had sent my world crashing down. The phrase that still haunted my dreams.

I love you, *but.*

My mind kept snagging on it, like the time my antique lace cape got caught on a nail and tore in half. It had proved impossible to mend.

'Rosh? Shit, I'm sorry, I shouldn't have blurted it like that . . . Just listen, please?'

I gave one slight nod, then, regaining some control over my body, lowered myself to sit beside him.

He licked his lips. 'I thought it would be easier, when you left. That I'd start to get over you. But I've been miserable without you. And even more miserable seeing this place empty of your stuff today. It's . . . because I love you.'

'You love me,' I said hollowly. '*But.*'

'What?'

'That's what you said . . . before. That you love me. *But.*'

'Did I? I guess I meant *but* you want the wedding and baby stuff.'

My eyes shot to meet his once more. 'And you don't.'

His hands were in his hair again. 'If we keep talking, we can find some kind of compromise. I'm sure of it.'

There wasn't a middle ground between married and unmarried. Only delaying getting married by staying unmarried, but I'd pinned my hopes on that for too long already.

'We can't,' I said, knotting my arms around my body, left hand on right bicep, right hand on left, and squeezing my clammy flesh. 'Not now we both know that what we want and what we can offer doesn't match.'

'We both want each other,' he urged.

'You want a version of me who's content to keep things open-ended. I want a version of you who's enthusiastic about marriage.'

Nate choked, but cut it off before I could work out if it was wry laughter or a sob, and buried his face in his hands. 'Rosh, I *wish* I felt differently. I *want* to feel differently. But I

84

don't know how.' His cheeks were crumpled when he raised his head. 'What about . . . how about you?'

I forced myself to inhale, to ensure that my brain was fully oxygenated as I formulated what I must say. 'I don't know how to feel differently either,' I said slowly. 'But I don't think I want to. I think . . . I really think we've got to get over how possessive we still feel about each other, somehow. Or we'll never be free to find the one whose wants match our own. Tomorrow I'll move into my new place, and you'll be here without reminders of me everywhere you look, and that needs to be our fresh start.' Meeting his eyes was painful. 'We've got to go no-contact.'

CHAPTER 8: LIVE-IN GIRLFRIEND

The minibus juddered over the track, forcing me to slow to a snail pace. The uneven ground was less of a hindrance to Mr Holt, driving a battered Land Rover, and I was concerned I'd lose sight of him altogether. Then again, I reasoned, my new home couldn't be much further on. He'd already led me halfway up the long driveway, down a fork and through a tangle of tracks within the woodland; we'd join the road that skirted the west side of the Sylverley estate imminently.

My new home. Which I'd accepted sight unseen. As much as I told myself that it had been the responsible thing to do, getting out from under Abi and Herbie's feet as quickly as possible, deep down I knew that it was really motivated by desperation. I needed a distraction from the hole Nate had left in my life, and this new start was it . . . Compared to that, the state of the cottage didn't matter.

I eased around a bend into a clearing. Mr Holt's vehicle was pulled in just ahead, in front of some chocolate-box cottages. There were five of them, not so much in a row as in a higgledy-piggledy line. They were all timber framed with thatched roofs, with the usually ubiquitous Bath stone only evident as paving slabs leading to their front doors. I could only identify clear signs of occupation in two of them; one in the centre had all the windows open, and another, which was set further back from the track so it was half swallowed by the woodland, had a pair of muddy boots beside the front step. Two others were entirely closed up, with boards nailed across the windows. It was presumably the cottage at the far end, then, that would be mine, and I parked close to the front path.

Mr Holt gave me the key as I hopped down from the minibus. It was long and iron, and attached to a wooden key fob. I jogged up the path, half in disbelief that I was moving into such a picturesque place. 'Perky seriously undersold this,' I murmured as I reached the oak front door. It had different dimensions to modern ones, being shorter but rather wider, which only increased my sense of being in some kind of fairy tale. The key turned easily in the lock, but there was a squeak as I pushed the door open. I paused, one foot poised to step inside, looking around.

'I'll get a drop of oil for those hinges,' Mr Holt puffed, coming up behind me with the two largest of my suitcases.

It clicked me out of my reverie, and I stepped inside, still taking in the interior. The windows were small and rather dim, with smeared marks like they'd been cleaned in a hurry. There was a soot-stained stone fireplace, faded but good quality furniture, and ancient beams across the ceiling, each thicker than my waist.

I squinted around for a light switch, discovering it at the bottom of the narrow staircase, and illuminated the space as Mr Holt entered, crouching to fit under the door lintel and hauling my cases through onto the flagstoned floor after him.

I wandered through to the rear and found a tatty kitchen. The tap was dripping into an enamel sink, which was chipped and rather stained. The freestanding fridge-freezer and electric oven looked at least twenty years old, but the correct time blinked on the oven and the freezer was cold inside. The back door had a key in the lock.

I trailed my hand up the bannister as I ascended the narrow staircase, and felt a splinter of wood catch in my index finger. I sucked it out as I explored, finding more beams and sloping walls, encompassed within which were two bedrooms and a tiny bathroom with a sink, bath and pull-chain toilet. The bigger bedroom had larger windows, and faced southwest, so it would be flooded with light once the glass was properly clean. I instantly christened it my sewing room; the smaller front bedroom was more than ample for me on my own.

Mr Holt's heavy feet came up the staircase. He dropped the case with a heavy thud, and the ancient floorboards shook.

'You just be directing where you want each box, when I bring it,' he said, stomping back downstairs.

I wasn't sure the floorboards would take more quaking. And the place had been cleaned, but not Irish-mother-standard cleaned. I wanted to get at least my workspace spotless before I unpacked my treasured sewing supplies.

'Please don't worry about it,' I called, pushing the cases against a wall, then scurrying down after him. 'I'd rather bring them in one at a time.' My spirits were rising at the task ahead of me. It was, I thought, because I'd had entirely too much time lately for thinking. The physical challenge of turning this from an empty cottage to my new home would take all my energy, leaving none for replaying that conversation with Nate, and whether I'd chosen wrong by not giving us another try.

Mr Holt was hard to persuade, and insisted on at least showing me how to light a fire in the hearth and where the fuse box was. He explained ponderously that he and Mrs Holt, who he referred to as *her indoors*, lived in the cottage in the middle of the row. The electricity for all the cottages ran on a generator, as the electricity firm was being slow to run mains to this side of the estate, which was why the renovation had stalled after re-thatching the roofs and repairs to the drains and chimneys. He'd make sure I had electric heaters by the autumn, since there was no other source of warmth beyond the fire.

'And being it's the last Sunday,' he added suddenly. 'There's high tea in the house at five.'

'Sorry, the last Sunday? Oh — in July you mean? And *the house*?'

'Sylverley,' he said, boggling like I'd asked what number came after three and before five. 'We call it the house, being as how the whole estate is called Sylverley. Her indoors does high tea for everyone on the last Sunday of every month, and she said to tell you you're to come.'

* * *

I began by shifting furniture around to suit my purposes, creating more sewing space by taking the single bed in the back room apart, to be reassembled in my bedroom. I scrubbed the workroom from beams to floorboards before beginning the long job of hauling bales of fabric and mannequins and sewing machines upstairs, almost slipping a few times on the stair-treads, polished smooth by centuries of feet.

Moving into the bedroom, I put the bed back together, pushed it against the single it matched and stretched a mattress cover across them to create a double of a sort. There was only one wardrobe but I'd expected that, and brought several freestanding hanging racks, which I built and pushed against the longest wall. I made a mental note that the bedside tables I'd left with Nate would be useful, though having insisted on no contact, I'd have to let an appropriate length of time pass before texting to request them.

After eventually completing the upstairs I took a break for a cup of tea, with water boiled on the hob in the metal kettle I found in a cupboard. There was no microwave, and I wrote a list of urgent purchases before returning to heave in and unpack the final boxes. There was a couch in the lounge that I initially thought I'd beg to have removed, but after heaping throws and cushions on it, I decided I could live with the lumpiness.

After I'd completed all my unpacking, I surveyed my new home with my hands on my hips. It wasn't yet perfect, but for one day's work, it was pretty damned homely.

Leaving it for conversation with strangers up at the house wasn't an enticing proposition, but I needed to eat, and driving back into Bath for groceries or a takeaway would be just as bad. So I pulled off my jeans and considered what to wear. High tea meant a big spread of food at teatime, rather than a formal sit-down meal, but I was never again going to expose myself to Sylverley staff's ridicule by being under-dressed, so I chose a full-circle skirt and Liberty print blouse. It was stylish but demure — the kind of outfit I'd wear to meet prospective in-laws.

As I walked up to the house I fell in behind a group of gardeners, following them round to an entrance at the rear, which led into the sub-basement level. There I lingered on the threshold of a long, whitewashed room, with windows set high in one wall, and a plain fireplace on the other, too small to heat the whole space in the winter. Those features made me certain it had been designed as the servant's hall; the only living space available to the majority of Sylverley's residents' through most of the estate's history. It would have been used for their meals, as well as the short periods of time they got to relax and gossip, with prime positions near the fire taken by the senior staff while scullery maids lingered nervously on the fringes, aware of their red-raw hands and intimidated by the throng of their seniors.

I took a deep breath, put my raw hands in my pockets and pushed away the comparisons. I could empathise with the scullery maids of the past, but I wasn't an unschooled teenager, away from my family for the first time. I had skills that earned me my cottage, and money in the bank. I even had the claim on a wedding in one of the spaces upstairs that scullery maids would have barely been allowed to venture into. So I marched up to join the end of queue for the buffet, passing long tables filling with staff in a jumble of different uniforms; grey suits, teal polo shirts and fleeces, chef whites and black boiler suits with discreet logos. Those reaching the buffet piled a tray with food before peeling off to join one of the tables. Some scurried to those wearing the same uniform, but more seemed to deliberately break away to sit with other staff, so the uniforms gradually intermingled.

'Yahoo, Róisín, over here!' Perky called, waving wildly from her position towards the front of the queue. 'I've saved you a place in line,' she added, with deliberation, as the teenage boy behind us made signs of preparing a complaint. She raised an eyebrow at him, and he went quiet.

'Thanks,' I murmured. 'Mr Holt mentioned that I should attend, but then I wasn't sure . . .'

'Of course you should.' The delicious smell from the buffet was nearly as reassuring as her firm words. 'Was moving in day tough? Did you get through most of your unpacking? And what d'you reckon of the cottage, and of our spread of grub?'

I hummed noncommittally, wishing I could limit her to only three questions on any one subject at any one time.

'Her indoors says there's a tray held back for Róisín,' Mr Holt said, coming up behind us. His booming voice made us both jump slightly. He didn't wait for a reply before tramping back to the middle of one of the tables, where he'd left a plate, piled high with steaming bangers and mash, and a fork stuck into the middle of it.

'I'll retrieve it . . .' Perky stalked off behind the buffet. 'Save my place in the queue, please,' she called back over her shoulder, with a hard look at the teenager.

As the queue shifted forward I slid my eyes around the room. When they reached a golden head over broad shoulders, I snapped my gaze back to the buffet. Tristan Nash was here, then. I was wondering if I was brave enough to go to sit near him, when Perky returned, carrying a covered tray.

'Mrs Holt dished you up some of the best of everything — she was keeping it warm to deliver if you hadn't turned up for tea.' I muttered a thank you as I accepted the tray, and turned, faltering as I found the back of Tristan's head again. He was amidst colleagues in boiler suits and fleeces.

'There's a place for you beside the seat I saved!' Perky called, pointing at an empty chair, next to one with her suit jacket slung over the back. A few of the other managerial staff were immediately opposite, including Amelia, who broke off the chat to introduce me to a girl she called, 'Lola-Pop — our head of visitor experience'.

'Róisín, have you had a chance to check your email?' Amelia added. 'I've sent you a map of the estate, with the side gate highlighted, which you can use for direct access to the cottages, to bypass queues on the main drive. Your visitors can use it, but I've also attached a number of free tickets. And you've probably noticed already that mobile reception over by the cottages is patchy, so switch your phone to Wi-Fi calling.'

I put the Wi-Fi password into my phone, pleased that I'd be able to video call Mam and take her on a tour around my cottage, then flipped off the fitted lid of the tray, discovering cutlery, a small plate filled with a cornucopia of salads and a larger one with some sort of nut roast and pasta with tomatoes and the most disgusting food on God's earth — black olives. They were chopped up small, so they resembled dead woodlice stirred through the penne. And worst of all, there wasn't a single potato in any form.

'Mrs Holt plated up a little bit of every vegan option for you,' Perky said, planting her tray down. The most delicious smell wafted my way from her slices of beef, Yorkshire pudding and roast potatoes, all sodden with gravy. And she had a bowl of trifle, with a thick layer of fresh cream above cherries and chocolate sponge. My stomach grumbled a protest.

'That was lovely of her,' Lola-Pop put in. 'I swear that woman's a modern day saint.'

I gave them something approximating a smile, and dug into my salads. Confessing to not being a vegan now would harm my reputation more than standing on the table and drop-kicking a kitten into the fireplace. Instead I'd have to phase it out . . . maybe start with backsliding to vegetarianism in a few months, so I could at least have trifle.

I speared a grape. 'So does this happen regularly? Mr Holt didn't explain much.'

'Yes indeed,' Perky said. 'Most of us have Mondays off, since we're closed to guests then, so after closing on the last Sunday of each month, we celebrate making it through another twelfth of a year. Of course, some of the grub's left over from the orangery or private events, but that just means more choice.' She sliced her beef into thin strips, dunked one into the gravy pooled beside her Yorkshire pudding, then ate it, her eyes almost rolling with pleasure. 'This is so good . . .' Her eyes popped open. 'Is that rude in front of a vegan?'

'It's fine,' I assured her quickly, comforting myself with a forkful of the hazelnut mush on the other side of the plate from the woodlouse pasta. It was tastier than anything Herbie had ever served, but I needed more carbs. 'You know, your roasties look delicious. I'm going to re-join the queue—'

'They're cooked in goose fat,' Lola-Pop said. 'And the chips are cooked in the same deep fat fryer as fish, and the mash has butter in — I assemble the ingredient lists for allergy sufferers,' she added.

I subsided miserably back into my seat as the conversation moved on to gossip, cloaked with the respectability of filling me in on what was happening in my new home. Two of the gardeners had got together, which had been predicted for a while, but also two chefs, which hadn't, and was widely expected not to last.

My gaze drifted back to Tristan, who had moved to talk to another group. 'He seems . . . sociable.'

Amelia snorted and Lola-Pop giggled.

'What did I say?'

Perky sighed, then filled me in. 'He's all business, that's all. So sure, he talks to everyone at times like these, but only about work.'

'Doesn't socialise with mere mortals,' Lola-Pop said.

'Doesn't socialise with *anyone*,' Amelia corrected, around a mouthful of mash.

'He's a good boss,' Perky said quickly. 'And expects even more of himself than he demands of us. But he's . . . insular.'

I transferred my eyes to my food. 'How many people live on the estate?'

'With Bath such a short drive, most of us travel in daily,' Amelia said. 'So there will only ever be a few of you here overnight.'

Perky dunked Yorkshire pudding into her pool of gravy. 'But don't worry — the Holts live two doors down from you, so you'll always have someone close at hand.'

I smiled my appreciation for her reassurance, then parted my lips to enquire where Tristan lived. But he stood up at that moment, and took his tray to the edge of the room, where he stowed it in a trolley. Rather than ask his colleagues, I could time my exit to strike up conversation with him directly.

I murmured an excuse about needing to get back to unpacking, then picked my way toward him. There was no rush, as Tristan had paused to speak to Mr Holt. I slowed my steps slightly, listening hard.

'—the feasibility of rewilding the northern fields . . .' Tristan was saying.

I was out of earshot by the time Mr Holt replied, but as I slid my tray into the trolley I glanced back, and caught Tristan clapping Mr Holt on the back, indicating, I thought, that it was the end of their conversation. I could head out then, and linger in the corridor as if I wasn't sure of the way out of the building.

I was nearly at the door when it opened. A small figure stood there and the room became stilted with silence, every conversation abruptly ending and faces going blank as the raven-haired woman entered. Below a fringe, her face was pulled taut by cosmetic surgery, which didn't disguise the paper-thin fragility of aged skin.

She gazed around imperiously. 'Where's Mr Nash? *I need* Mr Nash.'

As it hit me that this must be Suzanne Sylvers, the widow of the late owner, who left Sylverley to be run by a trust rather than his second wife, she turned her attention to me suddenly, and scowled. Thankfully a moment later Tristan reached her side.

'How may I assist you, Mrs Sylvers?'

'I had more unwelcome visitors this afternoon. *Your* tourists, infesting *my* private apartment. The *Sylvers family's* private apartment.'

'Sorry to hear that.' Tristan's voice was more constrained than concerned. 'Someone must have left the internal door unlocked again. Apologies — and I'll have a bolt added to your side of it.'

Her chin retreated into her lace collar. 'Who's that girl eavesdropping? Yet another new member of staff? No wonder you needed to sell all my family's heirlooms.'

Tristan turned and met my eyes for a split-second. His level eyebrows drew together, before he returned his attention to Mrs Sylvers. 'That's Ms O'Reilly, who's staying in one of the cottages while doing some freelance design work.'

She sniffed. 'O'Reilly? One Irish redhead on the estate wasn't enough for you, Mr Nash?'

Tristan's lips thinned into a hard, narrow line as she turned on her heel and stalked out.

'Sorry about that, Róisín,' he murmured, under the muffled collective sigh and clatter of cutlery as everyone resumed their meals. 'She was trying to rile me — it wasn't personal to you.'

I shrugged. 'No offence taken.'

He held the door open for me and I slipped through, smiling. 'Thanks. Oh, and where's this other Irish redhead?'

He palmed the back of his neck as he followed me along the flagstone passage. 'Uh . . . right now, she's in my cottage — which is at the opposite end of the row to yours.'

He did live on site, then. And just a few doors away from me. But . . . with a live-in girlfriend.

He cleared his throat. 'That's why I needed to apologise. She's, uh . . . she's a red-coated Irish wolfhound.'

I pivoted and stared up at him. His expression was neutral, entirely under his control, but he'd flushed slightly.

'Right,' I said rather helplessly. 'Well . . . At least Mrs Sylvers didn't call me Sylverley's second redheaded bitch, I suppose.'

95

AUGUST: TEN MONTHS TO GO

CHAPTER 9: OUT OF MY LEAGUE

'Is this urgent? I'm busy.'

'Why would I have called back three times in a row if it wasn't urgent?' Gemma snapped. 'And you're not busy. You never start work this early.'

'I'm busy with something else.'

'Planning things for a groomless wedding doesn't make you busy, Róisín.'

I dropped my pencil onto the huge sheet of cardboard I'd been sketching on and spun to stare through the window, which was open to encourage a breeze. 'Are you watching me?'

'You're just predictable, that's all. You don't get up before nine if you can help it, and then you drink tea and faff around with your personal projects until you're awake enough to work.'

She was correct, except that I was sleeping so terribly that I wasn't getting up until ten. Living alone was taking some getting used to — especially at night. I lay awake listening to the creaks of the cottage's old timbers settling, and woke when the absurdly early sunrise filtered through my bedroom window, taking ages to get back to sleep. I'd made curtains a few days ago, but found myself still disturbed at dawn, first by Tristan calling *'Here, girl . . . come along, Bear,'* to his massive Irish redhead, and then the grumble of Mr Holt's Land Rover. Tonight I was intent on closing all the windows, however stuffy that made my bedroom.

'What's the emergency, anyway?' I asked, lifting my pencil again, and glancing over at my laptop. I was turning all five digital mood boards for Sylverley wedding ideas that I'd made before my first visit into larger physical copies. It was much easier to refine them when they were on a larger scale.

'I didn't say emergency, I said *urgent*. I've found you a date!'

'Ugh.'

'Way to sound grateful, Róisín. Do you know how many hours I've spent messaging the friends and relatives of complete muppets?'

'You offered!'

'And you agreed, so now you're going out with Frankie. He's not a historian but he does like old buildings, as you specified, since he works in property.' At her triumphant tone, I rolled my eyes, wondering why I'd trusted the most literal person I knew with my love life. 'He's thirty-four, very much wants to settle down and doesn't have any communicable diseases — well, as far as his sister's aware.'

'*Probably* not diseased? What a catch.'

'He *is* a catch — well, comparatively. Until him, mankind have been conspiring to send me their worst candidates. I've chatted to a bloke who reckons you're too old for his thirty-nine-year-old friend, a woman searching for a wife for her gay son and a girl finding dates for her flatmate after he was banned from Tinder for posting dick pics.'

'This app sounds like a shit show. Delete my profile and stop—'

'I'll delete it after the date,' she bargained. 'If you like Frankie and book a second date to see him. Or if not, I've got plan B sorted — the next Soulmates Speed Dating event. It's a fortnight on Sunday.'

'I'm busy that night.'

'Liar!'

'I'm not lying. It clashes with an ongoing . . . commitment here at Sylverley, on the last Sunday of every month.'

'What kind of commitment?'

'A social thing for the staff and residents. There's not many opportunities to get to know—' I stilled my tongue from saying *him* in the nick of time. Revealing there was an attractive man here would be tantamount to inviting Gemma to barge into his cottage offering an arranged marriage. Though she was unlikely to actually encounter him in his cottage since he worked constantly, returning in the dark and leaving at dawn. 'To get to know people here,' I finished lamely.

Gemma snorted. 'Not a priority, compared with finding *the one*. So a date with Frankie tonight—'

'*Tonight*? You never said that!'

'I said the chat was urgent, duh. You have to meet him at Rivers Street at 6.45, as he's booked a table somewhere special. And you know what's on Rivers Street . . . oh, come on, Róisín, try to keep up. That little French steakhouse with a Michelin star — it's meant to be amazing. I said you'd just moved house so had budgetary constraints, but his sister said there was no need for you to worry about it being an expensive evening — which is code for Frankie picking up the bill, by the way. So you'll meet him tonight, then book a second date with him *or* go speed dating in a fortnight, and then — and only then — can you see Esme.'

'I can't believe you're using your daughter as bait like that!'

'Yes, you can.'

I snorted, but then relented. 'Fine. But then I want you to bring Esme to Sylverley.'

'She'll be there as soon as you want to invite her, after the second date or speed dating. Have fun tonight!'

* * *

As I circled for a parking space, I chanted to myself, 'You'll like Frankie, you'll book to see him again,' because the only thing more sickeningly nerve-wracking than meeting a man I didn't know would be meeting multiple men I didn't know at high speed.

I was so intent on positive affirmations about how much I'd like Frankie that I forgot to actually look out a parking space long enough for the minibus, and by the time I'd found one I had to leg it, and dashed into Rivers Street in a sweaty mess.

'Are you Róisín?' a man called from across the street. 'I'm Frankie!'

I raised a hand in acknowledgment, and crossed slowly, trying to get my breath back. Frankie was wearing an ill-fitting shiny suit, so I focussed on his hair (close-cropped, conker brown) his eyes (screwed up against the sun, nice shade of blue) and his features (decent face, sticky out ears).

'All right?' he asked, and I noted that his West Country burr was stronger than Nate's, then squashed the comparison and swore to myself not to repeat it.

I stuck my hands in the pocket of my jacket. 'I'm good, thanks. You?'

He grinned. 'I'm well pleased you agreed to come out with short notice.'

'I'm pleased to be invited.' As I spoke, I took a few steps towards the discreet entrance for the steakhouse.

Frankie was walking too, but in the opposite direction. 'Come on,' he called back. 'We've got to get our order in before seven.'

I assessed and reassessed as I followed. A bit further down there was an Italian place that Nate once described as—

'Stop thinking about Nate,' I hissed to myself, as Frankie continued past the Italian restaurant. Which meant we were going to one of the overpriced cafés that trapped the tourists coming round from the Royal Crescent.

'Here we are,' he said, pushing straight into a pizzeria wedged between two cafés. I'd never even noticed it before. But maybe it was a little-known gem, I reassured myself, and much nicer inside than the rather dingy exterior. I entered behind him and glanced around: deserted tables, covered in oilcloth and laid with plastic cutlery and disposable napkins. Even the yellow carnations in little vases were artificial.

'Table for two,' Frankie was saying to the waitress, who nodded over at an empty banquette.

'Frankie?' I asked with caution. 'My friend seemed to think this had to happen this evening because of something special?'

'Yup. As I told my sister, I've got a special.' At my blank expression he added, 'A special offer, for in here, tonight.'

'Ah. The message I got was a reservation, somewhere special.' I tried not to gaze around too pointedly as I spoke. It was a miscommunication, not a deceit — I didn't need to be blunt about this place not being special at all.

But if he took any offence, he hid it well, just shaking his head slightly. 'My sister should be better at this by now.'

'She's set you up on a lot of dates, then?' I asked dryly.

'Twelve and counting. I'm determined to find a girl and settle down.' His expression was alarmingly conspiratorial.

'It's my first one,' I said hurriedly. 'So I don't know what it is I'm wanting. Beyond making it to a second date, that is.'

If he noticed my hint, there was no sign of it. 'Two menus,' he hollered at the waitress. 'And some drinks. A jug of tap water and—' He broke off to raise an enquiring eyebrow.

'A lemonade, I guess,' I said, loud enough for the waitress to hear, so Frankie wouldn't yell it at the top of his voice. 'I heard you're in property, Frankie. Is there a particular period of architecture you're interested in?'

'Whatever type earns me the most commission tends to be my favourite,' he said cheerfully. 'Right now that's a 1970's semi out in Radstock. Get this — I sold it to new owners two years ago, they decided to get a divorce and came back to me as clients, and I just sold it on to first time buyers.' He slapped the plastic table between us, and guffawed. 'Two lots of commission in as many years.'

'You're an estate agent,' I said, pointlessly.

'That's right.' He took that as a show of interest in the property market, and began a lecture about the rise and fall of the price of flats in Bath, not even breaking off as the waitress delivered our drinks and two menus. If I hadn't already ruled him out as potentially *the one*, rudeness to waiting staff would have done it, but that didn't rule out a second date, I calculated. It would still be much less unpleasant than speed dating, especially if I could arrange to meet him in a location where I didn't have to inflict him on others. A walk in the park, perhaps . . .

I interrupted him to thank her for the slightly sticky menu she handed me, and Frankie pulled something from the inside pocket of his jacket, unfurling it for her perusal.

'I've got this voucher — two mains for the price of one, for orders made before seven. So make sure you chop-chop back over here quickly to take our food order.' As she stalked off, grumbling slightly, he turned back to me. 'So I heard you've recently moved? How much did it cost and when do you plan on stepping up to the next rung of the property ladder? I'll give you my business card for when you're ready to go on the market, and you must—'

'No need. I'll be renting for a while yet.'

His mouth dropped open. 'You rent? You *rent*? You know what we estate agents call renting, don't you?' He of course didn't wait for my reply. 'It's paying the mortgage of someone richer than you every month, that's what!'

The waitress's return saved me from the bother of replying. I hadn't even glanced at the menu, but it didn't matter. All I wanted was the smallest, simplest pizza on offer, so the evening only lasted long enough to arrange to meet again. I could cut that second date short — maybe by getting Abi to phone me with an "emergency", and get to see Esme, my duty discharged. I pushed aside the problem of how to find *the one* without Gemma, to deal with another time. 'I'll take a margarita, please — the smallest size you do.'

'If you get a small margarita then I only get a small margarita!' Frankie said, at a volume marginally lower than his usual foghorn, which I gathered was intended as a whisper. 'The voucher specified two for the price of one on the *same main*!' He raised his voice again. 'Two extra-large meat feasts, but with extra ham instead of pepperoni — I don't like spicy muck.'

'Please don't write that down,' I said to the waitress, scanning the menu. 'I'm afraid I don't eat meat,' I said with artificial sorrow, for no other reason than to repay Frankie for ordering on my behalf so peremptorily. 'It'll have to be an extra-large veggie supreme. And I love spicy food so I'd want an extra topping, of chilli.'

'If the lady gets chilli as an extra, can I swap it out for ham on my veggie supreme?'

She assented, probably to shut him up, and Frankie returned to his monologue about property prices, this time with asides about the vulnerability of tenancies and how anyone can save a deposit with proper money management. I zoned out by plotting revenge against Gemma. To make the punishment fit the crime, it should involve being stuck with Frankie for a very long time in a very small space. Like a coffin.

When our pizzas came Frankie's face lit up. There was blessed silence as he sliced up his hammy veggie supreme, tore a wedge free, folded it in half lengthways and shoved it into his mouth.

'This is lush,' he said, his mouth still half full. 'How's yours?'

'Not so bad,' I choked, surprised that flames didn't burst from my throat. Extra chilli really meant extra chilli in this place. I glowered at Frankie's pizza, wishing I had his ham topping instead.

'Too spicy?'

'Not at all,' I said, before glugging back lemonade.

'What's that like, then?'

'Like yours, only less hammy.'

'The drink, I mean.'

'Oh.' I placed my glass down. 'It's lemonade. So, it's like . . . lemons.'

'Ha!' he said. 'Good one! It's nice, then?'

'Uh, sure?'

He took that as an invitation to reach over and grab my glass. Throwing his head back, he took a long slurp. 'I see what you mean.' He wiped around his mouth with the back of his hand. 'Very nice, that is.'

Instantly I changed my mind; speed dating had to be considerably less painful than this. I gestured over at the waitress. 'Could we have the bill, please?'

'You've only eaten one slice,' Frankie pointed out.

'Sorry about that. But I'm . . . not feeling well.'

'It'll be the spice,' he said, tapping the side of his nose and leaving a greasy mark. 'Should have listened to me. You'll have the runs all night. But before you go we need to talk about this second date you went on about.'

Rapidly, I prepared a response. *It's not you, it's me*, would be kindest. Or, *I've only recently broken up with the man I thought was* the one, *and don't feel ready to date after all*, which was still kind, and much more truthful.

'Listen, don't take this the wrong way, but me and you—' Frankie gesticulated between us with his dirty fork — 'it's not gonna happen.'

I sagged with relief. 'I know. We're not right for each other at all.'

He blinked, seemingly taken-aback. 'Well, that's one way of putting it. But truth is, I'm looking for someone who's, you know . . . on my level. A homeowner, with a bit of ambition and all that. I'm out of your league, love.'

At that moment the waitress returned with our bill. I glared at my disposable plastic cutlery, wondering how much damage it could inflict on a human body, as she handed it to Frankie.

'I ordered tap water, and my pizza's covered by the special offer.' He jerked his chin in my direction. 'The bill's for the lady to settle.'

CHAPTER 10: UP CLOSE AND PERSONAL

My phone chirped.

I felt for it without opening my eyes, switched off the power, and sunk back into sleep.

An alarm clock beeped. I swung down to retrieve it from the floor beside my bed, blearily wishing I had my bedside tables from Nate's, clicked it off and dropped my head back to my pillows.

A siren shrieked, and I sat bolt upright, wondering if an ambulance was on the track outside the cottage. In the meagre light filtering through the curtains, I spied the laptop on the opposite side of my bedroom. Stumbling out of bed, I cursed the diligent Róisín of the night before as I silenced it, and, finally knowing why I'd made efforts to rouse early, switched to cursing Perky bloody Perkinson.

Her email suggesting dates and times for me to measure the staff needing historical garments had offered flexible dates (*any weekday works!*) but distressingly rigid timings (*8.30 a.m. sharp please!*). I couldn't think of an acceptable excuse for a later start. Not when I was living and working on site, rent free. So I'd committed to Wednesday at eight thirty, and spent Tuesday adding finishing touches to my array of costume designs, and devising methods of waking myself early enough to be alert by half eight.

* * *

Perky had directed me to the estate offices, in the west wing of the house. I entered through a side door at sub-basement level, ascended a bare stone staircase and then a carpeted one, and along corridors that increased in width and natural light. The estate offices were on the second floor and blended ancient and modern, with laptops set on huge mahogany desks, and filing cabinets beside leather Chesterfield couches.

Perky was waiting, and showed me into a room further along the corridor, which was dominated by an ornate four-poster bed, draped in maroon velvet.

'One of the few guest chambers in this wing that we could afford to include in the first phase of the renovation,' she explained. 'It seemed best for the fittings, given your requests.'

She motioned between the full-length mirror I'd needed, which was foxed with age and propped against a wall, and a small, level platform, just a foot above the carpet, to make it easier to take measurements.

Setting my basket down on the bed, I fanned out my designs, each for an individual from the list of approximate heights and ages Perky had compiled when she first commissioned the costumes. 'Who am I starting with?'

'Me?'

I circled *female, age 30, five foot four*.

'Then Lola-Pop,' Perky continued. 'Next Amelia — who's got the day off so coming in especially — and Mrs Holt. And the boys last of all.'

'Okay,' I said, rubbing my temples as I tried to match the names to the brief descriptions.

Perky stepped onto the platform and I passed her the design I had in mind. As I talked her through it I slung my measuring tape round my neck and put my pencil behind my ear, then began to measure every facet of her figure, working downwards from the crown of her head. Perky's efficient approach to her own work extended to mine, so her questions were straightforward, and she rotated her body and raised her arms co-operatively at my requests.

'How's the grand plan going, Róisín?'

'Sorry?'

'Your plan — to find a groom for the wedding.'

'Oh. Well . . .' I lassoed her around the waist. 'I had a date last week — he wasn't the one for me, but you know, getting back out there was . . .' *Shit, hideous, revolting.* 'Good. And I'm going speed dating next week.'

Lola-Pop's arrival cut off any further questions, and Perky swept out as I offered the younger woman her concept sketch.

'Oh my God,' Lola-Pop said, staring at the colour drawing. 'My boobs are a lot bigger than that.'

'I'll redraw it to your proportions after this.' Her expression remained doubtful. 'Look,' I seized back the paper and sketched another version of the gown beside it, shaped for more of an hour-glass. '1810 is the look Perky wants, but there are a few options within that to suit different body types.'

'I like that more,' she admitted. 'Does it have a corset? I don't want to be uncomfortable.

'I'll be making stays, which are similar, but well fitted — which they will be — there's no discomfort at all. Step onto the platform, please. Could you hold your arms out at ninety degrees?'

* * *

When I was finished I started to write her name at the top of the sheet, but hesitated after *Lola*. 'Lola what?'

'Pardon?'

'What's your full name? I take it 'Pop' wasn't on your birth certificate.'

'Oh, neither's Lola. I'm Amanda Blenkinsop.'

I scrubbed out Lola. 'Isn't anyone at Sylverley called their actual real name?' I muttered.

'I am,' Amelia said, entering. 'I used to try to get the others to call me Leggy, rather than boring old Amelia Legg. But fun nicknames are a boarding school thing, that stick for life.' She gave a small sigh. 'I went to a girls' day school and it'll always show.'

I wondered if it showed that I went to an inner-city comprehensive, then dismissed the thought, waving off Lola-Pop and appraising Amelia. She was in her own clothing rather than Sylverley uniform, wearing jeans and an oversized blouse. 'My measurements will be more accurate if you wouldn't mind taking that loose top off?'

She stripped down to a tank top and I showed her the design I had in mind before taking her measurements. When I was finished, and had them all noted neatly down, I handed her back her blouse.

Mrs Holt was next to step onto my platform, in a mixture of embarrassment and pleasure that as head of catering she was deemed to need a historical gown. 'The visitors barely see me,' she twittered.

I pressed gently on her shoulders, which she kept hunching. 'Try to stay relaxed.'

'Of course,' she said, immediately scrunching up the top line of her shoulders again with anxiety. I needed to distract her from thinking about being measured. Since I had something to ask her advice on, I began with that.

'My friends and goddaughter are visiting Sylverley next Tuesday, and I've been meaning to ask what you thought about booking a table in the orangery.' I explained that Esme would adore the afternoon tea menu, but that the step in and out of the glass doors was potentially a problem, since some of the time she had to use a wheelchair. 'She has a form of cerebral palsy that causes her mobility to be highly variable. Sometimes she can walk unsteadily, other times she's in a wheelchair. And she's getting to the age where she's fighting for independence, so hates being carried.'

Mrs Holt tilted her head to one side, as she considered, but the rest of her body was much more relaxed. 'How old is the little darling?'

'Six. So the wheelchair's not that big, but it needs more space than you'd think, for a decent turning radius.'

'I could make space for it, and we've got removable ramps. But a girly of six doesn't want to be stuck in genteel surroundings like the orangery. What about I provide a nice full picnic basket for you and her, and book a table for two inside so her parents can get some quiet time alone?'

'That's a lovely idea,' I said, measuring her hips as she provided her own distraction by listing what she liked about the changes I'd wrought on my cottage.

'Clean windows and the little curtains peeping from behind them make such a difference,' she concluded, tucking the wisps escaping from her bun behind her ears. 'I've told the cleaning team to get access to Tristan's cottage and get that shine on his glass. It's so dreary in there — not that he seems to notice.'

'Well, he's not in there much,' I said, inching my looped tape up to her waist. 'He seems incredibly busy.'

'All work and no play, that one. It's a shame, with looks like those.'

I murmured a non-committal sound. I didn't disagree with her verdict, but I didn't want to be thought to have noticed more than Tristan's unflagging diligence, in pursuit of profits or perfection — or probably both.

I waved her off and welcomed a diffident young man, who was Lola-Pop's deputy head of visitor experience, and conducted many of the VIP tours. I scrunched up the military-inspired design I'd come up with before I'd met him, rapidly assessing that he'd look best in something much simpler. And black and white, rather than colourful — almost parson-like. I stayed silent as I took his measurements, certain he'd get embarrassed if I was anything other than gravely professional.

There was a short lull afterwards, and I wandered to the window, wishing someone would bring me a cup of tea. Outside, the lawn rolled down to the woodland that sheltered the cottages, though I couldn't see even the rooftops, through the thick summer foliage of the trees.

The sash windows encompassed sixteen glass panes, a patchwork of original glass, of variable thickness and marked with whirls and pits, and much more recent replacements. The outlook was slightly distorted through the aged originals, and as a figure strode toward the building, I had to shift my eyes to a modern pane to confirm his identity. It was Tristan. He glanced at his wristwatch then increased his pace, clearly late for something. And my next individual, *male, age thirty-four, six foot two* was late for me . . .

I allowed myself a moment of panicked reproach for not even considering that one of Sylverley's employees I'd be designing and sewing for would be Tristan himself, then pulled myself together. By the time he entered, a professional smile was smooth across my lips.

'Good morning, Tristan. Remove your jacket and tie, please.'

'Sorry?'

'I can't get accurate measurements over those,' I explained, with so much patience it almost sounded exaggerated. His eyes were wary. Then he shrugged off the jacket.

'Thanks,' I murmured, as he draped it over the back of a chair. Not wanting to make him feel scrutinised, I transferred my eyes up to the ornate plasterwork on the ceiling, admiring the intricacy.

He followed my gaze. 'We got lucky — the plasterwork's only needed minimal repairs.'

In my peripheral vision, I was aware of him quickly releasing his tie. 'It's stood the test of time, like so much here at Sylverley. I really think it's one of the finest examples of a house of this kind.'

As he opened the top few buttons on his shirt, he gave a slight snort. 'Believe me, Sylverley has more than its fair share of problems. The initial round of restoration didn't include nearly as much of the house as had been hoped, and the grounds need three times more gardeners than budgets allow.'

'Visitor numbers seem very healthy, in such early days, so at some stage the budgets can increase, right?'

'In the longer term,' he conceded. He shook his head suddenly, as if clearing water from his ears. 'Where do you want me?'

'Not on the platform yet — I need to start from the top, and you're much taller than me.'

I didn't measure around his head — the men would get top hats supplied by a milliner, so I only needed to reach as far as his neck. So close, it was impossible not to notice that there were blue flecks in his ambivalent irises. I lowered my eyes, and noted that the light tan on his face and neck ended just beneath his collar bone.

'You normally wear a sixteen and a half inch shirt?' I didn't need to double-check my measurement, but it was something to break the awkward silence.

'Yes.'

I took refuge in describing his costume as I moved behind him to measure his shoulders from blade to blade. 'A tailcoat's essential for the period — I'm open to your input with whether to go for charcoal or navy or black. And breeches to just below your knee or long pantaloons.'

'I'd much rather wear the latter.'

'Good choice.'

'Why do you say that?'

I glanced into the mirror and caught sight of his face. Thinking I was behind him, his expression was less guarded than I'd even seen it before, displaying lively curiosity.

'Fashionable men would have preferred them in the evening,' I murmured, because I wasn't going to say that tight pantaloons would look better on Tristan's long, shapely legs. They'd taken off with men who wanted to show off their leg muscles — with padding for those who skipped whatever

112

was the Regency version of leg day at the gym. 'Could you raise your arms, please?'

He obliged, holding his breath to stay entirely still as I wrapped my tape around his chest.

'Arms down,' I said, before lowering my tape to his waist and returning to my plan for his outfit. *It was because he was the boss*, I told myself. I wanted him to notice that I shared his professional perfectionism, as he had the power to commission more costumes for Sylverley in future. 'You'll have a high-collared waistcoat with an open neck, and a cravat in . . .' The plan had been Sylverley teal, but I changed my mind, in favour of bringing out the blue in his eyes. 'Pale blue silk. A white linen shirt goes under that, with full sleeves.'

He grimaced. 'I've seen pictures of those, with frills at the cuffs and collars.'

I measured the length from his wrist up to his shoulder. 'Don't worry. By the early nineteenth century there were minimal frills. The English upper-class was intent on self-preservation, in case the French Revolution spread over the channel. Though I don't think evening wear with clean lines rather than flounces would really have been much protection from the guillotine.'

I was concentrating on exactly where a collar would need to hit to be most flattering to Tristan's bone structure, and caught his sudden wince. For an aghast second I thought I'd pricked him with a pin, before coming to my senses. I couldn't have hurt him with a soft tape measure. It must have been a wince of boredom at the history I was spewing. Or at having me so up-close in his personal space.

At that notion, my face heated. The concept of personal space necessarily melted away for me when I was doing fittings, but not always for my clients. And this one was the boss here.

I kept him literally at arm's length as I completed the first set of measurements, then asked him to step onto the platform, ruing the stiffness in my voice. *Just talk like a normal person*, I chided myself, as I sank into a crouch.

I'd done so many fittings that I barely needed to think anymore, trusting the muscle memory in my fingers as I flicked the measuring tape around living, breathing mannequins. But as I anticipated measuring the distance between Tristan's lean hips and ankle, I dropped the tape, and in my scramble to lift it, the pencil fell out from behind my ear.

I knotted my newly-clumsy hands into fists, then splayed them wide, quelling the tremors.

'Could you—' My tongue rebelled, refusing to form the words *spread your legs*. 'Could you just step your right foot out a little . . . And then the left. Thank you.'

As I raised the tape again I wondered if he was looking down at me, or watching more cautiously in the mirror, or just staring straight ahead. I didn't dare glance up to see.

'Tristan—' Perky said, entering suddenly, making me jerk. 'Oh, sorry. I thought you'd want a heads-up that Mrs Sylvers is on the warpath.'

I stiffened. Since Mrs Sylvers had turned her ire on me for no perceptible reason, I'd successfully avoided her as I explored the house and estate, running off in the opposite direction any time I heard her voice in the distance.

'She's headed in here?' Tristan asked.

'I'm afraid so,' Perky said. 'I tried to intercept her, but she'd already heard that you're up here—'

The door, which Perky had left ajar, was flung wide open.

'*Mis-ter Nash*,' Mrs Sylvers said, overly enunciating every syllable. 'I just overheard some surveyors outside my windows. They seem to be under the impression that I — *the last remaining Sylvers* — would be relocating from the family apartment in the east wing, where the previous four generations have resided. Worst of all, someone seems to have confused me with an — an *equine*, and dares plan to move me into *a stable*.'

I felt Tristan's legs tense, and took the opportunity to lift the end of my tape close to his crotch, safe in the knowledge that he was distracted.

'I'm very sorry, of course,' he said with calm courtesy, 'that you heard about this before I could explain it to you myself, Mrs Sylvers. But let me reassure you that the conversion of the stables will be stunning, with five bedrooms, and nearly as much square footage as you have already. As you can see, I'm . . . engaged at present. But if you go through to my office I'll be with you to show you the plans in . . .'

I realised he'd dropped his eyes to me and cursed him internally. I didn't want to draw the old bat's attention again.

'I'm done,' I said, committing his inside and outside leg measurements to memory, rather than scrabbling around for my sheet of paper.

'Right now, then,' he said to Mrs Sylvers, stepping down from the platform and pulling his jacket back on. I thought he was following her without another word to me, but at the last instant he turned back from the doorway.

'Róisín, next Sunday's the last one in August.'

'I know. I can't make high tea that day. I'm . . . I'm going speed dating.'

He gave one inscrutable nod, then left.

CHAPTER 11: MADE FOR EACH OTHER

The restaurant was lit up like fairyland, with strings of lights adorning the exposed roof trusses. A long bar ran down the middle of the room, surrounded by various shapes and sizes of tables, set in front of bare brick walls.

A chalkboard at the bottom of a metal spiral staircase advertised that the speed-dating event was happening upstairs. I climbed up slowly, my heels striking the metal treads like hammers on an anvil, preparing to scarper at anything alarming. At the top, I discovered women sitting alone at small tables while a gaggle of men stood uneasily at the far end of the room. A woman in a large, flashy engagement ring swooped on me.

'Name?'

'Róisín O'Reilly.'

She consulted her clipboard then gave me a badge, which proclaimed that I was Róisín in a swirly font.

'I'm Carmen, and you're the last of the girls. It's so nice *slash* satisfying,' as she said *slash*, she chopped sideways with her hand, 'to have a full house. Please get a drink at the bar and take it to table thirteen — lucky for some!'

I bought a non-alcoholic cocktail, since I needed my wits about me, before wandering to my table. They were well-spaced, limiting the chances of the occupants listening-in on other conversations, and rather than a clichéd red rose, each had a lavender plant as a centrepiece, with the table number chalked on the pot.

I took my jacket off and hung it on the back of my seat, then turned my mobile to silent and drew my notebook out, opening it at the right page. Missing Sylverley's high tea to attend this had made me determined to make the most of speed dating, and I'd spent hours listing innocent questions that might elicit the essential information I needed. *Have you ever done anything like this before?* was my opener, to reveal the length of their commitment to finding a romantic partner. If they seemed serious rather than after a one-night stand, I'd launch into: *What do you do for a living?* so I could immediately weed out estate agents. Any men who'd made it, unscathed, over those two hurdles I would ask: *Have you any holidays booked?* allowing me to confirm availability for the wedding date.

Carmen was at a microphone stand. 'Welcome to Soulmate Speed Dating everyone!' The sound system made her high-pitched voice sound like she'd been gulping down helium. 'I can promise you a really fun *slash* purposeful evening, with plenty of eligible men *slash* women for you to meet!'

As she rabbitted on, I turned my attention to the men lingering against the far wall. Several immediately stood out to me as completely not my type, but there was one toward the back that caught my eye for all the right reasons. Someone shifted to one side, and a clear line of sight opened to him. Between dark red hair and a firm jawline, his mouth was quirked in amusement, and his eyes were dancing . . . and fixed on mine. I lowered my eyes to the floor, then took a quick, deep breath, reminded myself why I was there, and shifted my gaze back to him. At my smile he dropped one eyelid into a wink, and a firework went off in my innards.

'The procedure is very simple,' Carmen was saying. 'Girls, stay at your tables; boys, check the number on the

117

back of your name tags. When I ring my bell, go straight there to meet the lovely lady. When the bell rings again, move onto the next table, and so on.'

Rustles and low murmurs marked the checking of numbers. I glanced at the man, who held up eight fingers.

'Thirteen,' I mouthed.

He tapped his watch and winked again. I got the message: it would take a little while, but he was looking forward to meeting me.

'As you boys make your way over to the correct numbered table, please all listen to a final few top tips. If you've prepared for this by planning conversation starters then well done.' I sat up a little straighter, and centred my notebook in front of me, as an inordinately tall man came toward me, a determined look on his face. 'But if you've planned mundane questions like what do you do for a living and where do you go on holiday then scrap them now. You'll be instantly forgettable *slash* only remembered for being dull.'

I slapped my hand over the notepad as the man, with a nametag labelled *Phil*, bent almost double to fit his lanky frame onto the seat.

Carmen raised her voice above the hubbub. 'Finally, remember to note down the name of everyone you feel is a potential match. If any of them has also written down yours, you'll be given one another's full names and contact details. Now only one instruction is left — have fun!'

She rang a bell, and the conversations grew instantaneously louder.

I pushed my notebook into the handbag at my feet. 'How you doing?' I asked, stalling as I sought a non-boring question.

He half-smiled, but didn't meet my eyes. Deciding he was shy, I thought a moment, then tried harder.

'Uh . . . would you rather fight a tiger-sized duck or a hundred duck-sized tigers?'

Following his eyes, I realised his uncomprehending stare was directed at the name badge on my chest.

'It's pronounced *Rosheen*,' I prompted.

His eyes remained, fixed and unmoving, on my chest. I leaned slightly toward him, and his mouth flopped open. Wondering if he had suffered a stroke or something, I examined him carefully. Could he really be entranced by my name badge . . .

No! He was staring at the bit of cleavage that showed at the top of my blouse.

Slowly and deliberately, I did up my top button.

'Tigers,' he said without shame, his eyes still hovering on my chest.

I laced my voice with as much displeasure as possible. 'Pardon?'

'I'd fight all the duck-sized tigers. Ducks are all pecky. They scare me.'

'QUACK!' I said, loud enough to make him flinch. 'Now stand up and move on to wait for the lucky lady at table number fourteen, Phil,' I hissed, removing my name badge. By the time I'd got it to balance against the lavender, the buzzer went off again.

A man in a bicep-swollen T-shirt wandered over. He was pushing at the upper end of the thirty to forty age band, but since he wasn't perving at my chest he was a welcome improvement.

'You're not wearing that badge,' he said, as he sat.

'Well spotted . . .' I checked out his. 'Dave.'

He peered at my name. 'Roy-see-een? That's complicated isn't it?'

'Not complicated, just Irish.'

A gleeful expression, like I'd fallen into his trap, spread across his face. 'But we're here in England, speaking English. So how about I call you Rosie?'

I crossed my arms. 'Absolutely not.'

He recoiled from my glare, then shrugged and swivelled in the chair, moving his whole attention onto the poor woman at table fourteen, who was squirming under pervy Phil's gaze.

We sat in stony silence until the bell sounded and he stood up so fast his chair made a scraping sound. 'Bye, Rosie.'

I ignored the pathetic parting shot, in favour of smiling at the thin, nervous-looking man holding out his twigletty hand as he came toward me.

'Rosie is it? Nice to meet you.'

I knew he was only parroting what he'd heard the last loser say, but I was beyond reining in my annoyance. So I scowled as I shook his bones. 'Actually it's *Róisín*.'

'Sorry! I'm very sorry! Maybe I should . . . just wait for the next . . . uh . . . lady . . . from . . . from over there at the bar . . .'

He clearly wanted to flee. And as nervous as he was, I'd never be his type, even if he was mine — which he very much wasn't.

'Good idea.'

I sipped my cocktail, regretting that I hadn't got a fully-loaded one, and stared around the room, trying to distract myself by searching out the gorgeous man. He was only two tables away, leaning against his chair back as the pretty blonde across from him giggled. When I examined the slight smile on his face it was easy to damp down the spark of possessiveness, somehow certain that his expression was conveying politeness to cover boredom. And when his eyes flicked over to meet mine, I was certain of it.

Carmen interrupted my attempts at batting my eyelids at him. 'Is everything okay, Róisín?'

'Not really. The first guy I met is a perve.'

'Argh — sorry. I'll eject him at the next bell. And let me have your drink replenished . . . virgin cosmopolitan, was it?'

'I'll have a proper one this time, please.'

She nodded as she sailed away, and a few seconds later the bell pealed once more. The guy at table twelve got up slowly, and walked over at a snail's pace. I wondered if he was always this slow, or whether word about me had gone around . . .

As soon as he spoke, it was clear. 'Hull-oooooh,' he said, managing to drag the two syllables out over the course of thirty seconds. 'I'm sorry . . . but I don't know . . . how to pronounce your . . . name.'

'It's Rosh-een,' I said quickly, trying to lead by example. 'Irish, y'know.'

'Hello Róisín,' he said. I wondered if his next question would be worth waiting for. 'What . . . do you do . . . for a . . . living?' he finished at last.

I gave an internal scream. He'd missed the memo that this question was boring. And, indeed, that the operative word in speed dating, is *speed*.

'I make clothes,' I said, making it sound as dull as possible so as not to invite any follow-up questions. 'How about you, Dan — what job do you do, and what do you enjoy doing when you're not at work?'

As he launched into the minutiae of his book-keeping role, I lowered my eyes to the table, then gave in to curiosity and looked through my lashes at Mr Perfect, now with my neighbour at table twelve, a rather haughty-looking brunette. He still wasn't close enough for me to make out his name, but by straining hard enough I heard a bit of conversation. Haughty Brunette was doing all the talking . . . something about horse trekking in Andalusia. He didn't look in any way scintillated, though I glanced away again as his eyes turned towards me. Making eyes at each other from across the room was one thing, but now a meeting was imminent, nerves were shooting off in my stomach.

I pushed away my glass, and tried to concentrate on ponderous Dan.

'I suppose . . . that when I'm not . . . balancing accounts, adding to my . . . collection . . . is how I . . . spend time.'

'Collection?' I asked mechanically.

'My collection of . . . acronyms,' he said. Slowly, of course, but amiably enough. 'I spend an . . . oh.' Gradually he moved his hand to his forehead, then struck it. 'I'm dominating the entire conversation . . . again. Please, tell me more about you . . .for example, what's your favourite . . . acronym?'

The plaintive *again*, moved me enough to think. 'Uh . . . maybe OMG? But unfortunately, Dan, our five minutes are almost gone.'

He continued speaking as he rose. 'OMG is technically . . . an initialisation; an abbreviation where you . . . say the individual initial letters . . . rather than taking those initials . . . and pronouncing them as . . . a word. It's the difference . . . between NASA, an acronym, and DVD . . . an initialisation.'

'I get it. FFS is an initialisation, and DILLIGAF an acronym.'

'Exactly,' Dan said, rotating towards table fourteen. My eyes met the hottie's, as he paced towards me, grinning.

Please say my name right, I chanted internally. *Please, please, please say my name right.*

His eyes alighted on the badge I'd propped against the table number, and his smile widened. 'How do ye do now, Róisín? How did ye find the acronyms?' The dozen words were enough for me to place him as not just Irish, but from Northern Ireland. He misinterpreted my raised eyebrows, and hurriedly elaborated. 'I swear I wasn't listening in — it's just that I've been behind him all evening, so everyone's mentioned it. D'you mind if I sit down?'

'Not at all,' I croaked. 'Please do . . . uh . . .'

He pulled his name badge from his pocket ruefully, before dropping into the chair. 'I had to take it off, because it was getting to me that everyone was pronouncing it so weirdly.' He scooted the chair in tight and leaned his shoulders all the way toward me. His voice lightened with merriment. 'I'm Oisín, and it's nice to meet ye, Róisín.'

His hoot at the near-rhyme our names made was impossible not to join in with, and our combined laughter caused the potential couples at other tables to swivel in our direction, staring.

'So I take it you're Irish too?' he asked.

'What gave it away — the name, or the hair?' It struck me that without an explanation for my accent, he might assume me to be a plastic Paddy, and I added in a rush: 'I was brought up in London but born in Derry, and my mammy lives back there now.'

'Derry, is it? I was raised just down the road in Strabane.'

I settled more comfortably into my seat as our conversation developed a natural flow, and the coincidences about our lives stacked up. He also had three siblings, also went to university in England before moving to Bath, and also phoned his family more often than he flew back to see them. The biggest difference I uncovered was that he referred to Northern Ireland as home. He was so easy to converse with that I almost launched into how homeless I felt, stopping myself at the last moment, since it was too heavy for speed dating. I must only have a few minutes left, and I had a lot to get through, to ensure he fit the brief before I fell for him.

I snorted internally at myself for the *before*, then concentrated on his adorable anecdote about his niece.

'So what are you looking to get out of this?' I blurted.

He shrugged easily. 'I went home, a few weeks back. When I returned to Bath I got to thinking. Well, after my eardrums had recovered . . .' I smiled in recognition. 'I don't know how to explain it, but my flat felt empty. I'd been so busy at work for so long that I hadn't made time for anything serious, and it felt like about time.'

I fist pumped under the table, then crossed my fingers. 'What line of work?'

'Property.'

My mental image of him as my groom crumbled; another estate agent, just like Frankie, who was certain that I wasn't in his league. And Oisín was hotter, funnier, and much more polite than Frankie — I really wasn't in his league in any way.

'Oh?' It came out in a quiet sigh. I stared into my cosmopolitan. 'Estate agent? You probably snapped up a bargain on your flat.'

'I pay silly money,' he said, laughing again, 'to rent a tiny place.' I looked up at him sharply. 'And no, I work in the non-lucrative side of the property business. I'm an architectural investigator of heritage buildings. Basically uncovering evidence for when they were built, and why, and how they've changed and evolved. My particular field is the 18th century, hence ending up in Bath.' His voice trailed off. 'Sorry, the minutiae is dull—'

'Not for me! I'm involved in heritage history as well — I'm a fashion historian.'

'Seriously?' He was laughing again, his head thrown back, eyes sparkling. 'I can't believe this — it's like we're made for each other!'

The bell rang, but it sounded muffled, as though my head was under water. *Like we're made for each other* rang in my ears as he looked askance over at Carmen.

'I'm really not ready to move on,' he said.

'I don't want that either,' I breathed.

His eyes flew back to mine, gently probing. 'I'll be writing Róisín down — and only Róisín, aye?'

I smiled at him. 'Only Oisín for me. And maybe, let's talk more afterwards?'

He exhaled, long and deep. 'I'm already looking forward to it.'

He stood and made his way to the next table, then, with a final show of reluctance, doubled back and pushed the chair opposite me deep under the table. 'Don't want to make things too easy for the next fella,' he said, with a wink.

* * *

After the final bell I rushed to the loo to make space in my bladder for another drink or two, and reapplied my lipstick. Emerging, I saw Oisín at the bar, craning his neck around the upper floor.

'There you are!' He rose from the bar stool and pulled a second one out for me, then jerked his chin at the full glasses on the bar. 'I took a guess that ye're still on the Cosmo's, but I can get you something else if—'

'This is perfect,' I said, because it was a bit soon to tell him that *he* was perfect. Generous, polite, handsome, funny, wanting to settle down, and a frigging architectural historian . . . If anyone would appreciate getting married at Sylverley even more than me, it was this man. And although I had no intention of bringing up the whole wedding thing yet, I wanted to drip Sylverley into conversations from the get-go. Thankfully, living there made that easy.

'Which part of Bath do you live in?'

'Upper slopes of the centre. My flat's on the top floor of a town house, so there's lots of stairs, but it's worth it for the period features.'

'And the views.'

He hummed agreement, shifting his bar stool a little closer, so his knees brushed against mine. 'Where d'you live yourself?'

'For ages in Widcombe, but I recently moved out of the city.' I took a deep breath. 'To a cottage within the Sylverley estate — have you been there since the renovation?'

'Not yet, but I heard that the new management made an impressive start—'

Just as I'd got the conversation where I wanted it, Carmen bustled up, a sheet of paper in each hand.

'Looks like it's news to neither of you that it's a match,' she said, beaming between us. 'Oisín, written down by . . .' She rotated her wrist to check the other side of the paper, where I'd written my full name and contact details. 'Ms Róisín O'Reilly. And Róisín, written down by . . .' She flipped the other sheet, 'By Mr Oisín O'Reilly — is this a prank?'

She glanced around as if checking for hidden cameras, but Oisín and I were staring at each other. Both red-haired, history-loving O'Reilly's from Northern Ireland.

'My father was from Derry, and you're from Strabane,' I said, to reassure myself as much as him.

'Mam's from Strabane. Dad's originally from Derry. Seamus Paul O'Reilly — have you heard of him?'

'I only know a few of my relatives on that side,' I said, already fumbling for my phone. 'My dad died when I was a teenager. Excuse me.' I half-turned away as I pressed to call Mam. It went straight to voicemail, and I tried Aoife's mobile instead.

'Hi, Róisín.'

'Is Mam there? I need to check something.'

'*Mam-my, Róisín for you,*' Aoife screeched.

I jerked the phone from my ear, my head ringing. 'Thanks for screaming in my ear.'

'I didn't, I called down the stairs. Oh, here's Mammy coming up — No, actually she's out.'

I twisted further from Oisín and Carmen, lowering my voice. 'She can't be out if she was just downstairs. Take your phone to her and say it's urgent.'

That time I moved my handset away in time, so I heard her screech of *it's urgent, Mammy* from a safe distance.

'Sorry, Róisín,' she said. 'She says you can't go saying it's urgent when you haven't called her for so long that she presumed you dead.'

'I spoke to her last week!'

'Aye, you did not. Nearly three weeks ago now, she says. And you didn't reply to anything on the group chat. She's raging about it.'

'Shite. Well, tell her I'm really sorry, and I'll phone back for a long catch-up tomorrow. But this really is important. I need to know if she knows a Seamus O'Reilly — Seamus Paul O'Reilly. From Derry, now living in Strabane.'

'Hang on—'

I pressed the phone hard against my ear to catch Mam's reply. 'Tell her I'll expect her call in the morning before I start my shift at half eight. And of course I know wee Seamus — he's your daddy's cousin.'

I screwed my eyes up as I cancelled the call mutely, not turning back towards Oisín.

'Looks like we're . . .' I swallowed, then continued hoarsely. 'Looks like we're second cousins.'

126

CHAPTER 12: CAN'T GET YOU OUT OF MY HEAD

'So, you were right about lots of fish in the speed-dating sea. But it turns out they're bores, perverts—' I dug my toe into the gravel path — 'or my blood relations.'

Gemma had taken one look at me and dispatched Esme and Joe to look around the rose garden, then marched me in the opposite direction debrief. 'Seriously, you got the hots for your long-lost cousin?'

'Second cousin,' I said sharply. 'And I only had the hots for Oisín until I found out who he was. I'm not sure which of us was most revolted, afterwards.'

'*Oisín*, and on your dad's side — so he's an O'Reilly too?' Gemma spluttered. 'You sound like virtually the same person.'

'You don't know the half of it.' At her enquiring raised eyebrow, I reluctantly elaborated. 'We're both historians, and look so alike we could be siblings.' My voice was so glum that any of my other friends would have offered me a shoulder to cry on. But Gemma being Gemma, she howled with laughter. 'Oh shut up, Gem — it was awful.'

'Did you tell your mother?' she asked when she recovered.

'Hell no! Thankfully she was too busy threatening me with dire consequences for not replying to her messages to ask why I'd wanted to know. Apparently she was on the verge of flying over.'

'But hottie Oisín . . . he's only a *second* cousin?'

When I got what she was hinting at, a primeval shudder ran through my body. 'No, Gem! Just . . . no. Even hearing him described as a hottie repulses me now. And he felt the same way — we agreed never to mention it if we ever encounter each other at weddings or funerals back in Derry, and he sprinted out of there like the place was on fire.'

'And you drowned your sorrows at the bar?' As I parted my lips to ask how she guessed, she added, 'Oh come on. I've known you almost fifteen years, I can tell when you're hungover. And given it was two days ago, that was some monster drinking session.'

'I hung out with another woman from the speed dating for a while,' I admitted. 'She'd gone for the Dutch courage approach and arrived addled by vodka, then decided this guy who's obsessed with acronyms was cute. Just as she was sobering up she realised he'd written her name down too, and had her contact details.'

'A guy obsessed with *what*?'

'You didn't mishear — acronyms. And he was far from the worst. Though to be fair, they kicked out the creepy pervert.'

'No wonder you ended the evening without any phone numbers.'

'Uh . . . yeah . . .'

Gemma narrowed her eyes. 'What aren't you telling me?'

My sunglasses weren't enough protection from the searchlight of her scrutiny. 'Nothing significant. A few drinks in, I got chatting to this American guy, who hadn't been at the speed dating.'

'And he gave you his number?'

My memories of later in the evening were hazy, but I was confident enough of the answer to shake my head. When I woke up the morning before, my bedroom spinning, I'd recalled him hailing me a taxi outside the venue, and saying we'd talk soon. But there was no new number in my phone, and no piece of paper in my bag or pockets.

'Fairy Godmother — *Fairy Godmother*!' Esme was calling, walking haltingly toward me, Joe hovering behind in case she stumbled. 'Look at me — I've walked all round Sylver-lily's pretty roses!'

'Brilliant!' As I gave her another reminder of how to say Sylverley, Gemma hissed at Joe to go get the wheelchair from the boot, before she suddenly flagged. He muttered back truculently that it might undermine her confidence and I drew Esme away from them, ostensibly to point out the woodland through which my little cottage was located. As she jabbered away about how it made me like a proper fairy godmother from a storybook, I kept an eye on her parents. If they were amidst a big row, maybe lunch for two in the orangery would come as entirely the wrong type of surprise. But before I could tell how serious it was, it ended, with Gemma stalking back toward the car park.

'Come on, sausage,' Joe called. 'Let's go over towards the woods. If you get tired, we'll wait on a bench for Mummy to catch up with the chair.'

'I'm a girl, not a sausage,' Esme said scathingly, taking an unsteady step, and then another. 'Don't stand so close, Daddy.'

As he backed off, she increased in pace, until she was a few metres ahead of us.

'This is the furthest I've seen her walk in months,' I breathed.

'It's a good day,' he said distractedly.

'Is there a but?'

He raised his shoulders, and for a few minutes I assumed that was all the response I'd get. 'But . . .' he said at last. We both glanced at Esme, who had drawn even further ahead, and was humming. 'Bad days get harder as she gets bigger. Carrying her up and down the stairs especially.' He rubbed his forefinger and thumb across his eyes, then corrected himself. 'Well, Gemma having to carry her, since I'm at work. And then Esme gets accustomed to that and kicks up a fuss when I try to take over at weekends.'

Before I could reply, he'd sped up to remonstrate with his daughter about having a little rest. Esme ignored him, insisting on continuing to walk unsupported.

When I caught up with Joe, he cleared his throat before speaking. 'I know I upset you, by never telling you that Nate had expressed doubts . . . no, let me finish. I thought he needed a bit longer, not that he had cold feet entirely, and I'm really sorry.'

'It's fine.' I didn't know it until after I spoke the words, but it was entirely true. 'It doesn't matter anymore.'

'He came for dinner last week,' Joe blurted.

'Joe,' I began, but he ploughed on.

'When Gemma let slip that you were dating again, he looked sad. I thought maybe you'd want to know—'

I interrupted more forcefully. 'Well, I don't. I've just uprooted my business — my whole life — because Nate spent years too cowardly to be honest with me. Literally the only thing I want to know about him at this point is whether I can pick up the bedside tables I left there. If you want to do me a favour, ask him if I can collect them. Aside from that — stay out of it.'

'Fuck's sake, Joe,' Gemma panted, coming up behind us at jogging pace with the empty wheelchair. 'I told you not to bring up Nate. And good job sticking close to your daughter, father of the year.'

I turned my head with such a jerk that it hurt, discovering with relief that Esme was okay, just drawing rather a long way ahead. Joe was already sprinting off, to get away from his wife's wrath as much as to look after Esme, I suspected.

'I'm really—' Gemma began.

'You don't need to apologise for Joe,' I said quickly.

The look she shot me was incredulous. 'Why would I? It was him who was an insensitive idiot, not me. I was about to say I'm really hungry now — what's that face for?'

'I'm weighing up whether you two need Esme and me as buffers, or if the surprise I've organised would go down well.'

'Your guess is as good as mine, to be honest,' she said morosely.

Gemma was blunt about everything except her own emotions, so generally her problems had to be cautiously cajoled from her, like tempting a tiger into a cage with a trail of delicacies. 'If talking about it might help, I'm here to listen,' I said softly.

She released a long breath. 'Well, it can't make anything worse, at least.'

She fixed her eyes on her husband and daughter, now quite far ahead of us. 'This summer holiday's been tough, with no respite, but Joe still having to go into school, since he took on running summer catch-up sessions. I'm exhausted from hauling Esme in and out of the bath and bed, and then we snipe about who's the most tired, and I get resentful that he gets to go to work, and he gets resentful that I get so much more time with Esme. More often than not our volume rises and we wake her up, and then we drop everything to reassure her, and none of it ever gets resolved. God . . . I'm sorry.'

'Hang on, why are you doing all that lifting anyway? Didn't the occupational therapist say you needed a hoist and stairlift and all that other stuff in her report last year?'

Gemma gave a strangled laugh. 'Our application for those adaptions was turned down by the council. We don't meet their criteria because we're renting — we can't prove we've got a secure enough tenancy for the adaptations to definitely benefit Esme rather than the landlord.'

'That's crap!'

'That's the law,' she corrected bleakly. 'We've appealed, of course, and joined the very long waiting list for a charity who might be able to help. But in the meantime, we're stuck. Joe thinks he needs to earn as much as possible so we can save up to buy a place in five years, rather than ten, and I think we need him at home more.'

She slapped her face with both hands, and her voice strengthened. 'I don't want to harp on about it. He's got this week off, and it's beautiful here, and come on, what's this surprise?'

My plan went down so well that within ten minutes Esme and I had found the picnic baskets, rugs and cushions laid out in the private part of the woodland, and her parents were waving as they headed into the distance for their lunch à deux.

Esme laid back until she was spread eagled across the picnic blanket, staring up at the sky.

'Not hungry yet?'

'No,' she said, unusually brief.

I reclined back into a mirroring position, squinting against the sunlight, despite my dark glasses. 'What are we looking at? Aeroplane, bird, images in the clouds?'

'Not looking at anything.' She sighed like the weight of the world were on her narrow shoulders. 'Just thinking.'

'Ah, thinking. Always important, that.' Esme didn't reply, which was so unusual that I probed a little deeper. 'Esme — you know I'm always here for you, if there's anything you might want to talk about?'

She raised her head at that, then wriggled to prop herself up on her elbows. 'That would be good, Fairy Godmother. I *do* have some questions.'

I groaned. 'I fell straight into that trap, didn't I, you merciless little assassin. Okay, fine, but remember the rule that—'

'I know, I know! Only three questions at one time on a subject.' Her voice, as she geared up for the inquisition, had risen to a shrill pitch, and I winced.

'Yup. And for today only, there's a special extra rule, that we use our indoor voices even though we're outdoors.'

'Why?'

'It doesn't matter. Come on, what's on your mind?'

'It's to do with Nate.'

'Oh.' I stretched and propped my shoulders up on the cool bag, playing for time. 'Well, I don't think I'll be able to help with things connected to Nate anymore. You should probably save those questions up until you see him next. Look — that cloud in between Sylverley's two sets of big chimneys looks like a dinosaur, don't you think?'

Esme followed my finger to examine the cloud I was pointing at. 'It's more like a dragon. But anyway, here's my first question about Nate. It doesn't matter if you don't have a very good answer. You can just try your best.'

I blinked, then laid back down on my back. 'Thank you for the encouragement. Come on, first question about Nate, then. I'll answer if I can, but no promises.'

'Okay. Number one why is Nate being so greedy about cakes?'

I rolled onto my side to face her. 'I'm sorry, but I was right, I can't help at all. I haven't seen Nate in a while, so your guesses will be as good as mine.'

She gave a huff of displeasure. 'I hate it when grown-ups won't explain things.'

'It's not that I won't — I honestly can't,' I assured her. 'It sounded like gobbledegook to me.'

'What language is gobble-gook and what does it mean?'

'It's not another language, just silly slang, and it means nonsense.' Seeing her mouth snap back open, I added hastily, 'And I'm only answering two more questions about slang.'

'I don't want to talk about that. I want to understand what Mummy and Daddy was saying about you and Nate.'

'They were saying stuff about me? Was this to Nate?' The query escaped before the guilt of pumping a child for information kicked in. 'Actually, Esme, don't answer that—'

But she was already shaking her head. 'It was after Nate went home. And it wasn't 'zactly about you. It was . . .' She waved her hands in the air. 'All that gobble-gook about Nate and then a bit about you afterwards. First Daddy said he feels bad for Nate and Mummy said well I don't because, because of something like he wants to have cakes and eat other cakes, and then Daddy said Nate and Róisín need to talk, and Mummy said *do not get involved, Joe* in her scary voice.'

I mused on that. Gemma thought Nate was trying to have his cake and eat it, from the sound of it, which was true — or at least it had been, until I ended our relationship.

'What's a prickle?' Esme asked suddenly.

My head spinning slightly from the rapid change of direction, I squinted, and raised the sunglasses to rub my eyes. 'It can be a spine in a hedgehog's back, or a thorn in a plant. And you know what? I'm ravenous even if you aren't. It's picnic time.'

Rummaging through the cool box, I discovered carefully wrapped delicacies in far larger amounts than the appetites of one adult and one child, and brightened. There were enough of the egg sandwiches, sausage rolls and bite-size cakes that I didn't even bother unwrapping the vegan stuff.

Esme accepted a plate of food, and my help to get inclined against a few cushions. 'Is there anything else a prickle can mean? Because I don't think Mummy was calling Nate a hedgehog or a plant. She said *he can be such a prickle*, and — oh no, you're choking!'

'A bit of sausage roll went down the wrong way,' I managed, between splutters. 'Listen, Esme, you know it's not polite to listen in on Mummy and Daddy's conversations when they think you're asleep.'

'Such a lot of things aren't polite,' she said glumly, picking buttercups.

'True,' I said, weaving the flowers into a circlet. Especially Gemma calling Nate a prick. 'Do you want to wear this crown?'

Before I found out if my diversionary tactic away from all things Nate had worked, something huge and red hurtled towards us, barking.

Esme screamed, and scrabbled backwards in alarm.

I leaped to my feet. 'Sit! Sit, Bear. Sit, you naughty girl!' The dog didn't obey my command, but it did slow her enough for me to grab her thick leather collar. 'Sit!' I roared.

She gave a huff of annoyance and then sat, right in the middle of the picnic rug.

Esme, who was cowering behind me, burst into tears just as Tristan came into view around the bend in the path.

He was clearly engaged in outdoor estate matters — instead of the ubiquitous suit he was wearing jeans, and a linen shirt with sleeves rolled to the elbow.

'Sorry!' he called, his jog accelerating, so that a few seconds later he was beside me, taking a firm grip of the collar as I eased my hands free. I swung around and gathered Esme up into my arms.

'I'm so sorry she scared you,' Tristan said. 'But do you want to know a secret? Even though she's really big, she loves children.'

Esme's lower lip wobbled. 'To eat?'

'No!' he spluttered. 'Never! She only eats kibble and dog treats.'

'Bears shouldn't steal poor doggies' treats!'

Tristan's mouth twitched, and I had to place my finger in the dip above my top lip, to keep from laughing. 'She's a dog *named* Bear, Esme,' I managed eventually. 'Not an actual bear.'

Tristan had gathered himself together, too. 'She loves playing with children, and getting cuddles. She's a complete softie — just a big one. Look — Bear, give me your paw. Paw!'

'Watch, Esme,' I said. 'The dog's shaking hands — it looks really cute.'

She eventually peeped through her thick lashes, and smiled uncertainly at Tristan, solemnly shaking hands with the huge Irish wolfhound. I saw his gaze drift to the empty child-size wheelchair beside the blanket, then snap to mine. Now I knew it was there, I could see the blue in his eyes again.

'Keep looking,' he said. 'She's got another clever trick. Bear, lay down. Lay down and roll over.'

The huge beast lay down, covering the whole width of the picnic blanket from front paws to back paws. We anticipated the consequence instantly, and I hopped off the rug with Esme in tow, as Tristan said, 'No! Bear — stop!'

His words were in vain. Heeding her master's first command, Bear rolled onto her back, ruching up one side of the rug so that our plates went flying, and obliterating the food on the other half as she landed on top of it.

* * *

'Poor doggy, you didn't do it on purpose, did you,' Esme crooned. She was safely ensconced in her chair, and with Bear lying beside her she'd found she was at the perfect height to stroke between her ears. 'But no more barking, we have to use our indoor voices.'

'I'm so sorry she intruded on your picnic like that,' Tristan said, stooping to lift up a flask. 'If I'd had any idea that anyone was picnicking in the private woodland, I'd have kept her on the lead — she's a sucker for sausage-meat.'

'No real harm's done,' I said, scooping squashed sandwiches back into their brown bag.

'Aside from a child getting the fright of her life that a bear was attacking her. By the way, these brownies are smashed to oblivion, but this box of cauliflower fritters looks unscathed, if you're still hungry.'

'Of course the—' I cut off the groan that the brownies had been decimated and the cauliflower had survived, recalling that he thought I was a vegan. 'Let me introduce the two of you properly. Esme — this is Mr Nash, who's the boss here at Sylverley. Tristan, this is my goddaughter, Esme Burrows.'

Both of them rolled their eyes. 'Not Mr Nash — *Tristan*, please,' Tristan said.

'And I'm not a goddaughter,' Esme huffed. 'I'm a *fairy* goddaughter because she's my fairy godmother, you see.'

Tristan assured her that he quite saw what she meant, then offered her the cauliflower fritters.

'She's quite something,' he murmured.

'She's a little tyrant, and I adore her.'

I braced myself for what would come next — a politely expressed but intrusive question like what's wrong with her, or why the wheelchair. But when he spoke it was to exclaim on a box of fairy cakes that had survived.

I offered them to Esme, then scarfed two down while Tristan wandered over to a bin with all the detritus we'd collected. Esme offered him one as he returned, and it surprised me when he accepted.

'Why not, it's a beautiful day for a picnic,' he said, lowering himself onto the cushion beside me.

'Sylverley's always beautiful,' I said. He snorted slightly, and I smiled, recalling his complaints about the place the last time I admired it, while I was measuring him for his costume. 'Well, for those of us who don't have to worry about all the budget constraints.'

'Or worse — deal with the dodgy drains,' he said, stretching, then settling himself more comfortably.

'Do you even like Sylverley?' An instant after blurting the question, I wished I could take it back. He worked almost every hour of every day — of course he liked it.

'No one's ever asked me that before,' he said slowly.

'Sorry—'

'It's fine.'

I couldn't resist. 'The question, or Sylverley?'

He snorted again at that. 'The question. Sylverley is . . .' His voice trailed off, before strengthening. 'I can recognise Sylverley's beauty, of course.'

Before I could point out that his statement didn't actually answer my question, Esme spoke up. 'Fairy Godmother, have you got one yet?'

'I've had enough to eat, thanks.'

'Not cakes, silly. I mean a boy to marry, for your wedding.'

'Oh. I'm still working on that, I'm afraid.'

'I told Fairy Godmother she had to find one, so I can still be her bridesmaid,' Esme told Tristan.

'Did you?' he said, smiling. 'Of course you did.'

My phone rang and I sliced my eyes from his profile to wrestle it from the deep pocket in my dress. 'This'll be Mummy,' I said to Esme. 'Gemma, we're just finishing up—'

'Err . . . is that Róisín?'

I checked the screen. An unknown mobile number. 'Who is this please?'

'Jason.' There was a beat of silence. 'You gave me your number on Sunday night?' His accent, even more than the verbal prompt, was the trigger for everything to fall into place.

'The American.'

'Present and correct,' he replied, laughing. 'Róisín, I can't get you out of my head — when can I take you out?'

SEPTEMBER: NINE MONTHS TO GO

CHAPTER 13: LEAVING ME HANGING

In the first week of our acquaintance, Jason and I exchanged dozens of messages. He worked as a management consultant, commuting into Bristol from his home in Bath. He thought my cottage sounded quaint, my business charming, my accent delightful, and by mid-week, he'd overcome my caution and weaselled out of me that my sparse memories of the latter part of Sunday evening didn't include a clear sense of what he looked like. A grinning, white-toothed selfie flashed back within seconds, and then twenty minutes later, a message.

—*Kinda leaving me hanging here ;) D'you like what you see?*

'Do I like what I see?' I asked myself, scrutinising the image. He was leaning back in one of those steel and leather executive chairs, his feet propped up in front of him, maybe on a desk. His white shirt only emphasised his dark hair and tan, and his features were large but well balanced above a lantern jaw.

—*Of course I like the way you look x*

It was easy to type, and to repeat the next day when he phoned during his lunch break, since he was objectively attractive. But his appearance made me uneasy because it matched the rest of what he was projecting, that he wasn't just American; he was upbeat good-humour, perfect smile and suntan, all-American. He even sent me a video of the best fourth of July fireworks he'd ever seen, set to a soundtrack of the Star-Spangled Banner, apparently completely unironically.

I had nothing against Americans, but couldn't quite get past the fact that they habitually married another American in a black-tie reception at a swanky hotel near one or both sets of American parents. It seemed unlikely that one of their menfolk would want to marry a pissed woman he met in a bar in a foreign country. Let alone at a wedding ceremony in that foreign country within nine months of the drunken encounter.

Nine months. I was a quarter of the way to my wedding date, and no closer to finding the one than when I started.

I seized my phone and enquired which evening he was free to meet up next week. Ruling out anyone who seemed as keen on me as Jason did would be stupid, with the deadline so rapidly approaching. And after all, he could be an orphan, with no family to pressure him into ditching the desperate foreign girl. Or the secret heir of an elderly English godfather, whose inheritance he could only claim once he had discovered and wed the love of his life—

I was snapped out of it by the ping of his reply.

—*Work's insane next week — the week after?*

It was the first hint of another potential downside of an American — their propensity to be workaholics. And as another week slipped by, the evidence mounted. Jason's selfies were taken against the backdrop of his office, and phone calls came during his lunch break, or on his commute home, at past nine. Once he called just after six in the morning, telling me that he'd dreamed about me, and now, working out in the gym, couldn't get the thought of me out of his head. 'I felt the need to tell you how desperate I am to see you again. I've cleared my calendar for Friday afternoon . . .'

'You never ever, need to tell me anything before 9 a.m.,' I croaked, ending the call and dropping instantly back into sleep. When I woke up properly I discovered an apologetic text. Not only was he sorry for calling at the crack of dawn, but also the tentative date he'd proposed wouldn't work out after all. A networking conference had popped up, and it would help achieve his aim to be made his firm's youngest partner . . .

I'd had enough, and slammed my phone back onto the bed, fully intending to block him once I was alert enough to work out how. But by the time I'd made a strong cup of tea and had a lukewarm bath, I'd received another of his grinning selfies and a suggestion of meeting a week on Saturday.

—*Can't. I've got to help my pregnant friend out by taking a tour group around Bath.*

—*Lucky tour group. Okay, this Saturday then, at 6?*

—*Fine. But don't cancel, or else.*

His reply paired scared and crying-with-laughter emojis, which didn't give me much confidence. It was his final chance, and he barely seemed to realise.

I'd had so little faith in the date going ahead that even a few hours before we were due to meet, as I pieced together the lilac raw silk which was to become Perky's gown, I felt a steely determination rather than nerves. Jason would cancel, and I'd block him from my phone and my mind, then think about how to meet more men. But when the anticipated message arrived, it was only directions of where to meet him — at a car park on the northern slopes of Bath.

—*Where are we going, though?*

—*It's a surprise! A nice one!*

I gritted my teeth. Americans and their bloody enthusiasm.

—*That doesn't help with what I should wear . . .*

His reply was another selfie, taken down the length of his body. He was wearing chunky ankle boots, dark jeans, and a flannel shirt beneath a leather jacket. The late-thirties American male's version of warm, comfortable and casual.

My version of warm, comfortable and casual was vintage corduroy trousers in deep red, with a shirt and a loose-knit mohair jumper. I parked further away than where Jason had recommended, to avoid explaining why I was driving a tour group minibus, then jogged to our meeting point and scanned around. Unable to find him, I checked my phone, poised for disappointment.

As I confirmed there was no message, I heard him call, and swivelled. Before I knew it he'd pulled me in for a tight hug. 'You're a sight for sore eyes,' he said in my ear. And then, as he released his hold on me, 'I love your sweater — it's so soft.'

'Thanks,' I murmured, as I took an unsteady step back. Nerves had descended in one fell swoop.

If Jason also suffered from nerves, he hid it well as he jerked his chin up the hill and asked how my day had been.

I stammered something, and turned the conversation to him, so I could steal glances as he talked. Three or four inches taller than me with a broad build and easy confidence. Although we'd met before, I'd been in no fit state to assemble all those pieces of him, and now that I was suddenly putting them together, the combination was more attractive than I'd anticipated.

He paused his story about booking the afternoon off work, so he'd be certain to be available for our date. 'I'm talking too much,' he said.

'Not at all. I was just . . . uh . . .' I glanced around. Heading up the slope, away from the city centre, was the opposite of what I'd expected. 'I was looking for clues for where we're going.'

'Ah,' he said, halting our march up hill. 'No visual clues yet, but I think maybe some others, very faintly.'

I listened, hard, in the lull after a car vroomed past, and caught the distant strain of amplified music. Not a melody, just the pulse of bass. I inhaled deeply as I considered where it could be coming from, and captured a slight scent on the breeze. It was sugary sweet, but mixed with something less pleasant . . . acrid even. 'I smell a petrol station, and sugar. And I can hear music. But up there is only . . .'

'Only the park,' Jason confirmed, recognising that I'd got it.

As we pumped our legs up the final slope, the thump of the music got louder, the intermingled scent of candy floss and diesel fumes strengthened, and brightly-lit rides loomed over the canopy of the trees.

'This was inspired,' I said, laughing as we reached the clearing where the travelling fairground set up several times a year. 'Can we go on the dodgems first?'

Cramming into one together was a tight squeeze, and with the length of Jason's thigh pressed against mine I felt myself flush, then was suddenly glad that the evening air was so cool. He offered me the steering wheel but I demurred, smiling, and he grinned back, then grasped it and pressed down hard on the pedal. He spun us headlong into another dodgem and I shrieked in his ear, which only made him laugh harder.

Jason clambered out first when we slid to a halt, and held out a hand to help me. When I was on my feet he tightened his hold on my hand, rather than releasing me.

I raised an eyebrow at him. 'That was a bit of a smooth move.'

'Yeah? Well, I've got a few more of those up my sleeve,' he said, dipping his head. Our lips were about to meet, when the man running the dodgems screeched. 'Pick a car, any car, quick as you can. Hey, lovebirds — move on or give me another token!'

'Not so smooth that time,' Jason grumbled, sweeping me off the circuit. I hoped being so awkwardly interrupted wouldn't scare him off trying again soon. Maybe I should take the initiative, in case it had, I mused, as he moved his hands to my waist to assist me down from the platform of the ride. 'You're freezing — you should have told me!'

Before I could reply, he'd peeled off his leather jacket, and held it open for me. 'Oh, I really can't—'

'Course you can . . .' His face clouded with concern. 'Or you mean ethically you can't wear leather — are you vegan?'

'Absolutely not!' I shoved my arm in, my body temperature increasing immediately from Jason's lingering body warmth.

He slipped both hands under it, around my waist. 'Now where were we . . .'

'Róisín!' I heard someone yell. 'Oy, Róisín!'

I recognised the girl as a former employee of Nate's, in the café. 'I haven't seen you in ages,' she said, eyeing Jason. 'How's Nate doing?'

I'd heard several variations on that question since our break-up. Mostly it was asked in all innocence, by an old acquaintance who genuinely hadn't heard what had happened. This was different — she'd spoken slyly, and I knew her motivation was making things awkward for me.

'I wouldn't know, since we broke up more than three months ago.'

I stalked away, aware that Jason was in tune enough to have kept step with me. I didn't have to wait long to find out what he thought.

'That was masterful,' he said, catching up my hand again. 'What d'you fancy a ride on next?'

I shot a glance at him, but there was no hint of him intending that as an innuendo. 'Something mellow,' I said shortly. 'So my blood pressure can recover.'

'I've got just the thing.' He led me past a hook-a-duck stall and helter-skelter, populated by whizzing, squealing children, deeper into the crowd, towards the busiest central section, where a large Ferris wheel was picked out by gaudily coloured bulbs.

'Just think,' he said, when we were ensconced in a swinging seat, and starting our first ascent. 'If things had gone differently at the speed dating, you'd be sitting here wrapped up in your cousin's coat right now.' I'd forgotten telling him about the horror of matching with Oisín, in the bar, and I buried my face in my hands. 'And I'd be standing alone beside the cotton candy concession, having just noticed your flaming hair and red lips, as you made eyes at another dude.'

'I'd be retching if I was snuggled up like this with my second cousin, not making eyes at him.' But with a few weeks of distance, my revulsion had lowered enough for me to be able to laugh, somewhat reluctantly.

'Ah, but poor Jason wouldn't know that. He'd just be pining after you, until he decided there was nothing for it but to wait until your seat lowered close to the ground, then take a running jump, and leap up here and squash between you and your beau . . . well, cousin.'

I laughed harder. 'I've seen *The Notebook*, you know. You're ripping off the way Ryan Gosling risks his life to get Rachel McAdams to agree to a date, but we're already on a date.'

A self-satisfied smirk spread over his face. 'Why, yes we are. And I hope I don't scare you off by admitting that I never want it to end.'

'That doesn't scare me at all,' I murmured, fist pumping internally. This was the perfect start to the kind of relationship that would result in an engagement by say, Christmas and then marriage six months later. We could even put a funny and romantic spin on the early part of our relationship, for the grandchildren. The awkward speed dates became a funny anecdote that caused our meet-cute; Jason's crazy work schedule was the hurdle we leaped to get together despite the odds, and the interruptions of our attempts at a kiss was the first battle we'd fight, side by side, to stay together.

We soared upwards again, stopping abruptly to discharge two sets of passengers and let more take their places. The sky had darkened since our arrival, giving the illusion that the fairground lights had brightened. It wasn't a bad outlook for a first kiss, and I turned to Jason. But he was shifting slightly in the seat, making it rock more than I was comfortable with at this height. 'What's up?'

'My phone's vibrating. Must be my boss . . .' I must have looked forbidding, because his explanation turned to apology. 'He has poor boundaries.'

'So do you, if you answer it when you purposely took the afternoon off.'

His smile was rueful. 'You're right — I'll ignore it. You're good for me, Róisín.' His tone was soft, his eyes open and disarming. 'Are you . . . would you . . . be interested in inviting me back to your place? I'd never usually suggest that on a first date — but then again I've never felt this magnitude of emotions on a first date before. It doesn't have to be about . . .' he bit his bottom lip, then released it. 'There would be no expectations, overnight. Whatever you're comfortable with. But I want a proper introduction to your life — to see your quaint little cottage, and . . .' His voice trailed off as my lack of response became evident. 'I'm really sorry if that was too forward—'

'Jason. It's fine.' I drew in a long, slow breath. It *was* too forward — we hadn't even, quite, kissed. But there was mutual attraction, and he was falling for me, and I needed to find the one . . . 'I'm not offended. Just . . . the evening's only just begun. Let me think about it for a while?'

'Of course — take as long as you need.' He crossed his eyes slightly. 'Even the thought of getting you alone is making me incoherent.' I smiled, and he smiled back. 'Decided yet?' he added lightly, which made me laugh so hard that our swing rocked again as it made its final, slow descent to where the bar across our laps would unlock, and the adult and child at the front of the queue could swap into our seat.

'I could murder some chips,' I said. Jason stiffened and I glanced at him as I corrected, 'French fries, I guess you say, only I don't want fries, I want fat, chunky chips from the burger van by the drop slide.'

He didn't even look at me. Just continued to stare ahead, his jaw locked as though he was frozen. I followed his gaze to the people awaiting their turn on the ride. A woman, looking bored, and a little girl in a bright pink gilet, jumping up and down with excitement. They had similar blonde curls, so were probably mother and daughter — from a further distance I could easily have mistaken them for Gemma and Esme. As I noted the differences (the woman was pretty, but not Gemma-pretty; the girl was younger than Esme, who couldn't bounce in wellies like that), I saw the woman's gaze fall on us. Her mouth dropped open, and then she shook her head from side to side.

'Jace,' she said, unsteadily. Her voice rose. 'Jason!'

He slithered his arm away from my back and wrestled with the bar across our laps.

'It's not like it looks,' he said. 'Honey, I can explain.'

The little girl's eyes were pinging between the two of them, then landed on me. 'Mom? Who's that with Daddy?' she said uncertainly.

'My work trip got cancelled so I returned to the fair, but by then you two had left — or I thought you had — so I rode this Ferris wheel alone, only this girl was nervous,' Jason babbled as he finally won his release from the swing and shot to his feet like I was a grenade, primed to explode. 'I sat with her to coach her through her fear of heights . . .' On and on he went, as he ushered his family away, the little girl confused, the woman dazed.

They were almost out of sight when I remembered that I was still wearing Jason's leather jacket. I stood and pulled it off, then stalked to the nearest bin and shoved it deep inside, with the rest of the rubbish.

CHAPTER 14: LIGHT MY FIRE

Abi often likened guiding a large group of tourists to herding cats, but in my opinion it was much worse. At least if a cat walked in the opposite direction from where I was leading it, right into the path of a bicycle, it wouldn't berate me for getting it run over. And on top of the normal exertions of a full day of tour guiding, I was out of practice at talking at the top of my lungs, in the rain, while wearing a heavy costume based on a Regency riding habit. My myrtle-green jacket was fitted to my torso, and matched the voluminous skirt of my dress, which had a simple bodice top, hidden under a ruffled muslin blouse. I'd made the outfit some years earlier with rainy-day tours in mind, hemming the gown and petticoats a few inches short, so I didn't need to hitch them up constantly to dodge puddles, but that still left me shielding myself from raindrops and pigeon poo with a parasol.

The group had booked the full VIP tour of Bath with a costumed historian before Abi had thought to remove that option from her website. Since her expanding belly no longer fitted into the outfit I'd made her, she had asked me to conduct the tour. It only lost me one potential sewing day, I'd figured, when I put it into my diary. But then I'd lost the best part of another week, stewing rather than sewing. Every time I closed my eyes I saw the devastation on Jason's wife's face, and after fitful nights I spent the daylight hours mulling over my gullibility, and how close I'd got to becoming the other woman.

I fixed a smile on my face to hand out my business card to those of the group who'd admired my outfit, then slumped back into the minibus seat. I wanted nothing more than to return to the cottage and see if physical exhaustion led to much needed deep sleep. But Joe had finally arranged for me to collect my bedside tables from Nate, and then I had to drop by Abi's to debrief her on the tour and get changed into my day clothes from that morning. The biggest downside of living alone, now I'd got used to it, was not having anyone to help me with getting in or out of my costumes.

My jaw almost cracked open with a yawn, and that decided it: I messaged Joe asking him to rearrange with Nate for a later date, then Abi that it all went fine and I'd come for my clothes and a proper chat soon. Once back at Sylverley, I could ask Mrs Holt to unlace my back-laced bodice, which was impossible alone.

* * *

The whole estate closed early on Sundays, so Sylverley's grounds were deserted, and as I bumped over the drive I was free to stare up at the elevated house, tinted mauve in the muted half-light of dusk.

As I turned down the track to the cottages, I didn't see the usual light from their windows filtering through the woodland, and drawing closer, I heard someone call out. I put my foot down, trundling over the bumpy terrain until I reached Tristan, kneeling beside his giant of a dog in a small circle of light from a torch.

'What's up?' I called, opening the minibus' door almost before I'd pulled to a complete stop.

'Bear's ill — I'm worried her stomach's twisted. It can be fatal for this breed.'

'And the darkness?'

'Power cut — must be something up with the generator. But the Holts are in Bath, and I haven't had a chance to investigate. Not with Bear like this.'

I was already checking my phone, which had no connection. Reliant as we were on Wi-Fi calling, it was no wonder that without electricity we were cut off entirely. 'What can I do?'

'Stay with her, while I run up to the house for my vehicle.' Bear whined, and he bent closer to her, then swivelled back towards me, his voice thick with urgency. 'No, if I'm right, every minute counts. Would you lend me your minibus?'

I hated having to hesitate. But it didn't belong to me, and he wasn't on the insurance. Thankfully there was an obvious solution.

'I'll drive you there.'

* * *

The vet confirmed Tristan's suspicions, and rushed Bear into surgery. There was nowhere for us to wait, and we were urged to return home, the vet promising to phone the instant there was news. Tristan was silent for most of the journey, speaking up only as I pulled into the side gate of the estate.

'Róisín, I really can't thank you enough.'

'It was nothing—'

'You probably saved Bear's life, and I've not managed even polite conversation in return.'

I shot a quick glance at him; he still looked careworn but was less pale now that Bear was in the right hands. 'You've been in shock. Make sure you stay hydrated and warm.' Recalling the power cut, I added doubtfully, 'Well, as warm as you can.'

'My log fire was burning all afternoon,' he said, as I slowed to a halt on the far side of the track, equidistant between our front doors. 'I'd just banked it when Bear had the seizure, so my place will still retain heat.' He glanced between our cottages, book-ending the row. All five were dark and uninviting, so the Holts couldn't be back yet. 'You were out tour-guiding all day?' At my nod, he pulled his torch from his coat pocket. 'I'll help set you a fire, but it'll take a while to overtake the chill. In the meantime, you're welcome to come to mine.'

I declined, then regretted it when I unlocked my cottage, and realised it was even colder inside than out. Automatically, I flipped the light switch. It remained pitch black, beyond the small pool of light that Tristan was directing from the torch.

I blew on my hands. 'Is your offer still open?'

'It definitely is,' he said, training the torch beam on the candles on my mantlepiece. I hurried to light them. When I straightened, he was holding out his torch and his key.

'Let yourself in, while I light your fire — there's no point both of us freezing in here.'

'I can do it myself.'

'I know you can,' he said simply. 'But it's my fault you've arrived home so late. So indulge me, please?'

I considered for a moment, then accepted the torch and key and ventured outside again.

In line with Tristan's prediction, a glow emanated from his fireplace. I stoked the embers to a flame with the nearby poker, added a dry log, then sank onto his couch, which was similarly lumpy to the one in my cottage.

He entered a few minutes later, with two of my candlesticks in one hand, his other palm curled protectively around the single flame from the conjoined wicks. 'The site plan involves modernising the cottages so we can rent them out commercially as holiday lets,' he explained, retrieving a box of candles from a drawer below his coffee table and lighting them from mine. 'But until power companies get services to this side of the estate, there's no point. No paying guest would put up with the lack of central heating, let alone the risk of blackouts, from relying on a generator.'

As the illumination increased, there was finally enough light in which to examine his lounge. It was a similar size to mine, but very much emptier. What furniture there was had the same faded and scuffed grandeur as mine, but there were no added touches of comfort, with bare windows and a minimum of possessions — half a dozen books on a shelf and just one picture on the wall. There was more evidence of Bear's habitation of the place than her master's, with a fluffy dog bed the size of a single mattress and several massive bowls.

I slipped off my shoes and tucked my legs under the full sweep of my skirt. 'What made you decide to get a wolf-hound — have you always liked giant breeds?'

He separated my candles and set one of them on the mantelpiece. 'She was here at Sylverley before I was. Edward Sylvers got her as a puppy — for Mrs Sylvers, I believe, but she'd lost interest by that stage. Hadn't realised how big she'd get, apparently.'

'Irresponsible cow.'

From his quick glance at me, I gathered that I hadn't muttered that quite as quietly as I thought, so I rushed on, since he always seemed at great pains not to insult her, however much she deserved it. 'So you decided to adopt Bear?'

'I couldn't let the beautiful beast go off to a shelter,' he said, as if it was as simple as that.

'How long ago was that?'

'Getting on for two years ago, when I moved in to oversee the renovation from on-site.' He disappeared through the doorway that must lead to his kitchen, and I took the opportunity to direct the beam of the torch to the lone picture on the wall. The frame was ornately carved wood, but it hung slightly askew. Within it was a pen and ink drawing of Sylverley, its simplicity emphasising the stark symmetry of the building.

Returning with two glasses and a bottle without a label, Tristan followed my gaze.

'I found that here when I moved in,' he said quickly, like he was defending himself against an accusation of theft.

'Lucky you.'

He deposited the glasses on the coffee table, glanced around as if for another seat, and then sunk onto the opposite end of the sofa. I cast a sidelong glance at him, recalling that he'd never answered my question, during the picnic with Esme, about whether he even liked Sylverley. 'I can never decide if my favourite thing about Sylverley is the classical symmetry, the warmth of the Bath limestone, or the way it's set perfectly within the landscape . . .'

He poured an inch of amber liquid into each glass. 'Or the leaking roof on each wing, the ancient lead plumbing, the viperish wife of the late owner . . .'

I accepted a glass with a sigh. 'Fair enough. I'm not exposed to all that side of things.'

He slugged half of his drink back then refilled it and set it on the coffee table. I tilted my glass up cautiously, letting the liquid just wet my lips. It was smooth, then strong, and I quirked an eyebrow at him.

'Whiskey? Bit of a liberal interpretation of staying hydrated.'

'Ah,' he said, looking pleased with himself. 'But you also ordered me to stay warm, and there's no electricity to heat the kettle.'

I took a proper sip, feeling the burn as I swallowed, then the pleasing unfurling of warmth in my stomach. 'Definitely more warming than tap water,' I conceded. 'Where were we?'

'Sylverley's my job,' Tristan said shortly. 'So of course I'll mostly experience it like a millstone around my neck. But more interestingly, it's your wedding venue. How's the search going?'

I pulled my drink up to conceal my expression. I couldn't confess that my love life was a disaster zone when he was already shaken about Bear. 'Watch this space,' I said, gripping the glass hard and seeking a change of topic. 'I'll scour the cupboards in my cottage, now I know you found a picture in here. I'd love to find any kind of link to someone who lived there in the past — I wonder a lot about the generations who inhabited it before me.'

'All I know is that they were built for the family's servants, to attend them in the old medieval structure that

Sylverley replaced, or to tend the land. And unfortunately records on Sylverley employees haven't been preserved in the way that details of the family and their guests were.'

'That happens at every stately home. It's such a shame, given that they're so much more revealing of the true differences between life now and then than those of grand families, like the Sylvers.' I caught the flare of his nostrils and an indentation of lines along the sides of his mouth; he was suppressing a yawn. My earlier tiredness had been melted away by the heady combination of whiskey, wood-smoke and late-night conversation with the man I'd wondered about for ages, but he was just bored. 'Sorry, I should get back—'

He laid his head on the back of the sofa, but twisted his head and shoulders towards me. 'Please, finish your point. I'm genuinely interested.'

'Okay, well . . .' I marshalled my train of thought. 'Estates like Sylverley are such a strong link to the history of a nation that it's easy for the majority of visitors to engage their imaginations, and picture themselves here in the past. But they're generally imagining themselves as the landed gentry, living here in opulence. When really it's more likely they're descendants of the much more numerous population — the multitude of serving staff, sharing attic bedrooms, or cottages like these, and spending their days working their fingers to the bone.'

Tristan had gone very quiet. 'You've thought about this a lot,' he said eventually, as he bent forward for the bottle. He tilted the neck of it toward me, and I stretched out my glass so he could top it up.

'During my degree, the more lectures I had on English kings and queens, the more interested I got in regular people of the past.'

'Leading to your business focussing on the clothing people wore in different eras . . . Surely the kind of thing you're wearing now would have only belonged to the elite, though?'

I smoothed my skirts, suddenly aware how ridiculous I must look. 'Sure, but they didn't stay in the hands of the rich.

Fashion filtered down. Ladies gave their discarded gowns to their maids, who sold them on to women without enough money for custom-made. They in turn sold or donated their old garments. It was like how hand-me-down clothes go to the next sibling, in a large family, but for the whole of society.'

He smiled at that. 'That sounds like bitter experience talking. You're from a large family?'

'Eldest of four. So the others got my hand-me-downs, until all of them got taller than me — getting younger siblings' hand-me-downs is its own particular ignominy, I can tell you. It's what made me save up for my first sewing machine, actually. What about you — brothers and sisters?'

'Only child.' When he didn't add anything else, I got the hint, and rose to my feet.

'I should get back.' I turned toward the door, then wavered. 'Any idea when the Holts are returning?'

'I'm wondering if they've gone away overnight, at this stage, so unfortunately the generator might not be back on until the morning.'

'It's not that. I need . . .' My voice trailed off. Sleeping in my bodiced gown would be less uncomfortable than explaining that I couldn't unfasten it to the only person around to help. 'Never mind. Do let me know the dawn update on Bear—'

'Please, Róisín, if you need anything, however big or small, it would be my pleasure.'

'Oh it's nothing big . . .' I grimaced helplessly, then lowered my eyes to my hem. 'I'm laced into this outfit. I was going to ask Mrs Holt to unfasten the back.'

'Ah. I see.' Even in candlelight, his swallow was palpable. 'Can I . . . offer assistance?'

I examined him for sincerity. 'You really wouldn't mind?'

He raised his shoulders. 'Not if you don't.'

'Thank you, then,' I murmured. Turning my back to him, I shrugged out of my jacket, then rapidly unbuttoned my ruffled-front shirt and, before I could chicken out, slithered it off. The sleeveless bodice of my gown exposed little more of my back than a sundress, but above the fullness of the gown's skirt, I felt half naked. I had to screw my eyes shut and take a deep breath before I could pull my hair over my shoulders, to give him full access to the lacing.

'Right,' he said after a moment. 'It's a bit more complicated than I expected.'

'You haven't encountered a boned bodice before, huh?' I tried to speak lightly, but I could feel his breath against my neck, and my voice came out sounding strained. 'If you find the long ribbon tucked into the top, then untie the bow, you can unlace downwards — like you would a tennis shoe.'

'Like a tennis shoe . . .' he echoed rather uncertainly, but then I felt a pull at the top of the bodice, right below the nape of my neck, and a fleeting touch from his warm fingers as he scooped the ribbon free. A shiver rippled up my spine in response.

'I've got the bow,' he said. There was a fainter pull. 'And that's untied. Uh . . . ready for me to start unlacing?'

'Yes, thank you,' I said, more steadily than I felt. 'You'll need to pull the bodice quite hard, to get enough slack to free the ribbon.'

I thought he might speak again, but instead I felt the pressure of his hands alight between my shoulder blades. The ribbon was threaded through twelve pairs of tiny holes and at each of them he needed to work his finger under the criss-crossing ribbon. There was a light tug, and then another.

'Harder still,' I murmured. 'It won't hurt at all — I'm used to it.'

His right hand alighted on my waist, steadying me as he tugged more firmly, then moved up so he could slide a finger under the ribbon. I knew when he'd pulled the length of the ribbon through the hole as the top of my gown loosened.

His hand returned to my waist and the bodice tightened again. This time I braced myself for his searing finger on my bare skin, and he paused. 'Okay?'

'Fine. Keep going.'

His hands retreated entirely as he pulled free the length of the ribbon, and my gown loosened again. I clutched it at the front, so it couldn't fall down.

Manipulating it to create slack became easier with every loosening, and Tristan changed tactics; instead of dropping a hand to my waist, his knuckles brushed against me, then he hooked a finger under the ribbon and finally came his tug to release it, before the cycle began again.

Knuckles, a little lower each time. His finger, skimming down my spine. The release of the ribbon and answering slackening of my gown. And underlining it all, the dancing candlelight, crackle of burning wood and Tristan's breath, descending down my back as he bent to concentrate on the fiddly task.

Amidst the intoxicating assault on my senses, I'd forgotten the importance of holding my gown up at the front, and as he reached my lower back my gown suddenly plunged. Grabbing it with one hand, I slammed my other arm across my breasts, then hauled the bodice back up, breathing hard.

'Sorry,' I said, eyeing the distance to the door. But rushing off in the dark was impossible, so with my arms crossed over my bodice, I rotated, and glanced up at Tristan. His face was flushed — from embarrassment, I thought. But in the instant before I spoke, I reassessed his expression, and the apology died on my lips.

'Róisín, I should have told you earlier,' he breathed. 'That your outfit is beautiful. *You* look beautiful.'

His flush had deepened, but it wasn't signalling embarrassment at all.

I barely dared to breath; movement and speech both seemed impossible.

'I was thinking it, Róisín.'

At that, we locked eyes.

All it took to signal back, was an upward tilt of my chin, and then his arms flew around me, his hands flattening on the bare skin of my upper back as he bent, down and in, and our lips met.

Tristan is kissing me, I thought, in the first, dazed, split-second. *Tristan Nash, who can be distant almost to the point of aloofness, is slowly and deliberately kissing me.*

A few seconds later it was replaced by an even more astonishing thought; I'm *kissing Tristan back* . . . The reality of how pleased I was about that made me arch into him, and his kiss deepened in response.

And then there was only incoherent sensation; the warmth of his hands, smoothing across my shoulder blades, the heat of his lips, moving with startling intensity, and my ragged breath, and his.

Our lips stilled at the same moment, and he pulled back. I closed my eyes, wishing more than I'd ever wished for anything that he wouldn't step away, stammering excuses. But instead, I felt his lips on each of my cheeks, then my forehead.

I opened my eyes. 'Hi,' I murmured, nuzzling into his neck. The softness of his skin there contrasted with the faint stubble I'd felt on his cheeks.

'Hi,' he breathed back, bending lower again, his lips returning to mine.

Beep. Beep-beep.

The sound sliced the air, and our lips stilled. Then the intruding blare of *beep, double-beep* came again, and as if we'd been hit by a flood of icy water, we sprang apart.

'Is that . . .' Tristan rubbed across his eyes, as if waking himself up. 'Is that a car horn?'

'I think so,' I said thickly, my pulse pounding in my ears. 'Or . . . no. Not a car.'

The blare on the horn, followed immediately by a double blare, and then repeating the sequence again, was Nate's hallmark.

'I think . . . I think that's my ex's van.'

CHAPTER 15: SINCE YOU'VE BEEN GONE

Tristan's level eyebrows drew together. 'Your ex? Were you expecting him?'

'Not at all.' So close to him, I was dazed and I shifted back slightly. 'I was meant to drop by to collect something. I guess it's about that . . .'

'Róisín!' Nate yelled, from the track outside, and Tristan and I both flinched.

'I'd better go out there,' I breathed. 'I'll be back shortly, okay?'

Tristan's eyes bored into mine, then he caught up my discarded shirt and jacket, and wrapped each in turn around my shoulders. With the shirt tucked into the bodice of my gown, it was a little more secure, and I only needed to hold it up with one arm.

As Tristan passed me his torch he took my hand in his own and flipped it gently. He dropped a fleeting kiss on the inside of my wrist. 'I'll be waiting.'

* * *

Squinting against the brightness of the van's headlamps, I stalked to confront Nate. He was sitting on the driver's seat with his door open and his feet planted on the track, his head bent over his phone.

'What the hell are you doing here?'

He glanced up. 'Rosh! I was starting to panic.'

It was hard to think. 'That doesn't in any way answer my question. We agreed on no contact, so what are you doing here?'

'I'm doing you a favour. Joe said you needed these bits of furniture urgently, so I thought I'd deliver them.'

The remaining disorientation from the kiss was being rapidly displaced by exasperation. 'If it was really urgent why would I have left them with you for nearly four months?'

'Well, I also wanted to check you're okay, and to see where you're living now,' he said, staring over at Tristan's cottage.

'That's the cottage of another staff member, who I was just visiting. Mine's at the opposite end of the row. But it's late, and I'm not expecting you.'

'Keep your hair on, Rosh.' He lowered his voice to a mumble. 'I waited ages for you, and then I didn't see Joe's text about you coming next week instead until I was halfway here. I was hardly going to turn home then.'

That was the truth of it. Inquisitiveness about my life, paired with sheer disorganisation. He'd probably let his phone run out of battery again, so there was no chance of him seeing Joe's message until he'd plugged it into the charger in his van.

I sighed, trying to expel some fury along with the spent air. 'Whatever, Nate. I was in the middle of . . . something, so if you were interested in seeing anything but the outside of my new place, you're out of luck.' He opened his mouth, and I cut him off crisply. 'Seriously, just open the back so I can get my stuff out, then go home.'

As I spoke there was a gust of wind, which stirred the jacket around my shoulders. I tightened my hold on my gown, recalling how precariously I was dressed; I wouldn't be able to carry anything without losing my grip on my clothing. 'Actually, I have to get changed first.' I'd already turned toward my cottage, and added, over my shoulder, 'Put the bedside tables at the side of the path. I'll be back out for them shortly.'

I ignored his grumble about how only Rosh insists on a change of outfit for every single thing she does, as I bobbed the light of the torch over the path to my front door. But by the time I'd reached it, his mutters had turned to heavy breathing, and I glanced back. He was following me, staggering under the weight of carrying both bedside tables at once.

All I could think was what Tristan must be thinking, if he was watching. And for sure, if *he'd* left, right after that searing kiss, in response to another woman's arrival, *I'd* be watching.

'Come on, Rosh — switch the light on,' Nate panted, as I hovered indecisively on the front step.

'I can't. There's been a power cut.' I trained the torch on my door, wrestled open the handle and then shone the light on the ground, to help guide Nate in.

'You're here in the dark, and not bothering to lock up?'

'No one ever comes here.' Before he could counter this with the fact that he had, I continued quickly. 'And anyway, I usually lock up. As I said, I'd popped into one of the other cottages.'

'Hmph.' He didn't look convinced, but he was in no position to argue. 'Where d'you want these anyway?'

'Just leave them at the bottom of the stairs—'

'Don't be a doughnut, Rosh,' he said, rolling his eyes. 'You'll never get these up that narrow space on your own.'

That was the whole point, you kiss-blocking eejit, I wailed internally, as he tramped up the stairs, panting under the weight of what I'd intended as an excuse to invite Tristan back to mine.

'Where now?' Nate hollered. 'It's blacker than coal up here.'

I snapped out of it and scampered upstairs. 'To your left,' I said, directing the light from the torch into my small bedroom. I remained on the landing as he thudded them into position, either side of the bed. He glanced around

162

before retreating out. On the small landing we were too close together for my liking, and I stepped back, which caused the door to my sewing room to swing open.

'Let me see,' Nate said, peering over my shoulder. Gritting my teeth, I turned and flashed the light into my sewing room. Now he'd got upstairs he would insist on staying for the grand tour, and it was quicker and easier to get it over and done with than argue about it.

'You've taken the little room for yourself, and given the big one to your sewing machines,' he said, smiling.

'*Typical Rosh*,' I put in, before he could. '*Always so predictable.*'

'Well, yeah,' he said, chuckling a little. 'What are you working on anyway?'

'The costumes that got me free rent.' I bobbed the light along the row of empty dressmaking mannequins, the one I'd adjusted to Perky's proportions, and had fitted her lilac silk dress to, which was complete, aside from a small amount of hand sewing. Beside it was Amelia's mannequin, in the yellow dress I was part way through. Stretching behind them both was the table I'd pushed into the corner, propped along the back of which were all the large mood boards I'd made, with ideas for my wedding. Scraps of fabrics showing potential colour palettes intermingled with silk flowers, my sketches of outfit designs, and my photos of various locations within the estate.

Barely an instant after the light bathed it all, Nate exhaled heavily, and I jerked the torch away. He was silent as I led him back downstairs, not speaking until I pivoted for the front door.

'No, Rosh.' He caught up my arm. 'I don't want to leave yet. I need to . . . we need to talk. Please?'

I couldn't see the expression in his face, but the tone of his voice went beyond a plea, verging on desperation. Confused, I inclined my head towards my couch.

'Okay?'

'Jeez, this is uncomfortable,' Nate muttered. I whirled, preparing to tell him that this conversation was only happening at his request, but saw, before I spoke, his wriggling attempt to find a non-lumpy spot on the couch. His remark was aimed at my furniture, rather than the stilted atmosphere between us. I smiled wryly, which turned unbidden into a yawn.

'I've got to get out of this outfit,' I said, yawning again. 'I'll be back in a minute.'

When I returned, in a pair of silk pyjamas that fulfilled the triple brief of cosy enough for a power cut, decent enough to wear in front of Nate, and attractive enough for when I eventually got to resume my . . . whatever was happening with Tristan, Nate had moved into an upright chair, which he'd lifted closer to the fire.

'So what is it?'

He glanced around the dimly lit space. 'How's your family doing?'

'Fine,' I said stiffly. 'Excited about Aoife's wedding.' That gave me a notion for what this could be about. 'Oh God — has something happened with yours? Your dad's lungs—'

'He's fine, and so's Mum,' he said quickly.

I breathed out, long and slow. 'Good.'

Nate drummed on his knees.

'Nate?'

'Sorry,' he said. 'Ugh. I don't know how to start.'

'Then it's not that important, is it?' I said, aware my voice didn't sound as exasperated as I felt. Even my vocal chords were weary. 'Listen, I've had a very long day and it's not over yet — I've still got something important to . . . handle. So explain whatever the issue is quickly, or leave.'

He bent forward and ran both hands through his hair from forehead to the nape of his neck, then repeated the motion. 'The mood boards,' he said at last.

'What about them.' I spoke tersely, with no inflection: making a statement, not asking a question, to be clear that this was none of Nate's bloody business.

'I don't know,' he said, repeating the gesture with his hands and his curls. He was going to pull it out at this rate.

'I guess I . . . *shit*. I guess for the first time since you've been gone, it just became real.'

'*It?*' Despite myself, I felt myself pulled into the conversation — more due to his obsessive motion than his words. 'My wedding, you mean? It's been real since my name was drawn and I had a phone call to inform me.'

A call from Tristan, I thought, who had congratulated me on my *upcoming nuptials*. So he was more aware than anyone that I was committed to getting married here at Sylverley. And he'd kissed me anyway.

I didn't dare join the dots between those two things. Not until I'd talked to him. But it was impossible not to smile.

Nate shook his head vehemently. 'It was theoretical, back then. Now — this is it. You're planning it.' I thought he had finished, but more sound burst from him. 'You're getting married, Rosh. You'll be a wife. *Another bloke's* wife.'

Maybe, I thought, if his facial expression wasn't obscured by shadow, and my weariness wasn't so extreme, I could think of something to say. Nate had had his chance to marry me — a decade's worth of chances, in fact. He'd made it very clear, when I won the prize, that he didn't want to: 'I love you, *but* . . .' was branded into my eardrums to prove it.

'Earth to Rosh,' Nate said suddenly, and I returned my attention to him.

'What?'

'You've stared into the fire for, like, five minutes, without even commenting on what I said.' Then he sighed. 'I know about the American.'

I blinked. 'I literally have no idea what you're talking about.'

'Lorna said she saw you at the fair with a bloke with an American accent, and that you and him seemed really loved-up. I was desperate to see you tonight to find out if it was serious, but I don't need to ask, now I've seen the mood boards . . .'

'She was as wrong as it's possible to be,' I said flatly, being too exhausted to express myself with the vehemence

165

his dogged questions deserved. 'But for what it's worth, I'm not with that man, and I never really was.'

'But the mood boards . . .'

'Ideas, that's all. For if . . .' The sentence died on my kiss-scorched lips. For most of my search, *if I meet the one* would have been correct, but the situation had abruptly changed. 'For *when* I get engaged.'

'You're single,' Nate said slowly.

I didn't know how to reply to that, but since it was none of his business, I didn't need to, and instead stalked over to wrench open my front door. 'Time to go, Nate.'

As he thumped to his feet, I saw headlamps sweep around the corner, and one of the estate four-by-fours pulled up along the track. The bulky form of Mr Holt heaved himself out before lumbering up to Tristan's cottage. Nate came up behind me, and I pushed the door wide for him.

'See you soon, Rosh.'

'I don't think so.'

There wasn't enough light for me to catch his expression, before he turned and stomped over to the van. The engine roared within seconds. I forced myself to wait until he'd driven it out of sight before I pulled my thickest cardigan on, grabbed his torch, and flitted towards Tristan's place.

He was exiting his cottage on Mr Holt's heels.

'Róisín,' he said, sounding relieved. 'Everything okay?'

'Fine.' I didn't want to be too direct with Mr Holt within earshot, but I had a burning need to reassure him. 'Like I thought, my ex decided to deliver some of my stuff that I'd left there for too long. Any news on Bear?'

'Not yet. And sorry, our . . . uh . . .' He broke off to glance at Mr Holt, who had waited beside his vehicle. 'Mr Holt reckons we might be able to get the generator restarted together.'

We couldn't continue our . . . whatever it was, immediately, then, and I gritted my teeth. 'How long will that take?'

He was already moving away. 'No idea. Listen . . . you should get some sleep. We'll catch up properly in the morning.'

* * *

Bright light was filtering through my eyelids, and my pillow had ruched up to form a hard bolster beneath my neck. I rolled onto my front, and fell out of bed—

I made a hard landing onto stone, not the rug covering the bare boards in my bedroom. And the ceiling above me was made up of thicker beams. I must have fallen asleep on the couch, without even closing the curtains.

An instant later, my heart in my mouth, I was scrambling to my feet, testing the limits of my stiff limbs. The last thing I recalled was deciding to ignore Tristan's entreaty to sleep, and wait up for his return. Instead I'd drifted off on the couch, without even closing the curtains.

I had to see him urgently — check how Bear was doing and that Tristan wasn't annoyed about Nate interrupting us.

Certain of all that by the few seconds it took to reach the door, I blinked as I stepped out. It was well past dawn, I assessed from the height of the sun — at least mid-morning.

My muscles protested as I raced down the path, craning to see if he was around. But I could only see Mr Holt, examining the reddening leaves of the huge tree on the opposite side of the track from the cottages, muttering about ash dieback. Still half-winded from my spill onto the floor, I ran out of breath, and slowed.

'I got the generator restarted,' Mr Holt called as he spied me.

'Great! Sorry, I can't stop to chat, I've got to see Tristan.' I added, rather desperately, 'To see if there's any news on Bear, you see.'

'She made it through surgery all right. The boss said to tell you that when you were up and about, and that the vet reckons the odds are good for a full recovery.'

I span, as if I might find Tristan coming up behind me. But of course he wasn't in sight, and as my eyes shifted to his unlit cottage, my brain caught up with me.

'Tristan's already left for the vet's then?'

'That he has,' Mr Holt agreed.

I ground my teeth, ticking myself off for not making it an open-ended question. I needed to know when to expect him back. If I'd just missed him, I calculated rapidly, maybe I should follow in the minibus, to offer moral support while he visited Bear. 'What time did he head off?'

'An hour past dawn.' The desperation in my gaze must have been strong, because after a glance at me, he added, 'Nigh on three hours ago.'

'There's no point me following, then,' I murmured, and louder, 'Thanks for passing his message along, Mr Holt.'

I released a long, slow breath, and shook tension from my shoulders. I could bathe — in warm water, thanks to Mr Holt — and dress in something nice, then await Tristan's return with a pot of tea. I waved my thanks at him as I turned towards my front path, noticing that to one side of my front door were my candlesticks, that Tristan had carried over to his cottage the night before.

Mr Holt added something, and I swung back. 'Sorry — what was that?'

'What was what, love?'

'Could you repeat what you just said — something about Tristan?'

'Oh,' his weather-beaten face cleared. 'I just was to thinking aloud. It was three hours ago he left, and it's round about twenty minutes into the surgery. So he'll have reached London by now, or near as not.'

I fixed my eyes on a thin line of birds in the sky, high and remote, as I fought for composure. Eventually I managed to ask, 'London, Mr Holt?'

'Or thereabouts. Tristan said he'd be heading off there straight from the vet's.'

It took a little time to tease out a full explanation. It seemed that as they restarted the generator, Mr Holt had gained the impression that Tristan had plans to go to London before realising Bear was ill. Hearing she'd recovered he'd decided to go ahead, taking Bear with him for a second opinion from a London vet. He'd left quickly, in a hurry to see her, only pausing to give the verbal message on her prognosis to be passed to me.

I swallowed heavily. 'Do we know how long he'll be gone?'

Mr Holt shook his head, his attention already refocussed on the tree.

I had no reason to disbelieve Mr Holt, but I couldn't work out why Tristan hadn't mentioned an upcoming trip away, nor why he hadn't spared a few seconds to knock on my door and explain — or at least left me a note, tucked between my candlesticks. Leaving me just those few words of benign reassurance about Bear, via Mr Holt, gave the impression that our encounter meant nothing to him.

For a stricken moment I wondered if that was it — he just didn't give a crap, then dismissed the fear. A kiss as bone-melting as ours couldn't possibly be meaningless.

So what then . . . he was offended that I'd fallen asleep — despite telling me not to wait up? Or he was upset by the appearance of my ex? It could be either, or some other issue entirely, and there was no way I could set things right until he returned.

My eyes alighted on my phone, and I caught it up, laughing at myself. I didn't have Tristan's mobile number but I did have his Sylverley email address. I could assure him I'd got the message about Bear, and how pleased I was to hear it, to get a conversation started. I turned the volume to max so I'd hear a swish for incoming emails, plugged it into the wall and smiled expectantly.

The swish sounded barely a minute later: *Out of Office Alert from Tristan Nash. No access to office emails due to annual leave. Please contact Miranda Pangbourne-Perkinson in my absence.*

No return date was stated.

CHAPTER 16: WHEN YOU KNOW, YOU KNOW

A day and a half later, I pushed Amelia's gown away, struggling to concentrate on the awkward sleeves. I ran my hand over the bale of navy velvet intended for Tristan's tail coat, stroking it like he'd stroked down my spine. Maybe a hundred miles away in London he'd give an answering shiver in response, and lift his phone to call me . . .

I glared at mine, but it remained silent.

With an apology to future Róisín, who would have to pull some all-nighters to make up for me dropping even further behind schedule, I awarded myself the rest of Tuesday off, seized my handset and set off on a walk around the estate.

I tried to pretend to myself that I'd chosen the least scenic route, skirting the edge of the lengthy drive, out of interest at how many weekday visitors Sylverley was getting these days. Not at all because it increased the number of staff members I'd encounter. And my eyes swept from side to side to admire the profusion of autumnal colour displayed by the trees, not to disguise my intention of oh-so-casually bumping into everyone I found. The dark green of the evergreens, under which a few of the cleaners were huddled for a tea break. A fiery red maple, beside which a gardener was digging. And the diffident young tour guides, talking beneath a burnished gold beech. I greeted each in turn, then led the discussion toward their boss, but they were blank-faced over when he'd return, and I gathered nothing more than what I already knew, that he was 'on annual leave in London, Perky says'.

Slowing my steps as I returned to the cottages, I glanced over for Tristan's torch. It was still where I'd left it, squarely in front of his door, so he hadn't returned through the side entrance. I sped again, my mind skipping ahead to the excuses I could make for an intrusion into the estate offices — or perhaps I should try the orangery, in hope that Mrs Holt knew more details.

Then the woman herself bustled out of her cottage, a woven laundry basket between her arms. I waited for her to reach me on the track, then seized the opportunity, and the basket. 'Let me help you with that.'

'Thank you, dear,' she said, blinking. 'But it's got to go all the way up to the orangery.'

'I don't mind walking further, I'll bring it.'

Stepping out with shorter strides than usual, to keep side-by-side with her, I opened my mouth to ask for news on Bear, but Mrs Holt piped up first.

'There was a bit of a do, last night,' she said darkly. 'Forty people celebrating a golden wedding anniversary, or such like, in the orangery. I offered to work late, but Perky said she had it in hand. *Had it in hand,*' she repeated, huffing with displeasure. 'Someone forgot to put the stained linens — stained with *red wine,* no less — in the wash, so I had to bring them down to steep them in bleach in my own kitchen. All while prepping for lunches, afternoon tea, and another of Perky's events for tonight. I've warned her that I want no more of that under-supervision of the kitchen staff, or Tristan will hear of it the minute he's back—'

'When will that be?' I blurted in desperation. 'When will Tristan be back?'

'Here now!' Mrs Holt's voice had risen to the same shrill pitch that my mam used to signal someone being in

Significant Trouble. Before I could stammer an apology for the rude interruption, I saw that her gaze was focussed on a young gardener standing off the path, ankle deep in shrubbery. 'Here now, what are you doing smoking on the job? No point showing me empty hands like that — I saw it with my own two eyes — have you dropped it in that bush?'

She dished out a piece of her mind to the stammering young gardener, insisting he trample out the cigarette then take the laundry from me and deliver it up the hill. As she resumed her slow march, I scampered after her, explaining that I wanted a bit more exercise.

Mrs Holt accepted that without comment. 'The problem with all the young 'uns,' she said, with a nod after the gardener, already well beyond earshot. 'Is that with the cat away, the mice will play, and all that.'

That was another opening, and she was slightly puffed out from her tirade, so there was a gap in which I could take it. 'When do we expect him to return? The cat, I mean. Or, you know, the man and his dog?'

'Only Perky seems to know, and she hasn't told me.' Mrs Holt glanced back at me and heaved in a breath. 'You're looking peaky. Make sure you come to last-Sunday high tea at the weekend, so I can feed you up.'

* * *

Constantly checking my phone for texts and refreshing my email was incompatible with my preference to avoid the O'Reilly group chat when the conversation was focussed on Aoife's wedding, and unfortunately she'd seen something in a bridal shop that she never stopped going on about. Mam refused to let her buy it on the basis that she'd get something nicer and cheaper if *Róisín does a wee bit of work to make you a dress.*

'*Wee* bit of work,' I muttered, holding up two pinned pieces of the velvet for Tristan's frock coat. Typically for velvet it had slithered and wasn't quite straight, so I pulled out the pins, stabbing them back into my pin cushion. Since it was impossible not to think about Tristan, I'd devoted the rest of the week to his outfit, but, also since it was impossible not to think about Tristan, I kept making mistakes, so progress was slow. Another message from Mam popped up on my phone, this one just to me, in a side-bar from the family group to insist I back her up over £800 *for a bit of net*.

Through gritted teeth, I asked Aoife for a photo of the gown she liked, so I could see how to copy it, then discarded my phone and Tristan's velvet and wandered over to my desk to scroll through the news on my laptop. Before I knew it I'd navigated to a search engine and input *Tristan Nash*.

His online presence was minimal, with no social media — he wasn't even plastered all over Sylverley's website, only meriting a brief mention in the *About Us* section. I added *Ashgrove Trust* to the search, and found the management company. They had a brief biography of him, as the general manager of Sylverley House and Estate. He'd attended university in Scotland before doing a decade working his way up at a company I'd never heard of. Another search elicited the information that it was a financial advisory firm, and I wondered if his background being finance rather than heritage history perhaps explained his attitude towards Sylverley, with the pressures of its problems blinding him to its beauty.

I found a few lines within that firm's annual report, noting Tristan Nash's swift departure to take up a new role in a different field, and leaned back in my chair, considering. With seemingly no hankering for historic houses, something had perhaps happened — in his old job or his personal life — to cause the abrupt change . . .

My phone chirped again and my heart leaped as I dived to check it. It was an SOS from Abi.

* * *

She was waiting on the pavement outside her house, her arms folded over a new garish cardigan, buttoned perilously over her expanding belly. As I pulled in, she gesticulated wildly for me to flip the switch that unlocked the minibus doors, then instantly pulled open the passenger side and heaved herself up into the seat. Slamming the door behind her, she pounced on the silver foil wrapped package on the centre console.

'Róisín O'Reilly, you're a flame-haired goddess,' she said with a groan of desire. Then she glared at me from under her untidy fringe. 'Come on, I'm desperate — get me out of sight!'

'Seatbelt.'

After she clicked it on, I indicated and pulled away from the curb, aware of her casting sidelong glances at me.

'Why are you moody?'

'I'm not! I'm just . . . uncomfortable with the subterfuge.'

She pulled at the edge of the foil and breathed in deeply. 'You wouldn't be if you knew how badly I've been craving this.'

'Making me feel like a dealer doesn't help, actually.'

She unfurled the foil and cupped the contents lovingly. 'My own personal dealer of bacon butties. That's your official job description for the next three months, by the way.'

I halted at the junction at the end of her street. 'Official — so you'll be announcing my new role to Herbie, committed vegan and love of your life?'

'Unnecessary, Róisín.'

'Where are we going, anyway?'

'Left,' Abi said, and I pushed the indicator down. 'No, actually right.' Rolling my eyes, I pushed it all the way up, and held a hand of apology to the car behind me. 'Actually I don't really care. Just out of sight of all my neighbours, in case they don't know that snitches get stitches.'

'How charming.' I spied a gap after the passing car, switched yet again to indicate left, and turned into the road. 'You know, you seem to be channelling Gemma today.'

'Thanks,' Abi said serenely.

'That wasn't really intended as a compliment, and since you don't much like Gemma, you know it.'

'I do like her! She's a great mum, and she's as determined as anything. I just struggle when she does her . . . you know, passive-aggressive thing.'

That made me snort. '*Passive* aggressive? Actively aggressive, more like. She's never expressed herself passively in as long as I've known her.'

Abi glanced out of her window, then past me out of mine. 'Do you think I'm safe from prying eyes now?'

Before I had even formed a reply, she bit into the roll. Ketchup oozed out the far side of the bread.

'Careful of the upholstery — napkins are in the glove compartment.'

Abi didn't pause to get them, just chewed her mouthful, swallowed, then bit off another hunk of bacon and bread. I indicated, then manoeuvred into the next side street, and found a space long enough in which to parallel park. Once the handbrake was on and the engine off, I leaned over her protuberant belly to grab the napkins, and dropped them where her lap used to be. 'Here.'

'May I remind you that we're in my vehicle,' Abi said, around a mouthful. 'And I think life's too short for worrying about clean upholstery.'

'I wonder what Herbie would think about bacon grease stains?'

She scrabbled for a napkin, hastily wiped her fingers, and wrapped another one around the roll. As she continued eating, I checked my phone. More wedding gown snark between Mam and Aoife, each entreating the rest of us to join her own side. And a text from Nate, asking how my bedside tables were settling in to their new home; he'd clearly decided that our moratorium on contact was over.

'Who you messaging?' Abi asked, scrunching up her rubbish and licking ketchup from the back of her hand.

I dropped my phone back into the cup holder. 'Literally no one. Did the bacon hit the spot?'

'It did, but I wish I'd reminded you I've got two babies inside me. Fern and Frond seem to want a butty each. Maybe we could swing by a takeaway . . .'

I infused my voice with syrupy sorrow. 'I would if I could, but I've got to get back to my work commissions, I'm afraid.'

'Ha!' Abi said. 'You're lying — I see it on your face. Come on, let's get round to that place on London Road—'

'No need.' I flipped up the centre console, to reveal a second and third foil wrapped package, on top of another pile of napkins. 'I fancied one as well. And I guessed you'd want two.'

As she tore off her wrapping and bit into one, I side-eyed her. 'Tell me *Fern and Frond* is just because you've cycled back to F in the alphabet thing, and not what you've settled on?'

'You don't like them?' Abi said through a gob-ful of bacon.

'Not Frond. Fern's sweet.'

'Well neither's on the shortlist. Top contenders right now are Poppy and Bay.'

I'd bitten into my butty, so could only show enthusiasm by widening my eyes.

'You hate them. What — too boring? Does it help if I explain that it's short for Bay *hyphen* Leaf and Poppy *hyphen* Seeds?'

I swallowed my mouthful. 'The short versions aren't boring at all. I think,' I added cautiously, 'they're much better than the hyphenated versions, which are a bit . . . too obviously inspired by a herb garden.'

'Hmm.' Abi munched down a few more mouthfuls. 'Is inspired by herbs a bad thing, though?'

'Maybe it depends whether the herb's already a given name, like Rosemary, or something that would be considered batshit as a name, like, uh . . .' I snapped my jaw shut against *Poppy-Seed and Bay-Leaf*, and pictured Nate's huge herb and spice cabinet in the kitchen of the café. 'Uh . . . Hyssop and Borage.'

'Borage,' Abi said dreamily, 'and Hyssop aren't batshit at all. They blend the natural world, and human refinement.'

'Poppy and Bay are honestly much cuter,' I said firmly, as she yawned. 'They not letting you get much sleep?'

'Never. But last night their father was to blame. He fancied aubergine wedges at midnight, and used wax paper rather than baking paper in the oven, so I was woken by the fire alarm. It was an hour before we cleared enough smoke to shut it up.' She darted a look at me. 'I swear on Mother Earth, I love him like I've never loved anyone, but occasionally he's a complete numpty — have you noticed?'

'Err . . . kind of . . .'

'Every time he goes on about what a magical babymoon we'll have, in the weeks after the birth, I wonder how he'll cope in those early days.'

'He loves you too, and that's what mainly counts, right?'

She shrugged. 'Usually, yes.'

'And you don't only have him to rely on. I'll come as soon as you want, and stay as long as you want.'

'Really?'

'Of course. Though if you could keep them inside you until close to the due date, so I can hand over my Sylverley costumes first, it'll be easier. If not, I'll figure it out, though. Finished?' As I collected her discarded wrapping and greasy napkins, my phone pinged again. I started, then glanced at the message, which was from Gemma, offering to hit the date-my-friend app again. I groaned. 'Gemma wants to pimp me out to more estate agents.'

'Tell her no!'

'I am,' I said, pressing in *no thanks* with my thumbs, backspacing and changing it to *hell no*.

'Seriously — you've realised she's wrong with the whole love-is-a-numbers-game thing?'

'I wouldn't put it that strongly. Let's just say . . . her plan resulted in a succession of disastrous dates, culminating in one — which I fixed up myself, so can't blame on Gemma — with a man who turned out to be married, with a kid.'

'What a scumbag! But it's not your fault—'

'It was. If I'd caught all the red flags, I could have made bunting long enough to festoon across Sylverley's ballroom.'

'Still not your fault,' she insisted. 'And I'm glad you're not going on her set-ups anymore, but getting your fingers burned is no reason to give up on the idea of meeting *the one* in time to use your prize.'

I grasped the top of the steering wheel and stroked my hands down to the ten-to-two position, then back up to meet again at the top. 'I know. I haven't.' I sucked in a deep breath. 'Don't get excited and go into premature labour — it's really early days and I don't know if anything will come of it . . .'

She sat bolt upright. 'You've met *the one*!'

'Did you hear my careful introduction about how it's early days and—'

'Fine — you *might* have met the one, But seriously, when you know, you know. So, do you know?'

I pressed my lips together and raised my shoulders in a mute shrug, but it was impossible to suppress my smile entirely.

CHAPTER 17: FAVOURS

By the end of a full week without Tristan, it was clear how integral he was to the smooth running of Sylverley. In his absence, the usual practiced perfection unravelled a little more each day, like a hem with a loose thread. A visitor's child got lost and the police were called before he was discovered asleep in one of the bedchambers, sucking his thumb under an antique coverlet in a four-poster. Two gardeners had a fist fight in front of the orangery, when it was full of patrons for lunchtime service, and had to be suspended from duties. And Mrs Holt's sous chef sneezed near Mrs Sylvers, who screamed that he was a plague rat, in the wake of which the chef walked out, refusing to ever return to Sylverley. It left Mr and Mrs Holt and the other senior staff run ragged, dealing with problem after problem, so as the week went on it got increasingly difficult to engineer casual-appearing encounters in search of any updates on when their boss might return.

Eventually I gave up all pretence, and admitted to myself that I was incapable of thinking about anything but him. To prevent me getting even further behind on the costumes, I'd capitalised on that by putting in long hours on his, and both the shirt and tailcoat were complete, and the waistcoat cut out. I'd just pinned the pieces together when my laptop chirped, and I shifted my eyes to the screen. It wasn't an email from Tristan, but only an incoming video call from Aoife. I leaned over with one hand and clicked to accept.

'What is it? I'm working.'

Mam peered into the camera, so all I saw was her long nose. 'Aoife, this is broken,' she screeched. 'I can see our Róisín, but I can't hear her.'

I hastily lowered my volume.

'I told you I'd connect you to her in a minute, Mammy,' Aoife shrieked back. 'I'm just making a wee sandwich.'

'Sandwich? I brought you in chips and battered sausage.'

'Connor's eating it. I'm dieting for my wedding, aye? Chips are wile unhealthy.'

I wished I had some popcorn. At a safe distance, as I was, this was as entertaining as the cinema.

'Get on with yourself calling chips unhealthy indeed!' Mam shrieked back. 'I remember you spending at least a year munching away on crayons, and you never would listen when I said they weren't good for your health.'

Aoife appeared in the background, her hands on her hips. 'That was when I was four, Mammy! You can't keep bringing it up—'

'Aye, I can,' Mam said. 'And if you don't come and make this machine work I'll tell wee Connor about the time I was called into St Mary Magdalen's to hear that you were force-feeding crayons to the other weans. I never lived it down with that snotty teacher.'

Aoife whirled back out of my view and Mam hollered exasperatedly after her. I grabbed a sheet of paper and pencil, wrote: *turn the volume up*, and held it up. When Mam eventually glanced at the screen she wrinkled her nose, then rooted around in the drawer under the desk. As she pulled out a pad, I groaned, then flipped my paper over and scribbled quickly.

I can hear you! Just turn up the volume. 2nd button from right on top row.

'Hello,' Mam said suspiciously. I waved and nodded, then pointed above my head, to the left. 'It hasn't worked. Hello, hello?'

'Hello,' I said, and she jumped.

'Jesus Christ don't shout,' she shrieked. 'You'll deafen me.'

'Maybe press the button below it a few times . . . that better Mammy? What's up?'

'It's about Aoife's wedding—'

'Of course it is,' I muttered. 'Sorry, Mam, carry on.'

'Well, she wants a buffet, after the sit-down dinner, but the hotel want to charge us six pound a head extra — six whole pound! So I was thinking we could whip out some Tupperware onto the tables — you listening?'

'Yes, Mam,' I said, transferring the waistcoat and my scissors to beneath the table my laptop rested on, so I could trim the seam before bagging out.

'Good. So tell your Nate we want three dozen of those sausage rolls he does in that café of his.'

'Nate and I broke up back in the summer, remember?'

'Of course, I'm not an eejit. But sure, that doesn't mean he can't help us with a favour.'

'It kind of does, Mam.' She had the expression that meant she wouldn't take no for an answer, so I raked through my brain for another excuse. 'I couldn't bring them with me on the plane, anyway. I've got a conscientious objection to sausage rolls, since I've gone vegan.'

'*Vegan?*' She went pale. 'Why on God's sweet earth would you do that?'

'It's no big deal—'

'Here, Aoife — *it's an emergency* — *come here now!* I don't know how to break this to you, but your sister's gone vegan. I have to say, I never thought I'd live to see the day a wean of mine refused butter or meat, but I suppose it's what comes from bringing her up in England. We never should have left Derry in the first place, and then—'

'It was a joke, Mam,' I said hastily. 'I still eat butter and cheese.'

181

'All your ancestors died in the famine, you know, Róisín,' Mam said darkly. 'They'll be rolling in their graves at you starving yourself willingly like this.'

'I'm not vegan!' I called louder, and she sucked her cheeks in, which was the ultimate signal of impending wrath.

'Then why did you say you were?'

'Stupid joke. I've got to go. Talk soon, okay?'

I pushed the lid down on the laptop, unsure whether to laugh or cry, and checked the time. It was the last Sunday in September, and I'd determined to attend high tea; in the absence of information on Tristan, there was nothing for it but to pump Perky for information myself.

* * *

The effect of Tristan's absence was evident even in the old servant's hall, with the array of food less abundant than when I'd attended in July, after several apparent disasters in the kitchens. Each long table was filling with members of separate work forces, rather than the prior jumbled camaraderie. Fleeces of the grounds team at one, with the far end of it taken over by the boiler-suited maintenance crew. Cleaners and kitchen staff took over two more tables, leaving the one closest to the food to be inhabited solely by those in smart Sylverley trouser or skirt suits, though even that had a few empty chairs in the middle, delineating a split between the front of house and management teams.

The separation into tribes might have made me back out, awkward about finding a place to sit, except that I was on a mission, and already knew my place: as close to wherever Perky sat as I could inveigle myself. So I joined the back of the queue, scanning round the room to establish whether she was already there. She wasn't, so I murmured something about waiting for someone, and let those joining the queue behind me filter ahead. Before long it was only single stragglers entering, and continuing to linger would look odd so I seized a tray and stepped up to the buffet table. I filled a plate mechanically, my eyes fixed on the door, but Perky still hadn't appeared when I reached the end of the buffet.

Taking a deep breath, I strode to the gap between the two groups of suits. I planted my tray on the table and myself on the chair closest to the management group, and waited for the few of them I knew to notice me.

'Neither of those are vegan,' Lola-Pop said eventually, nodding at my tray. I had a plate of pasta bake, oozing with melted cheese, and a bowl of cherry trifle. 'There's mozzarella in the pasta and cream in the pud.'

'I switched to vegetarian,' I said.

'You're not vegan anymore, when there are such benefits to the environment from a plant-based diet?'

I stared significantly at her plate of roast beef and gravy.

'I'm anaemic,' she said hurriedly. 'If it wasn't for my iron levels, I'd turn vegan like a shot.'

I concealed my smile behind a forkful of gooey pasta bake, side-eyeing her as I chewed. 'Any news on Bear?'

'Perky said she's recovered.'

'Great. And what about on when Tristan will be back? I need to consult him about an aspect of his costume.'

'Perky, yoo-hoo!' she shrieked, swivelling in her seat. I jerked around, to see Perky marching toward us from the buffet. She must have entered directly from the kitchen, because I'd barely taken my eyes from the main door. 'Róisín's asking when Tristan will be back . . .'

'Because I'm onto making his costume, and I've got an urgent query,' I added in a rush.

'He's taking some long-overdue annual leave,' Perky said, as she sat down in the empty seat at my other side. She broke off to pointedly exchange greetings with the front of house team, who'd been exiled by management — or who had exiled management. 'He's not confirmed his specific date of return, I'm afraid, Róisín. What's the issue with the costume?'

'He never confirmed whether he wanted full-length pantaloons or knee-length breeches,' I explained, crossing my fingers under the table. 'I need to check directly — on the phone would be fine.' Hopefully this excuse was personal enough for her to refer me on to Tristan, but mundane enough that she wouldn't follow it up by mentioning it to him herself. Once I had his phone number, I could text him asking how Bear was doing, and let the conversation take its course from there.

'No need for that,' Perky said. 'Surely it wouldn't cost much extra for you to make him a pair of each? Do that, then — and itemise them on the final invoice, so I can show him it was his own fault that the cost rose.'

'Great,' I said, uncrossing my fingers and plaiting my hands together hard. I lowered my voice. 'That's only part of the issue, though. I've got to know . . . to know if Tristan wants the groin area padded or not, in the pantaloons. Some men prefer it for . . . decency's sake, since they're cut on the bias and very tight.' I'd had to go so personal that she couldn't answer for him, but the instant the ludicrous excuse passed my lips I was desperate to gulp it back.

'Oh.' That perturbed even Perky. 'Well, I still can't give you his number — it's for dire emergencies only and surely you could add any,' she cleared her throat, 'necessary extras at a later stage, if required.'

'It doesn't work like that — if I leave space for padding and he doesn't want it, the fabric would sag.' For some reason my hands got in on the action, spreading in front of my hips to draw attention to the area under discussion. Her face was so aghast that I relented slightly. 'Listen, if he's back this week then it should be fine, but more than that and it'll hold up everything. Do you really have no idea at all when he'll return?'

Her face cleared slightly. 'Strictly between you and me,' she said in an undertone, 'he's back on Tuesday.'

'Tuesday,' I breathed. *Tuesday, Tuesday, the-day-after-tomorrow is Tuesday.*

Perky's eyes tightened slightly, and I hardened every muscle in my body against the threat of exposing any more of my reaction.

Amelia passed us, then paused. 'Perky, did you see my reply to your email? I'm really sorry, but overtime's impossible tomorrow — my parents are visiting Bath and they'll disown me if I cancel again.'

Perky's grimace seemed more resigned than surprised. 'Thanks for letting me know.' As Amelia left, she rubbed her face, muttering to herself about cancelling a tour.

'Tours on a Monday?' I asked, with most of my attention on my pasta. 'Aren't you closed except for events?'

'It *is* an event booking — an exclusive tour for a historical society, followed by a three course lunch. The kind of thing we'll be wearing our costumes for, once they're ready.' She poked at her food disconsolately, then laid her fork down without eating anything. 'Everyone's even busier than usual, from covering Tristan's tasks, and I can't really blame them for not wanting to sacrifice their day off to assist Mrs Holt. But she can't prep and serve three courses for twenty completely alone, and I can't assist her and conduct the tour at the same time.'

I made a sympathetic sound as I finished my pasta and dug into the trifle. 'Mrs Holt should make this for their dessert — it's amazing.'

'She won't be making any dessert at all now everyone's refused the overtime,' she said with a groan. 'I'll have to refund their sit-down lunch and offer a light finger buffet. Tristan would loathe me doing that so last minute — it's beyond unprofessional. But what else . . .' Her gaze focussed on me, then sharpened. 'Róisín, do you happen to have plans tomorrow morning?'

I swallowed a cherry whole. 'Sewing,' I said, when I'd recovered. 'So I hit your deadline.'

'But you said you're working on Tristan's costume, and you don't know yet about the . . .' She cleared her throat, 'Hip-region padding. So surely it wouldn't be a big deal to take a few hours off to help—'

'I can't cook,' I said. 'Like, really, really can't cook. I'd be next to useless at assisting in the kitchen. No, worse than useless — an active liability. And I've never been a waitress.'

'But you have been a tour guide, I seem to recall.' She smiled so wide that it exposed her large teeth rather alarmingly. 'You must know the house pretty well, at this stage, and you're a heritage historian for goodness' sake. Come on, conduct the tour — as a favour for Sylverley, please?'

It was *for Sylverley* that made me relent, I told myself. Killing time while waiting expectantly for Tristan's return had nothing to do with it, and neither did the hope that Perky would relay back to him that I'd nobly stepped in to assist.

'Fine. But seriously, just this once.'

'Jolly good. You should wear one of your historical outfits,' Perky added, biting into her sausage roll at last. 'And by the way, it's a bit shabby that you've let your veganism slip so soon after Mrs Holt named the plant-based afternoon tea after you. Can't you at least make a pretence at it?'

OCTOBER: EIGHT MONTHS TO GO

CHAPTER 18: DREAM MAN

'Sylverley is Palladian revival,' I said in my clearest tour-guiding tone, 'inspired by ancient Roman styles, and built in the 1750s for the Sylvers family on the site of their Tudor mansion. As you saw from outside, the exterior is well proportioned but in no way fussy — all the decorative richness being saved for the interiors.' I ignored the attempt at an interruption from a Texan in her fifties, who'd already interrupted twice on the steps of the portico. 'We'll begin with the primary reception rooms, which are the dining rooms to our left, the drawing rooms to our right, and ahead, the grand ballroom, beyond which is the library. As we entered Sylverley up the steps of the portico, you'll have noted that we are on the first floor. Below us — yes, what is it, sir?'

The elderly gentleman hadn't interrupted before, and I was allowing each of them two interruptions. 'What you call the first floor in British English is what we call the second floor in American English. So perhaps best to keep things clear by giving it the original name — the *piano nobile*, which is translated to the stately storey, and—'

It was my turn to interrupt. 'Thank you for the reminder. Now as we move into the dining room — yes, to our left everyone — it's important to note that the kitchens are far below us in the—' I turned that into a cough, and switched to a term that wouldn't elicit a correction, 'Far below us in the *sub-basement*. We can gather from this that the food served at even the grandest of occasions was at best lukewarm by the time it reached the table. It begs the question as to why the wealthy landowners commissioning these houses were happy to suffer such an inconvenience. Was it worth sacrificing hot soup on a cold day, in order to live in a strictly proportioned home with classical lines?'

Having spoken quickly, to get through my spiel without being corrected yet again, I paused for breath. Glancing around them, I realised I'd got lucky, with my rhetorical question sparking a debate between two or three of them that quickly drew in the others.

As Perky had mentioned, the tour group was formed of members of a historical association. It was only when I'd greeted them off their coach that I'd learned that it was an American historical society and they were on a whistle-stop trip around English stately homes. Their national traits combined with their collective passion for history caused a fizzing enthusiasm which was manifesting in constant corrections and multiple clarifications.

I wandered to the window and glanced out, then screwed my eyes up and reminded myself that there was to be no watching for Tristan today. After spending the night dreaming about him, I was concerned at my own obsession, and banned myself from thinking about him. Even thinking about thinking about him. That was allowed to begin tomorrow, when he should return — but I wasn't allowed to think about that yet either.

I turned, pushing the pins to tighten the pleat in my hair. Rather than spending an hour in front of the mirror wrestling my hair into an authentic up-do, I'd twisted it up simply, but red tendrils kept escaping, so I pushed them behind my ears then smoothed the length of my skirts. I was wearing one of my favourite costumes, an empire-line gown made of a fine lawn cotton, patterned with tiny cornflowers.

There was only so much discomfort I was prepared to go to as a favour to Perky, though, so I'd left off the proper boned stays in favour of a pliable, quilted corset.

The debate was turning into a squabble, with raised voices, and I stepped in hastily. 'If you'll come this way, ladies and gentlemen, I'll show you the red dining room, which is even larger.' There was little movement, and their discussion continued. 'If we take too long in these initial reception rooms, I'm afraid our time in the library at the end will be curtailed.'

Library, to a huddle of history buffs, was of course a magic word, and it elicited absolute silence, followed by a speedy shuffle through the double doors.

'That was nicely done,' the group leader said, pausing at the threshold. 'You're very good with them.'

Until then I hadn't taken any particular notice of him, beyond noticing that he was male and perhaps in his late twenties, with an English accent. But his voice had an attractive, mellow timbre, and now I couldn't keep myself from scrutinising him from beneath my lashes. Under sandy brown hair and thick eyebrows he had green-blue eyes, which were on mine.

I shifted my gaze away. 'Uh . . . thanks.'

'Róisín, didn't you say? I'm Henry Inglis.'

'Hi,' I murmured, as I swept past him into the next room after the rest of the group.

'Ladies and gentlemen, as you see, the table in here has been laid as if for a dinner party. It's based on surviving records of an event held here in 1767.' My voice sharpened: 'I know I don't need to ask such an esteemed group of visitors not to touch any of the antique silver.'

The elderly gentleman retracted his hand hastily, and the group leader hastened toward him, remonstrating quietly. I directed the group towards a slightly moth-eaten tapestry, embroidered with the Sylverley family tree, then approached the two of them. Their conversation broke off, and the older man apologised to me — though he didn't say what for — and stepped to join the others gazing up at the tapestry.

'Sorry about that,' Henry said. 'Hank sometimes can't resist a touch. I've reminded him that we've negotiated special access — but not that special.'

I nodded, and called the group to gather beside the double doors to the grand ballroom, enjoying their gasps as I flung them open. The central circular space, surmounted by a dome, almost spoke for itself, but they were paying for a full guided tour so I launched into details about the design and then a potted history of some of the events the Sylvers family had presided over through the centuries.

'It's such a shame no one throws parties like those these days,' a woman said with a sigh. 'This ballroom's crying out to be full of fancily dressed people.'

'Maybe not quite on the scale of the past, but there are big events in here sometimes,' I assured her. 'I've attended one myself.' I regretted that a moment later, when questions shot at me from five different directions.

I didn't want to recall my arrival in borrowed clothing, or the sickening nerves I'd experienced. And I mustn't think about Tristan's steady reassurance as he'd escorted me in . . . before my mind continued running away with me, I shook my head.

'No, I didn't wear this gown . . . it was back in June, to celebrate that Sylverley had recently opened to the public . . . yes there was dancing I believe, but I wasn't in attendance for long.' That caused another volley of questions, and rather desperately I announced that it was time to ascend the great staircase, where they could wander round the galleried landing and in and out of bedchambers. 'Please stay close, in case you want to ask me anything — and remember not to touch anything,' I added, side-stepping to follow closely behind Hank, just in case.

I bumped into Henry, who'd clearly had the same thought, and we exchanged slight smiles before heading after Hank.

'I meant it earlier, by the way,' he said as we ascended the stairs. 'You're good at both leading the group and imparting the right kind of information. Not many people can do both equally well. Have you been tour-guiding for long?'

I side-eyed him, then decided to let him in on the circumstance. 'I don't actually do it at all, anymore. I'm just lending a hand today, after a few . . . temporary staffing blips, here at the estate.'

'Ah,' he said. 'But you're a historian — I can tell.'

'My day job's fashion history,' I confirmed, as we reached the top of the wide staircase, and watched Hank, who was reading the sign beside the blue bedchamber, which described that it was used by the Prince Regent — later George IV — during his visit to Sylverley in 1816.

'Hence the frock,' he said, with a glance at the pleated muslin. 'You designed it?'

'And made it, actually. What about you — do you run tours full time?'

His eyes crinkled with humour. 'Not at all. Funnily enough, I've also stepped in at the last moment.'

Before I could ask about his day job, I noted that the group had spread out extremely wide, with some already approaching the first corner of the landing, where they'd be hidden from my sight. I raised my voice again, drawing their attention to some original bell pulls to tempt them to wander back toward me to see them. Once I'd penned them in one area I suggested we all waited to head to the other side of the galleried landing together. They could explore the other bedchambers before we headed down the other staircase and entered the library via the grand ballroom, where we would spend the rest of the hour.

As we rounded the gallery, those furthest ahead of me stopped beside the entrance through to the east wing, which had a discreet *private* sign. Too discreet, it turned out, as one of them tried pushing on it.

I sped towards them. 'We can't enter there, I'm afraid. It leads to the private family quarters.'

It was the first thing I'd said all afternoon that provoked a widespread flurry of surprise.

'The family? The *Sylvers family*, are still in residence?'

'Is Lord Sylvers at home?'

'Would they come and *meet* us? Should I *curtsey*?'

'Do they still eat cold meals in those huge dining rooms downstairs?'

I held a hand up, only venturing to reply once the questions had stopped. 'The Sylvers family were landed gentry, not nobility, so they've never had titles. The current occupant lives in an apartment in the east wing, beyond this door, and is very private. That's all I can say, I'm afraid, and if you want some time in the library before lunch, we need to keep moving.' Mrs Sylvers was well known for accusing tourists she encountered of being worse than cockroaches. While I didn't know if she'd react like that to enthusiastic Americans who bowed and scraped and called her *your Ladyship*, it seemed prudent not to hang around long enough to find out.

* * *

The library stretched along the back of Sylverley, formed from three rooms, interconnected by deep arches. The floor was covered in parquet, the tiny wooden blocks laid in an intricate geometric pattern, and the ceiling was cross-hatched with blackened oak beams. Full bookcases lined the walls, displaying spines in a rich palette of shades. And overhead, high windows along one wall were inlaid with jewel-like stained glass. Sunlight streaming through the panes reflected different coloured shapes onto the floor like transparent rugs.

'As you can see, ladies and gentlemen, the library isn't built in the same architectural style as the rest of the building for the simple reason that it's several hundred years older — being one of the few remnants of the earlier house on this site, which was purposely retained and amalgamated within the new building.' I stepped onto a circle of sapphire, beside a door that led into the garden. 'Do take your time to look around

— without removing any books, of course,' I added, for good order. 'Or if you'd rather make the most of the sunshine, you could wander through the rose garden.' I opened the door and paused as they cooed over the view it framed: formally laid out rose bushes in the foreground, and behind them the glinting glass of the orangery, where their lunch would soon be served.

As the group dissolved into smaller clumps, I strolled among them, making my way eventually through the connecting arches to the opposite end of the library, where there was a mirroring door leading to the lawn on the westward side of the estate, before returning to a good vantage point in the middle. Rotating to check that Hank was behaving himself, I saw Henry approach. Although he was looking just past me, I had a curious sense that his eyes had been on me.

'I can't thank you enough for the tour, Róisín,' he said, outstretching his right hand.

I shook it. 'No problem. It's not difficult to show beautiful Sylverley off.'

Rather than releasing my hand immediately, he held onto it for a beat or two longer. 'Will we have the pleasure of your company during lunch?'

He wasn't unattractive, but all I felt was suddenly very tired, and I put my relinquished hand behind my back, entwining my fingers. 'Afraid not. As I said, I'm just helping out briefly.'

'Then you certainly should join us for lunch, so we can express our gratitude for your endeavours.'

Before I could reply, the Texan woman waved in our direction. 'How would I find out more about the specifics of the Prince Regent's visit to Sylverley, Henry?' she hollered.

'Don't know off the top of my head, but I could do a little research once I'm back in Oxford, and email you?'

My confusion must have been evident on my face, because he explained. 'Anne writes Regency romances, and is constantly after research material.'

'It wasn't that . . . I was wondering about — your day job involves history? And in Oxford?'

'Ah. Well, yes,' he said, as though it was something he should apologise for. 'I'm in the history faculty.'

I had to tighten my legs to stop myself physically kicking myself. Henry Inglis — *Dr* Henry Inglis, surely — was an Oxford University historian. He was polite and attractive. And we were in a library. This was the dream man I'd described to my friends, in the dream setting I'd come up with. And he was even showing interest in me.

I stared at him, willing attraction to stir within me. To feel something — anything. I jumped slightly as Perky breezed in the eastern door, clapping her hands and announcing that the eminent guests were welcome to make their way through the roses to be seated for lunch in the orangery. I snapped out of my reverie and moved to stand where I could say goodbye to each of them as they exited, handing out my business card and accepting hugs from some of the women.

Henry brought up the stragglers then lingered a moment with a sweet hesitancy. 'You're sure we can't persuade you to join us, Róisín?'

'I really don't think—'

'Of course you should!' Perky said, coming up behind him and stretching her eyes at me. 'You've got loads in common with . . . all of them.' She stared at the back of Henry's head, then back at me, as though I could possibly have missed which of the *all* of them she actually meant.

'I'm afraid I'm busy.'

Perky literally pounced on me for that, nipping forward and seizing me by the arm. 'Too busy to eat, Róisín?'

I was tempted to announce that yes, I was too busy even to eat, because I was so behind with the outfits she'd commissioned. It might work to squeeze an extension out of her. But then I'd have to join them in the orangery. With my mind already agonising over what Tristan's absence meant and if he really would return tomorrow, it was the last thing I needed. So instead I cast around for a way to excuse myself. My eyes alighted on the next best thing — a way to get rid of Henry.

'Err . . . I fear that Hank is assessing the viability of taking a cutting from one of the rosebushes.'

As he rushed off, stammering an apology, Perky's disbelief was evident. 'What the hollyhocks, Róisín? You urgently need a husband, and he seems really into you!'

'But I'm not into him,' I said shortly.

'Why not? He admires Sylverley and he's photogenic—'

'Which might make him the perfect groom for a wedding — no, that's not a concession about anything, I said *might*. But he's . . .' *Not my type*, I'd intended to say. But a better, more accurate, answer formed on the tip of my tongue. *He's just not Tristan*, I swallowed back.

Rolling her eyes, she swung away towards the orangery and I was alone with my thoughts. Or rather, with the single thought that seemed to be preventing me from stringing any other words together. He's just not Tristan.

Desperate suddenly to escape into air and sunlight, I pivoted toward the door at the opposite end of the library; there was a direct route back to my cottage, and minimal chance of bumping into stragglers from the tour group. Or so I thought until, pacing through the first archway, a tall figure stepped over the threshold. One of the group must have wandered all the way round the outside. But this man was wearing an impeccably cut suit rather than—

My mouth went dry and my feet stopped their motion, as recognition hit me.

Tristan.

CHAPTER 19: BELONGING

The abrupt immediacy of his presence rendered me dizzy. But then a compunction to see if Tristan was really here — or if this was an apparition, conjured by my desire — fuelled my hesitant steps forward. Tristan moved at the exact same moment, his longer legs propelling him through the first room in just a few strides.

We passed beneath the arches flanking the central space of the library at the same time, both coming to a halt just before we crashed in the middle. As it was, we hovered either side of one of the illuminated rugs of light, reflecting the stained glass above us, just in front of the double doors to the grand ballroom. It had been on the other side of that vast, domed space that we had first properly met, as the suddenly-single winner of a wedding, and the Sylverley representative responsible for awarding it.

I had known nothing more of him, as he escorted me in, than his name. But proximity had changed that, and now I was aware of our similarities — like professional perfectionism, whereby nothing but best efforts would do — and our differences, like my passion for Sylverley in comparison with his stated aversion. There were other things I had come to know of him, too. His reserve, which bordered, at times, on isolation. How much I enjoyed looking at him, with the meticulous cheekbones and eyes that shifted slightly in shade in response to the colour he was wearing. And the long, lean dimensions of his body, which I'd spent all week moulding velvet and silk to fit.

But, setting eyes on him for the first time since that kiss in near-darkness, it came to me how much more I'd learned of him that evening. The deep affection he had for Bear, who I could only hope was okay. The dexterity of his long-fingered hands, unfastening my gown. And the pliable warmth of his lips and tongue, as they had melded with mine . . .

The temptation to kiss him overwhelmed me; to leap the rectangle of reflected ruby sunshine on the ground between us, and rise onto the tips of my toes to crash my mouth against his, then pretend I needed help to get this gown off.

Before I could decide whether this was the best or worst impulse I'd ever had, he spoke.

'Róisín. How are you?'

'Fine,' I said. My tongue felt numb. 'And you — and Bear?'

He turned his back on me, and my stomach gave a sickening lurch. What I'd heard was wrong, and his dog was not recovered but dead, and he didn't want me to see his grief, or — but he had put his fingers in his mouth, and his whistle pierced the stillness.

Bear appeared in the doorway, then lolloped across the library in her master's footsteps. She was looking healthier than ever, her coat deep red and burnished, eyes alert and damp tongue lolling. She accepted my scratch between her pricked ears, then lay in a patch of purple sunshine.

I wanted to tell Tristan that I had missed him. But as I glanced up at his expressionless face, I lost my nerve. 'I'm pleased to see you back,' was all I managed to stammer.

His lashes swept down over his eyes, then rose again as he met my gaze. 'Pleased to be back.'

Still not a single hint of what he was feeling. I fixed his eyes, hazel against all the wood, with my own. 'I heard that you wouldn't be returning until at least tomorrow.' *Pick up on the hint, Tristan. I went to the bother of sussing out your movements.*

He raised his shoulders, then dropped them, but his expression was unchanged. 'I gathered I had a lot to see to, so thought I'd better come and get a head start on the mounting paperwork while the place was empty.' He added, drily. 'So the coach in the car park came as a bit of a surprise.'

'Perky arranged a private tour and lunch for some Americans . . .' I broke off as he nodded.

'So I gathered from Mr Holt — sorry, I interrupted. You were saying?'

'That was it really. I took them on a tour to help her out. Hence playing dress-up . . .' I ran a hand down my historic gown, my whole face flushing with heat. The last time I'd seen him, I was wearing another of these, and he'd complimented it . . . complimented *me*.

'It looks . . .' He broke off and paused before beginning again. 'It makes you look like you belong here.'

His face was inscrutable, so beyond the slight pause there were no clues as to how I was meant to take that.

And I'd stared at him for too long without verbal response, I realised abruptly. Before the gap in the conversation became uncomfortable, I drew in a long, slow breath. 'I'm . . . I really am pleased to see you.'

'It's good to see you too,' he said, with a slight incline of his head, and an even slighter smile. My heart thudded in my ribcage. Good to see you . . . as in, *I missed you, I'm delighted to find you immediately on my return, and I'm desperate to kiss you too?* Or good to see you . . . as in *I'd better respond politely to what you just said to me?*

I wouldn't know unless I asked, so I parted my lips—

'Tristan — thank God!' Perky called through, from the threshold between the library and rose garden. 'Pardon my French, but I thought I caught a glimpse of you in here and our guests would love to meet you.'

He blinked. 'Technically I'm still on annual leave,' he said mildly.

'Then you shouldn't have come into the house.' She heaved in a deep breath, battling to control exasperation, or perhaps concern. 'Go back to your cottage, or London, or wherever, if you need a longer break. I'll cope here somehow.'

It was the plaintive *somehow* that seemed to catch his attention. He palmed the back of his neck, and smiled at her apologetically. 'I'm sorry, you caught me off guard. Of course I'm here to get stuck straight back in.' She tried to interrupt, but he raised a hand to stop her and returned his attention to me. 'I need a few minutes with Perky . . .'

'Of course,' I said, stricken sick that he didn't even want to talk to me. 'I'm off anyway—'

'No — please, Róisín. If you have time, would you mind waiting?'

Finally, I thought, relief firing up inside me. *Bloody finally, he would reveal his feelings for me*. I nodded, smiling, and he strode towards Perky in the doorway.

'I'm not interested in a meet and greet with these Americans,' he was saying. 'But I'll crack on, at my desk, with everything labelled *important*. If you can give me a bit of time after you've waved them off, I'd appreciate you casting an eye to make sure I haven't missed anything direly urgent.'

Perky could do one better, she announced, brandishing her tablet as she launched into a list she had kept of the most crucial issues needing his input. I turned away to examine the contents of the closest bookcase. The shelf at my eye-line was filled with the complete works of Stanislas de Boufflers, and I peered closer at the spines, as if absorbed by the titles, despite my inability to decipher much of the French they were written in. She was still speaking in her assured drawl as I got to the end of the shelf, so I continued to the one at the same height in the next bookcase, which contained books even harder to mimic interest in: a leather-bound set of law reference guides, in Latin. Thankfully the conversation seemed to be drawing to a close, with an agreement to meet in the estate office later.

'At three, then,' Perky said. 'By the way, Róisín needs to ask you . . . something about your costume.' Feeling all my blood flood to my face, I was glad my back was still turned on them. 'Oh and Róisín — he asked for your business card. Can I give it to him?'

'Sorry?' Tristan and I said together.

'Dr Inglis! He wants a date rather than a costume, I'm guessing. Did you know he's a history fellow at Oxford? He's bloody perfect for—'

'You date him, since you like him so much,' I called curtly. 'I already told you I'm not interested.'

As she stalked away, Tristan's forehead scrunched almost imperceptibly. 'Thanks for waiting.'

'You're welcome,' I murmured. Bear ambled to her feet, yawned and came to stand by me. I rested a hand on her furry nose. Her presence helped me to be bold. 'I don't really need to consult you about your costume. It was an excuse to try to get your phone number. I just — I wanted to tell you that I'm sorry we were interrupted, y'know . . . that night.'

His level brows drew so close together that the skin between his eyes ruched up into a deep vertical line. 'We can just as easily discuss what needs to be discussed now, Róisín. There's really no need for an apology. Or, at least, not from your direction.'

'Discuss what needs to be discussed,' I echoed uncertainly.

'The last time I saw you,' he continued carefully, like he was measuring the weight of each word on his tongue. 'You were so amazing — helping me transport Bear like that, then keeping me company, after we returned. I can't apologise enough for getting a little drunk and emotional.'

Drunk. It stung more than a slap, and I flinched, then tried to cover it by crossing my arms.

'Kissing you like that was inexcusable, Róisín, and I'm sorry.' His voice was steady, his face collected, though pale; while maybe not quite as calm as he looked, he was far, far calmer than he had any right to be.

'Inexcusable — and *you're sorry*?' At my voice, his eyes snapped to the beamed ceiling. 'So what . . . what if I'm . . . *not* sorry about the kiss?'

His reply was slow in coming, and his eyes returned to mine first. 'Please know . . . I didn't intend to hurt you.'

So that was it, then. He wasn't apologising because he mistakenly thought I regretted what had happened. He knew now that I didn't, and was apologising nonetheless. This wasn't a misunderstanding but a very deliberate rejection.

My earlier temptation had been to run to him, but now a stronger urge overtook me, to sprint past him, getting out of his sight at such speed I'd leave smoking scorch marks across the parquet. But I had some tattered dignity to retain, so I made do instead with cutting my eyes away and arranging my facial muscles into an approximation of a smile. Painfully, I forced them to stay like that as I bent at the knee, my back straight in the gown, to give Bear a stroke along the ridge of her back.

'I'm glad you're okay,' I murmured into her fur, before I rose. 'Thanks for the apology, I guess,' I said to Tristan. 'See you around.'

As I made my retreat, I hiccupped, and hiccupped again.

* * *

In bed, with the covers over my head, I had to face it: I'd been wrong about everything. Pathetically wrong, all year. First, fixating on a wedding when Nate didn't want to marry me. Then, blinding myself to the red flags that Jason wasn't single. And now misreading an embarrassing fumble in the dark with Tristan as something momentous.

I wondered if his apology would have been less agonising without the interminable wait for his return, then dismissed the thought, because focussing on pain just made it worse. I'd learned that when I only began to recover from the agony of the break-up with Nate after we cut contact. So now, having repeated the same mistake, and imagined feelings for me that weren't there, I could only take refuge in the same recovery programme. I'd avoid Tristan until his rejection didn't sting anymore. It had even worked as far back as coping with Dad's death; I still avoided looking at his photos and talking about him as far as possible. If I could numb myself to that then I could get over this, by not seeing, hearing or even thinking about Tristan.

Which wouldn't solve the problem of how pathetic I'd become, in pursuit of a groom. I'd have to switch it up, and develop some new strategy if I was going to find the one for me, in time for the wedding. But unfortunately, I was already behind with the costumes for Sylverley, thanks to wasting time pining after Tristan in his absence. So any new strategy would have to wait until I'd completed the commission. If I ignored the rest of the world to get my head down over my sewing machine, I could finish the outfits on schedule, pocket the balance of what I was owed, and refocus on finding *the one*.

I threw back the bedcovers, resolving to take the rest of the day to deal with practicalities that would free up the rest of my time for sewing. I texted Gemma and Abi a warning that I had to devote my time to a massive work deadline and would only be available in an emergency, considered saying something similar on the family group, then rejected the idea. It would only draw attention to me: better to stay silent. I checked out of the front window that the coast was clear, then sprinted to the minibus and headed out of the estate by the side gate. I wrote a mental shopping list of sewing supplies as I drove to my favourite haberdashery, and from there went onto the supermarket. I plodded around with a trolley then joined the end of a check-out queue, before cutting out and doubling back to load up on more tea and chocolate biscuits.

I returned to the estate with my eyes peeled, preparing to circle round if it was necessary. But there was no sign of life outside the cottages. It was as I reached into the rear of the minibus for the carrier bags that I heard, in the distance: 'Here, Bear — good girl.'

My stomach lurched. I closed my eyes for a few seconds, debating the merits of diving into the minibus to hide, or rushing indoors and coming back for my purchases later. Then I hissed at myself, 'No more being pathetic,' seized all the bags in one go, slammed the minibus door with my hip, and strode into the cottage.

It was such a heavy load that the plastic handles seared indentations into my palms. The stripes stung for hours and didn't fade away entirely for several days.

CHAPTER 20: SEEING SOMEONE

Holed up in the cottage, I set to sewing all day, every day, ignoring my previous habit of taking a few hours to properly wake up first. To hold my body clock together I used tea, regularly spaced like pins in a hem. The first cups I tipped from a flask on waking, drinking so quickly I barely tasted it, and slurping especially loudly if a sound of a man calling his dog intruded from along the track. I had a mug at eleven and another as the lunchtime tin of baked beans or soup bubbled on the stove. In the afternoon I took a tea-break every hour, walking around to stretch my limbs as the kettle boiled. The last I made at the same time as the flask for the next morning, and drank in bed, once it was completely dark, a soothing distraction from the cramps in my fingers and my neck.

I never ventured further than the woodland behind the house, and then only for brief periods during the working day, after furtive checks that no one was in sight. I checked my phone and emails only once each evening, adding a thumbs up in the family group every time Mam sought my opinion on any aspect of Aoife's wedding. I replied with brief reassurance to Gemma's occasional texts (*still working hard? let me know you're not dead*) and the links Abi sent (*chakra affirmations to release and balance workaholism*) but ignored Gemma's queries about what was happening with my search for *the one*, and Abi's about how it was going with the man I'd mentioned.

With other big projects I'd completed each outfit before turning to the next, but now I'd done the opposite, beginning with the costumes I hadn't yet started, so that I didn't have to touch a certain not-be-thought-about man's half-finished trousers for as long as possible. By tomorrow or next week, or certainly by December, I'd be over him, I vowed to myself, every time my eyes slid to the sheet-covered shape of a mannequin in a velvet frock-coat. Completely and utterly over him, aside from perhaps a remnant of embarrassment, at my pathetic over-reaction to one kiss.

Every week the weather grew colder and the days shorter, until I was setting my alarm for dawn to capitalise on every chink of daylight, and going to bed early. Even so, there were a few hours to fill each evening, when the pads of my fingers were smarting and I needed a distraction from the outfits and — all the things I mustn't think about. I tried re-watching period dramas on my laptop, but somehow their usual magic of whirling me away into the romantic escapism of the past was dulled. Instead I kept fixating on irritating trivialities, like how much Pemberley's roof would cost Mr Darcy to maintain, and couldn't look away from the costume errors, which I normally managed to ignore.

The distraction that eventually developed came from the absolute last direction I'd have predicted. It began when I clicked through the *stream again* suggestions, and saw an action film that I certainly hadn't watched before. Checking the settings, I made the unwelcome discovery that my laptop had been logged into Nate's account on the streaming service, rather than my own. Worst of all, I'd rented the new version of Emma the evening before, and it had been charged to his credit card, rather than my own. I typed and deleted a dozen different messages, thought hard, then pressed in a simple *Sorry about that,* and sent it. A minute later I sent another.

—*I've logged out now, and I'll transfer you the money.*

—No problem. Of course you needed some space, after everything.

—Hang on, I replied before I saw your second text. What login/ money?

—I rented a film before I noticed my laptop was logged into your account.

He replied with a gif of a bank robber, sprinting away with his loot, then added.

—It's four quid. Don't worry about it.

I put my phone down, smiling, then rose and added another log to the fire from the pile I'd hauled in from beside my front door. Mr Holt had left a neat stack there every few days since the weather turned.

Nate had messaged again by the time I sat back down, to tease me about perving over Mr Knightly, and from there, light chat continued. We didn't text every evening, but more evenings than not, and over the next few weeks, our to and fro of messages went on for increasing lengths of time.

* * *

Three weeks into our renewed communications, the screen of my muted phone lit up one evening with an incoming call from Nate. I ignored it, and he didn't leave a voicemail, but Gemma texted a few hours later.

—Nate reckons Herbie told him you're seeing someone? Who??

I glowered at my phone, slammed it down, and stood up. It had poured all day so I hadn't been outside, and I felt suddenly claustrophobic. Striding to the front door, I threw it open and stood there in my nightshirt, closing my eyes against the wind whipping against the bare skin of my legs, neck and face as I inhaled fresh air.

Someone coughed.

I opened my eyes, heart racing, to see a pool of light out on the track. It took a few seconds for my eyes to adjust, and then I made out the silhouette of a huge dog, and her master. Tristan had a torch in one hand and Bear's lead in the other. The light was too dim for his expression to be clear, though his head was tilted in my direction.

Before I even had time to remind myself not to be pathetic, instinct had kicked in, and I'd raced inside and slid the bolt across the door with trembling fingers. I took a deep breath, then phoned Abi.

'Why the hell is your husband telling Nate something you swore to keep a secret?'

'What?' It was Herbie who'd spoken; he must have answered Abi's mobile. 'Who is this?'

'Look at the screen, Herbie.'

There was some crackling. 'It says Róisín — hi, Róisín! Abi's in the shower. Shall I tell her to—'

'You can help, actually. What did you say to Nate?'

'Nate?'

I inhaled, long and deep. 'My ex.'

'Oh, that Nate. You know, I saw him earlier at the farmer's market that has this amazing stall that sells Jerusalem artichokes.'

'He's claiming that you told him I'm seeing someone.' There was silence. 'Why would you do that, Herbie?'

'He asked,' Herbie said simply. There was no hint of defensiveness in his voice. 'And I said I reckoned so. Abi had been really happy one day, and she said it was because you'd met someone, and she thought it had happened our way — through serendipity, not a set-up.'

'She was happy because—' I cut myself off starkly. She was happy because she'd eaten two bacon rolls, and giving away my secret was the first excuse she came up with. But despite the fury coursing through me, I had no intention of lobbing a hand grenade between my heavily pregnant friend and her husband.

'I'm really sorry. I didn't know it was a secret,' Herbie said. Defensiveness had finally crept into his voice, though it was clearly defence of Abi, rather than himself. It made me feel utterly empty.

'There's no secret, it's just *wrong*. I'm not seeing anyone.'

'But Abi said that you said that—'

'I was wrong,' I corrected bleakly. 'I thought I had a connection with someone, but I didn't. It fizzled out before it even began. Tell Abi that, please.'

I hung up, and washed my face in water cold enough to scare away the threat of hiccups. Afterwards I found another text had pinged through from Gemma in the meantime.

—*Is that why we haven't seen you in ages? You're secretly loved-up with some mystery man? (Tell me now or I'm coming over.)*

—*No! Herbie was wrong. There's no mystery man and I'm genuinely only busy with this commission.*

—*Would you swear that on your vintage Chanel handbag?*

—*I swear on vintage Chanel that I'm completely single.*

—*Fuck. I'll have to break it to Esme. She heard us speculating who you could be seeing, and drew a picture of herself as bridesmaid to a fairy godmother marrying a prince with a pet bear!*

I switched my phone off after that, until a few days later when I had to pay for my inattentiveness to the family group chat by joining in a video call on my laptop. While nodding along about which of my brothers should walk Aoife down the aisle with as much neutrality as I could muster, I scrolled through emails. They were mostly junk, except for a reminder from Mrs Holt about the upcoming last-Sunday high tea, which I deleted especially viciously. I held my phone out of view of my laptop's camera to switch it on and check my messages. There was an abject apology from Abi; I repressed my urge to reply with a pig emoji and instead tapped in that she got lucky — no real harm had been done. Finally, there was a message from Nate.

—*I hear Abi's hipster was wrong. I guess it serves me right for talking to your friends about you.*

—*Yes and yes.*

After pressing send, I blocked him.

* * *

On Sunday morning Mrs Holt cornered me at my back door, expressing concern at how busy I was, and pressed me to attend high tea. I made up an excuse about having plans in Bath with my friends, leaving me with no choice other than to collect my coat and keys and leave in the minibus.

Even as I idly debated at whether to drop by Abi's house or Gemma's, I knew I couldn't actually see either of them. Abi would gently dig into why things had fizzled out with the . . . situation I'd mentioned, and Gemma would lambast me for taking a break from searching for my groom.

'I'll come up with a new strategy soon,' I promised myself. My voice sounded hollow, as did my footsteps, as I trailed around the fashion museum alone.

When I exited it was pouring with rain, and I got my feet wet in a deep puddle hidden by the minibus' shadow. I switched the wipers to full pelt, and even so was struggling with visibility. A flash of lightning lit the sky, and thunder rumbled in the distance. Swearing, I pulled in at the largest supermarket and dashed inside to buy a torch and more candles in case the storm triggered another power cut. Whether because of my lack of culinary skill or my mood, everything I'd cooked lately had tasted of ash, so I grabbed food that required minimal effort. I even found tins of sausages in baked beans, which I could warm on a saucepan over the open fire if there was no electricity to power the oven or microwave.

I rushed back to the minibus, streaming wet, and drove back to Sylverley at little more than a snail's pace, entering via the side gate, so the first cottage I reached was my own. My stomach lurched at how dark the windows were. There had indeed been a power cut, and having left in such a hurry I hadn't taken heed of . . . the warning I'd once been given, and laid a fire. It would take me ages in the dark, and I'd be freezing all evening.

An instant later my eyes reached the other cottages. The empty one beside mine was dark, as it always was. The Holts'. . .

The Holts' cottage had an illuminated upstairs window. And the one on the far end of the row, that I never looked at unless I could absolutely help it, was all lit up. The generator hadn't failed again — I'd just forgotten to leave a light on — and there would be no need for anyone to offer me a warm refuge.

I squashed away a traitorous sense of disappointment, took a deep breath and parked down the side of my cottage, before staggering in the back way with my haul. I was so wet and miserable that I went straight to bed with tea and chocolate.

NOVEMBER: SEVEN MONTHS TO GO

CHAPTER 21: EVERYTHING I EVER WANTED

The storm rolled away the next day, but the sky remained swollen with grey clouds, and there was barely a dry day for the next week. If anything it seemed a positive sign — my cottage was cosy and dry, and it made it easier to absorb myself in the costumes if even stepping outside was unpleasant.

With Lola-Pop's gown finished I launched into Mrs Holt's. I wanted to clad her in teal because it was a colour that suited her, but also because I thought she'd be more confident in a fancy gown if it had a slight resemblance to the work uniforms, and she could pull it on like a mask. I'd sourced raw silk in the exact shade of Sylverley teal some time earlier, but a matching muslin had been harder to find, and I'd resorted to purchasing fabric dye. Rooting through the cupboard under the sink, I found the bucket and plastic gloves left there by the cleaning team. Up in the bathroom, I filled the bucket with warm water and, after donning the gloves, stirred the powder into the bucket with a wooden spoon, then dipped in the corner of a length of white muslin. Pulling it back out, I approved the colour then plunged the rest of the fabric in.

If I'd been rattling away on the sewing machine like most other mornings, I might not have heard the tap at the front door right away. But above only the drumming rain on the roof, and my own breathing, it startled me into stillness.

There was another tap, and then a third, louder, and my pulse pounded in my ears. I shook my rubber gloves over the bucket, then scurried through to my bedroom, where the curtains were half-closed and flattened against the wall. I held my breath, willing whoever it was to go away. But instead, he or she knocked harder.

I inched a curtain from the wall with my elbow, then peeped through the chink I'd created. The figure almost directly below me had their hood up. But I identified him an instant later by his vehicle, out on the track.

A van.

If I didn't respond, he'd return to it and start his irritating horn honks.

I parted the curtains properly and opened the casement. 'What are you doing here, Nate?'

He glanced to one side, then the other.

'Up here,' I added, irritably. 'And I'm busy, working.'

His neck craned back, exposing his face to mine — and to a lot more rain. 'I need to talk to you.'

I spread my rubber-gloved hands, indicating for him to go ahead.

He licked his lips. 'Not like this. Come down — please, Rosh? It's important.'

I heaved in a deep sigh. 'I need a few minutes.'

I didn't purposely go slow as I lifted the fabric from the dye, wrung it out and spread it to dry over the base of the bath, but neither did I let the knowledge of Nate getting soaked outside pressure me into cutting any corners. I glanced in the mirror above the sink as I tipped away the bucket of dye. My hair was escaping a messy bun and I was wearing my oldest leggings and T-shirt. It was just as well that it didn't matter what Nate thought of how I looked anymore. I started to peel off a rubber glove, as I trudged downstairs, then pulled it up again with a snap. Keeping them on would emphasise how inopportune his timing was. On the other side of the front door, Nate was dripping wet under his unzipped-hoodie. His curls were tied back in a bun, which I'd only ever seen him do before when he was undertaking a complicated task that called for intense concentration, like a fiddly new recipe.

'What is it?' I said, standing stock-still in the doorway, to prevent him coming in. More likely than not, he was here to lambast me for blocking his number on my phone, and he could do that on the doorstep.

He swept a bouquet of flowers from behind his back. 'These are for you.'

It was so far from what I'd anticipated that I took a half-step backwards, blinking.

'Peonies are your favourite, right?'

I eyed the bright, multi-coloured stems he stuck out toward me. 'Peonies are indeed my favourites.' I was going to leave it there, until I spied the price tag on the cellophane. It was bright orange — a sale label, signalling that they were half price. 'Though these are zinnias.'

His face was so crestfallen that I accepted them quickly, inhaling their scent before I turned to set them on the side table. 'Thank you, Nate. And you'd better come in . . .' I broke off as I turned back and found him lowering himself onto one knee on the damp doormat.

'Rosh, you're the one for me. I know it, now.'

My stomach clenched. 'But . . .' I managed eventually. 'But we broke up.'

'That was the biggest mistake of my life.' Nate's large brown eyes met mine. I couldn't tell whether all the beads of liquid in his lashes were raindrops. 'I want a reconciliation. To get back together. And I want to marry you, in front of everyone we know, here at Sylverley. Rosh — will you marry me?'

'You're proposing,' I said, my head reeling. 'You're proposing to me, after everything. And when I'm wearing rubber gloves!' I pincered my stained old T-shirt and pulled at it. 'I look like shit, and *you're proposing!*'

'I'll ask again after you've changed into whatever the perfect proposal outfit is, if you want,' Nate said, smiling up at me. 'It'll knacker my knees to wait for you in this position, though. Can I get up?'

I glared at him. He smirked back.

It was me who blinked first. 'I suppose you'd better come inside.'

I didn't offer him a hand up, just swung back into the cottage, leaving the door ajar behind me. I started towards the stairs, then stopped and whirled toward him. He was just inside the threshold, bent double to take off his boots, the door still open behind him.

'You don't need to ask again — I know my answer already.' I held myself very still, preparing myself to deal with whatever the fallout was. 'It's a no, Nate.'

He put one Chelsea boot down neatly against the wall and calmly commenced prising off his other one. His eyes remained on mine, steady and unflinching, which was so far from the reaction I expected that I assumed I hadn't been clear enough.

'No,' I repeated, my voice only quavering slightly. 'I can't marry you. We broke up for — why the hell are you smiling? If this was some kind of prank—'

'It wasn't.' He placed his second boot beside the first, then straightened to his full height, though he didn't venture any closer to me. 'Believe me — I'd be smiling wider if you said yes. But I expected you to turn me down, even before everyone warned me that you would.'

'Sorry — *everyone?*'

'Everyone I confided in that I was going to do this, which was basically just Joe and Gemma. Joe thought you'd say a flat no, and Gemma reckoned you'd refuse to even listen to the proposal, or if you did, then chuck things at me once you heard it.' He thudded the door shut behind him, laughing a little by the time he swung back round toward me. 'Just saying no is by far the best of those outcomes, so yeah, I'm smiling.'

My head was swimming. 'I don't get it. Since . . . since you were certain I was going to turn you down, why did you bother asking?'

He raised his shoulders, suspending them high and taut for a few seconds, before releasing them. 'They thought you'd *start* by turning me down. Which, as Gemma pointed out to me rather brutally last night, is no more than I deserve after keeping you hanging for so many years. But the first step in changing that is telling you I was wrong, and that's what I'm here to do.'

I cut my eyes away from him and crossed my arms across my chest, then, recalling the ridiculous rubber gloves, peeled them off. 'And *that's what you're here to do*,' I croaked. 'Like it's as simple as that?'

'Exactly.'

Floundering for something else to say, I merely stared at him. His smirk didn't even lessen.

'Gah!'

I turned back to the stairs and sped up them without another word.

* * *

'Perfect proposal outfit,' I ground out, surveying my wall of open hanging rails. 'I'll give you perfect proposal outfit, Nathan Slater.'

I wasn't quite sure what constituted the perfect proposal outfit, but it certainly involved tactile fabric, colour and a bit of flesh on show, so I sought out the opposite. If I'd had a roll of bin bags to hand I might have fashioned the plastic into a neck to toe dress, but instead I slithered into corduroy trousers and a ribbed black jumper with a polo neck — as far from the perfect proposal outfit as I could muster with no notice.

'He bloody proposed,' I muttered as I stared at myself in the full-length mirror on the front of the wardrobe. 'Nate bloody proposed to me.'

It was everything I'd wanted, for more than ten years of my life. But it had finally occurred, five months too late, so I'd said the only thing that made any sense.

Downstairs, the latch on my front door clicked, as if it was being opened, and then thudded shut.

I raced to the window, holding my breath. Nate had proposed — then thought better of it, almost immediately?'

But instead of leaping into the driver's seat, he was opening the back of the van. He hauled out a couple of hessian bags, which had a baguette and a frying pan handle poking out of the top. Whistling, Nate wandered back towards my cottage with the haul of food.

I listened hard. Could he be leaving food on my doorstep before he left, or . . .

An instant later I had my answer, with clicks as the door was unlatched, then Nate's footsteps as he entered, and finally the slam of the door, reverberating up the stairs. He must have kicked it shut behind him, as was his habit when his hands were full.

Returning to the mirror, I examined my reflection as if it were that of a stranger. A stranger with lank hair, so in need of a wash that it was closer to brown than red. There were shadows beneath her eyes and her skin was sallow. Black really wasn't her colour.

I pulled off the jumper and replaced it with one which was a cashmere-cotton mix. Navy this time — a little less forbidding than black. And with a shawl collar, it revealed a sliver of the pale skin of my neck.

In the bathroom I combed my hair then twisted it up and pinned it. I pinched the apples of my cheeks and slicked on mascara and tinted lip balm. Then I took a deep breath, and descended the stairs.

Nate had taken off his hoodie, rolled his flannel shirt sleeves to the elbow, and put an apron on. His back was to me as he beat eggs beside my stove.

'You know you had no real food in at all?' he said over his shoulder. 'Lucky for you, I'd planned ahead.'

'For what?'

He turned and smiled. 'For brunch.'

When I didn't respond, he swivelled back to the eggs, giving them a final whisk then tipping them into my sole saucepan. 'You've got actual tins of spaghetti hoops in the cupboard. And those disgusting sausages in baked beans. I always thought Joe and Gem were exaggerating when they said you served those as meals as a student.'

I'd steeled myself for declarations of love and commitment from Nate. Not for teasing.

'I like them.'

He missed my warning undertone. 'Of course you do,' he said with a laugh. 'You've got rotten taste.'

His words stung, and I flinched. 'I don't know why you're bothering to cook for me, then.'

His back stiffened, but he removed the pan from the heat and switched the hotplate off before he turned again.

'You all right, Rosh?'

I couldn't suppress my snort. 'What the hell does that mean anyway?'

'What?'

I glared at him. '*You all right?* It's what you've always said, to kind of acknowledge that you might have said something that perhaps caused me to not be all right. And you know what? No, I'm not all right! And yes, it's *your* fault!'

He bit on his lower lip contemplatively. 'I'm sorry,' he said.

That was new, and I looked at him steadily. 'What are you sorry for?'

He sucked in a deep breath. 'I guess . . . for hurting your feelings, by teasing you like that. For turning up here unannounced. I just couldn't think of a way you'd agree to see me, after you blocked my number. And . . . and for taking you for granted for so many years. I'm really, really sorry for it all.'

It was only two steps to the closest stool at the scrubbed pine table. On it, was a steaming cup of tea. It was strong, with just a splash of milk to take it to the colour of saddle leather. Shakily, I took the two steps, sunk down onto the stool, grasped the mug and took a fortifying sip.

It wasn't just the correct shade, but exactly the right temperature; no one but Nate ever made me tea with precisely perfect tea:milk ratio. I wasn't sure that anyone else had ever even tried to.

Nate knew me like no other, and wanted to marry me. And, even more momentously, in many ways, he was sorry.

'You should have started with that, Nate,' I breathed. 'You should have started with *sorry*.'

* * *

We agreed to wait until after we'd eaten to resume our discussion of the heavy stuff, and instead caught each other up on the intervening months of our lives, beyond the snippets we'd shared in text messages. Or rather, Nate caught me up on his life, since every time he asked me a question I answered as briefly as possible and revolved the conversation back to him. It wasn't that I didn't want to open up in general, but that I had so much I didn't want to discuss, and little else to say.

I mulled over what Gemma could have told him about my attempts at dates as I chewed another mouthful of smoked salmon and scrambled eggs, then dismissed it. I didn't think she'd discuss it with him but even if she had, I was safe from him discovering the most shamefully pathetic aspects of my conduct because I'd never confessed those things to Gemma. She had no idea how close I'd come to leaping into bed with a married man, nor my overblown reaction to a kiss, setting up a near stranger as the one for me, and imagining a future together . . .

'You're shivering,' Nate said. He seized my empty mug and made me more tea. I watched his back as he made the quick, efficient motions, wondering how many cuppas he'd made me over the years. He'd brought me one in bed virtually every morning that we'd lived together, plus several more most days. So three a day, multiplied by . . . a lot of days.

I hadn't thought about that, and all the other things he'd done for me over the years, when he'd said that he didn't want to marry me. Nor when he'd been in touch, through the months apart, trying to keep some connection to me. And not even when he'd knelt in the rain to propose. I'd said no without giving it any thought. It was only when I heard him leaving the cottage that a panicked pang of regret had hit me.

'Thank you,' I said, as he returned to the table, holding the tea toward me, handle outward.

He sat down and drummed his hands on the edge of the table. 'You're quiet, Rosh.'

'I know.' I laid my knife and fork vertically across the plate and pushed the whole thing into the middle of the table. 'I've got a lot to think about.'

He mirrored my motions with his cutlery, slid his plate away, then planted his elbows in front of him, rested his chin on the back of his hands and met my gaze. 'Is one of them whatever happened with . . . whoever things fizzled out with. Before it . . . fizzled out, had it got serious?'

My throat tightened, and I gulped some tea without blowing first. It scalded my tongue slightly and I glugged back orange juice, grateful for the excuse to stall. 'It ended virtually before it even began,' I said eventually.

Relief was evident in his face. 'So it *wasn't* serious? I was worried I'd lost you to . . . whoever he was.'

'It wasn't serious,' I confirmed, hating myself for it. I was pretty sure he was asking whether I'd slept with anyone, in which case I was telling the truth. But with Tristan, it had felt serious on an emotional level, to me. Even though it was one-sided, and I was stupid and wrong and it had caused me nothing but hurt . . . 'I liked someone,' I blurted, my eyes on my plate so I didn't have to see Nate's relief drain away. 'I liked someone a lot, at one point . . .'

'The someone — the one it then fizzled out with?' His voice was almost gentle, but not quite, with an undertone of stiffness.

'Yes.' I met his eyes. 'Nothing happened. Not . . . beyond one kiss. And then it was over. But I liked him.'

Liked. Past tense. It was as close to the truth as I could get without falling apart at the seams.

He nodded. I couldn't read the expression in his eyes.

'Nate? If hearing that makes you want to take back the thing you asked me, then that would be fair enough.'

'Of course it doesn't. You liked someone and kissed him — I'd imagined a hell of a lot worse.' But as he spoke, he scrubbed at his hair, releasing a few dark spirals from the elastic, and I suddenly wished that I'd never admitted it in the first place.

'I've put that behind me. I don't want to discuss it again.'

'Me either,' he said wryly.

'What about you?' I tried for a tone of levity, but instead my voice come out all tinny. 'Any confessions about our time apart?'

'I've been entirely single, Rosh. Not looking. Just moping around, missing the woman I love.'

I took cover behind my tea again, not replying until I'd taken a few slow sips. 'You knew you loved me, all that time?'

'I told you I did. Told you I would.' It was the closest he'd got to an accusation in the entire conversation.

I bit the insides of my cheeks. 'You said *I love you, but* . . .'

'And you just heard the *but*, when the important words were the ones I said first!' He pulled the elastic from his hair, onto his wrist, then raked both hands through the curls, from forehead to the nape of his neck. 'Sorry to snap. It's my own stupidity I'm frustrated by, not your caution. Even as I said that *but*, all those months ago, I was regretting it. You'd waited for me, trusting me. And I got scared when you won the wedding, and said that stuff, and blew it.'

'You did blow it. Rejecting a wedding — and marrying me entirely, it . . . it really hurt.'

'I know.' He dropped his arms to his sides, heaving out a long sigh, then offered me his hands across the table.

I studied them for a few seconds. The white scar from when he'd been learning knife skills, a new burn mark on his thumb. He had rejected me, but he wasn't anymore. He was offering up everything I ever wanted with him, just like he served me up brunch.

I slid my hands into his palms, resting my fingers on his lightly.

His smile was watery. 'You know I came here to tell you I was wrong before, and how much I want to be with you. If I haven't made it clear enough already, then hear this: there's nothing I want more than to be with you again. I'm even excited by the thought of getting married. And I totally get that while I've been working up to this moment for a while, it came out of the blue to you, so I can't expect you to leave your new home to move right back into the flat—'

'This cottage will never be my home,' I said quickly. 'It's just the place I happen to be living.'

'Then I hope you'll move back in soon,' he breathed. 'But I won't press you for an answer, and I told Joe and Gemma not to hassle you about all this either. Before I go, though, I just want to confirm that my hope is correct, that your *no* wasn't a definitive for all time no, but instead, like . . . a maybe?'

It hit me then. Finally — *finally* — everything I'd wanted for so long was within my grasp. A handsome groom, enthusiastic about marrying me next June, but not only that. Also, by forgiving Nate, and moving on with him, I'd be erasing all my pathetic, desperate behaviour from the past six months, so I could finally forgive myself. If I could just say the word, and embrace my happy ending.

Embrace Nate.

My stomach twisted and my tongue stalled. I couldn't do it. Not with a tiny, shameful part of me still insistently wishing it was someone else across the table.

But I wasn't going to say no again, and let Tristan, who didn't give a shiny shite about me, steal my happy ending with Nate.

I just needed to buy a bit of time for my heart to catch up with my brain.

'Maybe,' I said unsteadily.

I couldn't have given away how close to a *yes* I was, I observed with relief, or he'd have looked disappointed rather than pleased.

'Good,' he said, his hands tightening around mine. An instant later and he'd risen to his feet and come round to pull me to my feet, stepping in close and lowering his mouth.

His lips grazed mine, and I jerked my head to the side.

'What?' he grumbled.

'You just said that you understood how I'd need time, and then you try to . . .' I bit back *maul me* just in time. 'I need time to get my head around *all* of this, not just the proposal. And space,' I added deliberately.

He shifted back slightly. 'I guess I was just hoping . . .' He shook his head, then held his arms up in mock surrender. 'Time, and space. If that's what you need, it's what you'll get.'

'It is. Aside from anything else, I've got costumes to finish by the end of the month.' I decided not to mention yet that after handing them over, I'd be moving in to help Abi with the babies.

'Is that, don't call me, I'll call you?'

I smiled rather ruefully. 'Yup.'

'But you will call me, when you're ready? Or text, or email — or write a letter? Anything, as long as it begins *yes, Nate, I'll move home and marry you.*'

I rolled my eyes. 'I think you should go now.'

'The washing-up—'

'I'll do it.'

'Can I ask one final thing, first?' He raised his index finger, pointing above him. At my bedroom.

I bristled. 'How the hell does *time and space* translate as jumping right back into bed—'

'Totally not what I meant, Rosh. I know you've come up with lots of ideas for your wedding. For *our* wedding, hopefully. As soon as you're ready, I want to see the mood boards. Just say the word.'

225

CHAPTER 22: A COUPLE

I arranged Mrs Holt's teal gown on her mannequin, and scrutinised the hem for loose threads. I'd snipped off the last of them when my phone rang. My guess was that it was Nate, finally cracking; it was ten days since his proposal and he wasn't nearly as patient at waiting as he thought he was. As I bent over to silence it, I saw Herbie's name on the screen, and snatched it up instead. 'Is Abi all right?'

'Oh no, this isn't Abi, it's Herbie.'

'I know that; your number's programmed into my phone. I asked if *Abi is okay?*'

'Ah. Well, that makes more sense.'

'So *is* Abi okay?' I said through gritted teeth.

'Of course.'

His vagueness had reached epic heights, and if I ground my teeth any harder, I'd have to spend a lot of money I didn't have at the dentist. 'Well, nice chat, Herbie. I'd better get back to work—'

'You can't come, then? *Abi,*' he hollered suddenly in the distance. 'Róisín can't make it.'

'Herbie,' I yelled down the line. 'HERBIE!'

There were some scuffles, then Abi spoke. 'Why can't you make it over?'

'I never said that, Herbie just didn't . . . whatever. You want me over at your place, now? Do I need to bring . . .' Unsure whether Herbie could hear, I didn't dare say bacon butties. '*Snacks?*'

'There's nothing you need to bring.' Her voice was curiously weak, now I came to think about it. 'Just hurry, please. It's an emergency.'

The line went dead.

Emergency. I re-dialled, then leaped to my feet and sprinted downstairs, the phone jammed under my chin. It rang and rang, as I shoved my feet into ankle boots.

'What kind of emergency?' I asked, as the call was answered. 'Are you in labour?'

With the phone pressed hard against my ear, I heard a shriek, and stiffened. Abi was yelling — and Abi never yelled. 'Bloody hell, you are in labour — I'll be there within half an hour!'

I shoved my arms into my coat, grabbed my bag and sprinted for the minibus. Jumping inside, I shoved the key in and rotated it. The engine spluttered, then died out.

I took a deep, calming breath, then tried again. The second splutter was even shorter, and death came faster.

I thumped on the steering wheel, cursing the stupid vehicle to hell and beyond, then attempted to start the thing again, even as I recognised the futility. This time, there wasn't even a splutter.

Sagging, I considered my options. The problem could well be the battery, since I'd driven the thing so little lately, and always with the lights and heating blaring, thanks to the cold weather. In which case, if Mr Holt had jump cables in his four-by-four, jump-starting it could be much faster than phoning round for a taxi prepared to come all the way out from Bath.

Before I'd even made a conscious decision, I was marching up the path to the Holts' cottage, and hammering on their door. 'Please — I need some help!'

Mrs Holt answered. 'Róisín, dearie, what is it?'

'Minibus won't start — I *think* it's just a flat battery — and I've got to get into Bath urgently — my friend's in labour, and she's having twins, and I promised to be there . . .'

'No need for any panic; I'm sure you can borrow one of the site vehicles. Now my Humphrey's over at the house, but he should be nearly finished, so if I ring up there, he can deliver one of them down here for you.'

'Thank you,' I breathed, as she turned away. 'Thank you so much.'

I returned to my cottage, rather than waiting in hers, using the time to bank the fire and pack a holdall. I rushed back outside the instant I heard a vehicle bumping over the track.

Mrs Holt was standing in her doorway, illuminated by the rectangle of light thrown from the lamps inside. I couldn't make out her first few words, over the four-by-fours' engine, and heaved my holdall up onto my shoulder to pace closer. '. . . offered to drive you straight there. And leave the minibus key with him, so he can sort out your battery later.'

'I'd much rather just borrow it,' I hollered, but, with her duty done, she'd already returned to the warmth of her fire.

The car pulled into the space beside the Holts' cottage and backed straight out, so it was facing in the opposite direction. Toward the front gate, which was a faster route into Bath than the side gate, when there were no visitors' cars clogging up the drive.

Mr Holt braked, then leaned across the front passenger seat to open the door for me.

'Thanks for being prepared to drive me.' I chucked my holdall into the footwell, and clambered in after it. 'But if I could just borrow—' the word shrivelled on my tongue as I glanced at him.

Because the driver wasn't Mr Holt at all, but a slimmer, fairer, younger man, and he was already rolling the car forward.

'What are you doing, Tristan?'

'Getting you into Bath as quickly as possible?' The light was dim, but I thought his eyes flicked in my direction, before returning to look out of the windscreen an almost imperceptible instant later. 'Mrs Holt was highly distressed to hear that her husband currently had his arm down a drain, so couldn't come to the phone immediately. When I asked if I could help, she explained what you needed.'

'What I needed was a jump start of the minibus. *She* suggested I borrow one of these Sylverley vehicles, which would be fine. I really don't need a lift.' *Especially from you*, I thought, and it seemed to hang in the chilly air, unsaid.

He drew the car to a halt and turned toward me, and I stared down at my hands, refusing to face more of his coldness from the library. 'Mrs Holt doesn't hold a license, so she hadn't considered that you're not one of the named drivers on the estate's motor insurance.'

'Shite.' It hadn't occurred to me either, though it should have. 'Do you have jump cables in the boot? I really don't want to . . .' *Sit beside you in the dark, in a cruel parody of being a couple.* 'Put you to the hassle of taking me.'

'Afraid not. And it's really no hassle. I owe you one for when you helped me rush Bear to the vet, due to the same technicality.'

I swallowed hard. That trip to the vet directly led to what I really, really mustn't think about. However many memories threw themselves into the forefront of my mind, triggered by his voice and scent and close proximity after more than a month of distance.

He drummed his long fingers on the steering wheel. 'So? Okay for me to drive on?'

I inclined my head, before recalling, flustered, that he wasn't looking toward me. 'That's fine. Thanks.'

'You're very welcome.' Perhaps I'd been more successful in keeping the begrudging note from my voice than I'd thought, because his own tone was light and unoffended as he accelerated.

I fixed my eyes ahead, and promised myself that, somehow, this would be okay. If I kept my eyes averted from him, and conversed as little as possible, I'd maintain the facade of the physical distance I'd so carefully established since I'd recognised my own pathetic desperation. That would be enough to protect me from sinking into deeper feelings for him . . . into wishing things were different . . . into obsessing on the all-too-short period when they had been . . .

He cleared his throat as he turned from the drive onto the road. 'It should be me thanking you, to be honest.'

His throat. I'd nuzzled into it, as I caught my breath from our kiss. The softness of his skin there had contrasted with the faint stubble—

I had to stop replaying the memory, before it seared so deep I saw it every time I closed my eyes.

But it was impossible to *not* think about an image, just from choice. I'd have to replace it instead. Overlay it with something one hundred per cent unsexy.

'It got me out of assisting Mr Holt's attempt to unblock the drains,' Tristan continued. 'Especially as I'm pretty sure we need to call the professionals back in.'

Drains. I closed my eyes and pictured a drain, backed up with gruesome sludge; imagined the foul scent emanating from it.

'Are you okay, Róisín? You look a bit queasy.'

'Yeah. Just . . . motion sickness.'

He dropped down to third gear. 'Because I was taking a country lane too fast. Apologies. We'll be on the main road shortly.'

'It wasn't the speed. Go as fast as you want.' *As fast as you can, so I can get out of here*, I whimpered internally.

'I haven't seen you around much lately,' Tristan said abruptly.

I gave a disinterested hum. 'I've been working flat out on the costumes. Perky wants them by the end of next week.'

'I've been wondering about your accent,' Tristan said into the silence, a short while later. 'Occasionally there's a hint of Irish, especially in your intonation, but other times I don't hear it at all. Have you lost it since moving to England?'

I considered and dismissed half a dozen different ways of wording *none of your bloody business*. He was putting himself

230

out for me, even if it was his escape from blocked drains, so I couldn't sit here refusing to converse, however much I wanted to. 'I was born in Derry, but I've lived in England virtually my whole life.'

'In the West Country?'

'London.' The one-word answer felt too stark. 'I moved to Bath after uni.'

'And you mentioned being from a big family — do you go back to London to see them often?'

I bit my lip. The only time I'd mentioned my family was on the evening-I-must-stop-recalling. 'They're all in Derry these days,' I said flatly. I don't know why I continued beyond that. Maybe because so many people had greeted the information with awkward silence, that I thought it might shut him up. 'My mother moved my siblings back there after my dad died.'

'I didn't know you'd lost your father,' he said softly. 'I'm so sorry to hear it.'

I clenched my jaw so tightly shut that it took a minute before I could reply. 'It happened a long time ago. It doesn't matter anymore.'

He slowed for the roundabout ahead. 'It always matters. Sorrow of that type becomes easier to bear, with the passing of time, but it never leaves.'

I couldn't miss the recognition in his voice. 'You've lost someone close to you too. A parent as well?' By gluing my eyes to the taillights of the car ahead, I managed not to glance at him as I waited for his reply.

'Yes,' he said. And then, with as much reluctance as if I'd torn the words from his throat with a rusty knife, 'My mother died when I was twelve. I return to Kent regularly, to see my grandparents.'

Grandparents, not father. Before I found the right words with which to ask, he nodded at the *Welcome to Bath* sign we were passing. 'Where do your friends live?'

I wasn't sure afterwards if my downfall was triggered by our similar tragedies, or just the illumination from the full-beam headlamps of the oncoming car, but suddenly I was staring at him. His shirt was thin and faded, like it had been sun-bleached during years of wear, which drew attention to his muscles, bunched across his shoulders. The sleeves were rolled up, exposing his forearms. The hairs on them were a brighter gold even than the hair on his head.

Then the car and the moment passed, and he was plunged back into near darkness. I twisted sharply towards the side window, scrunching up my eyes.

'Róisín? Where do your friends live?' he asked again.

'They're in Lansdown,' I said hollowly. 'Drop me along the London Road, I'll walk the last bit.'

'In the dark?' he scoffed. 'What's the address?'

'I don't need dropping at the door—'

'What if her labour's been speedier than expected, and they've already gone into hospital? You don't have transportation to get home.'

'True,' I agreed. I checked my phone, but there was nothing more from them. And I'd just about make it there within thirty minutes, thanks to Tristan. 'I've got a key to their place, though,' I said, propping my head on the window. 'So I'd be fine to walk the last part, but if you really don't mind dropping me the whole way, I'd appreciate it. I should get there quickly.'

'You're worried about your friend.'

'And her babies,' I breathed.

'Was that *babies*, plural?'

'They're having twins.'

We sat in silence as he traversed several sets of traffic lights.

'Would you rather be left alone to think, or distracted? I could put on the radio, or we could talk about . . . I don't know.'

'Talking about *I don't know* sounds scintillating,' I said, far more breathily than I'd intended. Within the confines of the city, the car interior brightened every few seconds when we passed one of the regularly spaced street lamps, and I looked through my lashes at his hands, gripping the steering wheel. Then his wrists, which flexed as he spun the wheel to avoid a wobbly cyclist with no lights.

Nate would have beeped his horn. Tristan just released a *pssh* sound from between his teeth, and continued on more slowly.

Nate. I hadn't thought about him once, in the whole journey. Nor before, when I'd needed an urgent lift. I'd considered calling a taxi to come out from Bath, but not asking Nate, who loved me, and had proposed to me, just days earlier.

'We could distract you with discussion about something interesting, then,' Tristan said. 'To be honest—' I caught his glance at me — 'there's something I've been wanting to say. But now might not seem to you to be the time, in which case, it can wait.'

'What kind of thing?' I asked idly, my mind still on Nate. Maybe his proposal, and my *maybe*, was too recent for my brain to have caught up.

Tristan slid us through a green light, indicating to turn right. 'It's regarding what happened after we were last alone in a vehicle together.'

'What?' I glanced at him, then did a double take. His lips were pinched tightly together, like that time in the library. And he wanted to talk about . . . my breath caught in my throat.

Jay-walking pedestrians left us stranded past the green light but unable to turn right, and the prolonged tick of the indicator switch seemed to echo the thrum of my pulse.

Tristan met my gaze head on, and I read apology in his eyes. Blood rushed to my head, and my cheeks turned to flame. He could tell I was still, pathetically, attracted to him, and planned to apologise, yet again, for the encounter that had left him ashamed and me aching for more.

'I don't want to,' I said quickly.

He nodded, just once.

Once the route had cleared and he'd manoeuvred us onto the side street, I told him Abi's address, then silently planned what to say. I left it for the very final moment, when he'd pulled up in the only empty space, much further down the street.

'I appreciate the lift, Tristan,' I said, fixing my eyes above his head. My voice was steady, but my nails bit into my palms. 'But you've already expressed your regret about . . . what happened, and there's nothing else to be said. I'm sorry it's awkward in the meantime, but rest assured, you won't be reminded of it for much longer.' I opened the door, and slipped out. 'I've . . . been offered a new place to live, so I'll be moving out of Sylverley as soon as I hand the costumes over.'

Before I'd made it two paces, I heard him call my name, and then louder, as I took a third step, and I whirled round. 'No offence, but your opinion on the matter really isn't of any interest.'

'It's not that. Uh . . . you forgot your bag.' He even had the gall to sound apologetic about my mistake, and I only narrowly suppressed screaming at the top of my lungs.

'Sorry,' I mumbled instead, as I leaned inside to grab it.

'Róisín? Phone the estate whenever you want to be collected — Mr Holt will happily come out.'

'No need. Nate will bring me.' His inhale was audible, and I added, 'He proposed, and I'm moving back in with him' — before I paced off again, this time with my holdall's strap clenched tight in my fists.

I didn't let myself break into a run until I'd rounded the corner, when I sprinted the final few steps, arriving at Abi's front door with my heart pounding.

They'd painted their front door in wavy zebra stripes since I'd last visited, but I barely even registered it as I rapped, then bounced up and down on my toes against the icy air.

'Hey,' Herbie said, opening it a crack. 'You came!'

'I did. Erm . . . can I come in?'

'Give me a minute.'

The door shut again, and I screwed my eyes up in disbelief at his lack of urgency when his wife was in labour. Even Herbie should be . . .

Hang on, I thought, reconsidering the phone call. I'd surmised that Abi was in labour, but neither of them had actually ever said so. If I'd interpreted the emergency wrong, and put myself through all that with Tristan for no good reason, I was going to sob.

'What's going on?' I asked, the instant Herbie answered the door again. His eyes were particularly heavy-lidded, I noted, as I followed him inside, and I sniffed suspiciously. 'Is Abi in labour, or what?'

He touched his fingers to his lips, then slowly opened their lounge door. Abi was reclined back in the armchair, her arms filled with bundles of hemp.

No, just two bundles, each swathed in a hemp blanket and cradled at a breast.

'Surprise!' she whispered, her eyes shining with tears. 'Borage and Hyssop came a few weeks early.'

CHAPTER 23: SWEET NOTHINGS

'I'm so sorry, little spice jars,' I whispered, bending over the cradle the twins shared. 'Please don't hate me for your names.' Hyssop emitted a tiny squeak, and Borage half-opened his eyes. I stroked from their downy foreheads to their noses with my forefingers, and after a few minutes they dropped into slumber, like their mother on the other side of the room.

'Do you want—'

I sliced a finger to my lips, and Herbie slapped his hand over his mouth.

'How did you get them to sleep?' he mouthed, out on the landing.

I didn't reply until we'd tiptoed down to the kitchen. 'Mostly witchcraft.'

His face fell. 'There's no point teaching me, then. I've never managed to awaken my supernatural abilities.'

'*Joke*, Herbie. You think I'm really a witch?'

'Why not?' He lifted the lid off the stockpot and sniffed appreciatively. 'My friend Cirrus is.'

'Well, I'm not.' I pushed up my sleeves and dug around for the plug in the sink full of encrusted dishes. 'Which means any tricks I've got with babies came from being the eldest in a big family, and are eminently learnable.'

'Even by me?'

'Definitely. Umm, are you sure adding more turmeric's a good idea? That soup already smells quite pungent.'

'It's porridge, not soup; for Abi, when she wakes up.'

'Lovely,' I said, with heartfelt pity for my friend, as I ran hot water into the sink.

Herbie hummed a discordant tune and flicked his long hair rhythmically as he stirred the concoction. When he eventually paused to taste it, he smacked his lips, then grated in copious amounts of root ginger. I blamed the steam from the washing-up for my eyes watering, and cracked open the window.

'Would you like some? I made plenty.'

My stomach gurgled a protest. 'I'm not hungry.'

'No, that's not it,' Herbie said, tilting his head and scanning over me contemplatively. 'There's something else blocking you from accepting.'

'You think?' I pushed the window wider open.

'I sense it,' he said. His eyes sprang wide open. 'Hey — maybe I've got supernatural abilities, after all? Becoming a father could have brought them to bloom.'

'Cool.' I scrubbed hard at a particularly grimy wooden spoon.

'They're still in a latent stage, though, because I can't get a strong sense of what your specific blockage is . . .' He tasted his concoction again, then opened the fridge, got a bowl of shredded kale, and tipped it in, then froze. 'It just came to me.'

'Yes?' I asked cautiously.

'You're sort of . . . feeling pain about something. Am I right?'

It was Herbie, so I could've said absolutely anything but for some reason my lips parted and I came out with the truth. 'Yes. Yes, you are, actually.'

He trotted over to the table, sat down, and pulled out the seat next to him. 'We should talk about it.'

'I don't want to.'

'Of course you don't. But you need to.'

I slotted the final dish on the draining board and fished for more utensils, but there were none left in the water. I was all out of distractions. So I dried my hands on a tea towel and, regretting it already, stepped over to sink into the chair. Herbie made a face like his son had while filling his nappy with meconium a few hours earlier. 'I sense I can advise, but only if you can give me a bit more.'

'That would be a hard no. Too embarrassing.'

He scrunched his face, and rubbed circles on his temples. 'I'll try my best,' he muttered. Then his voice rose, and he chanted gobbledegook. 'I'm getting nothing,' he said sorrowfully. 'Maybe if you concentrate hard on whatever this pain is, and channel it through to me silently, I'll come up with some advice.'

He shut his eyes and resumed his ministrations on his temples, and the chanting. Having distracted myself from thinking about Tristan by helping with the babies all night, the last thing I wanted to do was concentrate on it now, exhausted and sleep deprived. Nor did I want another crashing wave of guilt about why my mind immediately went to Tristan, not to Nate, who was offering up everything I'd ever wanted.

Herbie's face brightened. 'It came to me — the advice you need!'

Against my better judgement, my heart thrummed within my rib cage. 'What is it?'

He brought his hands together, like a priest preparing a benediction. 'A memory appeared in my mind,' he said, in a low, confidential tone. 'From the visit we once made to a shaman. He shared knowledge from ancient Native Americans, to crush certain jewel-like berries into an elixir, which has mystical cleansing abilities.'

'Cleansing abilities for what? I don't get it.'

His voice dropped lower still. 'We'd consulted him for a blockage that Abi was experiencing — the same painful feeling, deep inside, that you've described. She couldn't go at all.'

'Go where? Herbie, I'm mystified.'

'*Go* go. You know, *relieve* herself.'

Catching on, I didn't know whether to laugh or sob, and settled on a kind of exhausted indignation. 'Herbie, I don't mean I've got pain when I pee! And seriously, if the jewel-like berries were cranberries, then sure, drinking cranberry juice can help clear a urinary tract infection — but I hope you didn't pay that shaman too much money?'

'Oh no,' Herbie said blithely. 'He worked on a barter system. It only cost me a week's work.'

In anyone else's line of business, giving up the proceeds of a week's work for advice that could have been elicited from the top hit on google would have been highly alarming. But when I'd stayed with Abi and Herbie I'd learned his typical work output. 'In other words, he imparted *Native American wisdom*, and you gave him a cardigan?'

'One and a half cardigans.'

I suppressed the urge to ask him what anyone would want with half a cardigan. The conversation was bizarre enough already.

There was a rattling sound outside the room, and we both stiffened, listening hard.

'It's Abi,' Herbie said, leaping up and opening the door. 'Light of my life, you've awoken.'

I distracted myself from their croons of sweet nothings with my phone, forwarding the birth announcement, which Abi had texted to all their friends and family in the early hours, to Nate.

His reply blinked back within seconds.

—*Tell them congrats from me. You ok?*

—*Just knackered. Been up cuddling babies all night.*

A high-pitched wail drifted downstairs. It woke their sibling, who also started to cry, and we all sprang into action. I checked nappies while Herbie helped Abi into her rocking chair, then positioned each baby within a V-shaped cushion on her lap, so she could feed them in tandem.

'Any chance of a cuppa?' she asked, wincing slightly as they each latched and began sucking furiously.

'Dandelion root, lemon balm, nettle leaf or—'

'Nettle leaf's perfect.'

Herbie glanced at me.

'I'm fine, thanks,' I said hastily.

'I shouldn't have worried about him taking to father-hood,' Abi said, as he wandered out. 'Y'know, I appreciate your offer to stay as long as we need you, but you've got to finish those costumes, and I think we're going to be fine.'

'I don't—' At the look on her face, I forced myself to stop, and swallowed. She wasn't releasing me from the commitment because the twins' early arrival meant my com-mission wasn't complete. They really didn't need me here. 'You're right,' I said thickly. 'The four of you are going to be totally fine. I'll leave you to your babymoon.'

Thankfully her eyes had moved to the double photo frame on her coffee table. On one side it displayed a photo of what I knew to be the day they met; Abi in a pinafore and wellies and Herbie topless in a pair of fluorescent Speedos, their arms around each other. The other side contained their wedding photo; Abi in the one-shouldered wedding dress I'd knocked up with three days' notice, Herbie in a collarless shirt and braces, kissing her hand.

'Can you believe that day at Glastonbury was only the summer before last? Everything changed so quickly. So per-fectly.' Her smile faded a little. 'I want all this for you, too. I'm sorry it didn't work out with . . . whoever he was.'

My lips parted, to tell her it was fine, that I'd been wrong, that I was on the cusp of reconciling with Nate. But tears were threatening, and instead I excused myself and went into the bathroom, where I ran the cold tap until the water was freez-ing, then splashed my face. Then I pulled my phone out.

—Sorry for the lack of notice, but any chance of a lift home ASAP?

—Absofuckinglutely! See you shortly.

Nate's enthusiasm was puzzling; I'd half expected a whinge about being too understaffed at the café to give me a lift. He really did love me, if he was that keen to snatch

240

half an hour with me. It almost helped with the ache in my chest. Almost.

* * *

'I'll sort the minibus battery out immediately, so I can be right back here if there's a problem,' I told Herbie, as he saw me out the front door. Hyssop was swathed in a blanket against his chest, as he rubbed her back. 'So don't hesitate to call in an emergency.'

'Scout's honour,' he said.

I tore myself away and headed up the pavement to watch out for Nate where there was an empty space for him to pull in. But he came round it too fast to see me, and swung in front of their house, double-beeping his horn as he lowered his window.

'Why did you do that?' I huffed, marching back along the pavement. 'You could have startled Hyssop!'

'What?'

'She's fine,' Herbie called. 'Hi, Nate.' If he was surprised to see him, he didn't let on. Hyssop squawked as a strand of her father's waist-length hair fell forward onto her face, and Herbie tossed his head, flicking it all back.

Nate narrowed his eyes, then tossed his own head to similarly flick his shoulder-length curls. I rolled my eyes as I threw in my holdall and got in beside him.

'Abi doing all right?' he asked as he moved the van off.

I yawned, then inclined my neck to lean back against the headrest. 'She's taking to motherhood like a duck to water.'

He glanced either way at the junction, and turned the corner. 'Just as well, since she's ended up with twins, hey? What a nightmare.'

'Not really. They hoped for two children ultimately, so they're chuffed to have achieved that so quickly. And the babies are adorable.'

'Double the shitty nappies though. And they'll be knackered forever.' Before I'd decided whether I had the energy to argue the point, he slung an arm behind his seat and scooped up a paper bag, which he deposited on my lap. 'Thought you might fancy breakfast.'

Inside was nestled a warm pain-au-chocolat, the pastry flaking, the dark chocolate on either end glossy. 'You're the best,' I groaned, sinking my teeth in.

'Napkins are in the bottom of the bag, before you ask.'

I finished it all too quickly and wiped my fingers. 'That was amazing.' I darted a look at him, appreciating his profile, with a well-shaped nose over full lips. He was objectively so good looking; I had to find something to feel beyond gratitude. 'Thanks so much — and for the lift. It was a nice surprise that you could get out of the café so quickly.'

'Are you kidding? I dropped everything to bring you back home — I'd have closed the café for a while if it came to it.' He reached over and squeezed my nearer knee.

I stared down at it, then drew my legs together, angling them away from him. He returned his hand to the steering wheel, frowning. 'What's wrong?'

Everything. 'I'm . . . I guess I'm still not comfortable with the . . . touchy-feely stuff.'

The furrows on his forehead deepened. 'How's that going to work with one bedroom? The sofa bed's all well and good, but it makes my back sore after a few nights—'

'Nate,' I said uncertainly.

'And anyway, you need that room to work in so it's not—'

Impatience replaced my incomprehension. '*Nate!*'

He emergency braked, then stared at me. 'You can't yell like that at the driver, Rosh!'

'Pull over, please. We need to talk.'

'We can talk at home,' he said mulishly. 'We'll figure something out, with the . . . bedroom situation. You're coming back to me — that's the main thing.'

'Pull in, Nate. Now.'

As he found a space and reversed into it, muttering mutinously under his breath, I reread our message chain.

'Any chance of a lift home ASAP,' I said shakily, after he switched off the engine.

'I already am, Rosh.'

'No, I'm reading what I wrote. By *home*, I wasn't actually referring to your flat.'

His large brown eyes shot to mine. 'But you couldn't have meant Sylverley — you said it's not your home, just a short-term place to live, or whatever.'

'I know. I don't know why I typed that . . . tiredness, I guess.'

Nate flattened his hands and drummed them on the steering wheel. 'So you're not coming home? Not marrying me?'

I opened my mouth to explain. I was planning on accepting his proposal, and moving back to the flat, once the costumes were complete. But his truculent expression forestalled me. I snapped my jaw shut again and fiddled with the paper bag, empty of everything but crumbs and a napkin. 'We're arguing again — before we've even reconciled.'

'I know,' he said, on a sigh.

I thought about Abi's double picture frame, and crumpled the bag up, wadding it into a tight ball and squeezing. 'Nate? What do you really want for us — if there is to be an us — in an ideal world?'

'I want to be with you, like I keep saying. I don't know how to prove it except repeating it as many times as it takes—'

'That's not . . . I want specifics, about how you see our future panning out.'

He raked both hands through his curls. 'I guess . . . you moving to the flat again, obviously. And I'd like it if you'd let me put my grandmother's ring back on your finger, and we could tell everyone we know that we're engaged — for real this time. After that, it'll be fun to plan the wedding together — make the most of every freebie, max out the guest list, taste Sylverley's best food and wine and choose which we want.' He lowered his hands, stared at them like he didn't quite know what to do with them, then rested them on the

243

steering wheel. 'We'll have an amazing wedding day, and I'm not saying that because it's what I reckon you want to hear. I'm looking forward to it, too.'

'And afterwards? What would happen in the weeks and months after our wedding?'

He twisted his torso toward me. 'Why do I feel like this is some kind of test?'

I raised my shoulders; I wasn't entirely sure myself. I just knew that, since his proposal, something had been conspicuous by its absence. 'If there's a right answer, I don't have it either. But I think . . . I think I'll know it, if I hear it.'

'Bloody hell.' He scrubbed at his face. 'After our wedding . . . the honeymoon, of course. The café's done well lately, so we'll splash out on wherever we fancy. Seychelles, maybe? And then . . . back to the flat, and our businesses, and life goes back to normal.' I raised an eyebrow, as his voice strengthened. 'That's what I want, Rosh. What we used to have . . . plus the wedding day of our dreams.'

My eyes were stinging, and as I dug the heels of my hands into the sockets, silence descended.

'These aren't happy tears, right?' he asked eventually, as quietly as I'd ever heard him speak. 'Talk to me, Rosh. You owe me that much.'

It took some time before I could raise my head. 'You proposed marriage. But what you've actually got your head around is a wedding.' My voice had an unnatural, drained quality to it. 'And I know this is ironic, given everything that's happened, but . . . I've realised that finding the one for me doesn't mean finding a groom. Because . . . because an amazing wedding day isn't enough for me anymore. Maybe it never was.' I hiccupped twice in succession. 'What I actually need is an amazing marriage. And even if you wanted that too, and were excited about all the same things as me — like babies — it wouldn't be right. Because . . . I don't love you anymore.'

He thudded his forehead down onto the steering wheel. 'Fuck's sake, Rosh. Is this about whoever the twat was who you kissed?'

'My name's Róisín!' I'd spoken in one urgent, angry, exhale, and as I gulped in another breath, the fight drained out of me. 'Whatever. None of it matters now anyway.' All I knew was that it was over, this time for good. And that since I suddenly couldn't bear our proximity, it must be even worse for Nate. I fumbled for the strap of my holdall as I opened the door.

'So that's it,' he said as I stepped out. It didn't sound like a question.

CHAPTER 24: APPEALING

Gemma came into sight, her head above the cars parked on the opposite side of the street, and I stood stiffly, my limbs cold from the long walk to meet her. My oldest friend was striding to the pedestrian crossing, so within seconds I could unburden myself—

As she rounded the last car and pivoted to cross the road, I saw that she was pushing Esme's wheelchair. My goddaughter was swathed in bobbly hat, scarf, coat and mittens, her nose tilted into the air like a meerkat.

'Fairy Godmother — I came too!' she shrieked, when her eyes met mine.

'Shite,' I muttered, before setting my face into something that hopefully approximated a smile. 'What a nice surprise!'

Gemma's eyes narrowed as they drew closer. 'Liar,' she mouthed, and then, in my ear as we hugged, 'What the fuck's wrong?'

I shook my head. It was impossible to discuss without getting upset, and I had no intention of worrying Esme. I bent down to greet her, and when I stood again, Gemma was examining me critically.

'We're not going to a coffee shop after all, Esme,' Gemma said. 'Let's buy something to feed the ducks.'

* * *

Gemma snatched an opportunity for a private word as soon as we were inside Tesco Metro, where Esme rotated her wheels towards the dried food aisle.

'Sorry I had to bring her. We've got someone at the house, confirming the specifications for the adaptations, and Joe didn't fancy child-wrangling at the same time.'

'The council accepted your appeal? That's the first good news I've had in ages.'

'Nope. Bastards turned us down again. It's a representative from the charity visiting today — did I mention them before? They can fund part of it, maybe even all of it, if their latest fundraising campaign takes off.' She broke off to insist Esme put the Coco Pops back and picked up oats.

Esme wanted the coins to pay for it herself, and rolled up to the check-out.

'Send me the charity's details, would you?' I couldn't afford to contribute much — especially, I realised with a sinking heart, now that I needed to find a room to rent within a week, but I'd do what I could.

'Sure. But enough of all that — I'm just glad the form filling's over, and there's only builder's dust to contend with. Tell me why you look like you're responsible for killing someone?'

'Don't joke — that's not far off,' I said miserably.

Her eyes narrowed again, but then Esme's purchase was complete and we had a small girl observer once more, and kept the conversation neutral as we traversed to the park with an ornamental lake and large duck population. When Esme put the brakes on her wheelchair and threw her first handful of oats towards them, Gemma and I soundlessly moved back a few metres.

'You ended it with Nate, before it even began,' Gemma said, scrutinising me, as ducks waddled out of the pond to peck at the oat-strewn grass. Whatever she saw in my face was enough to confirm her suspicion. 'Bloody hell.'

Her dismay made me blink. 'Why are you pissed at me?'

'I'm not.' She tucked a tumbling strand of blonde hair into her hat, then pulled a face. 'I'm frustrated. He made me swear not to hound you about it, but I knew it was a mistake to agree. I reckoned there was time yet, though, that you'd stick your head in the sand for ages.'

I pondered on that. 'It all . . . came to a head, I suppose, because I certainly hadn't been planning to turn him down. Almost . . . almost the opposite.'

She snorted, and stomped over to check on Esme, scaring all the ducks back into the pond in the process. Esme crossly told her to back off, and she wandered back to me, scowling. 'I reckon, if I'd knocked your and Nate's heads together at the exact right moment, you'd be planning your wedding right now.'

'You're probably right.' I didn't add that if it had worked, within a few years we'd have been negotiating a divorce. 'But he's not the one for me, so I'm glad you didn't.'

'What made you suddenly so sure?'

I kicked at a pile of leaves. The top layer had lost their crispness, and the bottom ones had decomposed to slime. 'Who knows.'

'You do,' she said, unexpectedly.

I let myself recall the searing sensation of Tristan's lips on mine for a single second, before concentrating hard on the squelchy leaves. 'I'm not going there.'

She expelled air loudly through her teeth. 'Well, what's done is done,' she said eventually. 'At least there's still, what, over six months until the wedding date? I'll re-upload your profile to *My Single Pal* as soon as I'm home.'

I opened my mouth to decline. Then snapped it shut; Gemma was right, my wedding was six months away, and I had no groom. Either I had to sort my strategy for looking without being pathetic, or . . . or I had to face facts. I'd entered the competition out of desperation, and I no longer wanted to be desperate. 'There's no need.'

'Oh, come on. There's a zero-point-zero per cent chance of a serendipitous encounter with a hot historian in a library—'

'That's not true, actually. But it doesn't matter. My point wasn't that I'm quitting actively looking for a groom. I'm quitting even hoping for one. I've . . . I think I've got to turn the prize down.' Gemma's mouth dropped open, and I rushed on. 'You'll have to advise me how to break it to Esme that I won't need a bridesmaid anytime soon.'

'What's not soon?' Esme had wheeled over without either of us noticing.

'Err . . . the summer holidays,' Gemma said swiftly.

'But you know what *is* soon, Fairy Goddaughter?' I asked, grateful for her interruption. I was shaking slightly from my snap decision, and in no state to deal with further inquisition from Gemma on my motives. 'December! So have you thought about what you might want for Christmas?'

'Yup. I already told it all to Santa.'

'Did Mummy help you write the letter?'

'Oh no. I told him what I wanted tel — telly—'

'Telepathically,' Gemma put in wryly.

Esme crooked her finger, beckoning me, and I leaned down. 'It's a test, to check if he's really magical, or just a dressed-up man in a shop like what Tom at school said.'

'But . . . uh, how about you also write a list, in case you forget what you wanted?'

'We've tried that,' Gemma mouthed, which was backed up by her outraged daughter.

'Santa might read it, and cheat! So nope, the list is only in my head. And then if I get the toys I want, I'll know Santa's got real magic.'

'Give me strength,' Gemma muttered under her breath. From the set of her shoulders I knew she wasn't only referencing her daughter. 'Chuck the rest of those oats to the ducks right away, Esme, we're going home.'

'Can Fairy Godmother come?'

Gemma glanced at me, and I read the tacit permission in her eyes. Not just to come over, but to tell Esme, once I was there. I stared pleadingly back at her mother. 'I've got to get back to Sylverley. My deadline's in a week . . .'

'After that,' Gemma said grimly.

'After that,' I agreed.

Thankfully Esme distracted herself by burbling away about school as Gemma pushed her out of the park. As I trailed after them, Esme raised her voice to be heard over a peal of bells from the church up ahead.

'Oh, look,' she squealed, and Gemma stopped walking abruptly. The smartly-dressed crowd outside the church were applauding the bride and groom, who paused, beaming, under the porch as their photographer captured them from every angle.

The bells ended and they stepped forward, arm in arm, their guests throwing confetti into the air.

Esme gazed up at the multi-coloured strands fluttering in the wind. 'What's that pretty stuff called?'

'Confetti,' Gemma and I said together.

'Can you have confetti for your wedding, Fairy Godmother? *Please*?'

I exchanged a loaded glance with Gemma.

'Listen up, Esme,' I said immediately, to stop myself chickening out. 'I've got something a bit sad I need to tell you.'

DECEMBER: SIX MONTHS TO GO

CHAPTER 25: THE BIG DAY

Locking my own emotions up deep inside me had been the only way to get through confessing to Esme, and the numbness had lingered as I found a cab and returned to Sylverley, where I wrote a list of what I had to finish on the costumes. At the bottom I added three more items: *find somewhere to live, pack up cottage, inform Perky I can't accept the prize*.

I'd started from the top of the list, with the fiddly sleeves that still needed to be inserted into Amelia's gown.

Four long days later, five of the costumes were complete. Tristan's mannequin, however, was still swathed in a sheet. Before I could face it, I stuck my ear buds in and turned on a heavy metal playlist that I'd made to drown out my emotions when I had to finish making a wedding dress after an argument with Nate. It had done the job, making it so hard to concentrate on the garment that I had no brain space left to fret on anything emotional. I adjusted the volume until it was loud enough to deafen but not permanently scar my eardrums, then flicked the sheet onto the ground. His . . . *the* tailcoat and blouson shirt were finished, aside from a few hanging threads. The waistcoat needed top-stitching, and there were no form of trousers at all.

I cracked my knuckles, and began.

By Friday I had a banging headache and six complete and ironed costumes, hanging in a row within the protection of garment bags. I surveyed them giddily, then glanced at my list. After delivering them, the following morning, I could spend the rest of the weekend packing. But finding somewhere new to live couldn't be put off for a moment longer. Since Gemma had builders in and Abi was babymooning, I'd have to rent storage space for most of my belongings, and commit to a short-term room rental, within any shared house in Bath advertising a spare room. Once my final cheque cleared from Sylverley, I'd have hopefully found a cheap studio . . . Panic coursed through me, and I forced myself to slow my breathing until my heart stopped racing.

'One step at a time,' I muttered, opening my laptop. Before I navigated to a search engine, I saw that there were five missed video calls from Aoife. I hovered the cursor over her name. Clicking on it would be yet more avoidance of taking that first step. But *five* missed calls could be an emergency . . .

I connected the call. 'Everything okay?'

I knew before she answered that it was, from her contorted position on her bed, painting her toe nails. 'I saw some wile nice fabric for the bridesmaids' dresses, but Mammy wouldn't buy it unless I talked to you first.'

Her urgency was about her big day. Of bloody course.

'It's pink, and Mammy's concerned it won't go with your hair. I said it's not a problem, Róisín can just bleach her hair for my wedding, like. But Mammy said you might throw a fit—'

'I don't have time for this now.' My voice, which began as clipped as I'd intended, wavered, then grew thick.

Aoife moved closer to the screen, screwing her eyes up. 'What's wrong with you?'

I shot my index finger to the mute button, but my hiccup escaped too fast.

'*Mammy, our Róisín's crying,*' Aoife shrieked.

I went to slam my laptop shut, but Mam was there almost immediately, and she'd have only called back incessantly until I answered.

'God love you, Róisín, what's troubling you? Aoife, did you tell her to bleach her hair? I told you she *likes* being ginger, like your daddy.'

'It's not that . . .' I shook my head mutely rather than finish, knowing suddenly that if I let a single sound escape, a torrent of sobs would follow. But then it was too late, and the sobs overtook me anyway, and I buried my swollen face in my hands, hiccupping painfully. 'I won a wedding, but Nate didn't want to marry me so we had to break up. And then he did want to marry me but I'd . . . I'd made an eejit of myself with someone else, and I . . .'

'Aoife,' Mam said. 'Away you go to the kitchen and get my credit card. Never worry, Róisín,' she added into the screen. 'I'm booking you a flight. You're coming on home.'

* * *

I entered Sylverley's west wing through the entrance at the back, and trudged up the series of increasingly broader staircases, breathing heavily under the weight of six full garment bags.

'Drop them off, apologise for not finding a fiancé, leave,' I muttered, like a mantra, in time to my ascending footsteps. 'Drop them off, apologise for not finding a fiancé, leave.'

The door to Perky's estate office fell open as I knocked on it. Inside, she was waiting with what appeared on first glance to be everyone whose outfit I was holding. Lola-Pop was by the window, Amelia on the sofa and Mrs Holt hovered near Perky's desk. Lola-Pop's deputy was there, but he was the only man, I observed, with a sense of overwhelming relief.

'Congratulations, Róisín!' Perky said, rising from behind her desk, looking delighted and clapping her hands. The other four joined in with the applause.

'Uh . . . thanks.' I hadn't realised they'd been harbouring such low expectations of me completing the costumes on time. 'It's really no big deal, though.'

'Of course it is!' Amelia said, taking the garment bags off me and laying them in a row on the sofa. 'Do you have a ring yet?'

'Sorry, a ring?' I asked, removing my coat.

'Crikey, Róisín,' Perky said. 'Did I spill a secret?' I shook my head, in a vain attempt to clear my confusion, which Perky interpreted as a denial of her concern. 'Phew. Tristan told me the news of the proposal without so much as a hint of the fact that it might be confidential, and I couldn't help myself from passing the good news on to the rest of the team. We can't wait to get stuck in to organising your and Nate's big day!'

Me and Nate's big day . . . The words sunk in, and I felt sick. In the car, I'd told Tristan that Nate had proposed; even given the impression that I'd accepted. And he, naturally enough, had passed that news on to Perky. Meaning that after all my efforts for the past six months, I was exactly back where I started, not only with a prize I couldn't use, but everyone at Sylverley under the impression that I was engaged.

As I groped for a chair and lowered myself into it, Lola-Pop unzipped the garment bags and gave a gasp.

'These are gorgeous!' Amelia cooed. 'Look, here's yours, Mrs Holt, in Sylverley blue!'

The younger women lost no time in shooing away Amelia's young assistant and stepping into their gowns, cajoling Mrs Holt into trying hers on too. She retreated with it into the adjoining office. I had none of my usual pride in my creations as I watched them, feeling nothing beyond appalled numbness at the situation I'd landed myself in.

Lola-Pop shuffled towards me, her dress pincered tight under her arms to prevent it falling down. 'Róisín, I can't work out how this fastens.'

'You've got it on back to front,' I murmured, rising to gently tug the fabric round into place. My fingers fumbled with the hooks and eyes, my mind absorbed with considering the consequences of confessing that I'd turned Nate down, was as single as ever, and couldn't use the prize after all. On the upside, the whole thing would be over, and I could get on with my plan. Packing up and moving my stuff into the storage I'd booked for Monday, before flying off to stay in Derry until I could secure somewhere to live in Bath.

'Perky, did he also tell you I'm moving out of the cottage?' I blurted.

She was posing in front of the full-length mirror, dipping her knees in one direction and then the other, to get her skirts coiling around her ankles. 'Pardon? Oh, Tristan, you mean — yes, he mentioned that you're moving back in with Nate.'

Nope, I knew I should say, as lightly as I could: *Actually I turned Nate down. I need to apologise for not finding a fiancé.* But the numbness had spread to my teeth and tongue, and an instant later, I was glad of it. If I'd spoken, I'd have had to face their disappointment — or worse, their pity. And *even* worse, Perky would surely tell Tristan, who I could bump into around the estate in my final few days. Even the thought of that encounter made my toes curl with shame. 'I've got a removals firm coming first thing Monday morning,' I said instead, finishing the fastenings and reaching for my coat. 'But if issues arise with any of the garments, any of you must feel free to email me at any time.'

Issues seemed unlikely, but I'd give it a few weeks, just in case. Then I'd write an email, to explain and apologise. The whole disaster would be over, and I'd never need to have any contact with any of them ever again.

'I'm sure it'll all be fine,' Perky said, striding over to her desk. 'Let me write you that cheque before you go. Oh, and I know this is unlikely, but you don't happen to have another client with Tristan's proportions we could sell his outfit on to, do you?'

A bad taste stole up my throat. 'He doesn't *want* it after all?'

'More like, he doesn't have any need for it,' Amelia put in, practising a deep curtsey, which was only slightly wobbly. 'Since he's leaving.'

'Ashgrove will be recruiting a new general manager for Sylverley,' Perky confirmed bleakly, as she handed me the cheque.

I walked to look out of the window, to conceal my face, sure my expression would reveal how shaken I was. Staring at the expanse of undulating lawn, which appeared more white than green with the grass frost-tipped, I concentrated on breathing slow and deep.

'I have to admit, Róisín,' Amelia said with a sudden laugh, 'We'd pretty much given up on the PR opportunities stemming from the wedding competition. So pass our thanks on to Nate!'

'And would you get him to agree to take part in some interviews with the press, in the run up to your big day?' Perky added, rather gleefully. 'Just to think, girls, last week we'd resorted to brainstorming other ideas for raising our profile in the events market, and now the wedding's going ahead after all!'

I stiffened, so as to prevent my shoulders from slumping.

'My suggestion, to do a publicity campaign like at the Scottish castle I used to work at, could have worked,' Amelia said. 'I mean, as glorious as Róisín's big day will be, it'll only show off Sylverley as a wedding venue, when corporate balls and the like are an even more lucrative section of the events market.'

'That's a good point,' I said quickly, half-turning toward her with an intention of talking up her point. It wasn't just convenient for me if they decided to focus on events other than weddings, but it was probably best for Sylverley too. Large organisations could pay a lot more for a swanky function at Sylverley than most couples could ever dream of spending on their wedding.

'But that sort of publicity would have necessitated an advertising spend way out of Sylverley's budget,' Perky said. 'The whole point of our competition is that it garners us *free* PR — my friend at *The Telegraph* has already promised an article, and the local paper will give us a double-page spread — as long as Nate and Róisín agree to that interview.'

I screwed my eyes shut against her hopeful expression. 'I can't take any more,' I said, on a long exhalation of breath. 'Can I have a word alone, Perky?'

The others got changed out of their new gowns and left without too much prodding from their boss, so within minutes I was facing Perky, my mouth dry.

I pinned my gaze to the rug. 'I've got to confess that I'm not marrying Nate. It wasn't a lie when I told . . . I told Tristan that Nate had proposed. I think I was planning on accepting, at that point. But then . . . well then I realised that I don't love him.' I ventured a glimpse at Perky. There were circles of colour, high on her cheeks, and she had her hands on her hips. 'I'd forgotten even mentioning it to Tristan, or I'd have informed you the moment I turned Nate down. As it is . . . well, I can only apologise. And promise that I'll disappear now, so you never have to see me again.' A disparaging sound escaped Perky's tightly pressed lips, and I added, in a rush: 'Or I'll help you in any way I can. I genuinely think Amelia's right, that corporate event bookings could make Sylverley more money than weddings, so if you re-ran the competition, but as win a ball at Sylverley rather than just weddings—'

'No more competitions,' Perky snapped, before biting her lip, then sighing. 'Sorry. I shouldn't be rude. It sounds like you've gone through a lot in the past week or so. But we already considered rerunning the competition, in some form, when your hunt for a groom seemed to have . . . stalled. The legal advisor to Ashgrove cautioned against it. At least until after the year for you to claim your prize—'

'I won't suddenly meet someone and demand to get married here!'

'But legally you *could*, so it's not worth the risk of having two outstanding prize winners. After next summer we might get permission for another attempt, but we need to drum up business as quickly as possible.'

I pressed my fingers into my eye sockets, wishing my business was bigger. If I invited all the clients and potential clients from my mailing list, and begged them to bring their whole families, we'd maybe fill up a quarter of Sylverley's ballroom. Add in my friends and their colleagues and clients with their whole families, and maybe we'd get it nearly full. But which journalist, expecting photos of a wedding, would be satisfied with shots of a random bunch of people at a non-specific party? To get them to devote column inches, the event would need the heart-warming spectacle inherent in weddings.

Though not only at weddings . . . At that, an idea flew into my mind, as fully formed as a dress design.

'Perky?'

'Yes?' Her hand was on the door handle, and she didn't even glance back at me.

'Could I accept the prize, but not as a wedding? Have a different event — something as uplifting as a wedding, maybe even more so, so you can capitalise on the press interest?'

'A corporate ball won't—'

'Not that, exactly. A *charity* ball — with tickets sold to benefit the specific, small charity that is currently raising funds to support my goddaughter, and other children like her.'

Perky wheeled around and stared at me. 'I'm listening.'

* * *

My mouth was dry by the time I'd finished explaining, and I'd covered a dozen sheets of paper in sketches and notes.

I stayed quiet as Perky contemplatively leafed back through them.

'I really think it could be great,' I urged, when I couldn't take the silence for any longer. 'For publicity, *and* for the charity.'

Her gaze shifted to my phone, which was displaying a recent photo of Esme, adorable with a missing front tooth. 'I suspect you're right — so I'll support this. But I have to make it clear that I don't have the authority to sign off on it, Róisín.'

'If you put me in touch with the trust's legal advisor—'

'That's not who I meant.' At my blank stare, she elaborated. 'You need Tristan's approval.'

I barely held back a curse, and Perky's eyes snapped to mine. 'Is there a problem?'

Mrs Holt re-entered, bashful in her outfit, which gave me time to think. 'Of course there's no problem,' I said to Perky, kneeling to arrange the asymmetrical pleats in Mrs Holt's gown. 'I just reckon that with Tristan leaving, I'm better waiting to ask the new general manager.'

'But whoever's appointed won't know you from Adam. There's a much bigger risk they turn you down.'

Turn me down. I gritted my teeth.

'What's this about, girls?' Mrs Holt asked.

Perky glanced at me, then stated firmly that unfortunately my new engagement had fallen through before it even began, and then filled her in on my fledgling plan. Mrs Holt, who remembered Esme, immediately jumped on board. 'Of course you must ask Tristan's permission, and not whatever stranger gets his job,' she added with a sniff. 'They won't know the Sylverley way of doing things.'

'They'll learn it, in time,' Perky said, in a tone that seemed an attempt at reassurance, but rang rather hollow. 'But it'll certainly take anyone a while to get as on top of everything as Tristan is. And there's no saying what they might decide about a charity ball. Whereas Tristan's jolly likely—'

'Jolly likely to take offence at me even asking, since I'd first have to admit to not being engaged after all,' I said quietly.

'He's not like that,' Perky said, frowning. 'If he thinks it'll be good for Sylverley, he'll agree to it.'

Frustrated, I put on my coat, then gathered up the papers and my phone and stowed them in the pockets. 'Maybe I'll email him.'

'But your excitement about the plan is what convinced me, and that comes across so much more strongly in person—'

I paused at the threshold to lie with an entirely straight face: 'I'll think about it.'

CHAPTER 26: REVEALING

'So much for dropping off the outfits, apologising for not finding a fiancé, and leaving,' I muttered, as I stalked down the hallway. I'd been stuck in there for over an hour, and if Perky had her way I'd waste the rest of the day looking for Tristan around the estate, rather than packing, as planned. Not that there was a hope in hell of Perky getting her way.

As I neared the staircase, I heard Mrs Holt call my name. I continued striding, but she called louder, and reluctantly I spun.

'I just wanted to say thank you, dear,' she puffed, as she caught up with me. 'It's so beautiful, I can barely believe it.' She glided her hands over the teal silk of her skirt.

Instantly I felt ashamed at having pretended I couldn't hear her calling. 'It's me who should be thanking you, Mrs Holt — and Mr Holt, too. You've both been so kind during my time here. I made it safely into Bath to meet my friend's babies, and then came back to find the van battery fully charged. And then there's logs he chopped for me all winter, and your invitations to last-Sunday high tea — all of it.'

She gave me a hug, and said she'd pass the thanks along to her Humphrey. 'And you should get right along to have that chat with the boss,' she said, as she released me. 'He's in—'

My face must have given me away, because she stopped. 'Why not, love?'

'I . . . Well, I don't think he thinks much of me,' I said, flustered into a semblance of truth. 'It's better for me to take my chances with the new general manager.'

'Nonsense. As my Humphrey says, Tristan's a bit of a loner, but there's not many of him in a dozen. And he likes you fine. He drove you into Bath, didn't he? And those logs you said you were thankful for Humphrey chopping for you . . . that wasn't Humphrey.'

'Sorry?'

'Splitting the logs, and piling them up by your cottage every few days. It's the boss who does that.'

I stood, motionless, and short of any reply. The whole time that I'd been studiously avoiding catching even a glimpse of Tristan, he'd been going out of his way to do something for me.

'You'll find him in the private apartment,' Mrs Holt added firmly, moving out of sight.

* * *

I marched down the stairs, my eyes on the wide passage at the bottom, leading to the rear exit of the west wing. That's where I was headed. Not the narrow doorway into the foyer of the main house, via which I could reach the private apartment. Not when I'd rather walk through burning coals than initiate any conversation with Tristan, let alone reveal that I was completely and utterly single, and ask him for a massive favour.

Except that hot coals wouldn't help Esme right now, and a fundraising ball really would. If the charity had a lot more money, and a bigger profile, then the next time she needed an adaptation the wait wouldn't be nearly so long. And there were a lot more kids like her.

I paused at the foot of the staircase, then swerved into the doorway, passed the foyer, ascended the next stairs at a jog, rounded the galleried landing, then stopped abruptly in front of the door to the east wing.

A wedge was jammed under it, holding it ajar, and Mrs Sylvers was immediately inside it.

'I'll have the rest of your things delivered round shortly,' Tristan was saying, from somewhere within.

'As the last living Sylvers—' she snarled back, breaking off as her eyes hit mine. Without another word, she pushed past me, and stalked off.

And without another thought, I stepped in.

'As the last living Sylv—' Tristan appeared in the internal doorway and abruptly stopped speaking, his eyebrows drawing together. 'Róisín — what are you doing here?'

Wishing I'd not given way to impulsivity, I swallowed hard. 'I heard that it was you who's been chopping wood for my fire, and I . . . I thought I should thank you.'

His face revealed nothing. 'Oh. Well, you're welcome. Was that everything?'

'No,' I said, before I could chicken out. 'I need to . . .' I couldn't do it. 'I heard that you've quit.'

His eyebrows drew together almost imperceptibly. 'You were misinformed.'

'You didn't resign?'

'My contract was for two years. I've taken the decision not to renew it.' He stared at me for a moment, then retreated into the large room behind him, and held the door open for me. It had huge sash windows and a plasterwork ceiling of breathtaking beauty. It also had the distinct stench of rising damp, and was filled with wooden packing crates and tatty furniture. He didn't speak again until he'd reached the marble fireplace, which he leaned back against. 'There's something else you want to say, isn't there?'

'Yup. Uh . . . I don't plan to get married at Sylverley after all, and when I was just handing the outfits to Perky I came up with this idea for my prize which we think would be great for Sylverley and for—'

'Why not?' I couldn't read his expression. 'Why don't you plan to get married here?'

'Destination wedding, abroad,' I said, instantly hating myself. He'd hear the truth soon enough, from his staff, and wonder why I'd bothered lying. 'Which means Sylverley misses out on the PR opportunities of the competition. Unless my prize becomes a fundraising ball, on the same date next summer, to raise funds for the charity offering my goddaughter some vital support. You might recall meeting her—'

'I do,' he said impassively. 'Is Perky keen?'

'She said she supported it, yes. We drafted out some plans . . .'

He ignored the sheaf of papers I thrust towards him. 'I don't need to hear more. If you and Perky think it'll be a success, you'll make it a success.'

'Wow. Well, thanks.' I refolded the papers and squashed them back into my coat pocket, wondering how quickly I should make my retreat.

'When are you moving out, Róisín?'

The gentleness in his voice was unnerving. 'Monday. You?'

A muscle in his cheek twitched and he rubbed his jaw. 'Some time next month. Exact date depends on how quickly someone new gets appointed.'

'Right. Uh . . . I know this is none of my business, but I couldn't help noticing that all your staff seem pretty gutted. They'll miss you.'

He stared at the swirled marble of the fireplace. 'And I'll miss this place, on some level. But ultimately, Sylverley's more a millstone than an opportunity.'

It wasn't the first time he'd said that, and I'd never understood it. And with leaving soon, this was my last chance to discover why managing Sylverley wasn't the dream job for him that it seemed. 'I know you've felt the pressure of managing this place, but you're doing a great job of it. There must be more to it.'

His breathing was hard and fast, and his reply came at me in a staccato rush. 'You think I don't know my own mind?'

I examined him dispassionately. I'd only ever seen hints of this white-lipped fury from him before when Mrs Sylvers was accosting him. But he'd seemed to calm down after she left, so my presence — or something I'd said — had riled him up again.

'Sorry,' I said flatly, turning toward the lobby. At the last moment I whirled back toward him. 'Tristan, of course you know your own mind. But you're not being honest with the whole *Sylverley's a millstone* thing. Something motivated you to take the job here in the first place, and to devote every hour to making a success of the renovation and reopening. You even admired the house enough to hang a drawing of it in your cottage, for goodness' sake. There's no way that you feel pure antipathy.'

When he spoke, the fire had extinguished from his voice. 'And what about you, Róisín?'

'What about me? I love Sylverley — I've told you that before. I'm moving out . . . for personal reasons, as you know.'

He shook his head, just once. 'What do you think you have to do with this?'

'I . . . I have no idea.' A horrible suspicion crept up on me. 'Is it that you're so embarrassed that you're leaving—'

His eyebrows drew together. 'What do you think I'm *embarrassed* about?'

'What . . . happened between us. Or maybe awkward would be more accurate. Or sickened—'

'Don't be ludicrous,' he said, so scornfully it took a few seconds to register that this was a denial, rather than confirmation. He scrunched his eyes tightly closed. When he opened them, they met mine steadily. 'I'd like to talk properly about everything that happened between us, Róisín.'

I took a shaky step backwards. 'It isn't relevant anymore.'

'It is to me,' he said, his eyes still fixed to mine. And the expression in them seemed more pleading than pissed. 'Stay, please. Sit down, so I can put a few things right.'

I shifted my weight from one foot to the other, then nodded and picked my way through the boxes and furniture to the bare window seat furthest from Tristan. Slipping my coat from my shoulders, I placed it beside me, and smoothed the fabric of my full-circle skirt over my knees. 'I'm listening.'

He ran a hand through his hair. 'Róisín, did anything about that kiss — about that entire evening, in fact — hint towards me being in any way *sickened*?'

'Well, no.' I swallowed. If he was wanting an ego stroke for being a good kisser, he had to try further afield. 'The kissing was . . .' Mind-scrambling. Heart-scrambling. '*Fine*. You didn't appear sickened at the time.' My voice sharpened accusingly. 'But the next day you left. And when you returned, you put me well and truly in my place.'

'Not because I was sickened,' he said hollowly, sinking into the armchair that faced toward me. 'I feel terrible that you've been thinking that. Last week, believe it or not, I was trying to put it right. But before I could explain properly . . .' He spread his hands. 'You said your fiancé had won you back, and it hardly seemed appropriate, anymore. But now I find that I can't let you leave still thinking . . .'

When he didn't continue, I stared at him, but he'd transferred his gaze to the floor. 'What would you have explained, Tristan? If I was . . . If things were over with Nate — what would you have said last week?'

I thought for a moment that he wouldn't answer, but then he spoke huskily. 'That I kissed you because I was attracted to you, and I was entirely sober. That I left afterwards in a fruitless attempt to get my head straight. And that I returned with the intention of being honest with you about a commitment I'd made, which meant I . . . I, unhappily, wasn't free to pursue anything with you.'

My stomach churning, I half rose. 'You're married — or engaged?'

'Quite the opposite.'

I was overwhelmed with so much relief that as I sank back onto the window seat, I missed his next few words. When I caught up he was talking about what had happened in the library, on his return.

'—you standing there in that dress, like you were the lady of the house from two hundred years ago, I couldn't bear to make you think I felt nothing. If we hadn't have been interrupted, maybe we'd have had the conversation we're having now.' His lips were as thin as I'd ever seen them, his eyebrows a stark straight line. 'But Perky did interrupt, which reminded me both of my responsibilities, and that you had other options, and so I went ahead with rejecting . . . the truth of what had happened between us.'

Which explained my sense, in the library, that the conversation was heading in one direction, before abruptly changing. But I still didn't understand his broader point. 'You're saying that for some reason you weren't free to pursue things with me, implying that . . .'

'That I wished I was,' he said. '*Wish* I was.'

I don't know what my face revealed, but it was something that made him take in a short, sharp breath.

'I shouldn't have said that now you're engaged. Off limits . . .' He was suddenly very intent. 'But I need to explain. I behaved very poorly from the start. I'd noticed you, you see, when you visited the estate and I tried to turn you back to the delivery entrance. I noticed you, and thought about you, and again when you arrived in a tizz at the ballroom, collecting the prize, and apparently engaged.'

I was frozen in place, as he raised his eyes over my head, out into the view of the estate through the window. 'You admitted the next time I saw you that you were actually single, and my . . . my heart leaped. The most gorgeous woman I'd ever met had stumbled into my life, and she was single . . . but determined to get married within a year. And I . . . I couldn't offer that.'

He went silent, but I still couldn't move, let alone say anything, fixated by *most gorgeous woman I'd ever met*.

'As if it wasn't complicated enough already, Amelia and Perky decided on commissioning costumes from you, and offered the cottage. And I thought, well . . . I thought there was no harm in agreeing to their suggestion, and admiring you from a distance. I managed it, mostly, though not without difficulty, until that evening when you needed help with your dress . . . and I couldn't contain what I felt any longer.' He flopped his head onto the back of the armchair. 'As much as I've fought against it ever since, I constantly think about you. Despite my commitment to stay single.'

'This commitment?' The words tore free from me. 'It's like . . . a religious thing?'

'Ah. No. More . . . practical.'

We were on the brink of the truth, and I was desperate for it. 'Would you explain it properly, if I asked?'

He lifted his head from the back of the armchair, and gave me a smile of such sweetness that it stole every molecule of air from my lungs. 'For you? Anything, Róisín. But . . . you're engaged.'

I sucked in a deep breath, and then another. 'No, I'm not.'

He started slightly then became entirely still.

I stood up, paused until I was sure my unsteady legs could bear my weight, then made my way over to him. He rose an instant later, and propelled by longer limbs, met me in the centre of the room.

'Nate wanted us to get back together, and proposed, as I told you. What I didn't admit is that I said *maybe*, not yes. And the day after you gave me that lift . . . I said no — to all of it.'

'Why? Why did you say no?'

I let my eyes drift to his lips. 'I suppose for the same reason that I stopped looking for someone to marry after our kiss. So tell me, Tristan. Tell me why you have to stay single.'

His neck bobbed as he swallowed heavily. 'I will. I only ask that, whatever you hear, you wait until I've explained everything before you leave. It's all a bit . . . convoluted. Like a history lesson.'

I couldn't help but smile at him, though it hurt. 'The history of Tristan Nash?'

For a reason I couldn't divine, that made his jaw tighten. 'In a manner of speaking, yes.' He lifted a hand and I placed mine into it. He squeezed as if with silent thanks, then led me over to the armchair he'd vacated.

I scooped up the cushion as I sat. One half was worn pink velvet, and the other a needlepoint of pansies. It was home-made and early Edwardian, I thought. Possibly very late Victorian. I spared a second or two to wondering whether a woman of the Sylvers family had made it, and another to noting that it really should be preserved within a display case, before Tristan turned away, taking my attention with him. He took six steps towards the window, swivelled, then six steps back toward me.

'Mrs Sylvers said something as she left . . . This is relevant. I promise. What did you hear?'

'Something about *as the last living Sylvers*. I guess as a plea to let her remain in these family quarters?'

He took another six paces, before pivoting again. 'That is what she wants. But she wasn't referencing herself as the last living Sylvers. She meant someone else, who made the plan for the conversion of the stables.'

'Her late husband then,' I said slowly. 'I suppose technically she married into the Sylvers family, so he would be considered the last of them by blood.'

'Edward hadn't left edicts about precisely where Suzanne should live on the estate.' He made his sixth step toward the window, but stopped, rather than swivelling. 'He left it to the last member of the Sylvers family to decide, after his death. And that individual discovered that this east wing had to be renovated before the damp entirely took over. And wasn't sympathetic to Suzanne's view on moving to a luxurious former stable. Especially as . . . that individual lives with a large dog in a small cottage with no central heating.'

I clutched the cushion to my chest, as if it could stifle the pounding of my heart. 'I don't understand . . . *You're* living with a large dog in a small cottage with no central heating.'

His shoulders bunched under his shirt. 'Yes.' After that one word he remained, motionless and silent, staring out of the window.

'You're—'

He swung around then. The expression on his face was wretched. 'I'm Tristan Nash Sylvers. I've been concealing that from you — from everyone. And more than concealing — actively lying. Especially that evening, after the vet's, when I overtly lied to you about my reasons for hating Sylverley and . . . hell, Róisín, even the drawing on my wall. I've owned it my whole life, rather than finding it in a cupboard. And then, without setting any of that right, or apologising, I kissed you. Ever since, I've known you'd despise me if I—'

'Tristan.' It was a dry-mouthed intervention, and I wasn't sure he'd heard it until his jaw snapped shut. 'You're saying you are Edward Sylvers' long-lost cousin twice removed or something?'

'Try *grandson*.'

Tristan Nash Sylvers. Grandson to the late Edward Sylvers.

CHAPTER 27: FOR RICHER, FOR POORER

'Explain,' I said. 'Explain properly.'

Six steps, and then he was beside me. 'Edward and his first wife had a son.'

'I read about him. Edward Junior died of an overdose after his mother's death?'

Tristan sank into the armchair opposite, his eyes on the cushion on my lap. 'What you wouldn't have read is that he was married, shortly before that. They lived in a commune in Spain, after his father cut him off. To be fair to Edward Senior, I don't believe he knew that my mother — his daughter-in-law — was pregnant until my maternal grandparents made contact, some years later, after . . . after we lost her. I was twelve, and refused to have anything to do with him, or with Sylverley. Twenty years later I found out that he'd stayed in touch with them — had even sold off some land here to pay my school fees. So I made contact. He was very elderly, and I . . . well in a fit of emotion, I agreed to work for Ashgrove for two years after his death. To oversee the renovation, build a strong team, and think about whether I could manage the place long-term.'

'That's when you adopted Bear, too?'

He nodded. 'A month later, when Edward . . . my grandfather . . . had just died and Suzanne, my step-grandmother, didn't want her.'

'And all this is why Suzanne's such a cow to you?'

He shrugged. 'She stayed quiet about who I am, because she fears her lot will be worse under a new manager, with no familial links. But that doesn't stop her resenting every change I make.'

His gaze was still on the cushion. I slipped it behind my back, and captured his eyes with my own. 'Tristan? I promised to listen until the end. And we're not at the end yet, because I'm still bemused at *why* you concealed who you are?'

'I insisted on it, when my grandfather's lawyers were drawing everything up. I'd always preferred to use my mother's name anyway, and I was terrified of other people's expectations, if they knew everything. There would even have been press attention — whole articles on a long-lost Sylvers, rather than a dry line or two about Edward leaving Sylverley to be opened to the public by Ashgrove.' He shuddered slightly, then refocussed his attention on me. 'And I didn't want to swan in here like running the place was my birthright. Even though . . . well, even though it kind of was, I knew I wouldn't want to stay long-term, and thought it might be harder to leave if people knew who I was.'

'Why were you so sure of that?' I asked softly.

His mouth tightened. 'Have you heard people describe the sense of there being a wall between them and the rest of humanity? Especially . . . especially people with traumatic childhoods?'

I tucked my legs up under me as I nodded.

'I always felt that invisible wall, and I thought it would get stronger if the staff I hired, and suppliers and visitors, saw me as a Sylvers rather than just the manager. Only it wouldn't be a wall anymore, but a ninety-six room Palladian house. Very quickly I realised that I'd had it the wrong way round. Hiding who I was, meant that forming friendships would involve lying in a way that would ultimately just cause pain. So the barrier was there regardless, and there was nothing to do about it but limit the damage to others by avoiding friendships, and even more importantly . . . romantic entanglements, for the two years I was here.'

He frowned at me with furrows so deep that, until the few seconds when he began speaking again, I feared he might be upset with me. 'And then one night, after you'd saved Bear's life and my sanity, and I'd seen a tantalising amount of your beautiful pale skin, I ruined that pledge, and hurt the last person I'd ever want to harm.'

I had to lick my lips and think hard before I could reply. 'I wish you'd opened up to me earlier.'

'Me too.' His eyes were downcast again.

'Tristan? Would you come closer?' His head rose sharply and then he was moving to crouch at my knee. I had to swallow several times before I could continue. 'It's not only you who bears the responsibility for not opening up. That's on me, too. I was so intent on finding a groom within a year, that it blinkered me to what's really important. And *who's* really important. And bloody Nate bears some responsibility too, interrupting us like that, the night in your cottage.'

Tristan's smile at my indignation faded quickly. 'I knew immediately that he still loved you.'

'How?' I'd had no idea myself at that point.

'Because . . . why wouldn't he?' he said simply.

My heart fluttered, and then I held out my hands. I didn't dare voice my thoughts until he took them in his own, his eyes lustrous with an emotion I had a burning desire to interpret as hope. 'I was more hurt by being rejected by you after one kiss than by the end of a decade with Nate. No, don't apologise again. My point is that I'll never find anyone who feels as right for me as you do.'

He freed our hands, but a second later his were on my wrists, and he was gently pulling me to my feet as he stood himself.

'Let me say it, unprompted,' he murmured, 'so there's no shadow of doubt in your mind. Róisín O'Reilly, there's nothing I want more than to be the one for you, because all I've wanted, for some time now, is for you to be mine.'

I rose onto my toes, but still wasn't tall enough, so I encircled his neck with my arms and tugged, until our mouths met. Both sets of our lips were turned up, smiling, and it was a long time before we pulled back.

After I caught my breath, I dropped my arms and took a step back.

'I get why you're leaving Sylverley now,' I said, as his eyebrows drew together. 'Truly, I get it. After my father died I found it . . . less painful to avoid the rest of my family. At least, as much as they'd let me. But I . . . I've realised very recently that I need to change that. Spend more time in Derry, and find a way to live somewhere big enough to enable them to visit me more often. And I've got a couple of very important friendships in Bath, as well as Esme. But beyond that . . . there's no reason I can't move my business back to London, or wherever you plan to work next. I'm all in — *if* you are, too.'

Whatever he was expecting, it wasn't that, and his eyebrows drew even closer together. 'You'd do that — you'd follow me?'

I wasn't sure which of us moved first, but suddenly barely a millimetre separated us. It was still too much, and he shifted forward as I turned my head and arched into him, until the lengths of our bodies were pressed together, from our entangled legs, to my cheek against his chest. His heart was thrumming even faster than my own, and his oaky scent overpowered the musty damp.

'I meant it before — anything in my power to give you, I will. So what is it you want, Róisín?'

'Just you,' I murmured against the soft cotton of his shirt. 'Just you. Well . . . unless next summer . . .'

'Next summer? Oh, your wedding in June . . .'

Shock made me flinch, and he pulled back slightly from our embrace.

I kept my eyes from the foxed mirror on the far wall — I didn't need it to know that my face was pale, my eyes wide, my lips pink from his mouth. 'I wasn't asking you to be my groom — we haven't even been on a date yet!'

His sweet smile returned, and this time, it lingered. 'There's over six months for dating first.'

Blinking, I took refuge in practicalities. 'I'm holding you to the promise of a fundraising ball as my prize. So no, what I meant by next summer was . . . well, my sister's wedding in Derry, in August. If you'd possibly consider—'

He ran his fingers down my bare arms. 'It's a date,' he said simply, before grabbing me and sinking into the armchair, with me sitting sideways across his lap.

'Oof — careful! I'm not light.'

He just laughed, and wrapped his arms around my waist.

I breathed long and slow, trying to calm myself down after the wedding talk. 'So Tristan Nash *Sylvers*,' I said, relaxing against him. 'Where *do* you plan to look for a job?'

'If it suited you, I've got an offer to return to my former role, at a firm in West London,' he said, slowly. 'But for the first time in a long while, I find myself rethinking my decision to leave Sylverley.' I tried to suppress my increase in heart rate, but as close as we were, it was in vain, and he kissed the top of my head. 'Only if you were in favour, Róisín. London works too — in fact, in many ways, it would be much easier than this millstone.'

'Back to the dramatic metaphor.' I caught up one of his hands, examining it closely as I stroked his palm. 'Couldn't we keep it simple — you commit to another year or so, and see how it goes?'

'Unfortunately it's rather more complicated than that.' His voice was laced again with apology. 'I'm not quite sure how to tell you this.'

'The revelation of your real name wasn't nearly as terrifying as you'd seemed to fear, so I'm sure this won't be either.'

His eyes softened, but a muscle pulsed in his cheek, betraying his nervousness. 'I told you that I promised my grandfather I'd manage Sylverley for two years. That was a compromise, after I refused his first offer, which was . . . well, which was for him to name me as his sole heir. Under the terms of our eventual compromise, now that those two years are up, two things could happen. One is that I confirm that I don't want to run Sylverley anymore, in which case Ashgrove is incorporated as a heritage trust, ownership of the house and estate reverts to that trust, and I have no further involvement. The other option is in case I accepted my birthright, confessed who I really am, and took on the encumbrance of the rotting wings, the dodgy drains and the step-grandmother from hell. In which case . . .'

'In which case *what*?' I shifted to face him more squarely. 'What would happen, Tristan?'

'Ashgrove would immediately be dissolved, and ownership of the house and estate revert to me, entailed for the next generation . . .'

In the splintered silence I stared, slack-jawed, at Tristan Nash Sylvers, who was looking anywhere but back at me. First the rug, then the plasterwork, then a window. It was a long while before he spoke again.

'I wouldn't . . . couldn't take this place on alone. But you're experienced in the heritage side of things, which rather seamlessly complements my financial background. I have a suspicion that together we could make a bit of a success of it.' He rested his forehead on mine. 'Róisín, you love this place. Would you want to take it on with me? We'd be perennially broke and hounded by Suzanne at every step. But . . . maybe together we could cope with all that. If . . . if you want it for your children?'

I jerked back. 'Hell. No.'

'That's not the answer I expected,' he said mildly. '*Hell no* to children, Sylverley or both?'

'Hell no to you getting *me* to decide,' I clarified quickly, kissing one corner of his mouth in apology. 'It could only be a decision we made together, after a lot of careful thought. I should probably say the same about children, but frankly it's a firm yes from me, though I warn you in advance that

I have demonstrably terrible taste in baby names.' He tilted his head, so my kiss intended for the tip of his nose landed on his mouth, and his hands swept up my spine into my hair, pressing me closer. I was going to look a dishevelled mess whenever we left, but two could play at that game, so I pushed my hands through his hair in return, then, as we broke apart, slid his silk tie free of its knot.

'What *are* you doing?'

'Making you look as thoroughly kissed as you've made me. You don't mind, do you?'

'Not as long as it involves actual thorough kissing.'

I laughed, then sighed. 'You know how you promised me whatever I want? I'm absolutely gasping for a cup of tea.'

'I can resolve that with an immediate first date in the orangery,' he offered promptly. 'Or a visit to the less salubrious surroundings of my kitchen. Though we'd have to stop by your place for soya milk — I've only got the dairy version I'm afraid.' My shoulders shook as I choked with laughter. 'What did I say?'

'You exposed something I'd forgotten about. We're one short reveal from truth, all the truth, and nothing but the truth: I lied about being vegan, after I wore that stupid T-shirt, and Perky told Mrs Holt who so proudly named the plant-based afternoon tea after me. My favourite foods are, like, steak and cheese.'

'Thank goodness for that. I feared that becoming vegan myself would be the polite thing to do, but I couldn't quite bring myself to face it.'

As we laughed, I scrambled off him, and once he'd risen his hands were immediately back on me, smoothing up my arms, across my shoulders and down my sides. He wrinkled his nose.

'What?'

'I encountered a zip, so I'm guessing you won't need my assistance with this dress.'

'Indeed not. But I wear my historic gowns a lot, so keep your fingers limbered up.'

'Just say the word, and I'll tear them right off you.'

I smiled and kissed him, then pulled back sharply. 'You understand how many painstaking hours I spend on each historic outfit I make, right?'

'No tearing clothes?'

'Absolutely not.'

He kissed me again. 'It's much more fun unlacing you anyway.'

JUNE: 0 MONTHS TO GO

CHAPTER 28: PERFECT MATCH

Every single one of my wedding mood boards had showed the pillars flanking Sylverley's front gate entwined with ivy, and flowers to match the colour palette. But the seventh of June had become Esme's special day, rather than mine, and when I'd helped her create an Esme's-ball mood board, she'd decided on something with more impact. So the florist column on the spreadsheet had been renamed *balloon budget*, and now multi-coloured balloons were spiralled around the pillars.

The gate between them was closed, but between the wrought-iron bars I could see that the tethering of the balloons and streamers lining either side of the driveway had finally been completed. They highlighted the length of the route up to Tristan's house, which drew the gaze, even amidst all the colour, bathed as it was in soft summer sunlight.

'Okay,' I said into the walkie-talkie. 'Thanks for your endeavours, grounds team. The first glimpse looks fantastic, and we've done it with twenty minutes to spare before our guests start to arrive. We can open up the gates in five, four . . .' I thought for a second that there was feedback emanating through the walkie-talkie, then realised that everyone else holding one was joining in. 'Three, two, one . . .'

Others added their voices, and with a roar finished; 'OPEN SESAME.'

Mr Holt did the honours, heaving them each open in turn, and I eased my foot off the brake of the battered Land Rover.

'Looking good,' I called through the window as I inched past the security and ticketing teams, who were wearing vintage carnival-themed costumes and wide smiles.

'You too,' Amelia hollered back, and I snorted. I'd been too busy to change out of jeans and T-shirt, and unless I hurried, I wouldn't even have time to release my hair from the curlers they were pinned in.

The guest list had been a mess a few months earlier, with the great and good clamouring for tickets in numbers way beyond our expectations, which threatened how many places we could offer free to children with disabilities, and their siblings and parents. Then Amelia had volunteered to take over ticketing, and solved the dilemma in one fell swoop by tripling the ticket price. Since then, her smooth efficiency had freed me up to concentrate on other aspects of the event, as well as my most recent project, reconstructing servant's working and living quarters in the basement and attics, for guests to walk through.

I passed the car park, which had been covered with a striped circus tent. Guests could either park there and walk the rest of the way, or drive to the front of the house and leave their vehicles for the valets to move. As I was in a rush to complete the final check, I continued on up to the house myself, and threw the key to a smart valet, hired in via a local hotel, as I jumped down.

'Thanks very much.'

'I need your name for the label on the key, Miss?' the valet said. Before I could reply, a few of his colleagues hushed him.

'That's the boss! She's called Róisín. No, I don't know how to spell it either, just write *boss*.'

I smiled as I sprinted up the steps on one side of the portico. The other side was taken over by a ramp, so that every one of the evening's guests could enter through the main door. If we ever won the battle with the listed building officer, we'd make it a permanent change.

The balloon arch at the top of the portico featured white and metallics, signalling the thematic shift inside the house. The step through the huge double doors into the foyer was out of the early 1900s carnival outside, into the Rococo-style Venetian carnival of the interiors, with huge mirrored and feathered decorations, and even more gilding than the house usually displayed.

A member of the front of house team reeled off the practised welcome spiel, ending by gesturing towards the tables laid with a wide variety of highly decorative masquerade half-masks for those who hadn't brought one.

'Perfectly memorised, Ben. And these are set out beautifully, everyone. Thank you.'

I peeked into the ballroom, which was perfectly in order, since Perky was in charge there. Over the strains of the orchestra tuning their instruments, she updated me.

'The grounds team got the bushes in the rose garden lit up individually, and they've just finished festooning the path to the orangery. Along with the vintage fairground rides, it really looks like fairyland out the back.'

I held my thumb up, darted out again and jogged up to the galleried landing. Unlocking the private door to the family apartment, I checked in with the kitchens on the walkie-talkie. Mrs Holt assured me that canapés were on trays and ready to be served, and I breathed a deep sigh of relief as I strode through to the bedroom. It was the first part of the family quarters to be completed, and though the other eleven rooms were still full of building dust, so Tristan and I were months off moving in properly, it was convenient for stowing tonight's outfits.

My gown was still on the mannequin, but I found Tristan's suit gone. I should have been pleased that he'd got back from pacifying Suzanne so quickly, and was downstairs ahead of me, but I'd hoped to at least bump into him en route. The flurry of activity over the past few days had been so all-consuming that we'd barely had a conversation since my family arrived.

I wriggled into my gown, which was deep red and heavily embroidered, pulled up the invisible zip, and slipped the walkie-talkie into the deep pocket I'd incorporated for the purpose.

Sinking onto the stool at the dressing table I wrestled the rollers from my hair then tipped my head upside down and lathered the curls with hair spray. I rubbed off a fleck of mascara, added another layer of red lipstick, and exited the room barely ten minutes after I'd arrived.

At the top of the stairs, as I paused to raise the hem of my gown, the walkie-talkie in my pocket bleeped.

'The first guests are through the gates. Their ETA at the portico is three minutes,' Amelia said.

Perky chimed in, with her overly-enunciated orders. 'Everyone into welcome positions, please. Waiters with trays of canapés, champagne or mocktails, approach the doors in the blue dining room ready to enter the ballroom. Tristan and Róisín, get ready to greet guests.'

'Róisín's not quite—' Tristan broke off as I rounded the corner of the wide staircase. 'Scratch that, she's here now.' His eyes never left mine as I descended. 'You look stunning.'

'So do you. Someone very talented must have made your costume . . . My lipstick,' I added, tilting my head so he missed my lips.

He kissed my cheek, and then the other. 'It was actually someone too persistent, who ignored my entreaties to wear black tie, which I'm still convinced is what most of the other men will turn up in.'

'Herbie and Joe have definitely dressed up properly too,' I assured him for the umpteenth time, as I smoothed my hands across his shoulders, clad in a tight-fitting matador style jacket, that I'd edged in thick gold braid, a perfect match for the embroidery on my dress. 'Esme will be exceedingly pleased with all three of you.'

'Tristan? Róisín?' Perky's voice came again through the walkie-talkie. 'Are you in position now?'

'Almost,' Tristan said, towing me into the foyer and through the front door, to our agreed positions under the balloon arch, just in time for the first group of guests. The women were in Venetian-inspired dresses, but the men in black tie, so I studiously ignored catching my boyfriend's eye as we shook hands and welcomed them to Sylverley. Other guests were hot on their heels, and we soon had to separate to stand at either side of the portico in order to double how many people we could greet.

'Welcome to Sylverley. Thanks for coming and we hope you have a wonderful evening,' I repeated, hearing snatches of the same phrasing from Tristan, whenever I had a moment to breathe.

Only rarely did someone linger and say anything further; to me it was generally something about how well our costumes matched, though occasionally I heard comments to Tristan about his grandfather, and I'd glance over to see his easy acknowledgment.

The first arrivals who I knew personally were friends of Esme and her family, who'd attended the planning session a few months earlier. I thanked the mother for her suggestion of having a medical team in attendance in case of emergencies with any of the children, and crouched low to greet her adorable son, before they headed inside and I had to move on relentlessly to the next group.

Five minutes later I felt a hand low on my back. 'One moment,' Tristan said, holding up the line of arrivals with an apologetic smile, and turning to an elderly couple, who were staring up at the house. 'Róisín, my grandparents, Mary and Gerry Nash. Grandma and Gramps, this is Róisín.'

'We've heard so much about you,' his grandfather said, before muttering something to Tristan, their heads close together, as his grandmother leaned in and kissed my cheek.

'I can't believe it's taken so long for us to meet you, Róisín. That's a beautiful name you have. I'm Irish too, if you couldn't tell from the accent.'

Her Dublin brogue was faint but discernible, but even more than having something so major in common with her, it was their warmth towards me that I appreciated most.

'I can't wait to get to know you better,' I called after them, before Tristan squeezed my shoulder, and we plunged back into our duty.

'That's a wile weird smile on our Róisín,' my brother Ruari said, as he tramped up the steps a little time later. 'Don't you think so, Eoin?'

'Aye,' my other brother agreed. 'She looks like a constipated goldfish.'

'You try smiling for half an hour straight,' I hissed. 'Bet you'd end up with your cheeks frozen in place, too.'

'I remember that from my wedding,' Eoin's wife said sympathetically. 'You should have started off with a tiny little smile, not gone beaming at everyone from the off. Hear that Aoife, and wee Connor? It's a top tip for your wedding, now.'

Wee Connor, who was a foot and a half taller than her, just grunted as he examined the house.

'I'll remember it all right,' Aoife said. 'I wouldn't want my face to end up looking like Róisín's.'

Despairing, I poked Tristan in the side to get his attention. He waved at the couple he'd just greeted, then slipped an arm around my shoulders. 'Welcome to the ball, you lot, since we already welcomed you to Sylverley yesterday,' he said, grinning with an infuriating lack of the frozen-smile syndrome I was experiencing.

'How many bedrooms has this place got, then?' Connor asked suddenly.

'To be honest,' Tristan said, 'we've never really counted. You're welcome to try, once everyone's left later.'

'You'll regret that offer,' I said in his ear.

'See?' Aoife said triumphantly. 'I was right when I said Tristan's place isn't a house, it's a *castle*, wasn't I, Mam?'

'For sure it's big enough,' Mam said, then snapped her mouth shut.

'Are you okay?' I asked her. She shook her head, then switched to nodding vociferously.

'Perhaps you'd like to get inside,' Tristan said smoothly, 'before all the canapés are eaten?'

Reluctantly, I parted from him again so we could work through the queue which had built up behind my siblings. Once he had, the onslaught was ruthless for a while, until the flow of guests finally slowed to straggling latecomers.

Tristan glanced at his watch twice in close succession.

'It's fine,' I said. 'We built in fifteen minutes to welcome anyone who got stuck in traffic leaving Bath—'

'Or had to wrangle twins out of a minibus,' Abi puffed, pushing her double pram up the ramp. She was wearing the floaty dress she'd bought off the peg, turning down my offer to make her a costume with the dry observation that Herbie was going to enough effort for both of them. As he came into sight behind her, I finally understood what she'd meant.

He was in orange and purple from head to toe — in fact, from a foot or so above his head, where the three soft prongs of his jester hat stuck out, before curling under, and ending with a bell. His mask was decorated with harlequin diamonds and beneath it he had a stiff ruff, a striped tunic with blouson sleeves, and matching knee-length puffed breeches. Stockings and mismatched Crocs, one bright orange, the other dark purple, completed the ensemble.

'You look . . .' I struggled to find an apt term. 'Like you've gone to an awful lot of trouble.'

'All apart from the Crocs — can you believe I couldn't find a single pair of orange and purple striped shoes in any shop in the whole of Bath?'

'Astounding,' I said. 'Err . . . what made you decide on orange and purple in the first place?'

'He asked Esme, and she suggested it,' Abi said, with a significant look.

Tristan hid an explosion of laughter behind his hand, and I did the same by bending over the pram. 'I'm so sorry, little spice jars,' I whispered to Hyssop and Borage, as I always did, hoping against hope that they'd take after their parents enough not to hate me for suggesting their names. Borage gurgled at me, emitting the distinct whiff of eggy spinach, and I straightened before it could linger on my gown.

Tristan checked his watch again as they manoeuvred the pram into the foyer.

'We really are fine for time.'

'I know,' he said serenely, before pulling the walkie-talkie from his pocket. 'Perky, she's almost here.' My eyes shot to follow his gaze, on several minibuses, from the fleet that Abi had loaned us for the evening, making their way up the drive. The one in front pulled up at the base of the steps, decanting Joe's parents, Gemma's sister and her partner, and Nate and his recently acquired girlfriend. He nodded at me, and I nodded back then moved my eyes to the other minibus, which still had some way to come, so as not to appear to be examining his companion. From what I could see in my peripheral vision, as he helped her jump down, she was a pretty blonde.

'I'm still surprised he bought tickets,' Tristan murmured.

'Esme invited him directly, and you know how persuasive she is. Though that didn't stop him asking Joe if there was any chance of a mates-rate discount.'

'Surely not — it's for charity!'

We dropped that line of conversation as the second minibus stopped. Esme clambered out, and Gemma supported her arm as Joe ran round to the back. He returned not with her wheelchair but a brand-new walking frame. She planted it in front of her then leaned on it heavily as she shifted forward.

'I'm taking the steps, not the ramp,' she announced with determination.

The dress I'd made her, to her strict specifications, had a silk-taffeta bodice in iridescent white, over a tulle skirt in the peachy colour of ballet shoe leather. The crystal beads I'd sewn through the skirt shimmered as she climbed, planting the frame, leaning on it, then shifting her legs, one broad step at a time. Gemma and Joe trailed her, hand in hand, with their guests following.

As Esme reached the top, Tristan and I parted, heading into the foyer behind them all. The earlier arrivals were congregated in the ballroom, just as planned, and she glanced back at us quizzically. 'Daddy, you made us late with all those photos.'

'You're not late,' Gemma assured her. 'Come through these doors, and you'll see. Everyone's waiting for you.'

Tristan muttered into the walkie-talkie and the master of ceremonies spoke up.

'Ladies and gentlemen, girls and boys, welcome to Sylverley. I have the great pleasure of announcing our guest of honour, who is both the inspiration for this event, and one of the hardest working members of the event planning team. Please welcome, *Miss Esme Burrows*.'

The velvet curtains on the other side of the door recess sprung apart, and Esme and her family entered.

I grabbed Tristan's hand. 'Let's sneak in behind them.'

But he stopped me within the panelled embrasure, as the curtains closed once more. 'We need to wait for a minute.'

'Why? Oh hell, Tristan, we greeted everyone as they arrived precisely so that we didn't need to be formally announced. You know how embarrassed I get by that kind of thing.'

'Sorry,' he said, sounding entirely unrepentant. 'Let me distract you with reminiscing on the first time we stood here. You were under-dressed, and shaking like a leaf, and I was annoyed that the girl I hadn't got out of my head since encountering her in a van a few weeks before had come back to me — but engaged. It seemed the most horrific irony ever that we'd be facilitating your wedding here at Sylverley.'

I smiled, despite my annoyance. 'This time it won't take Perky shoving me in the back to get me through those curtains on your arm.'

'It might, if you don't like the wording of the announcement I gave the M.C. to read.'

'Sorry?'

Rather than explaining, Tristan dug the walkie-talkie from his pocket again. No — not the walkie-talkie, I realised, frowning. It was something much smaller. He concealed it in his palm, before he dropped to one knee, his face suddenly serious.

'Róisín.' His voice was steady, but his hands weren't as he took mine. 'Every day I'm more certain that you're the one for me, and more hopeful that you're certain that I'm the one for you.' His eyes were dark in the dim space, but the expression in them was in no way ambivalent. 'If you'll do me the honour of marrying me, I vow to spend every day of the rest of our lives proving to you that we're both right.'

My heart stopped. 'Sorry . . . are you . . . You want to marry me? *Right now?*'

The gravity in his expression morphed into humour. 'I assumed we'd allow ourselves a few months to plan the wedding. If there's going to be a wedding . . .'

'What? Why wouldn't there be?'

'Because, Róisín, my love, you haven't actually answered my question.'

'Oh,' I said shakily. 'Right. Well, yes — of course I'll marry you.'

He slid a diamond ring onto the fourth finger of my left hand, and I pulled it up to examine it. There were a trilogy of diamonds, the band was old gold, and it was a perfect fit.

'I had a piece from the Sylverley collection remodelled to suit you, but if you don't like it we could choose something new together—'

'Don't. I love it.'

He grinned up at me. 'And I love you.'

'Then stand up and kiss me.'

'Your lipstick—'

'I don't give a monkey's—' I said, kissing him as thoroughly as I ever had.

Something chirped. And then again.

'Tristan?'

'Walkie-talkie,' he said against my lips. 'Perky, with our cue, probably. Let's ignore it—'

'And leave three hundred and fifty guests, plus a hundred staff, hanging about for us?'

'Fine, fine,' he said, spinning us round to face the curtain before releasing his hold round my waist. 'No, I was on the other side, the last time.' He swapped our positions, then drew his eyebrows together. 'And what did I say? Wasn't it — *shall we?*'

I linked my arm through his. 'And we did this.'

'Shh,' he said. 'Listen for it.'

The Master of Ceremonies voice boomed loud and clear. 'Ladies and gentlemen, girls and boys, your—'

'And Bear,' a small girl added crossly. 'Bear's here too.'

'Ladies and gentlemen, girls and boys, *and Bear the dog*, one final announcement before the entertainment commences. Your hosts would like to thank you all very much for your support this evening, and here they are . . .'

Tristan's bicep tightened as the curtains opened, and a spotlight hit us.

'Mr Tristan Nash Sylvers and his *fiancée*, Ms Róisín O'Reilly.'

My feet felt glued to the marble, but without losing a beat, Tristan swept us into the ballroom, inclining his head slightly to wink at me. 'Suffering from stage fright again?'

'Suffering from an insufferably confident boyfriend more like,' I muttered.

'Confident in you,' he breathed, even as we continued forward in lockstep. 'And that's *fiancé*, thank you. You can't already have forgotten promoting me?'

A group of Sylverley staff called congratulations, and we both waved.

'No, but I changed my mind,' I said, once we passed.

Tristan laughed with so much delight that it was impossible not to join in. 'You didn't.'

'All right, I didn't. But be warned, my mam's going to kill you for telling her this at the same time as the rest of the universe.'

'Your mother learned about this several hours before you did,' he shot back, smiling at the woman in question, and his grandparents, who were beside her, right in front of the dais.

We stepped onto it in tandem. 'She gave me her blessing, but was so worried about letting something slip that she virtually resorted to muteness.'

I stared at him in outraged adoration as he pivoted us to the microphone.

'Thanks, everyone,' he said. 'To all of you, for being here, and to those of you who granted permission for this little surprise for my wife-to-be.'

He glanced at me as if I needed to add something, and I crushed his toes with a heel. He just smiled more broadly.

'You know I hate public speaking,' I muttered. The microphone amplified it, and the audience tittered.

Esme was at the foot of the stage, sitting down after the exertions of the walk, beside Bear, who towered over her. She grinned at me, and I gathered myself together to scan the crowds for the friends who'd supported me through the past year. Abi and Herbie were bouncing up and down with excitement, Joe was whistling and Gemma looked delighted. Nate was at the very back, one arm around his girlfriend. In his free hand he had a glass of champagne, and he raised it slightly in our direction, and smiled.

I took a deep breath. 'Many of you might have heard that I stood in this exact spot almost exactly a year ago, rather less suitably attired.' I squeezed Tristan's hand as I waited for the laughter to die away. 'On that occasion, despite being single, I accepted the prize of a wedding, and set out to find someone to marry within a year. That was as foolish as it sounds, but I got lucky. Because what I found — *who* I found — was this wonderful man, who's much more important to me than an opulent wedding.'

As we stepped down from the dais, I caught Tristan staring at me. 'You know you get me *and* an opulent wedding, my love?' he asked, over the orchestra starting up.

'I do, but . . .' I shrugged as he guided me to the dance floor.

'This event was so much work?'

'Exactly. Plus, I find myself much more excited about being your wife than a bride, and if we go simpler and smaller, we can get married sooner.'

'The soonest that's legally possible is two weeks.' He encircled me within his arms. 'I looked it up in case you were as keen as I am.'

'It's Aoife's turn first,' I reminded him, as we began to sway. 'But after her wedding in August, you're mine . . .'

THREE MONTHS LATER

As I pulled the straightener slowly down a strand of red hair, Tristan appeared from our hotel room en-suite, his hair damp and his chest bare, above a towel wrapped loosely around his waist. His level eyebrows drew together.

'You're ironing your hair?'

'De-fluffing it. This humidity has made it all . . .' I released the newly sleek lock onto my bathrobe-clad shoulder, then waved a flyaway strand at him. 'So I borrowed this from reception. Which reminds me to tell Perky that we should equip the cottages with — ouch!' As I'd reached for my phone, I'd caught the edge of my ear with the straightener. 'Jot that down for me, would you?'

'Didn't we agree not to work on honeymoon?' He caught my expression in the mirror and relented, retrieving his phone from the nightstand. I pincered another section of my hair between the ceramic plates. Behind me, Tristan's mobile emitted the swish indicating a sent email.

'You emailed me a reminder?'

'No, I asked Perky directly,' he said idly, rubbing his hair with another towel. The one around his waist slipped slightly, exposing the pronounced creases at his hips. 'To please order de-fluffing devices for all five holiday cottages in time for the October half-term bookings.'

'Seriously?' I couldn't help but laugh at the thought of poor Perky's reaction when she read that. 'They're called *straighteners*, Tristan.' I caught my ear again, and flinched. 'You're distracting me. Get dressed or I'll keep burning myself, and I want to look pretty for dinner tonight.'

'You always look pretty,' he said, ignoring my instruction. He captured my right wrist gently, then removed the straighteners from my grasp. 'And I like distracting you,' he added, bending to kiss my ear better.

For a brand-new husband of only eight days standing, he was pretty brilliant at it already. But we had a reservation at Seville's best restaurant, and three-quarters of my hair was still a mess, so I wriggled free. 'There's less than an hour before we've got to leave.'

'Exactly. Almost a whole hour.' Casually, he stretched up to the ceiling, and the low-slung towel dropped a little further.

I sliced my eyes from the mirror. 'I know what you're doing, and it won't work.' My gaze alighted on my pile of hair pins. 'Unless . . .'

'Unless?'

'Twisting my hair up only takes a minute or two.' I untied my robe as I raced to the bed, letting it gape open as I smiled up at him. 'Want to lose the towel?'

He dropped it to the floor in one swift motion — just as his phone rang.

'Please ignore it,' I begged, at the precise moment he announced, 'I'm ignoring it.' We sniggered and he switched it to silent.

Then my phone rang.

I flopped over to grab my handset. 'Was it Perky calling you, too? Hopefully she wanted clarification on what a *de-fluffing device* is, and there's not some huge emergency.'

I sent Perky to voicemail, my eyes on my husband, who knelt on the end of the bed, his eyes glinting with anticipation. 'Now where were we . . .'

His phone vibrated on the nightstand.

We both groaned. 'I give up,' I said. 'Just answer it.'

He grimaced, but retrieved the towel and wound it back around his waist, then perched beside me on the bed. 'Perky, please tell me this isn't going to interrupt my honeymoon in any significant way?' He listened intently, then sighed. 'She's right here. I'll switch to speaker.' His body language, as he reclined back on the pillows and snuggled me to his side, contrasted with his clipped voice.

I settled my head on his shoulder as Perky spoke. 'I'm so sorry, Róisín, but as Tristan just emailed, I thought it might not be the worst moment to impose.'

'Uh . . . actually we were about—'

'To go to dinner,' Tristan said, poking me in the ribs. 'Repeat the thing about Suzanne. *Who* did she eject from the estate this morning?'

'A courier, who was wandering around with a parcel addressed to Mrs Sylvers.' Perky added, significantly, 'From Northern Ireland.'

I sat up abruptly. 'Our ceremony photos!' In the pew during Aoife's wedding, Tristan had bent over and whispered a suggestion of continuing O'Reilly family tradition, and getting married in that same church, like my brothers and parents before us. When we approached the priest afterwards he'd mentioned a mid-September cancellation, and it seemed meant to be. A ceremony in Derry followed by a party in our newly-renovated private quarters at Sylverley the next day, had necessitated twice the planning, despite only inviting our nearest and dearest, but everything had gone without a hitch. Until now.

'He left under the misapprehension that Mrs Suzanne Sylvers is the only Mrs Sylvers and the package should be returned to sender . . .'

'She claimed she's the *only*—' Tristan spluttered.

I put my finger on his lips. 'Who cares what the old bat says? Perky, thanks so much for the heads up — I'll get in touch with the photographer immediately.'

'No problem. Ta-ta for now, both of you, and enjoy your . . . erm . . . *fluffing.*'

The line went dead and Tristan rolled his eyes at my laughter, then slid a hand under my robe. 'Please reassure me, Mrs Sylvers,' he breathed, walking two fingers down my navel, 'that *immediately* was a figure of speech . . .'

THE END

ACKNOWLEDGEMENTS

I'm indebted to my amazing agent, Tanera Simons, as well as Laura Heathfield and the rest of the team at the Darley Anderson agency. Also to my editor, Kate Lyall Grant, at Joffe Books.

This story's first readers were Stephen McCauley, Emily Rosal and Rebecca Lewis, who each went on to scrutinise several drafts with valuable insights and infectious optimism, as well as Allison Todd, who advised me on sewing when I quickly got out of depth, and Stephanie McCauley Martin, who helped with the Derry slang. As well as helping inspire this idea, Gigi McCauley corrected my punctuation and grammar with relish.

I can't thank my parents enough for nurturing their dreamy bookworm, as well as for bringing us up in beautiful Bath. And thanks to all the wider family in Oxford, Derry, Bath and beyond, for all the encouragement, especially my siblings Rachel, Laura, Emily and Jem. I'm grateful to writer pals for ongoing support, including my critique group and Write Magic, and to Ruth Jackson whose dating anecdotes helped inspire more than one of Róisín's disasters . . .

Finally, my storytelling owes so much to my husband, Stephen, and our children — Gigi, Billy, Celeste, Rafe and Kit — who make up for frequent interruptions with so much inspiration and love.

THE JOFFE BOOKS STORY

We began in 2014 when Jasper agreed to publish his mum's much-rejected romance novel and it became a bestseller.

Since then we've grown into the largest independent publisher in the UK. We're extremely proud to publish some of the very best writers in the world, including Joy Ellis, Faith Martin, Caro Ramsay, Helen Forrester, Simon Brett and Robert Goddard. Everyone at Joffe Books loves reading and we never forget that it all begins with the magic of an author telling a story.

We are proud to publish talented first-time authors, as well as established writers whose books we love introducing to a new generation of readers.

We won Trade Publisher of the Year at the Independent Publishing Awards in 2023. We have been shortlisted for Independent Publisher of the Year at the British Book Awards for the last four years, and were shortlisted for the Diversity and Inclusivity Award at the 2022 Independent Publishing Awards. In 2023 we were shortlisted for Publisher of the Year at the RNA Industry Awards.

We built this company with your help, and we love to hear from you, so please email us about absolutely anything bookish at: feedback@joffebooks.com.

If you want to receive free books every Friday and hear about all our new releases, join our mailing list: www.joffebooks.com/contact

And when you tell your friends about us, just remember: it's pronounced Joffe as in coffee or toffee!

ACKNOWLEDGEMENTS

I'm indebted to my amazing agent, Tanera Simons, as well as Laura Heathfield and the rest of the team at the Darley Anderson agency. Also to my editor, Kate Lyall Grant, at Joffe Books.

This story's first readers were Stephen McCauley, Emily Rosal and Rebecca Lewis, who each went on to scrutinise several drafts with valuable insights and infectious optimism, as well as Allison Todd, who advised me on sewing when I quickly got out of depth, and Stephanie McCauley Martin, who helped with the Derry slang. As well as helping inspire this idea, Gigi McCauley corrected my punctuation and grammar with relish.

I can't thank my parents enough for nurturing their dreamy bookworm, as well as for bringing us up in beautiful Bath. And thanks to all the wider family in Oxford, Derry, Bath and beyond, for all the encouragement, especially my siblings Rachel, Laura, Emily and Jem. I'm grateful to writer pals for ongoing support, including my critique group and Write Magic, and to Ruth Jackson whose dating anecdotes helped inspire more than one of Róisín's disasters . . .

Finally, my storytelling owes so much to my husband, Stephen, and our children — Gigi, Billy, Celeste, Rafe and Kit — who make up for frequent interruptions with so much inspiration and love.

THE JOFFE BOOKS STORY

We began in 2014 when Jasper agreed to publish his mum's much-rejected romance novel and it became a bestseller.

Since then we've grown into the largest independent publisher in the UK. We're extremely proud to publish some of the very best writers in the world, including Joy Ellis, Faith Martin, Caro Ramsay, Helen Forrester, Simon Brett and Robert Goddard. Everyone at Joffe Books loves reading and we never forget that it all begins with the magic of an author telling a story.

We are proud to publish talented first-time authors, as well as established writers whose books we love introducing to a new generation of readers.

We won Trade Publisher of the Year at the Independent Publishing Awards in 2023. We have been shortlisted for Independent Publisher of the Year at the British Book Awards for the last four years, and were shortlisted for the Diversity and Inclusivity Award at the 2022 Independent Publishing Awards. In 2023 we were shortlisted for Publisher of the Year at the RNA Industry Awards.

We built this company with your help, and we love to hear from you, so please email us about absolutely anything bookish at: feedback@joffebooks.com.

If you want to receive free books every Friday and hear about all our new releases, join our mailing list: www.joffebooks.com/contact

And when you tell your friends about us, just remember: it's pronounced Joffe as in coffee or toffee!